Urbanus
— the —
Kingdom Chronicles

Urbanus
THE
Kingdom Chronicles

Dwight O. Craver Jr.
Peter L. Colman

Library of Congress Control Number: 2016908948
ISBN: Hardcover   978-1-5245-0644-5
               Softcover   978-1-5245-0643-8
               eBook   978-1-5245-0642-1

Print information available on the last page

Rev. date: 06/01/2016

To order additional copies of this book, contact:
Xlibris
1-888-795-4274
www.Xlibris.com
Orders@Xlibris.com
741748

URBANUS—The Kingdom Chronicles by Dwight O. Craver Jr. and Peter L. Colman—Ramsgate Productions, LLC.

The creation of URBANUS—The Kingdom Chronicles was completed in 2016, and includes three distinct episodes: Episode 1—*The Perilous Journey*, Episode 2—*The Narrow Gate*, and Episode 3—*The Promise of Redemption*.

Nom Claritas Deo Anno—2016

For permission requests, write to the publisher at the address below:

Ramsgate Productions, LLC
2130 Columbus St., #3303
Dallas, Texas 75204

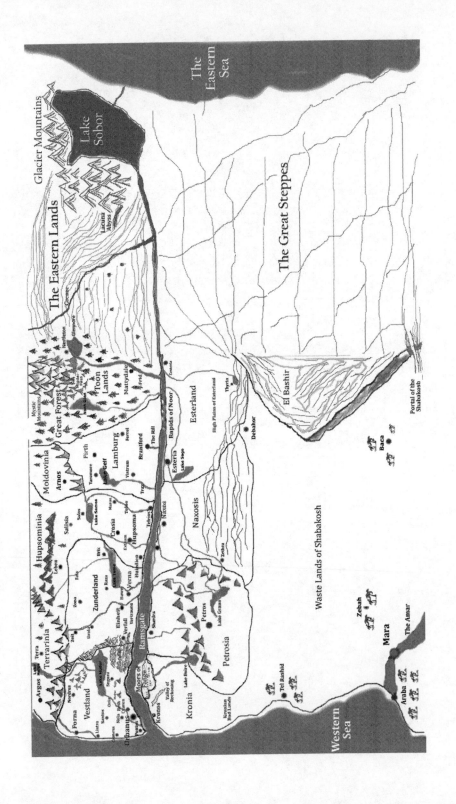

CONTENTS

ACKNOWLEDGMENTS

We want to thank our respective families who have always been a principal source of inspiration for our labors. We owe them a debt of love and gratitude for having patiently shared our own perilous and often unpredictable journey through unchartered territory. Without their love, support and encouragement this work would not have been possible.

We are also grateful to the countless unnamed personal friends, colleagues and mentors—men and women of strong faith and vision all—who have, with little or no hope for acclaim or achievement, freely and generously shared their own insights and collective gifts with two humble wayfarers in their life-long pilgrimage toward the 'heavenly city.'

Dwight O. Craver Jr.

Peter L. Colman

Episode I
The Perilous Journey

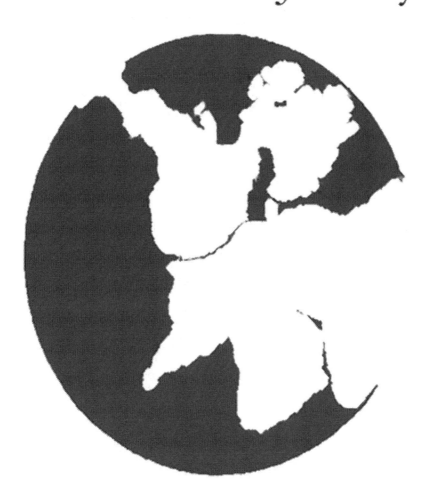

Storm Clouds Gather

The old man rubbed his wrinkled hands together trying to warm them. Time had been generous, if not kind, yet the years had taken their toll on the old wayfarer. His aging frame was weathered but lean, and he was almost completely bald except for the long whips of silver hair that circled his head like a halo. His gait was slow but deliberate, every step was punctuated with a groan, and every breath was an effort in the high altitude. Struggling to keep his balance, he leaned heavily upon his knurled staff. The weakness of his condition stood in sharp contrast to the strength of his will. Undaunted by the elements, he pressed forward, muttering to himself, "If only my strength would last until this mission is accomplished … just one more task before it is all complete."

Surveying the sky, he carefully considered the problem that the storm would pose. Deep in thought, his face marshaled a defiant gesture. Turning back was not an option.

"Where are they?" he wondered to himself.

No sooner were his words uttered than a company of men clad in green tunics and buckskins emerged like apparitions from the surrounding forest. In unison they pulled back their tunics revealing their faces and exposing themselves to the rain. The old man was startled, but he refused to let them know it. He recognized them, but revealing his mind was not the old man's manner. Quickly and without a sound, the forest figures fell into formation as one man and slowly walked together toward the stark figure, each waiting for the other to break the silence. Pausing for a moment, the old man spoke with a hint of jest in his tone.

"Late as usual, I see, but a welcome sight you are, nonetheless. Welcome pilgrims. I am glad that you finally decided to join me."

At the old man's side stood his long-time comrades, men of the Northern Kingdom known as Rangers. Their captain, Wain of Lair, was an unassuming man of average height and sandy brown hair that would have preferred the solitude of the Northern forests to adventure. Destiny had chosen otherwise. His brother, Lothair, was second in command. A tall, handsome man, his muscular stature and blond hair readily gave him an air of authority. His presence demanded attention.

The remainder of their rugged company included Lon of Mark, who was known for his wisdom. Lon was a practical, quick-witted man whose courage was second to none.

The heart and soul of the Rangers were the brothers Fairn. Swain was the oldest and the most reliable of the three. He was stubborn and dedicated, but possessed a very short temper. And then there was Hull whose massive size and strength marked him as a man of extremes. His appetite for food, drink and a good fight were well known, but, fortunately, his heart was bigger than his stomach. Boisterous and witty, he was a man you wanted at your side in a fight. Quill was the impetuous one, but equally insightful. Lastly were the men of Invar: Thrace, Doran, Jergen, Egbert, Derek, and Owen, all of whom formed the solid bedrock of the Rangers' legendary corps. Renowned smiths and swordsmen, their skill with steel was unmatched. The men of Invar seldom spoke, preferring action to talk. Warriors and woodsmen by trade, the Rangers were equally comfortable on horseback or on foot.

The Northern Rangers were a brotherhood, and like all true brotherhoods their kinship went deeper than flesh and blood. Their bond was one of self-sacrifice and a common spirit which knit them together in a way that family ties alone could not.

Wain and Lothair of Lair were two of three bothers born into the same family. Wain was the eldest followed by Lothair, and Horst was the youngest. It was said by those that knew the brothers of Lair in their youth that Wain was the adored child, Lothair the ignored child, and Horst the abhorred child.

Horst was rebellious and stubborn. He refused to abide by the values taught to him. He took every opportunity to go his own way, rejecting the ideals and character traits that would one day make him a Northern Ranger. Horst left home, disappeared, and became a wanderer. To this day no one knows what became of him.

Perhaps this explains Wain's deep concern for Lothair. Wain loved Lothair and as his older brother he felt an obligation to provide opportunities for Lothair and to protect him from Horst's influence. Despite Wain's loyalty to Lothair, Lothair seldom demonstrated respect and appreciation for his elder brother. Lothair was independent and a born risk taker, daring, rash, and always seeking attention. Wain, on the other hand, was self-effacing, humble and quietly confident. His deeds, not words, demonstrated the content of his character and courage. Wain and Lothair were blood-brothers born of the same parents, yet Wain felt a deeper kinship to Lon and Quill.

Northern Rangers were distinctively clad in high brown leather boots, leather pants and a forest-green hooded tunic. A vestment of leather, embossed with silver bearing the insignia of the Northern Kingdom of Aletheia, covered their chests and could be concealed under their tunic or exposed as needed during battle. Each Ranger carried their preferred weapon of choice, a composite bow and a quiver of arrows with bright blue feathers. They disdained the shield and spear, favoring mobility and stealth over fixed battle formations.

Additionally, each Ranger carried a double edged, straight-bladed sword forged by the smiths of Lair. The sword was renowned for its strength and sharpness. The gold and silver pommel was engraved with each Ranger's name and the insignia of King Sa'lem. It was said that these blades were blessed by King Sa'lem and were endued with spiritual powers. Attached to their belts was a single-edged knife with a slight curved blade known as the Noraxe. This was the distinctive emblematic weapon bestowed upon a Ranger upon his induction into King Sa'lem's service. Only a Northern Ranger was allowed to carry a Noraxe.

While their military skill was unmatched, their greatest strength was found in their personal integrity and code of honor. Upon entering King Sa'lem's service they took vows of loyalty, chastity and austerity. They accumulated no personal wealth or position beyond their rank as a Ranger. They had a singular focus that was captured in their motto: "Kingdom, Glory, and Dominion!"

Their history was long and storied, but in Urbania they were now the subject of fables. Their exploits had long provided the children of Urbania with bedtime stories, which no adult took seriously. The Northern Kingdom and its men of renown were just myths to the modern men of Urbania.

****

They marched until dusk. Hull searched for a favorable campsite and when he found one they settled down to cold food and the colder ground. Abner forbad them to make a campfire for he sensed that something was amiss, and they couldn't risk being detected. Cold food and the cold ground was the least of their concerns. But the night passed without incident, and with the break of dawn they resumed their journey.

"What a fair land this Great Forest of Urbania is," Lothair said to Abner.

"Indeed, it is, but its beauty is as fragile as its peace," he answered.

The Great Forest was a place of tall mountains, dense woodlands, and clear streams. Duty brought them here; they were not here by choice. There was no time for exploration. They had joined the old man for what he described as, "his last mission." They knew nothing more, but when men risk their lives for a cause, information is a good thing to have.

The Rangers silently polled each other. What was old Abner up to? He had told them very little about this journey. The old man would tell them but two things: where they were going and that if they failed, he was convinced the Kingdom of the South would overcome Urbania.

Over the decades, the growing darkness had gradually extended its grasp and influence over Urbania, and now her very foundations were threatened. Conspiring forces had long planned for this day. It was Abner's mission to expose them and ultimately stop them. Wain and his companions only knew that they were to protect Abner and to assist him in any way that they could.

Hull finally erupted, unable to conceal his curiosity any longer. "Wain, what are we doing here in Urbania?"

Swain, keenly aware that Hull was placing his huge foot into his mouth, interrupted him and diplomatically interpreted his brother's words.

"What he means to say is that he does not understand the reason behind our mission. We all think that the old man has been too closed about our place and purpose here."

Though the old man was several strides ahead of them, he heard every word. Turning around, he stopped abruptly and fixed his gaze on Swain. Abner's eyes seemed to pierce Swain's soul and sift his thoughts. The fire in old man's eyes burned like the forge of Lair. Nothing and no one would prevent him from completing his task. Hull knew he had made a grave mistake by his idle talk and now poor Swain was bearing the brunt of old Abner's indignation.

"Just what do you mean, Swain? I summoned you here and I told you all you need to know. Is it too small a thing for you to serve the interests of the Great King Sa'lem or must you also advise us and give us counsel?"

"That's not what I meant, Abner! Hull and I want to know more of the details. We are not trying to advise you as to what is best for Urbania."

"All in good time, my good friend," replied Abner. "You won't have long to wait for that. We can't be more than three days' march from the Ramsgate. Once there we can build a raft and reach the safe haven of Brantford on the Rill. True, we will be exposing ourselves, but I doubt that the enemy will venture to show himself in the light of day in Urbania. I understand your desire to know more, but trust me, should you be captured it would be better for you to know less than you do now. We must not delay any longer. There are too many eyes and ears in this place."

Wain reinforced Abner's words. "Enough talk! Let's get on with the march: Kingdom, Glory, and Dominion!"

In unison the Rangers responded: "Kingdom, Glory, and Dominion!"

Deep within the dark shadows of the forest, sullen eyes gazed to and fro confirming Abner's words of caution. As the unseen enemy scanned the trail for the slightest clue that would alert them to the presence of the travelers, they smiled with satisfaction. Suddenly the weather worsened, increasing their chances of intercepting the pathetic little band before they reached the Ramsgate.

It was still midday, yet the ominous sky grew darker. The old man and his companions were becoming increasingly suspicious that there was more to this darkness than met the eye. As their pace quickened, so did their alertness.

Suddenly Abner raised his arm and motioned for the company to halt. They stood motionless and made no sound. Deliberately, Abner broke the silence and beckoned Wain to his side.

"They are here!" he said softly. "I can sense their presence." And then the old man pointed, "There, over there! They wait to ambush us just beyond the bend on the high point of that ridge."

"Do you think they have seen us?" asked Wain.

"I think not. Either they know our destination, or they are scouting the forest for us, trying to cut off all routes of escape."

"Remain here, Abner, I'll take Swain, Hull, and the men of Invar and see what they're up to," Wain said.

High above the enemy's position, Wain peered cautiously over a protruding ledge. To his astonishment, he beheld sixty or more of the dreaded Sharokhan. There was no mistake. There were no uniforms quite like these, black leather trimmed in silver. Their black and silver helmets completely covered their heads, hiding their faces with black mesh. Each one wore a full-length hooded tunic that completely shrouded him in black. They were ghastly to behold. They appeared more like demons than men.

"What are they doing here?" Wain wondered. "Why would the enemy send his private guard after Abner? Abner might have proven to be a thorn in his side, but to send the Sharokhan into Urbania was something that the enemy had never done before! It was a great risk, a bold and desperate stroke! What had caused him to do it? Perhaps this was the reason for Abner's secrecy and concern!"

They were right. The enemy had not yet detected their presence; the Sharokhan's gaze was fixed on the road below. It pleased Lothair that the hunter had now become the hunted. He remembered a previous encounter with the Sharokhan. It was during the Great War, and he knew that this enemy neither surrendered, nor took prisoners. There were deep scars and old scores to settle with this foe.

"Remain here, Abner, I'll take Swain, Hull, and the men of Invar and see what they're up to," Wain said.

With a silent gesture, Wain signaled for the Rangers to ready their bows. Each man notched his distinctive blue-feathered arrow onto his bow. The tension in the air matched that of their bowstrings. Slowly and deliberately they drew back their arrows against their thick layered hardwood bows. In an instant, they released a lethal chorus of arrows in a simultaneous yet almost silent flight. Zzzzwwishhhhhh. Ten arrows screamed to meet their marks. Ten of the Sharokhan fell dead. The Rangers then moved with astonishing speed to a new vantage point and fired again.

Instantly, the enemy recoiled like a threatened snake. Volleys of black and silver arrows adorned with red fletches answered the Rangers' challenge. But the Rangers had already moved to another vantage point and again released their arrows with deadly accuracy. The men of Invar were eager to engage the enemy with their swords, but Wain would have none it for there were too few of them on this mission and he could not risk losing a single man. He signaled to the brothers Fairn to keep shooting from cover and to continue moving after every volley with such speed and dexterity that utterly confounded the enemy. The men of Invar held their ground, drawing the enemy's fire, hoping to divide their attention and confound their strategy.

The enemy appeared to be confused by their tactics and worse still, the storm, which had been the Sharokhan's ally, had now become its foe. The storm now afforded the Rangers cover, and their split-second movements could not be detected. Following Wain's orders, the men moved and released their arrows time and time again. As the lightning illuminated the sky, silky silhouettes could be seen moving about the rocks. Groans and the thuds of falling bodies filled the darkness as more of the enemy met their fate. Wain was pleased with the progress of the fight, but something disturbed him. "This fight is going too easily," he thought.

Suddenly Wain's body went numb at the realization that he was fighting on the wrong front. "What of Abner, Lothair, Quill, and Lon?" he thought. "It's Abner they're after!"

Lon sensed imminent danger, and instinctively reached for Abner, tucking and sheltering him safely behind a large rock. An arrow seemingly meant for Abner struck Lon in the left shoulder, bringing him to the ground. Immediately, Quill scurried to Lon's side and examined his wound. Lothair provided him with cover firing arrow after arrow.

"You'll be all right, Lon! Sit tight," said Quill. "I'll hold them at bay until Wain and the others return."

Before Quill could make a move, Lothair charged into the darkness leaving the others behind. The enemy charged after Lothair as Quill and Abner dragged Lon behind a great tree and attempted to cover him. At last, a blanket of silence covered the forest for what seemed like an eternity.

"I think they're gone," said Quill, "I think they've taken Lothair's bait."

But Quill's optimism quickly evaporated as he caught a glimpse of a black uniform. For a moment he paused in bewilderment, only to be rudely awakened by a throbbing arrow that plunged deep into a tree, inches from his face. Volleys of black arrows hissed like vipers through the air, proving only too well what Quill already knew; they were cutoff and outnumbered.

Another sound was now added to the battle as the sounds of steel against steel shattered the stillness with a dissonant clang, whoosh, swish, and clang! Quill knew that familiar sound. It was the steel of Lair. Wain had returned, outflanking the enemy and none too soon! Quill regretted that he could not join the fray but he had to stay with Abner and Lon.

The noise of the battle echoed throughout the forest. The clang of steel was occasionally punctuated by screams and groans. Quill could only hope that the anguish belonged to the enemy. Suddenly, an intense stillness shrouded the forest. It hung like a morning mist. Nothing moved. Everything was frozen and motionless. The eerie calm was more deafening than the battle. Gradually from the trees and shadows emerged the outlines of several figures. Quill's eyes squinted, struggling to see, and he wondered who or what would emerge from the mist. Slowly, Wain and the others labored toward them. They were cold, wet, and exhausted. Aside from minor wounds, they were none the worse for wear. Wain diligently counted heads. All were accounted for except Lothair. Where was Lothair?

Without hesitating, Wain left his comrades and set off looking for his brother, while Abner turned his attention to Lon's wound.

"It doesn't look good, not good at all. I'm afraid that the arrow was poisoned," said Abner.

****

THE RILL ON THE RAMSGATE

A great river may have as its source an insignificant and unimpressive stream. The same may be true of the river of time and the great events that stir and circulate beneath its currents. The constant ebb and flow of such events too often find their source in very humble beginnings. Such was to be the case in the momentous events that would unfold in the kingdom of Urbania.

Brantford was the capital city of the province of Lamburg. It was an agricultural region renowned for its production of grain and livestock. Despite its slow-paced lifestyle, whose internal clock kept time with the cycle of seed time and harvest, Brantford was a deceptively busy city nestled on the northern bank of the Ramsgate.

Flowing through its center was a current of water that had long been called the Rill, at least as long as anyone could remember. It was actually a small river and not a rill, but this proved to be of no real consequence for the townsfolk who referred to it as the Rill on the Ramsgate. As far as they were concerned, it was the Rill. It gave the city a tranquil beauty and congenial atmosphere that afforded a fine place for the town's folk to gather for commerce and conversation. Less than two dextors south from the city, the Rill emptied its waters into the Ramsgate. This location proved to be a very practical way of moving grain and livestock.

Brantford of Lamburg was surrounded by the fertile farmlands of the high plains whose soil was as fertile as it was vast. This natural resource made Brantford the commercial hub on a great wheel of farms and ranches that stretched for thousands of dextors. All the produce of the high plains eventually made its way to Brantford before making its final journey to the markets of the ten provinces of Urbania. Her strategic position made her the broker of the high plains.

****

"Daylin, breakfast is ready. Hurry or you'll be late again. Oh that boy, he's always daydreaming!"

Daylin paused and reluctantly closed his book, but his imagination remained wide open and his tired eyes were full of daring exploits. The very subject mesmerized him. It was a book of adventure and intrigue, of villains and heroes. He carefully earmarked the page and closed the book with a sigh of regret and an attitude of surrender to the reality of life's inevitable responsibilities. It was time to go to school.

"Oh," he thought, "I wish that I had just one day to myself, then I could read and run in the fields." But Grandmother had every moment planned, and Grandfather didn't believe in too much free time. Daydreaming didn't seem to fit into the Hanner schedule. "Work builds character, due diligence," Grandfather would say to Daylin at least twice a day. This was the way of the family Hanner, and he was resigned to it. Daylin dearly loved his grandparents and he knew that despite their strict ways, he was very fortunate to have such a good life within the secure confines and comfort of his native Brantford. It was the only real world he knew and it would have to do, at least for the moment.

The Hanner house was a large two-story dwelling. The bottom floor was built around a large kitchen with an enormous fireplace, a great room and a formal dining room. Grandmother often took in borders. The second story was divided into two parts with three bedrooms for the family on one side of the house, and three for guests on the other. Grandfather had his office on the first floor of the house and it was there that he conducted the daily business of buying and selling grain and livestock.

Everyone knew Jurius Hanner. He was a just and honest businessman who always kept his word. If you wanted the best price for your goods, you dealt with him. His character and wisdom in business skill were well known throughout the high plains and as far as the borders of Vestland.

Molly Hanner was a loving, caring woman whose generosity and desire to help the less fortunate was as well known as Jurius's business skills. Together they formed a team that excelled in offering hospitality and fellowship to the community and to the occasional traveler. The Hanner home doubled as an inn and boarding house, but few who stayed there paid their bills. The Hanners had a convenient loss of memory when it came to giving. Molly was fond of saying, *"Earn and build wealth, give and build a life."*

They understood all too well the effects of the Great War and what it had done to the hopes and dreams of the people of Urbania. The Hanners had lost everything in the conflict and they were profoundly grateful for the help they believed that they had received from the Brotherhood in Urbanus. It was the Brotherhood's kindness that had allowed them to rebuild their lives. Their home was a living demonstration of gratitude, as they dedicated themselves to helping others less fortunate than they.

The Hanner house had also become the meeting place of choice for many of the townsfolk. The makeshift inn was small but cozy. In the evening the men of the city often gathered for a pint of ale or cider and casual conversation in order to catch-up on the latest news from Urbanus. Molly's cooking was well known in Brantford. Her dining room was often a gathering place for those looking for a good meal and a refuge from the routine pressures of life. But there was an added benefit to their customary hospitality and generosity. The constant flow of people provided Jurius with ample opportunities for business deals. If you wanted to know the latest news, or just needed some sound advice, all that was needed was to ask the wise and well-traveled Jurius Hanner.

****

"How are the muffins, dear?" Grandmother asked.

"They're wonderful. You know how much I love blueberry muffins," Daylin said eagerly.

"Yes, I do and that's why I bought those fresh blueberries at the market. The merchant said that they came all the way from the Great Forest beyond the Noor."

Grandmother's description of the Great Forest and the Noor once again propelled Daylin deep into a daydream. Through the hypnotic properties of freshly made blueberry muffins, Daylin was soon transported to another time and place. There he stood in full battle regalia, against all odds, fighting alongside his companions, battling the superior forces of the enemy. With sword in hand, he advanced against the enemy position, "Onward men, follow me!"

"Daylin, Daylin! Wake up! Pay attention. Eat your breakfast and get on with it. Where are you, boy? Finish your muffin, drink your milk, and hurry up!" Grandmother lovingly scolded.

"Oh, my goodness, that boy, he's twelve years old and almost a man, and all he does is daydream," she said with a sigh.

She felt, but quietly suppressed a slight twinge of guilt for scolding him so, but what was she to do with him? He was brilliant, or at least he had shown signs of it, whenever he chose to concentrate on practical matters which, unfortunately, were very rare. He was destined for something special, she was certain, but what she did not know.

****

As Daylin walked into the schoolyard, he paused and looked back at the indomitable Ramsgate and, with a sigh of regret and resignation in his voice, he whispered, "Nothing ever happens here, I mean nothing!"

He didn't like school; it didn't challenge him. He didn't see the need to study grammar, literature and math. What good were they? He tolerated geography and science. At least they provided him with the necessary fuel for his one true passion—day dreams. He loved adventure.

Daylin was well-liked by his classmates, well, by most of them at least, and no one thought that it was strange that his grandparents were raising him. There were so many just like him, orphans of the Great War. He was blessed to have such a good life when so many other children had so little. He never knew what had happened to his parents and he never summoned the courage to ask.

****

The meadows and eddies of the Rill were Daylin's favorite secret spots. It was there that he could retreat from the monotony of the endless chores that Grandfather Jurius and Grandma Molly scheduled for his daily routine. But he still couldn't manage to escape his grandparents' gently overbearing influence, not even when he was alone in the meadow. Grandfather believed that diligence turned everything that it touched to gold, and that work was a tonic for young boys.

Daylin knew that his grandfather was right, but it was here that Daylin was free; this was his personal sanctuary and he loved it. This was his world. It was here that time stood still and he felt alive. He had calculated that if he used his time wisely and applied himself to his chores, there would be ample time for fishing and sailing. Here he was free from homework and he could dream to his heart's content.

Daylin loved animals and would often adopt them as pets to the displeasure of his grandparents. Stray dogs, cats, wounded birds and reptiles of every kind found their way to the Hanner home.

"This is not a farm or a sanctuary for every living creature in Urbania," Grandfather would say. However, their strict discipline gave way to their tender hearts and thus creatures of every kind could be found on the grounds of the Hanner's home.

Daylin was by nature quiet, gentle and sensitive. He was generally liked by all, but he never really fit in. While comfortable with his school mates, he preferred to be alone in the solitude of the Rill. He was different when compared to other children his age. He was precocious and introspective. "He's so much like his mother!" Grandma Molly would muse.

But there was another side to Daylin that was seldom seen outside of the home. Like his father, he was insightful beyond his years, and he loved to solve problems with a practical, hands-on approach. He displayed skill with tools and loved to build things for his personal enjoyment. They were the very creations that launched him on many an adventure that allowed him to escape the gravitational pull of Brantford's boredom.

When Grandfather Jurius went on business trips and things around the house needed repair, Daylin was at the ready. He could fix almost anything, and he loved to please Grandma Molly. School was another matter. In the classroom he was the definition of unrealized potential.

****

On one particular day, Daylin's routine daydreaming came face to face with a strange but irresistible realty. He had just settled into his well-worn oak bench seat and had slid unnoticed behind his desk. And then he heard something that made his ears perk up like a dog catching the scent of food. He overheard Vim Tuner say, "Its wingspan was ten dextars across, I'm telling you, at least ten dextars and not a mine[1] less."

"You're stone-cold crazy, Vim," Doron Fay said scornfully.

"No, I'm telling you the truth," said Vim. "Last night I went out behind the barn to fetch a harness that I had forgotten to store away, and I saw a creature flying over the eastern edge of Brantford. It was big, black and ugly. I've never seen anything like it. It was bat-like, but it had legs like a man. I don't know what it was, but it was real. I tell you, I saw it! I really did!"

"Right, you saw it and it was real," replied Doron with a characteristic dose of sarcasm. "Are you for real? My dad is right. You Tuners are the family from which the village gets its supply of idiots," snapped Doron.

"What are you talking about?" Daylin asked impatiently.

---

[1] A minex was the equivalent of 1.5 inches.

"He's been sniffing horse manure again! He's a moron. He expects me to believe that tripe about bat creatures!" Doron scoffed.

This was more than Daylin could bear; true or not, this was exciting! At last something was happening in Brantford. Brantford was the most boring place in all of Urbania and that's why he sarcastically called it, "Blandford, home of the chosen frozen."

"Daylin, Vim and Doron, stop talking and open your grammar books at once!" ordered their teacher. She spent more time admonishing these three partners in irresponsibility than she did in teaching the rest of the class.

Daylin did his best to concentrate on his studies that day, but he couldn't stop thinking about Vim's tale of the mysterious bat creature. He tried hard to appear that he was interested in learning, but it was proving to be a losing battle. So during lunch he pressed Vim for details, while Doron continued to mock both of them incessantly and without mercy.

****

Back at the Hanner residence, Molly was busy in the kitchen baking bread while Jurius was in the great room closing a grain deal with Vergil Bonner, when two strangers dressed in black approached the house. Carefully the dark figures scanned the house, peering through the windows for signs of life. The taller man was dark of complexion. His sharp, pointed, elongated features gave him an almost rodent-like appearance. His cold gray eyes penetrated whatever he fixed his gaze upon. The shorter man was heavy set and had a milky pale complexion. He had the pale appearance of a slug, or a sluggish mole that had rarely seen the light of day. He had a wide flat nose that sat on an oversized head that made him look top heavy.

After carefully surveying the house and the yard, the two men made their way to the front door. The taller man grasped the brass doorknocker and with a ferocious blow slammed it down on the door. The door seemed to groan under the abuse. The sound that this rude announcement made echoed throughout the house. Ramona, the housemaid, feverishly answered the door.

"Good day," she said breathlessly, pondering the situation. The site of these two grotesque individuals sent a chill up her spine. She had never seen the likes of these two before. There was something very strange about them, something very strange indeed.

"We were told that you take boarders. Do you have any vacancies?" The short man asked in high-pitched, squeaky voice.

"Yes sir, we do. Do you need separate rooms, or will one room do? How long will you be staying with us?" she asked.

"One room will do," the tall man mumbled coldly. "How long will we stay? Well that all depends, and that's all you need to know," he said with contempt. The cold stare of his gray eyes put fear in Ramona's heart and she knew that she should ask no more questions.

Romona called for Molly, who escorted the two strangers to the dining room where she explained the rules of the house.

"Lunch is at twelve, dinner at six and breakfast at seven. Do you understand that there's no smoking, and no guests are allowed in your room after dark. I do hope you enjoy your stay in Brantford," said Molly.

The two men abruptly stood up and stared coldly at Molly. They nodded their heads in agreement, but said nothing. Their faces were as distant and lifeless as their dispositions. They had no desire for conversation, and they went directly to their room.

"Strange, aren't they?" Molly said to Romona.

Jurius entered the room and asked, "Who are they?"

"I don't know," Molly replied. "I've never seen or met anyone quite like them before."

Jurius dismissed her comment, being preoccupied with the aroma of fresh-baked bread. He promptly put his arm around Molly and said,

"Oh, that bread smells divine. If there's a better cook in Brantford, I'll have to find her and marry her," he said teasing her.

"Oh, you'd say anything when you're hungry, Jurius Hanner. Wash up! Lunch is almost ready."

Jurius ate his lunch in his office accompanied by several of Brantford's prominent citizens. The strange stories circulating among the townsfolk and the surrounding farms dominated their meal. It seems that several people had seen what they described as a large bat the other night, and there were rumors of strange figures riding the back roads in the dark of night. Jurius was perplexed. As they pondered the situation, the two mysterious guests entered the great room and sat down for lunch. All eyes in the dining room were fixed on them.

The two strangers waited to be served. They seemed to communicate with one another without speaking a word. They knew that they were under scrutiny, but they paid no attention. They said nothing and no one at the table dared to introduce themselves. They knew that discretion was the word of the moment.

****

But Vergil Bonner could no longer restrain himself. He stood up and walked over to the window, looked through its glass, and pensively surveyed the sky.

"Things aren't right. I can't explain it, but there are changes taking place around here. Folks aren't as open and friendly as they used to be. Then there's the talk of night riders and unusual traffic on the Ramsgate. I've heard rumors of...."

"Rumors of what?" asked Theodus Cane.

"Rumors of ... hmmm, well ... of strange things happening in the Great Forest," he said with an embarrassed tone.

"Ah, not that again; that's the stuff of old wives' tales. Who could possibly verify the truth of those wild stories?" Theodus retorted.

"I will grant you that, sir, but when all these strange events are combined, they create some very interesting things to ponder, do they not?" he said, trying to convince the others.

Jurius cautioned them to keep their opinions and their imaginations in check. He counseled his friends to treat the matter with a calm detachment until they had more evidence. But, something *was* going on and, though mysterious, it was also familiar. It gnawed at him. And he knew what it was.

****

"Class dismissed," said the teacher. No sooner had the words left her lips than the stampede began.

"Freedom, freedom!" Daylin screamed. He ran out of the schoolhouse and into the road like a dog that had been kenneled for weeks. He ran all the way home. The news of the bat creature was still swirling in his young, fertile imagination. With reckless abandon he bounded into the yard of the Hanner house and dashed for the front door. But just then, and without warning, his tunnel vision rudely gave way and he ran headlong into the two strangers who were coming out of the house.

Daylin's face went crashing into the stomach of the taller of the two men. Before he could catch his breath, he found himself dangling from the ground, suspended by a single hand that held him by the throat. The fury of that man's gray eyes paralyzed him. He had never known fear quite like this. With a flick of his wrist, the stranger sent Daylin flying through the air and onto his back, gasping for breath.

Molly heard the commotion and came running. "What's happening?" she asked.

She was about to scold Daylin, but the terror on his face informed her that there was more to this than the mischief of a clumsy boy.

"Daylin, what happened?"

"I tripped coming in the house and accidentally ran into one of those two men. The bigger one choked me and then threw me down!"

The two men were already a long distance down the road, as Daylin explained the event to Grandmother Molly. The men never looked back, and Molly stood dumbfounded by their cold indifference. *How could they treat a young boy that way?* She thought.

"Who are they?" Daylin asked.

"I don't know, but I think for the safety of us all, we must soon find out," she said.

A Friend in Need

Wain and the others stood motionless, considering their options. Quill, however, darted into the woods, looking determined and intent on saving his comrade from certain death. Time was working against Lon and there was now another enemy to be reckoned with. Lon's condition meant they would be delayed, a delay that they could not afford. They had to reach Brantford on the Rill of the Ramsgate before the enemy learned of their intentions.

Wain cautiously made his way through the forest battlefield. The enemy had collected its dead and retreated into the forest. He hoped against hope that he would not find Lothair's body. Wain knew that he could not linger here for long." Thinking out loud he said, *"What was Lothair thinking in charging into the enemy's ranks like that?"*

But just then, Wain's thoughts were interrupted by the sound of cascading stones. High upon a ledge sat Lothair. He waved to his brother motioning for him to join him on the ledge. Lothair was fine and unscathed; it was a miracle. But Wain's happiness soon settled into a scathing rebuke.

"What were you thinking? What kind of reckless stunt was that? You saved Abner, but you're a reckless fool! How did you get away from them?"

Lothair explained that he had surprised the enemy by charging into their ranks. After killing three of them, he had retreated to his present position. He had been fortunate to find the ledge on which he had taken cover. It was Abner they were after; they had been so close to having him that nothing else had mattered. Lothair had indeed been fortunate. His explanation satisfied Wain. After all, Lothair was alive. His recklessness had saved the life of Abner and, at least temporarily, Lon's as well. The risk had produced a reward.

At last the sun broke through the clouds and Quill welcomed its warmth. The battle and his sprint into the forest had made him desperate with thirst. It was as if his whole body was on fire. He threw himself with reckless abandon face first into the first stream that crossed his path, and he drank until he could hold no more. Gasping for air, Quill collected himself.

As the ripples in the stream slowly subsided, his eye caught the reflection of a man. At least he thought it was a man. Instinctively, he rolled over and drew his sword. But there was no one there! Was he hallucinating? Were his eyes playing tricks on him? It must have been a shadow or the branch of a tree. No, he thought, I know it was a man! He had heard that the enemy employed strange creatures to do his bidding, and he was taking no chances.

Discretion would have to wait. Lon's need for treatment concerned him more than his own safety. Quill consoled himself with the thought that at least the figure that he saw was not wearing black. But what did he see? No matter; it was the herbs he needed. Quill searched diligently under ferns, and bushes. He knew what he was looking for, but this forest wasn't one with which he was familiar. There were so many new plants and herbs. Which ones were good for medicine and which were poisonous? Ah, this looks good he thought.

But just then a peculiar voice cackled, "No, you don't want to be using that one. It is more poisonous than the arrow your friend took!"

Quill turned around drawing his sword all in one motion.

"Who are you? Show yourself!" he demanded.

"Oh no sir, the question is who are you and what are you doing here? Is it not polite to introduce yourself when you stampede into someone's territory? Do you often go running off into someone else's forest not knowing where you're going or what you are looking for? That is not a wise choice, no, not wise, not wise at all! I could have been one of those nasty black ones, fortunate for you, yes, indeed very fortunate for you, that it is I."

Quill could not locate the voice. It seemed to come from everywhere. Was he so fatigued that his senses were playing tricks on him, or was this more of the enemy's wicked deceptions?

On a large rock above him, there sat a peculiar-looking man. He was not a mythical dwarf or an elf of fairytales; nor was he a midget for that matter. This was a man, but a very peculiar man indeed. He resembled an old owl perched on a tree limb, casually observing the goings-on of the forest. His large blue eyes scanned the forest floor capturing every movement. To Quill's surprise, he seemed as bewildered with Quill's appearance as Quill was with his.

The peculiar looking man was short, and dark of complexion. His hair and robust beard were dark brown and thick with curls. Between two large blue eyes sat a very large, bulbous nose that prominently occupied the majority of his face. He had a stocky muscular build that signaled he was no stranger to hard work. On his belt hung a sling and a leather bag of choice stones, and in his hands he grasped a knurled walking stick that could also deliver a devastating blow when necessary. To complete his wardrobe, he wore a full-length coat of wolf's hair, which made him appear like a large ball of fur with a very odd protruding head that lacked shoulders.

"So, you show yourself at last, do you? And what are you? Are you a man or a beast?" Quill challenged.

"What am I, you ask? What are you? You are indeed in need of manners. This is my forest; yes, it is my forest. You and those black nasty ones are trespassing and making all that commotion, scaring away all my creatures. You just can't live in harmony with the way things are!" the peculiar man exhorted.

Time was short and Quill could not bear to hear this round ball of fur make speeches while Lon lay dying. He interrupted, "You said that I was gathering the wrong herbs, that they were poisonous, didn't you? How did you know that an arrow struck my friend? Obviously you aren't in the employ of the enemy. Can you help me?

In one fell swoop the awkward looking man jumped down from his perch with a grace and ease that astonished Quill.

"Ahhhhaa, he said with a self assured air, allow me to introduce myself. My name is Macoot, and this is my forest. It's the land of the Toon. The people of Urbania talk of harmony with nature, but they have no understanding of the way things are. I have been given the stewardship of this forest! There is much to explain, my Ranger friend, but it will have to wait. Trust Macoot; it is time for me to help you. Time is short! Time is very short! Now, come over here. Do you see that little green and yellow herb? Pick two of those, and that long purple one over there, yes, yes, and get me three of those red ones and a handful the five leaf clover over there. Not there, over there! No, no, pay attention!" Macoot ordered.

While Quill and Macoot gathered herbs, the forest telegraph was busy sending out the alarm. In an instant the forest floor was pelted with pine cones cascading down from the trees around them. They fell from the trees like rain in a thunderstorm, filling the forest floor to Quill's ankles. To Quill's amazement, these were not ordinary pinecones. They possessed large eyes, ears, a diminutive nose, two arms and large hands. They walked on two legs while chirping and squealing their excited message to Macoot.

Quill could only muster a single question: "What are these things ... these creatures?" he asked.

"Oh, these are not *things*; they are the P'Ones. They are the forest sentries. No one enters the Toon forest without their knowledge. They are informing me of the enemy's location, and that your friends are in grave danger. We must leave now! Let's make a move!" Macoot ordered.

****

The Toon are a deeply proud and resourceful people, and people they are. They are not to be confused with the mythical figures of folk lore. The Toon are men, only they are different from the men of Urbania. For ages, they have ruled the great forest until becoming one with the landscape. They are master woodsmen, hunters and trackers, familiar with every twig and fern. Like the oak, firs and cedars, their roots run deep into the fertile earth. They know the source and course of every stream, the depth and invisible flow of every river current. They are intimately acquainted with every crevice, rock and ravine. These are theirs friends, and they are familiar to their slightest touch.

They are the guardians and caretakers of the forest glens and green towering leafy vales, drawing life and strength from the rich vibrant earth and sapphire forest streams. They are the living offspring of the verdant soil, the warm breath of every golden field and meadow and they are the ancient handlers of every savage species in the dense forest world that they call home.

They are cunning, clever and delightfully capricious. The Toon are the masters and minions of stealth—small and ruddy in stature, yet extraordinarily robust and agile, capable of running, gliding or bouncing through the forest maze, or even careening through timber and treetops with agile limbs, superhuman strength, and small silent feet. They are found everywhere and nowhere, all at once.

Their weapons of choice are surprise and cunning strength, but they are anything but passive and defenseless in the face of a real threat. They are fearless and loyal. They have worked hard to build a quiet happy life. And they will fight back to back to the very death and with every last fiber of their wisdom and strength to protect their fragile habitat and peaceful existence from any threat from the outside world.

At some point in their ancient past, when warfare had been more prevalent, the Toon had mastered the art and skill of the sling. The ancient art of slinging has a long, illustrious, near-mythical history. Few if any peoples of the earth have either known or preserved the mastery of such a simple, but lethal hand-held weapon. But, somehow, the Toon had rediscovered and refined this ancient, elusive art of warfare. Those who would trespass in the Great Forest, beware!

****

Wain looked at Abner in quiet desperation. Lon had been his friend since their boyhood days. Wain did his best to maintain his composure for the sake of the others, but only Abner could read the grave concern etched in Wain's face.

Swain spoke up, breaking the somber mood of the camp, "I'm worried! Where is Quill? He shouldn't have run off like that. What possessed him to do such a foolish thing?"

"He was following Lothair's example," Wain said.

The others patted Lothair on the back; they knew that his actions had been fool-hardy, but no one had dared to criticize him or question his bravery. It was a time for risk-taking, and they knew that before this adventure was over they would all take their share of risks.

"Herbs," said Abner, "He went for herbs. The right herb can break the fever. Swain did a fine job of removing the arrow, but unless we find an antidote for that poison there's little hope."

Lon, bathed with perspiration, trembled and groaned, drifting in and out of unconsciousness as the poison slowly worked its evil intent.

****

Meanwhile, Macoot gathered his ingredients and mixed them in a wooden bowl that he had fashioned from a log. He muttered to himself as he carefully blended the herbs, tree bark, and water into a potion for Lon.

"There, there, now that will do it," he said with satisfaction. "This potion has proven good in these parts for almost any kind of poison. Don't you worry any, Sir, I'll have your friend up and about in no time, in no time at all, or my name isn't Macoot."

Quill was doubtful, but he had no choice but to cast his and Lon's fate into the hands of this peculiar creature. He was still unconvinced that he was not an enemy spy.

"Then we had best be off; there no time to lose," said Quill.

Wain and the others kept their eyes focused on the patch of forest where they had last seen Quill. They debated among themselves as to their course of action.

"Should we go after him?" asked Swain.

"No," said Wain, "We can't afford to be separated or to lose a single man. The mission is already in jeopardy. We can't wait much longer."

No sooner had Wain finished his sentence than a pebble landed at his feet. He knew exactly what it meant. It was Quill's way of letting his comrades know that he was about to approach and that he needed their cover.

"Stand to," Wain ordered, "It's Quill, cover him!"

They readied their bows, watching for any movement. Quill came crawling into the camp on his elbows, grateful that the enemy had not seen him.

"Where is he?" asked Quill.

"Where is who?" answered Hull.

"You mean me, Sir? Yes, of course, me, Macoot of the Toon clan."

To their amazement Macoot seemed to appear out of nowhere. No one saw him enter the camp, but there he was and already moving towards Lon.

"What is that?" Hull inquired, staring at Macoot in utter disbelief.

"It's a long story," said Quill. "He says he knows how to cure Lon's wound; he has made an antidote for the poison."

"He's never been known to fail!" said Abner. With great relish he embraced Macoot. As Abner and Macoot exchanged greetings, Wain and the others looked on dumbfounded.

"Allow me to introduce my old friend, Macoot!" said Abner. "He's the leader of the Toon, the ancient people of the Great Forest. Their wisdom and ability to live in harmony with nature is legendary. At one time they inhabited all of Urbania, but presently they are only found here. They cannot exist outside of the Great Forest, for their very lives are intertwined with the living things of the rivers, glades and ravines. I have made many trips here over the years. I know the Toon to be a noble and honorable people. They are set in their ways, but they will help us in whatever way they can," Abner said.

Abner introduced the Rangers one by one to Macoot, who seemed to enjoy the acknowledgment as befitting his rank and importance among the Toon.

Abner's deference for Macoot was as admirable as it was surprising. There were so many things that the Rangers did not know about their long time friend. Like an onion, one had to peel back the multiple layers in order to know Abner.

"There are more of them?" Hull bellowed.

Abner's scowling eyes bore down on Hull, silently rebuking him for his ingratitude and lack of good manners. Macoot's smile signaled his hearty approval with the situation. These Northerners, he thought, needed a lesson in manners and hospitality which, of course, the Toon clan was very capable of providing.

Wain gave orders to prepare a stretcher for Lon. Each Ranger took his turn bearing the burden of their wounded comrade. As the little band made its way deeper into the forest, their apprehension and concern for Lon eased as they made good progress. Lon regained consciousness. They were all encouraged to hear him speak. Despite the rough terrain, they were making good time.

"It will be dark in about an hour," said Abner. "Can we reach the village before dark?"

"Yes, yes," said Macoot, "it won't be long now."

Quite suddenly a thunderous roar and a ferocious thrashing of the bushes broke the routine of their march. Before any of them men could grasp the situation, out from the thick brush charged a huge brown bear, which stopped and stood erect in the middle of the path. The men stood in awe of this towering beast. It was the largest bear that they had ever seen standing fifteen dextars[22] tall on its hindquarters. The bear was absolutely determined to prevent anything from passing by him on the trail. Roaring in proud defiance, it snapped its huge head back, threatening the men by bearing its long white fangs. The Rangers recoiled and attempted to ready their bows, but Macoot rushed forward placing himself between the Rangers and the huge beast.

Pointing a finger at the nose of the massive bear, Macoot demanded, "Now, you be still, Knarr! Stop it at once; do you hear me? I know you're upset with all the trouble these Northern folk have caused in the forest today. But these are my friends, so don't you be thinking of eating a one of them, not one, do you hear?"

Knarr appeared disappointed, as he reluctantly retreated and lowered himself in obedience to Macoot. Down he came, strolling up to Macoot rubbing his head back and forth over Macoot like a dog united with its master. Macoot grabbed Knarr by the ears and pulled on them playfully.

"You're a good old bear, a fine watchman you are. Nobody is going to slip past you, are they now?"

"He certainly has a way with animals," said Quill.

"Yes, this is, indeed, his forest. He is the steward here of both the woods and its creatures. They all know and love him and, fortunately for us, they obey him!" said Abner.

****

---

[2] A dextar was the equivalent of 15 inches.

In A Multitude of Counselors

Wisps of smoke on the skyline signaled that the weary travelers were approaching Macoot's village. As the sun set over the valley, shafts of gold and amber bathed the village. It was a cozy and hospitable place that the outsiders called Glennore, but the Toon called it Nestleton. Sturdy little cottages made of wood topped with straw roofs seemed to reach for the sky like haystacks. The sight filled the pilgrims' spirits with a rush of hope.

In the center of the village was an open clearing that was dotted with numerous open fires and ovens. Women were cooking food and game of every kind. They moved about furiously from fire to fire carrying platters of meat, freshly baked bread, and countless other dishes. Barrels of cider and wine seemed to flow in an endless stream into gaping pitchers. Serving hands to thirsty pallets quickly dispatched all of it. Such was the bounty of the forest. The aromas and sounds of the festivities were almost overwhelming for the weary band of pilgrims.

As they entered the village, scores of Toon surrounded them and heartily welcomed them. Macoot's wife, Ursula, waddled out to meet the great man with open arms and laughter. She was no more than three and half dextars tall and as round as she was high. Her face was a female version of Macoot's. Though it is always impolite to say that outsiders all look alike, whether your eye is trained or not, the Toon do look alike and they rather enjoy it.

"I see you found the old one," she said.

She promptly grabbed Macoot by the collar and planted a kiss on him, which sent the old boy reeling backwards. Macoot would have fallen if Swain hadn't caught him. The entire village broke into hysterical laughter at the sight and Macoot, who would never tolerate such an indignity at the hands of another, absorbed the indiscretion with a wink. Everyone knew that Macoot had one weakness: Ursula. He could never deny her anything. Their marriage and their home was the model upon which the Toon built their society. Macoot regained his dignity and responded to his wife.

"Yes, and fortunate for him that I did, those dark ones were going to have him sure enough, but these Northern folk are more than capable of holding their own. Fought a good fight they did."

Macoot's levity masked his profound concern for Abner and the pilgrims, for if the enemy took Abner, all hope was lost.

Macoot's words were met with cheers and celebration. It was a comical sight to see such a diminutive folk trying to carry Lon on a stretcher into Macoot's house. Little children tossed flowers in the air and laughed as Abner and the others made their way to the great hall. The Toon marched out ahead of Abner and his companions with Macoot leading the way. The Toon Elders, who in typical Toon fashion, praised Macoot for his bravery and wit, gave full credit to their headman for the victory. The Toon do not need a reason to celebrate, but this was no ordinary day. And as the Toon saw it, the enemy was trespassing in their domain and with the help of an old friend they had met the challenge. They were now safe and secure around their fires. This was worth celebrating indeed.

Macoot's house was far grander than any typical Toon cottage. That is not to say the Toon do not live well, for they do. They love nothing more than a good meal with family and friends. They are a gregarious people and if you should visit them, remember that time means nothing to them for the Toon prize security and peace. These values transcend all others for them. A Toon is not measured by what he owns, but by how much he enjoys it, and no Toon can enjoy what he owns, unless he shares it with others. Macoot was, on the one hand, the quintessential Toon and, on the other, its unrivaled headman.

Thus in keeping with Toon tradition his house was the meeting place for all matters pertaining to the Toon. In the middle of his spacious house was a huge hall with a table capable of seating seventy quests. The great room was constructed of massive timbers, the likes of which were seldom seen in Urbania. Two men could walk upon the timbers side by side across their one hundred foot span. These had been hewn from majestic trees of ages past. Macoot's guests marveled at the size and the splendor of this great room, but Macoot was about to indulge himself in what Toon do best, food and fellowship.

Macoot sat at the head of the great table, flanked by Abner on his right and Wain on his left. Family members cheerfully waited upon the pilgrims and the Toon elders. As food and drink filled their stomachs, music and dance filled the great hall. Children darted in out of the hall laughing and playing. Macoot raised his mug high over his head and declared, "A toast! To the Great King Sa'lem of the North and his servant, Abner, and to his friends, the Northern Rangers—health, peace and prosperity."

The great hall was filled with the sounds of gurgling throats as cider and wine celebrated Macoot's sentiments. Abner in turn responded with, "A toast to Macoot and the Toon, stewards of the forest and its creatures. Peace, blessings and security upon you in the name of the Great King Sa'lem of Aletheia and the Northern Kingdom."

Abner and the others drank, and the Toon applauded themselves for their contributions to the day's events.

Despite their fatigue, the children mesmerized Wain and his companions. None appeared to be over three dextars in height. Their rosy cheeks, thick heads of brown hair and round protruding bodies made them appear dwarf-like. Their high-pitched giggles blended in harmony with the music of the night and all agreed this was, indeed, a happy place. None could ever remember such a joyful time of celebration. The Toon knew what it meant to live in harmony with the earth and they knew the secret to a happy life: contentment. They were a most contented people.

But beneath Abner's placid smile lay a heavy heart. He wondered how long these children would continue to laugh. How long could this place would remain a refuge of peace. The darkness was encroaching. Even the outer most parts of Urbania were beginning to see manifestations of evil. For centuries it was believed that the great forest would never be penetrated by the darkness, but the darkness had come. The events of the day were proof enough. It did not take the old man long to regain his focus. His mission was his first priority, and he needed the Toon's help if he was to succeed.

"I need your help old friend," Abner said to Macoot.

"Yes, you do, old one. This time we must all stand together or Sanballat's plans will indeed prevail. What is it that you need of me?"

Quill and Swain could hardly believe what they were witnessing. This peculiar little man of the forest, to whom the recovering Lon owed his life, was the headman of all of this. Moreover, Abner was seeking his counsel and support.

To their astonishment, it was a role with which Macoot was more than comfortable. Appearances are often deceiving and this time was no exception. This strange looking little man was filled with wisdom and compassion. He understood Abner better than they, and he had a profound grasp of the crisis that faced Urbania.

Macoot signaled that everyone should leave the hall except the Toon elders. In a flash the gaiety of the night was replaced by an atmosphere of serious deliberation. All eyes turned to Abner.

"In the name of the Great King Sa'lem of the Northern Kingdom, I greet you and extend to you his profound gratitude for your help and hospitality this day. We are in perilous times. The Kingdoms are in conflict, and the provinces are on the verge of all out war; therefore, my Great King Sa'lem calls upon you to join him in defending Urbania from the enemy's evil plans. As the ambassador of my King, I am empowered to ask you to help my companions and me in our efforts to reach Brantford on the Rill of the Ramsgate. It will expose you and your lands as never before to the hostility of Sanballat of the Southern Kingdom. If you decline to help us, I fear that it is only a matter of time before the darkness engulfs your lands. Men of the Toon clan, we need you."

The great hall broke into a frenzy of conversation. Abner and Wain surveyed the room hoping that their request would fall on receptive ears. The conversations grew more and more serious. To the men of the North it sounded like the buzzing of bees. Abner's request had struck a blow at the very heart of the Toon's values: peace and security. Would they risk it all by helping Abner and his companions?

Macoot stood up; simultaneously, the cacophony of the room was exchanged for stark silence. All eyes settled on Macoot. The little man seemed to tower above everyone. He cleared his throat and then he spoke.

"The darkness from the south is encroaching on our lands. We have ignored it for far too long. Abner has come to us seeking refuge and aid. We must help. We have long sought the peace and the security of the forest. We live simply and treasure the permanence of the old ways. However, the times are changing. Our way of life is being threatened. Our lands are under the lustful eyes of evil men who will spare no expense or effort in their conquest. Our loyalty is with King Sa'lem of the North. The Toon will help you."

The issue was settled. Macoot spoke for them all and that was that. Macoot then sat down and rolled out a large map of deerskin. The Toon elders gathered around him and began to deliberate on the best route through the forest to Brantford.

"Where are the dark ones now?" Macoot asked.

One of the Toon scouts who had just returned from reconnoitering the forest and bearing news from the P'Ones answered him.

"There are three companies of the Sharokhan accompanied by Ghouls in the Western Forest. How many are guarding the northern Migdal Pass in the mountains we do not know. There are Sharokhan and hordes of Ghouls to the south on the north bank of the Ramsgate, and Black Ships patrol the river. The only way to avoid them is through the high country."

Pausing to ponder the situation, Macoot turned to the Rangers and then spoke.

"The safest route, although the most difficult, is east through the Mystic Mountains. You will then head south to the Migdal Pass. Once you pass through the Migdal Pass, you will need to proceed down the Frid to the Ramsgate. There's no safe route to the river except by way of the Migdal. The snows are beginning to fall in the high country, so your progress will be difficult," Macoot explained.

"Then the pass of Migdal it is," Lothair said, as if he were in command.

"If we must fight our way through, then so be it. Better to die fighting than to die thinking."

The brothers Fairn gave their boisterous approval to Lothair's bravado. Abner ignored Lothair's theatrics, turned his gaze away from Lothair, and spoke.

"There are highways in the wilderness to the east of Glennore that you know nothing of. What is seen is not always that which is and that which is, is not always seen. You look on what is seen, but what is unseen is what matters. The enemy is the master of deception. Do not believe your eyes alone; there is a vision of another kind that is required here."

The Rangers nodded their heads in agreement despite the mysterious nature of Abner's words.

"The enemy will never expect us to climb the high country this time of year to the Migdal Pass. If we can make it over the mountains and reach the Migdal, we might meet only light resistance. The enemy's main force is to the west and to the southwest between here and Noch Glen. His forces will be the weakest between the Migdal and the Ramsgate. He will be very confident that we cannot make it to the Ramsgate." Wain said.

"It's insane," cried Lothair. "It can't be done; it's suicide. Even if we make it through the high country, how will we get to the Ramsgate? Tell me, then what …? Will we swim to Urbanus? I need some fresh air." He then left the great hall and walked through the village, muttering to himself.

Lothair's abrupt change of mind left them speechless. His momentary bravado was cast aside and his attitude of distrust and suspicion were now revealed. He did not seem to care that his opposition to Macoot's plan would potentially undermine the Ranger's morale and jeopardize the mission.

While the others stood staring at one another baffled and bewildered, Macoot carried on undeterred, gazing long and hard at the map. He then said, "Nothing good thing comes from a divided mind. Let us discuss this in the morning after we have all had a good night's rest!"

****

The Hiding Place

Lon was now fully recovered from the effects of the poisoned arrow and was ready and eager to rejoin his comrades. One by one they were slowly awaking from the deepest sleep that they could ever recall. The beds of goose down seemed to absorb their weary bodies. It was as if they had slept for days instead of hours. To their astonishment, their wounds and injuries were almost completely healed during their sleep. To a man they felt renewed, almost reborn. After a hearty breakfast of eggs, ham, fresh bread, cheese and endless goblets of hot herbal tea, they gathered for one last conference with Macoot. It was time to plan their journey through the forest and down the Ramsgate.

Abner noted that the weather was turning colder. Macoot informed him that during the night the first snows of autumn had fallen in the high country and soon the forest would be snow covered as well.

"Macoot, how will we get through the forest and reach the mountains without being detected?" asked Wain.

"It won't be easy," said Macoot.

"However, there is a trail that the Elk use during the spring. I doubt that anyone except the Toon know of it. If it snows it will be hazardous, but it is normally smooth ground. The Toon will guide you as far as the mountains. You will have to climb the mountains alone. Once you are on the other side you should be able to handle any resistance that you encounter."

Lothair, who was in a better mood, interrupted Macoot and asked, "Once we're over the mountains how would we navigate the Ramsgate? We have no boats and what of the rapids?"

Macoot responded, "There is a village named Mattydale about thirty dextors from the edge of the forest on the Ramsgate. The men there are woodsmen and fine boat builders. They are trustworthy sorts. They have proven honorable in all their business dealings with the Toon. I have sent word ahead and I bartered with them for two of their best riverboats. They drove a hard bargain. If the enemy knew that they were helping you, they would suffer the consequences. But how they love our cider! Their boats are strongest of any in all of Urbania and fit for the rapids of the Ramsgate. When you enter Mattydale, go straight to the river and ask for Bjorn. He is the boat builder and a man whom you can trust."

Wain and Lothair double-checked the provisions for the journey. Swain, Hull and Quill loaded the packs on the mules. Thrace, Doron and Jergen busied themselves with sharpening the swords of the company. Egbert, Derek and Owen checked and rechecked the bows that would be their mainstay in time of trouble, and they gave particularly careful attention to the repair and making of arrows.

Abner slowly paced back and forth, deep in thought. Though present, he was far off in some distant inner realm pondering their future. He knew that the difficulties that they had faced were nothing compared with what was to come.

By late morning everything was ready. The Toon had outfitted the pilgrims with wolf skin coats, leggings, hats and gloves. All agreed that the pilgrims looked very much like the Toon and this was very satisfying for the Toon. Abner and his companions said good-bye to the elders and waved to the village folk who were there to see them off. Abner sat upon a mule, while Wain and the others set out on foot accompanied by a dozen Toon scouts. Macoot stood on the steps of his house and waved his good bye.

"Farewell and may the favor of the Great King Sa'lem be upon you." But in his heart he wondered whether he would he ever see his friends again.

As they made their way into the forest they could sense a dramatic change in the atmosphere. The beauty and peace of the place was now cloaked in shadows and foreboding. Everything in the forest seemed to be on alert. The creatures that normally scampered about on the forest floor gathering food were nowhere to be seen. The birds whose songs had filled the air were silent.

The only sound that could be heard was the sound of the pilgrims' feet carrying them toward the snow-capped mountains. Wain looked to and fro for any sign of the enemy, but no sign was to be seen or heard. He motioned for the others to advance while they moved as quietly as possible ever deeper into the forest.

Wain whispered to Abner that he feared for the safety of the Toon should they encounter the enemy. Abner responded with a terse reply, "They will disappear like the morning mist. Have no fear for them. So long as the forest lives, the Toon will live. It is we who need to take care, my friend. The enemy is concerned with us. The Toon are of no concern to him for the moment."

The journey lasted for several hours, but felt more like days. The air was filled with tension and a growing sense that sinister eyes were watching their every move. Finally, the mountains emerged into plain sight and they could clearly see the Migdal pass. Lothair tried one last time to convince Wain to reconsider the Migdal, but Wain would not hear of it. The enemy was sure to be plotting an ambush at the pass. Only by doing the daring and the unexpected could they hope to outwit him.

The Toon scouts stopped and pointed to the peak to the right of the Migdal. They instructed Wain to look for a stream along the right side of the mountain and a path that followed it. This was the path used by the Great Elk. It would allow them to climb the mountain and avoid the ambush below. But just then, and just as Abner had predicted, the Toon vanished like the morning mist!

As Abner and the Rangers approached the mountain, the terrain grew more difficult. The pack mules had trouble maintaining their footing, sending loose stones down the steep slopes and into the ravines below.

"If the enemy is near, he's sure to know where we are now," said Lon.

"Press on! There's no time to waste," said Wain.

It was just as the Toon said. The mountain stream ran alongside the path of the Great Elk. The sight of the stream brightened their eyes with renewed determination. The pilgrims pressed up the path toward the summit of the mountain. As they climbed it began to snow. The higher they climbed the harder the snow fell. The winds increased and whipped their exposed skins like the sting of a jailer's lash. Adding to their suffering was the combination of the altitude and the cold, which made breathing almost impossible.

This was no ordinary storm and they immediately sensed its source. The sky became black as pitch. Jagged lightning bolts flashed striking the trail ahead of them. A rogue wind and deafening thunder conspired to create a cruel chorus of what they thought were voices that mocked and scorned their every effort to move through the fierce tempest that engulfed them. Despite this, they stumbled and staggered forward. As the storm intensified so did the flow of voices that now resembled a warlock's incantations, spewing curses and draining them of resolve.

Abner's mule collapsed under him, sending the old man reeling to the ground. Wain struggled to reach him and with what little strength he could muster, brought the old one to his feet. The fierce winds made it impossible to keep the pack mules in line and they were lost in the blinding wind-driven snow, taking all their provisions with them.

Abner drew his tunic over his face and walked straight towards the side of the mountain. The massive wall of rock was barely visible in the blowing snow. As Abner approached it, he cried, "In the name of the great King Sa'lem of Aletheia of the Northern Kingdom, open!" With his knurled staff, he struck the rock. His words were immediately confirmed by a deep groaning sound. The earth rumbled beneath them and the rock face opened before them. A cleft in the rock allowed a shaft of light to protrude. To their amazement, whatever the light touched melted the snow and stilled the ferocious winds.

As they entered the narrow rock corridor, the exhausted pilgrims fell down as if dead, and gasped for air. The warmth of the light that bathed them was like nothing they had ever felt. It was far more than the warmth of a fire. It was as if they were being bathed in warm oil. As the storm just behind them intensified, a voice emanated from the massive rock.

> "Enter weary ones. Come and rest; eat and drink at the table prepared for you."

Fear gripped the hearts of Wain and his companions. They cowered before this awesome spectacle not knowing which was worse, the storm or the power of the presence that had beckoned them inside the mountain. Abner approached reverently, yet boldly bid his comrades to follow him farther inside the mountain. A small circular chamber emerged with a very narrow cleft on the wall opposite them.

"No weapons beyond this point," Abner commanded. Reluctantly, the Rangers laid down their precious arms and followed Abner. Each man entered farther through the narrow cleft in the rock. Abner's command to leave their gear in the chamber now seemed all but unnecessary as the opening was so narrow that they could bring nothing more than the clothes on their backs.

Once the last man had entered the cleft of the rock, the opening instantly closed behind them. Wain and his warrior comrades had never experienced such a feeling of helplessness. They were being led like children out of danger and into the unknown, cutoff and unarmed. Abner led the way down a long corridor. There were no torches lighting the corridor; the light emanated from the rock. At the end of the corridor was an opening that allowed entrance into what appeared to be another great chamber. As they approached the chamber they could see their images reflected back at them from the crystalline walls. Each man in turn gazed at himself in the glass-like crystalline and felt a strange sensation. It was if the depths of his being were being probed by the presence within the chamber.

In the center of the great chamber they saw a simple wooden table encircled by thirteen chairs. In the center of the table sat a large loaf of freshly baked bread, a great cask of wine, and a side of smoked venison. Abner instructed them to sit down. He broke the bread and served them meat and wine. While they ate and drank their wine, they carefully studied the chamber. The entire room was the brightest white that they had ever seen. The floor, ceiling, and walls were seamless and smooth like silk. No tools known to them could have created such a room. The chamber was bright and warm, yet they could not discern the source of the light or the heat.

Such a room was fit for a king; surely it required a throne, but there was no throne. As they ate their bread and venison and consumed their wine, they slowly surrendered to the peace and serenity that engulfed them. They were safe here, and a silent unanimous verdict was rendered by all of them—they wanted to stay right where they were. But Abner's voice boomed in dissent,

"It is time! We must go."

It was not an easy proposition to accept, but accept it they did.

The doorway by which they had entered the chamber was now sealed. But a new opening appeared on the opposite wall. Abner waved them toward the doorway, and down the corridor they marched. The corridor appeared to be nearly three dextors long; when they finally could see its end, they beheld a wall of solid rock.

At the foot of the wall they noticed that their weapons, which they had laid down earlier as commanded, were now neatly stacked in piles. Their bows were restrung and in superb condition. Their quivers were freshly oiled and their arrows sharpened. Each sword, Noraxe, knife and axe had been polished and honed to a razor's edge. They glistened like a polished mirror. What skill had fashioned such perfect blades they wondered? Each man took up his weapons and when all were ready, Abner placed his hands on the rock face and spoke softly, "Thank you Great Rock, thank for your shelter and help. Thank you for the meal that sustains us and for the path that is grasped by faith and yet not seen by the eyes of man. Show the way; lead us to the chosen place."

A pinpoint of light emerged from the center of the wall and slowly grew until it penetrated the rock. As they gazed through this curious window there was no storm to be seen. At the far distant edge of the forest they could see the river Frid. One by one they climbed through the opening and made their way down the mountain into the forest, prepared to meet the unknown.

But even now as they made their way towards the Frid, unseen malevolent eyes scrutinized their every move. One hundred or more of the Sharokhan, along with five hundred Ghouls, slowly encircled them. Large winged black creatures, called Artrax, circled over the trees, and then bolted downward turning and twisting with blinding speed. With each descent they gathered information on the pilgrims' whereabouts and this they reported to their fellows.

Wain knew that the situation was grim. He ordered his men to take a stand and create a circle. They used the trees for cover, placing Abner safely in the hollow of a great oak and then they waited. The forest was soon filled with the twang of bowstrings and the screeching of arrows. The trees around the perimeter of the pilgrims' defense were soon bristling with quivering feathered shafts. Several dozen Ghouls charged the perimeter seeking to probe a soft spot in their defenses.

One fell to Quill's well-aimed arrow piercing its forehead and two more fell at the hands of Jergen. The men of Invar made short work of the rest. The dismembered bodies of Ghouls littered the forest floor. Instantly the rancid odor of the decaying Ghouls filled the air. Ghouls have no life of their own. They are the bodies of dead men inhabited by demons. When they are dismembered, they decompose immediately, filling the air with the stench of rotting flesh and the sickening odor of sulfur.

The Sharokhan were intent on raining down a torrent of arrows on the outnumbered Pilgrims. Taking aim and drawing back on their bowstrings, they anticipated a swift end to their foe. But when the order to release was given by the enemy commander, and as soon as the arrows had left their bows strings, tens of thousands of oddly shaped missiles descended upon them knocking their arrows off their mark and blinding the enemy's line of sight. The P'Ones had arrived. Their chirping high pitched tones called out to their companions that it was time for a full scale assault.

But just then and without the slightest warning, a strange cacophonous sound echoed off the trees and the fury of the enemy's assault suddenly came to a halt. The forest floor began to vibrate. A soft rumble quickly escalated into a tremor that caused the forest floor to shake violently.

"What is that?" cried Hull.

Wain and the others looked to Abner for an explanation. Abner slowly emerged from the safety of a great oak tree.

"Perhaps, Macoot has a hand in this!" said Abner.

The rumble escalated to a deafening roar; it appeared that whatever the unseen force was, it was about to engulf them. The forest erupted with Ghouls and Sharokhan running to and fro. The scene was one of utter confusion, as the enemy broke ranks and ran for safety. Thousands of Giant Elk stampeded towards them. The greatest of their number charged the Captain of the Sharokhan, impaling him on his massive antlers. The other elk followed suit, tossing Ghouls and Sharokhan alike into the air like helpless mannequins, and then trampling them under their massive hoofs.

As the enemy fled towards the Frid, the trap was sealed. Old Knarr stood erect on his hind legs snarling in angry defiance. He was accompanied by hundreds of his gigantic brothers. The fleeing enemy ran straight into these guardians of the forest. Like faithful guard dogs, they pursued the enemy, tearing them to pieces with their gaping jaws and giant claws. Knarr and his kin chased down the trespassers until none were left.

Quietly and without fanfare, Macoot emerged from the forest, and with deep concern in his voice asked, "Are there any wounded? Are you all safe?"

"Yes, old friend, we are all safe thanks to you and your friends," Abner said with a sigh of relief. The enemy appears desperate in his attempt to stop us," Abner said.

"He is indeed, old one," Macoot replied.

****

"The Times Before Time"

As the grateful pilgrims moved on cautiously under the protective cover of the great forest canopy, a sudden chilling wind, *like a living thing from the distant past,* shattered the solitude of their simple respite. Their legs became weak, and their eyes heavy with fatigue. But they took courage in the warm memory of the mighty Elk, Knarr and his kin, and the gentle P'Ones, and pushed forward undeterred.

By the time the pilgrim's reached the Ramsgate's tributary known as the Frid, it was dusk. The green dark depths of the serpentine waters of the Frid seemed harmless enough, but even the Rangers kept their voices low and their weapons at the ready. The peaceful current of the Frid whispered caution with every ripple.

Discretion dictated that they camp until morning. Wain ordered the men to secure a camp site with an escape route away from the river should the enemy be lurking in the area. Against his better judgment, he ordered that they build a campfire. He knew that they had to choose their adversary: the elements, or the two legged variety. Wain feared for Abner, and so he chose to battle the cold of the night.

Adversity and fellowship reveal much about the character of men. Valor and vulnerability are two sides of the same coin and each was being displayed. The Toon are fond of repeating the ageless truth that "courage is just fear well disguised." As they settled in embracing the warmth of the fire enjoying their food, all eyes eventually turned to Abner; in the imposing silence, they all intoned the same question: "Why are we here?"

"I know, I know, and I understand your situation," the old weary warrior sighed.

"Perhaps it is best for me to explain our mission and your role in it. Only two of you fought in the Great War and the restoration of Urbanus. You do not know the story of Urbanus and its importance. I must begin in the era that the people of Urbania call, "the times before time," Abner said.

The old man settled in with the look of a weary but resolute wayfarer about to take a long and difficult journey. While leaning on his staff, he slowly laid his aching back against a large tree and with a wince of discomfort, began to relate the tale that few had ever heard before or since. Like a conductor of an orchestra, all eyes and ears where attuned to his baton. He had their undivided attention, and so he began his long and mystifying refrain:

> I must bring you back to the very beginning during the Age that is called the 'Eternal Age' when all that existed was King Sa'lem's Kingdom of Aletheia. All that is and all that shall be is due to the wisdom and power of the Great King Sa'lem. It was an age of unparalleled peace and tranquility, that is, until the rebellion.
>
> One of King Sa'lem's servants, much like you Rangers, but lacking your heart and spirit, arose and decided that he was equally suited to sit upon King Sa'lem's throne. The "Usurper," as he became known, was found out, but the poison of his treachery had already affected a vast number of the people of Aletheia. In His mercy, King Sa'lem did not destroy the rebels; instead, He chose to exile them. They were banished to the far southern reaches of the world and confined to the dry and desolate lands beyond the Shabakosh. Their realm is now known as the Southern Kingdom.
>
> The age after the "Great Rebellion" was called the Age of Knowledge. It was dominated by the region of Argos. As men multiplied during that period, so did their desire for land and wealth. Ten provinces arose around their geographic regions, all of whom contended for power and

supremacy. It was an age when men sought knowledge at the expense of goodness. They had hoped that their quest would bring peace and prosperity, but it was a vain imagining. They sowed pride and arrogance and reaped humiliation and conflict. It was an age when many believed that freedom was a means to do what they wanted to, rather than what they ought to.

What is now known as Urbanus, formerly known as Kampia, has always been defined and dominated by the Ramsgate. All the rivers of Urbania flow into it and eventually empty into the Great Western Sea. Urbanus is uniquely situated on the Ramsgate and has always been the ideal place to harvest the teeming treasures of fish that make it their home and spawning grounds. It was this natural resource that at first drew men to it. The great city that now occupies the riverbank was once a humble fishing village occupied seasonally by men from Argos. These fishermen risked their lives to harvest its bounty.

The dangers they faced were far more than the Ramsgate's treacherous currents, whirlpools and storms. The verdant landscaped was perforated with a labyrinth of limestone caves that were the wretched lair of dragons. In their hunger to exploit the Ramsgate and the land's rich resources, the hunters all too often became the hunted. Many a fisherman paid with his life for the opportunity to fish the teeming waters of the Ramsgate.

Like the ominous cracking of ice under one's feet, the talk of an ancient limestone lair that was once the haunt of flesh-eating dragons caused the weary wayfarers to listen intently. Wain and Lothair gazed keenly into the growing darkness of the Frid's waters, preoccupied with the danger before them, while their comrades keenly attuned their eyes and ears to Abner as if he alone existed at the moment.

The dragons made fishing all but impossible, so the distraught fishermen reluctantly yielded to their fears and decided to abandon their fishing station at Kampia. Except for one man, a man named Neri. Where other men saw problems, Neri saw a challenge; where they saw impossibilities, Neri saw an opportunity. Neri was different; suffering and hardship had fashioned him.

He was born in Esterland, but his parents had been killed by raiders from Naxosis; he was taken captive and subsequently sold as a slave to the fishermen of Petrosia. Until he was a mature youth he had suffered terribly. His masters' cruelty knew no limits. He was beaten, starved, branded and whipped at their whim. Despite this treatment, he worked from dawn to dusk, seven days a week. He did, however, learn much from his taskmasters who were expert fisherman. From them he learned the trade and, more importantly, he learned to sail the treacherous Ramsgate and to survive and survive he did. Rather than to despair and give up hope, he decided to plan his escape.

Neri absorbed himself in his work and became all but invisible to his masters. He did more than what was required of him, and this put him out of mind and sight. He became a harmless cog in a senseless machine, biding his time and waiting for the right moment to flee his tormentors.

Finally, the day arrived. Neri's masters where overjoyed on that particular day, for the fishing had been the best of the season. The boat was teeming with fish, and the fishermen had been completely absorbed in the celebration of their good fortune. The captain, whose name was Keil, was an obese, ugly brute that stood head and shoulders above his peers. He seldom bathed expect by chance that he fell overboard, and his long black beard was a rat's nest of uneaten bits of food and lice. In short, he was devoid of any qualities that would mark him as human.

Keil delighted in tormenting Neri, and would often deprive him of food and water for the slightest imaginary infraction. He drew sadistic pleasure in torturing his slaves, and had dispatched many of them in merciless fits of rage. But Neri carefully maneuvered around Keil's maniacal mood swings; he had learned over time that distance was the only safeguard against Kiel's wrath. This was not as difficult a task as one might think, since Keil's stench would announce his presence long before he made his appearance."

It so happens that the southern shore of the Ramsgate is no stranger to severe thunderstorms, waterspouts and whirlpools. Only a fool would sail its treacherous waters without a skilled guide, and even then there is no guarantee that one would return. The autumn of the year was the height of the fishing season on the south shore, and it was also the time when storms were prone to arise from nowhere, turning the placid waters into a churning cauldron of wave and foam. It was on just such a day that Neri made his daring move.

On one such day, a sudden thunderstorm arose, creating a fierce gale that threatened to capsize the vessel. All hands ran to their stations and attempted to down the sails and steer clear of the rocky shoreline. In the midst of the commotion and confusion, Neri boldly approached one fisherman after another, and when they were off guard, crushed their skulls with a mallet and then pushed them overboard. One by one they succumbed to his strength and determination; his hatred for them was peaked as he remembered every cruel act that he had endured at their hands. They were all taken off guard and dispatched into the waves of the Ramsgate. All but one, that is.

As the stormed abated and the skies brightened, Keil made a mad dash for Neri and grabbed him by the throat. His massive hands constricted Neri like a python; the power of his grip was crushing Neri's throat, causing him to drop the mallet. Keil cursed and spat as he hoisted Neri into the air. As his life hung in the balance, Neri looked into Keil's sullen eyes that spewed intense hate and disdain for the slave. In desperation, Neri reached for anything that he might use as a weapon. His hands fumbled along the deck rail as his life was slowly being choked out of him.

While losing consciousness, he felt a familiar object. He grasped the gaff hook and with a vicious blow plunged the hook into the back of Keil's neck severing his spine and paralyzing the brute. Kiel's eyes were filled with shock and utter disbelief. How could he have been done in by a slave? The gaff hook that now protruded through his Adam's apple answered his unspoken question. Neri threw him overboard while thinking that he would finally get the bath that he sorely needed. The bodies of his tormentors were now floating on the brackish waters of the Ramsgate surrounded by the protruding dorsal fins of hungry Bull Sharks.

Neri was now free, as were the remaining slaves onboard the fishing vessel. He trusted no one, but he needed them. So, he made them an offer: "What is your preference?" he asked. Will it be the sharks or a new captain?"

Neri now possessed a fishing vessel that would provide him with a means of escape and a livelihood to boot. Confidently he set sail for Kronos of Kronia, and there he recruited a fresh crew to fish the Ramsgate. He prospered in Kronos and became a highly respected fisherman. As his renown as a fisherman spread, he had his pick of able volunteers to staff his crew. The best fishing grounds were on the north shore in Kampia. His skill as a captain encouraged many a man from Kronos to join his crew and make the perilous journey to Kampia. It was in Kampia that his future began to unfold.

Yes, Neri was very different from these fishermen. His character had been forged in the fires of suffering. After all that he had endured, he would never consider backing down from mere dragons. So Neri appealed to his fellow fishermen to stand their ground and reconsider their decision to surrender in fear and flee. He wisely encouraged them to think like their foe."

"What motivated these dragons?" He asked. "What were their patterns of behavior?" Succumbing to Neri's reasoning, his once-reluctant crew of seasoned fishermen momentarily set their fears aside and began to calculate a response to the dragons.

And then Neri demanded, "Think! What was the dragon's weakness?"

The fishermen pondered his question and then responded, "It's their appetite; they cannot pass up a meal!"

"Then feed the dragons. Give them what they desire—fresh blood and meat," Neri counseled.

For days the fishermen studied the dragons' hunting patterns. They noticed that the smaller dragons would lead the attack; only when they had the advantage would the larger dragons close in. All would venture into the blood feast except for one dragon, the largest of their kind, some forty dextars in length; the one whom the fishermen named Komodus.

Komodus was as cunning as he was cautious, and would only join the feast when the coast was clear. He would then cast aside any dragon in his path and kill any that dare challenge his dominance. Neri carefully observed the dragons' behavior and crafted a plan.

Like a dog, the dragons needed to be trained to respond to a regular feeding time, along with a food that they relished. The obvious choice were wild goats since they were plentiful, roaming the hill sides of the Ramsgate. So, every day for several weeks the fisherman set goat carcasses and pots of blood to entice the dragoons and lure them from their lair. Neri needed to buy time in order to set in motion the next phase of his plan.

Next he instructed the fisherman to trade a week's catch of fish for iron bars forged by the blacksmiths of Shardra of Petrosia. The bars were fashioned into gates that would be dropped over the mouths of the dragon's lair. The fisherman assembled the gates and each day slowly moved them into position waiting for Neri's command.

Neri then ordered the fisherman to gather seeds from the Castor Oil plants that grew along the glens of the riverbank. These were ground into a fine powder and collected until a sufficient quantity was obtained. The deadly poison was then placed in sausage like casings and sewn into the carcasses of dead goats. When the bait was ready, the dragons were summoned by the odor of decaying flesh and fresh blood. It was a meal twice the size of their normal feast; this was a meal they could not resist. Knowing that they would all come salivating for a place at the table, Neri used the ruse to enable the fisherman to place the iron gates in their strategic positions.

And come they did, continued Abner. First the smaller dragons, and then their older siblings rushed headlong into the feast. As they gorged themselves, ripping and tearing the goat flesh from the bones, the fisherman dropped the iron gates over the mouths of the caves, thus sealing the openings closed. Only Komodus remained in his lair, surveying the action. His tongue flicked the air for the scent of blood and anything else that signaled danger. The timing was crucial as Komodus waited for the right moment to charge out of his lair.

At the precise moment, Neri gave the command, and the massive gate slid into position on sleds fashioned from logs fell to the ground. With a thundering crash that caused the ground to tremble, the cave's mouth was shut, permanently sealing it. Komodus roared in frustration; as the dust settled, the threat of the great dragon dissipated with it. Komodus was trapped in his lair while the remaining dragons filled their stomachs to the full with the deadly poison. One by one they fell snorting and choking, vomiting and rolling in agony upon the ground. Muffled grunts and groans gave way to death throes and one by one they fell silent, littering the ground with their carcasses.

The triumphant fishermen hailed Neri as Drakontas—"*The Dragon Slayer.*" With the threat of the dragons removed, the humble fishing village grew in size and reputation. It soon became apparent to all that a suitable name for the village was in order. The former fishing village of Kampia was now a small city in need of a name befitting its new stature. After some thought, Neri suggested the name Urbanus, after the species of butterfly that populated the northern shore of the Ramsgate. After all, Kampia the moth of a tiny fishing village had metamorphosed into a thing of beauty over night, and with it Neri's stature and importance. His popularity and esteem ascended on his new found wings of good fortune, and he was soon recognized as the first mayor of Urbanus.

Neri owed much to his old nemesis and captive house-guest, Komodus the dragon. The fear of his memory proved to be a more formidable defense against would-be enemies of Urbanus than her stone walls. The old dragon was fed a regular diet of fish and an occasional criminal. With his formidable appetite regularly sated, Komodus slowly acclimated to his permanent solitary haunt. To this very day, he prowls the limestone caverns known as "The Pit." The citizens of Urbanus affectionately call Komodus the "Watch Dog" of Urbanus.

As Abner's story continued to unwind, feelings that had once been confined to a past age before the great cataclysm began to take on a life of their own. It was ominous enough to have learned that ancient flesh-eating creatures had inhabited the primitive underworld of an otherwise peaceful and idyllic landscape. But it was a chilling thought that such a beast yet lived and was now the erstwhile custodian of the city's invisible underworld.

The weary pilgrims would have preferred that Abner discontinue his sobering account. After all, darkness had descended upon the Frid, and they were exhausted. But Abner closed his eyes and continued his fascinating account.

The dragons, though a grave threat to the original inhabitants of Urbanus, gave way to a new clear and present danger from the north. From the fetid depths of the earth came the Cannibas. They were a foul and savage scourge that raided by night from their stronghold in Beth Craven, feasting on human flesh as their bounty. Since ancient times they had avoided Urbanus due to the threat of the dragons, but they no longer feared what they could not see upon the land.

The people of Urbanus were now easy prey for these fiends with spiked hair, filed teeth and skin dyed blue. They raided at will and spared no one. The young, the old, the strong and the weak, were all on their menu. When the north wind blew over Urbanus the aroma of roasting human flesh could be detected. What had once been a hidden evil now resurfaced in a visible form that defied earthly imagination and every conceivable nightmare. The people were paralyzed with fear and once again looked to Neri Drakontas for an answer.

As was his manner, Neri carefully pondered the peril before them. He calculated that there was no adequate defense against the stealth and speed of these raiders. The people lacked sufficient time to build suitable walls and barricades. He knew that Urbanus had but one option—attack Beth Craven. In preparation for the attack, Neri sent scouts to the north. Beth Craven was a formidable honeycomb of tunnels and caves. The Cannibas had created secret passages that ascended vertically into the landscape. From these camouflaged strongholds they ambushed any unsuspecting victims.

In a moment of inspiration, Neri concluded that every living thing required rest and relaxation, and the Cannibas were no exception. They relished the aroma of burning flesh over their fires. Why not give them all that they could handle? The Cannibas raided by night, which meant that they rested by day somewhere in the fetid confines of their putrid dwellings. 'They have no appreciation for daylight,' reasoned Neri, 'so we shall brighten their day with this surprise.'

So being the practical man that he was, Neri used what was readily available to him. Along the banks of the Ramsgate one could find pools of oil and tar pits. He ordered the men of the city to gather all the vessels they could find and fill them with oil and tar, and then dilute the mixture with turpentine. To this concoction, he added alcohol and sulfur. In deadly jest, and as a begrudging tribute to his old adversary Komodus, he called the mixture "Dragon's Breath."

"Ready the wagons and secure the vessels," he ordered. We don't want to waste a drop of our precious cargo. We march as quietly as possible. Surprise is our ally and our advantage. Their arrogance will lull them to sleep. The wolf never expects an attack from the sheep!"

So they journeyed north-northwest along the banks of the Orta approaching Beth Craven from the north. They marched as quietly and as cautiously as possible. The Cannibas were either feasting or sleeping in a state of oblivious serenity that was soon to be rudely interrupted. Vessel after vessel of the Dragon's Breath was slowly emptied into the rock crevasses that hid the monsters. Torrents of the liquid cascaded down the crooks and crannies of their lair. Neri Drakontas then ordered the men to ignite the mixture. Instantly Beth Craven was turned into a flaming crematorium. While screams of agony coupled with foul curses echoed off the caves and their blackened rocks, the men of Urbanus listened contentedly to the sweet refrain of revenge, savoring the aroma of victory.

Yes, Abner droned, the victory over the dreaded Cannibas was a triumph for Urbanus and Neri Drakontas, in particular. He was heralded as the savior and protector of Urbanus, and offered the title of Prince and Ruler of the city. He accepted these accolades, and the path to prosperity and prominence was now etched in stone. Almost overnight, Urbanus became a haven of security and safety once again, and a realm of opportunity for all. The city became a province called the Vestland, and its influence spread to what became known as Urbania. Merchants, businessmen, traders and people from all over the world flocked there to enjoy the peace and prosperity it offered. But with unrestrained wealth comes the inevitable social and cultural lack of restraint. Wealth and power created a toxic brew that permeated Urbania, producing a stupor of crime and corruption."

Abner was now exhausted and could go no further with his story. "I will finish this tale later. There is much for you to know but that's for another time.

****

MATTYDALE

Abner had finished his long and detailed story. Many questions yet remained, but the weary Rangers had much to ponder, and sleep now held them in its relentless grip. Abner had surrendered to his fatigue and was sound asleep. As they lay down around the fire, Lothair, as was his habit, began to sing the songs of the Northland. His tenor voice filled the night air with peace and tranquilly. The weary warriors lay back and gazed into the starlit sky. His song sent them back into time and space where, as children, they were safe from care and harm. Lothair sang so beautifully, it was almost hypnotic. The pilgrims took their ease as Lothair emptied the contents of his heart singing in his native Aletheian language.

> Remember the former days, dear friends, days of splendor long ago,
> When our brother, the infant sun first cast its golden, glistening rays
> Upon the blushing, waiting, virgin soil...
> ...When every painted, plum'ed bird and fearless beast
> Danced and pranced in blissful harmony
> Upon the tender lap of mother earth...
> ...When sapphire seas and crystal streams,
> And fruit-filled trees and fertile life-full soil first
> Stirred and warmed the graceful, child-like soul of man...
> Sang and strung their playful melodies...
> Return with me, and listen, as when on that blessed, reverential day,
> Lace'd cobwebs drenched in morning dew

Sang and strung their playful melodies...
And in reply, ten thousand voiceless, like veil'd valley
flowers,
Flushed in tiny, blinding shimmering hues,
Plucked their sacred harps in breathless harmony...
Listen once again with me as every planetary orb and
yellow star
Tune their choral song in mesmerizing symphony
To the celestial music of the spheres...
Lift your hearts and watch with me as shepherd lads and lasses
Walk once more in purest innocence and perfect harmony
Upon the silken moss and friendly forest heath.
Return and see, with clos'ed eyes, th'eternal child of man
Romp and roam once more in fearless, unrestrain'ed joy
Upon the peaceful Northern glades...
Look! He stands there still, bright bedecked and bathed in
simple ecstasy,
And laughs and loves, and yearns to feel again the blessed sun's
Dark-disposing, dawn-begetting, fire-inducing rays.
Let the almond and the fig tree happily drink once more
From deeply down the secret hidden root...
And purest honey sweetly flow in golden rivulets from
Every shaded, sheltering tree and peace envelop'ed vale...
Let deer and bullock, sheep and goat, and every predatory beast,
Roam both free and unafraid on Northland's peaceful shore...
And every blessed child of man romp, and run,
And freely reign forever more.

And then, without the slightest warning while Lothair sang and scaled
the heights of poetic ecstasy, a rogue wind invaded the escarpment and
pierced the warm enclosure where the Rangers lay. A cold chill seemed
to seize the singer by the throat. As if helpless, and struggling in the
clutches of fear, Lothair continued singing under the control of the
malevolent power that possessed him:

"What hollow man is this among the fetid ranks of
mortal men?
Who dare seize the Muses' plastic harp, or weave a
threadless warp
Of pointless words and fruitless fantasies? And who is this
shallow form,

Bent and broken, like a warp'ed arrow in a blinded
archer's bow?
Who, with heavy, heartless voice, speaks of things
unknown, unseen... yeah, who sings of hope and light
When he in doubt and darkness dwells?"
Unyielding virtue blinds a man; those bend are those that stand
But can this hapless paper 'child' of whom the poet sings
Dare trust the feeble ramblings of such a mortal fool as he
who, himself,
Betrays the hopeless sheep within this feckless fold?

****

And then, just as suddenly, the frigid chill and hellish voice vanished
into nothingness as quickly as it had appeared. The cold emptiness
shook and shocked Lothair to consciousness. Fear and darkness had
loosened their death-like grip. Lothair lay still, as if dead, his corpse-
like shadow still flickering and shaking helplessly in the dying flames
of the midnight fire.

Struggling for warmth and comfort against the growing darkness and
silence of the night, he mustered what little strength remained and
offered a desperate plea, a prayer to the guardian of the night. And as
Lothair whispered the final lines of his song, mingling and sending
faint words heavenward, his heavy eyelids yielded to the encroaching
cold of night:

"Strong Keeper of the Northland's sweetly tun'ed sacred harp...
Blessed Songsmith, Sacred Tamer of celestial spheres...
O let us now but see once more, and dream, and hope again!
Bring us home! Take us back! Let us see and freely breathe again...
Awake and stir our yearning souls to heart-renewing songs
Of joyful, pain-free days and endless dawn...

As he finished his last refrain, his tired, weakened comrades
surrendered their weary bodies to the call of sleep, blissfully unaware
of his torment. His poetry and plea had filled the void created in their
hearts by their absence from their homeland. The loneliness and cold
of the night was now displaced with fond memories as they camped

under a blanket of stars. The men of the North slept peacefully while dreaming of the Northern Kingdom.

****

The morning sun bathed the forest and reflected off the river like the facets of a diamond. The intensity of the light penetrated the rugged travelers' eyelids, rousing them to meet the day. The Frid was an impressive river, but it seemed to grow in size as they contemplated their journey. Mattydale was still a half-day's march. Breakfast would have to wait, time was short. They broke camp in haste and marched down river to rendezvous with Bjorn, the boat builder.

As they marched, they wondered what they would find in Mattydale. Was it safe to enter the town? Had the enemy discovered their plans? Men have a marvelous capacity to invent what they do not know. As they marched their thoughts battled them as viciously as the thorns along the riverbank. Sensing their inner conflict, Wain from time to time punctuated the cadence of their march with words of encouragement.

"Be strong, men," insisted Wain, "Mattydale is just a few hours away. We have come this far. We will succeed. Take courage: Kingdom, Glory, and Dominion!"

It was approaching midday when Wain ordered Lon and the men of Invar to scout ahead.

"Check the town for any signs of the enemy, "Wain ordered.

A short time later, Lon and the others returned. "Everything looks normal, no signs of the enemy," said Lon.

"Good," replied Wain, "then we will proceed into the town and look for Bjorn."

The townsfolk paid them no particular heed, being occupied with their daily business. Occasionally, someone would bid them good day. Although strangers were not regular sights in Mattydale, the townsfolk did not embarrass them with impolite stares or by gawking out their windows as some might do. Mattydale was a small town bustling with craftsman and shipwrights. The townsfolk were curious but courteous at the sight of the new visitors.

The sound of tools could be heard everywhere. The smell of fresh cut timber filled the town like perfume as hammers kept cadence to the beat of progress. The fine tuned hiss of bench planes shaping the ribs of the river boats under construction dovetailed with the odors of turpentine and linseed oil wafting out of the numerous shops. Sawdust filled the streets of the town like a clean carpet of fresh flowers in a spring meadow.

Dominating the waterfront was a large old log building. It appeared to have been built at least a century earlier. It was the largest log building in the town. Its massive wooden doors were open, both front and back revealing craftsmen building riverboats for which Mattydale was renowned. On the porch loomed a giant of a man. He was nearly seven dextars tall. His full-length red beard resembled a lion's mane, and his huge arms bulged, making him as intimidating as he was impressive. His large calloused hands bore testimony that he was no stranger to hard work. Standing erect, he placed them confidently on his hips as he greeted the pilgrims.

"Welcome! You must be the men that old Macoot told me of. Not hard to tell; not too many strangers in these parts. It is good to see that you have made it thus far in one piece when so many want your heads for trophies. These are dangerous times, ya? My name is Bjorn Svengarrd. Come in and sit a spell. Have a mug of ale with me, and then I will show you what old Macoot has arranged for you."

Bjorn's shop was filled with numerous boats, all in different phases of construction. Some were finished and being oiled. Others were being fitted with final detailing. Some looked like giant skeletons whose ribs lacked flesh. The men who worked for Bjorn appeared content with their trade and their master. As he moved from boat to boat, explaining his craft to the pilgrims, Bjorn laughed and jested with the men who eagerly returned their master's good humor with jokes and teasing of their own. That Bjorn was loved and esteemed was clearly evident. The quality of their boats gave ample evidence of their skill and dedication to their craft. Bjorn then led the pilgrims into a large room off the workshop. It was filled with a dozen large round tables. He shouted, "Bring meat and drink for my friends."

On command, several women entered the room with large platters of venison, hard cheese, squash, beans, hot bread, and huge mugs of ale and cider.

"Recognize the cider?" Bjorn asked. "It's from the Toon, the best there is. Liquid gold, this stuff; folks in Urbanus would give a month's wages for one cask of this. Drink hearty, friends."

At that, Bjorn hoisted a large piece of venison to his mouth, smacked his lips together in sweet anticipation and tore into the meat with a savage passion that struggled to find his mouth through the maze of his thick red beard.

This friendly giant captivated the pilgrims. His heart was as big as his stature and his hospitality seemed to know no bounds. He was delighted to have guests at his table, and though he was a businessman, he certainly knew the value of fellowship and hospitality. There seemed to be no end to the number of questions he asked.

"Tell me everything," he said.

Wain and Abner knew that for Bjorn's safety, the less he knew, the better. Should the enemy discover that Bjorn had aided them, Mattydale would become an ash heap. Bjorn soon realized that he would not get the information that he sought, so he suggested that they go to the boats that he had prepared for them.

Behind Bjorn's shop were several large boat docks. Under the cover of camouflage and huge fishing nets were two newly constructed riverboats loaded with supplies.

"Here they are," said Bjorn.

"No finer boats on the Frid or the Ramsgate or in all Urbania for that matter. With proper care and caution, they'll handle anything that the

Ramsgate can offer. There are six water-tight compartments fore and aft that make them well nigh unsinkable. If you capsize they are easily be turned upright."

Bjorn took a deep breath and with a look of concern and hesitation asked the Rangers, "Do you have experience on the river?"

"Yes, we have experience on the water," Lothair replied impatiently, "But can they handle the rapids of Noor?"

"Yes, yes they can, but I caution you not to take the Noor head on. You have to know how to tackle those rapids. If you do it right, these boats will do just fine, but no boat can face the Noor head on. No boats, anywhere," Bjorn said sternly.

Bjorn informed them that enemy ships had been seen on the Ramsgate. He explained that they had entered the Ramsgate from the east and that they must have established outposts there. Until now they had not ventured up the Frid, but he told them to beware because it was only a matter of time before they did. He then gave them instructions to stay close to the riverbank until they reached the Ramsgate. Upon entering the Ramsgate the rapids of Noor would soon appear.

"No boat on the river can out-run these boats of mine. Keep your oars at the ready. Sails will do you no good along the high banks or in the rapids. If you are cut off, leave the boats and head inland; however, if you can make it to the center of the river, trim your sails and out run them. Remember what I am telling you now, do not attempt to take the Noor head-on, many a river boatman has perished trying."

"What if the enemy inquires about us and asks if we were here?" asked Lothair.

"Should anyone inquire about you, I will say that you were here and that like the lying thieves you are, you robbed me of two of my finest boats, along with enough provisions to get you to Urbanus," Bjorn explained.

"I certainly hope that they are as gullible as you are hospitable," Abner replied.

"Never mind me! I've had to deal with those Southern vermin before. They have threatened us, but they need Mattydale. We are a safe place on the frontier where information can be exchanged from many different sources. We mind our business, but we aren't blind or deaf. We know that there are some in Urbania doing business with the South. They wander into town pretending to look for work, but they're just spies, probably Ganza. We tell them what they want to hear and after a few rounds of Toon cider they're too happy to care. I believe that our good fortune will hold," said Bjorn.

"May it be so," said Wain.

He marveled at the courage and daring of Bjorn. He was not fearful in the least, but then no ordinary man would risk helping them. Bjorn, like Macoot, was a rare specimen of courage and risk taking. These two were the embodiment of the old proverb of the Northern Kingdom that says, "It only takes one star to illuminate a universe of darkness."

Wain, Abner, Lon and the Bothers Fairn manned one of the boats. Lothair and the men of Invar, manned the other boat. Wain gave the signal and the boats were launched into the Frid.

****

THE RAPIDS OF NOOR

The sleek riverboats cut through the water like a shark's fin. They were making good progress. The day was clear and the winds were light. All in all, it was a fine day to travel down the Frid to the Ramsgate. The Ramsgate has many faces and the one that you see, seldom prepares you for the one that is to come. Experienced river boatmen call her "the river of deceit" because she is constantly changing. Numerous tributaries flow into her, and she is dotted with frequent oxbows. The ever present sandbars, shoals, and rocks routinely maroon and sink unsuspecting ships.

The constantly shifting currents make charts obsolete over night and navigation a nightmare. Yet these are the simplest challenges that the Ramsgate and her many tributaries have to offer. Conquer these, and you are eligible for the rapids of Noor. It is there that the river descends thousands of dextars in a short span of several dextors from the high country of the mountains to the great plains of Urbania. It is there that the river is transformed from a gentle life-giving, flowing stream into a thundering torrent of churning death.

"How far before we enter the rapids?" Quill asked.

"It can't be long now; the current is increasing in speed. Tie down everything and hang on," Wain ordered.

Wain remembered Bjorn's advice, "Do not take them head on. You have to know how to tackle those rapids!"

He then waved to Lothair to follow him to the southern bank of the river in order to avoid descending the rapids from the center. As they maneuvered their boats to the southern bank, they dropped sail and readied their oars. The current was rapidly increasing and in their preparations to meet the Noor, they failed to notice a large Black Ship sailing directly towards them. The ship sported a large black sail bearing the red and silver crest of the Great Red Dragon, El' Shay'tan. A crew of nearly fifty Sharokhan, Ghouls and human galley slaves manned the Black Ship. The beating of drums and the splash of oars announced the enemy's presence. No sooner did they take note of the enemy ship, than volleys of black arrows rained down on them.

"Row harder, men. Better to take our chances with the Noor than with those devils, Kingdom, Glory, and Dominion," cried Wain.

Bjorn was true to his word; no other boats on the river could match his for speed and agility. The harder the galley slaves pulled at their oars, the faster the pilgrims' river boats seemed to cut through the water. With their gear tied down it was impossible for the pilgrims to return the enemy's fire. They had but one hope: to enter the Noor before the enemy cut them off. They could now feel the mist of the great rapids. The sound of white water growled with fury as the two boats approached the Noor. At the entrance of the rapids a rainbow arched its way over the river; its beauty stood in stark contrast to what awaited them as they entered the cauldron of foam and fury.

The two boats plunged down the rapids and out of sight of the Black Ship. The captain struck his fist against the railing and cursed in disgust. He then gave orders to bring the Black Ship about and take her out of harm's way. The galley slaves strained at the oars, but the current now dictated the destiny of the ship. The captain ordered the Ghouls to use their whips to encourage the galley slaves to row harder. The screaming men grimaced in agony as the whips cut deep into their flesh, but their efforts were in vain. Nothing could free them from the grip of the Noor.

Like a hungry crocodile, the Noor opened its gaping jaws anticipating a meal. The suffering of the galley slaves was soon to come to a merciful end as the powerful rapids devoured the Black Ship. Crashing against the rocks he ship's fate was sealed. Death came as a welcome respite for those miserable creatures. For galley slaves, life is a living death.

Wain could not see Lothair's boat as he and his companions lunged into the jaws of a huge rapid. Keeping the boats properly situated in the rapids was an enormous task. Their arms cramped under the constant strain of the oars. The cold water of the Noor saturated their garments and the wrenching force of the water never allowed them a moment's rest. Wain's boat careened off a rock and was sent out of control. The boat was catapulted upward and fell almost perpendicular to the water.

With a violent crash the boat came to rest on the bottom of a swell. Wain and those who had been in the stern of the boat struggled back to their positions. Lon and Hull struggled to keep their oars in the water and somehow they managed to right the boat and keep its nose pointed into the rapids. As they ascended the crest of a large rapid, Wain quickly looked back for Lothair, but he was nowhere to be seen.

****

BRANTFORD

Wain's boat was hurled down the rapids with such force that the boat was completely airborne. He wondered how much more punishment the men and the boat could endure. Abner hung on to the rope that was lashed to the side of the boat. Down the Noor the boat plummeted into a vast chasm of churning foam and then shot through the tube-like rapid into slightly calmer water.

"We're through the Noor," said Hull in utter disbelief.

"I hope your right. I've had my fill of these rapids," said Lon.

"Abner, are you all right?" asked Wain.

"Yes, a bit bruised, but I am nonetheless glad to be among the living," he said.

"Head for that shoal on the north bank and we'll make a campfire. We need to dry our gear and wait for Lothair," Wain said.

"Where are Lothair and the men of Invar? Did anyone see them in the Noor?" Wain asked.

"I lost sight of them after we almost capsized. I don't know if they made it through ahead of us or whether they're still in the rapids," said Lon.

"Or, worse," said Hull, "they never made it."

"Enough of that," snapped Wain sternly, "Lothair can handle a boat with the best of them; he'll make it."

With haste, they made for a prominent shoal and built a fire. The heat of the fire warmed their cold bodies' right to the bone. Cold, wet garments and exposure to the elements bring certain death in the high country. Hunger was the next challenge that they needed to remedy. Hull, who was always hungry, went into the nearby bush looking for game. A short time later, he returned with several rabbits. Once roasted over the open fire, they proved a tasty solution to their hunger. They were warm, their stomachs were filled, and their boat was still intact. Bjorn was right, his boats could survive anything. But one question remained unanswered: where was Lothair?

It was late afternoon and Wain needed to make a decision. Should they camp and wait for Lothair or should they move on? Time was not on their side. Abner had been concerned about the enemy reaching Brantford before he did. He would not share anything more than that, but he was deeply troubled.

"Look, there's an oar floating down stream and some baggage too, "said Swain.

Wain took Hull and Quill and immediately launched their boat into the Ramsgate. It was an oar from Lothair's boat, and the gear as well. Up the river they could see a capsized boat with several men clinging to it. It was Lothair, Thrace, Doron and Jergen. Egbert was bobbing up and down, treading water behind the boat, as Derek and Owen clung to a tree limb floating down stream. They were alive, but they wouldn't be for long. Wain and Hull strained on the oars to reach the men before they succumbed to the cold water of the Ramsgate. Quill threw a rope to Egbert and pulled him in. Next, Derek and Owen were rescued; Lothair and the others grabbed the rope and were towed to shore. Their numb, frozen bodies would not respond, and they needed to be carried to the life-saving warmth of the fire.

"More wood for the fire!" ordered Wain. The others immediately responded by building a roaring blaze that would warm a man at fifteen paces.

"What happened?" Wain asked.

"We must have been separated at the beginning of the rapids. I tried to follow your lead, but I thought it best to head for the north shore and wait until it was clear. The Black Ship that followed you tried to pull out at the last moment, but the Noor grabbed her and she went down. When we decided that the coast was clear, we entered the Noor and all went well until the last depression. Our weight was all shifted to one side. When we hit that wall of water, we couldn't recover. Fortunately, we capsized at the end of the Noor," said Lothair.

As their garments dried, Wain and Abner planned their next moves. The day was too far gone to travel the Ramsgate. Precious time was being lost and Brantford was still a half day's journey. They decided to send Hull to hunt for more game. They would dry their gear and, more importantly, rest. They would resume their journey at the first light of dawn.

The Ramsgate became wider and calmer as they traveled south toward Brantford early the next morning. Without the benefit of a favorable wind for their sails, or a strong current, rowing became a tedious task. When the wind came up, it grew cold. The clouds darkened, and large snowflakes filled the sky dancing on the air currents like feathers. Hour after hour they rowed against the cross wind, while the gale battled them for every dextor of progress.

It was mid-afternoon when they observed whispers of smoke rising from the north bank of the river. As they set their course for the smoke, a small river appeared. Soon, to their delight, buildings and docks appeared along the waterfront. What a welcome sight Brantford was to the cold and weary pilgrims! But Abner waved them on past the docks, to the disappointment of all. Abner had another destination in mind. Their fatigue demanded that they stop, but up the river they rowed, following Abner's lead. Abner stood in the bow of the boat looking carefully discerning the shoreline.

"There, over there," he said.

The Rill, as it was called by the city folk of Brantford, appeared far deeper than they anticipated, and it accommodated the draft of their boats with ease. This was Brantford, but where were they going? Onward they rowed against the cold wind. Suddenly, as in a mariner's dream, a large dock adjacent to an apple orchard appeared, circling and sheltering the fieldstone base of an immense dwelling.

They were spellbound. Speechless to a man, they could never have imagined such an imposing structure. Its majestic form dwarfed the fertile shore and spread a strong warm shadow over the small weary travelers like the boughs of the ancient oak from which its proud timbers were deftly hewn. Its weathered and rugged grain, but gentle form, blended into the quiet landscape like a precious stone protruding from a shallow forest stream.

"We are here," said Abner.

No one dare ask him, where they were, or why. They knew it was best just to follow and wait for things to unfold. Once the boats were docked and secured, the men followed Abner to the house. What a sight they were. Brantford had never seen the like of these travelers. Abner was not concerned with drawing undue attention from the townsfolk. He was a man intent on his mission. The inhospitable weather was doing an admirable job of keeping the townsfolk indoors. It was getting colder, and the house spoke of warmth and food. Abner paused and stared at the house. With a sigh of relief, he approached the front door and knocked.

"Yes, may I help you?" Romona, the house maid asked in disbelief.

She had never seen men dressed like these men and they were profoundly different in another way. Her apprehension was overcome by their kindness. "*What was happening to Brantford?*" she mused in silence. Strange things indeed were happening in recent days. Abner and his friends were an astonishing sight. But Abner's soft-spoken words immediately broke down the wall of fear that surrounded her.

There was gentleness about these rugged travelers; their eyes confirmed their words, and it was compelling. She did not understand the rush of emotion that filled her, but she knew that could she trust them.

Somehow she knew that they would do her no harm. They were not at all like the two men who hurt poor Daylin.

"Is Jurius Hanner at home?" Abner inquired.

"Whom may I say is asking?" Romona requested.

"Tell him that an old friend wishes to see him. Tell him that whoever receives him, receives his Master," Abner said.

Without hesitation Romona went straight to Jurius and relayed the old man's message. Jurius was sitting comfortably before the fireplace in his stuffed leather chair. It was a cold late autumn day that had been filled with the frantic pace of business. Jurius was enjoying a few brief moments of peace. Romona's entrance into the room with Abner's message shattered his solitude. Startled, Jurius muttered to himself, *"How could it be, after all these years? It's impossible. I thought he was ... I mean, ugh, I don't know?"*

"He's at the door, sir. He's waiting for you there ... and he's accompanied by, oh, oh, oh ..., well, please come and see for yourself," she stuttered.

Jurius got up and went to the main entrance of the house. There stood Abner and the band of Rangers. Jurius stared at Abner in utter disbelief. Surely he was dreaming, but this was no dream.

"Abner, it's really you! How many years has it been? I've had no word for so long. I thought you were dead. Why are you here? Come in, come in. How rude of me. Come in and warm yourselves by the fire. "Romona, Romona, quickly, bring food and hot tea," he said.

After instructing Romona to say nothing about the arrival of his guests, Jurius quickly escorted Abner and his companions to the Great Room. Cautiously, he looked up and down the halls, and quickly but carefully shut the doors to the Great Room. After his guests were seated, Jurius turned to Abner and waited for his explanation.

"Jurius, old friend, I know that my presence here is a surprise to you, but these are desperate times. The Great King, Sa'lem, has sent me here for two reasons. It is time for you to know things which have been long hidden from you for your protection. The Great King also requests your help in making known his will to the Brotherhood in Urbanus and to Prince Solon. You have influence with the Brotherhood, and you are respected in Urbanus. It is critical that they listen to what I have to say, and that they act on it. The enemy is about to launch a major offensive against Urbania. There is much to explain, but I must rest now," said Abner.

"Yes, by all means, rest," Jurius pleaded.

Just then, Romona entered the room with the refreshments Jurius had requested. The warmth of the fire and the hospitality proved a welcome respite from the cold. Their eyelids soon surrendered to their fatigue, and they slept were they sat.

****

"Abner, Abner, is it possible? You can't be serious." Molly said.

"Hush. Yes, he's here in our home and he has a dozen Northern Rangers with him. He says that he has things to share with us, things that we need know, but I think I know what he's going to say, and ..."

But before Jurius could finish his sentence Molly finished it for him.

"He wants you to help him, doesn't he? Of course you must, after all, he was responsible for rescuing us when all was lost. You remember, don't you? You must help him. What does he want?" Molly demanded.

"He wants me to deliver a message from the Great King Sa'lem to Prince Solon in Urbanus, and to appeal to the Brotherhood for their support. He said that the enemy is conspiring with traitors and is preparing to launch an offensive against Urbania. It sounds very serious. I'm not sure what I can do to help. The assembly is deeply divided into factions of diverse opinions and agendas. The Brotherhood has been closed to outsiders, tolerating no views at odds with their own," Jurius explained.

"I don't know what we can do, but whatever we can do; we will do in order to help him. We owe a debt of gratitude to King Sa'lem and to

Abner. We will do what we can but what do you think he wants to share with us?" she asked.

"I think it concerns Daylin," Jurius said apprehensively.

****

Jurius quietly opened the doors of the Great Room. Abner was awake and sitting before the fire, deep in thought while his companions peacefully slept away their fatigue. Jurius cautiously entered the room and approached Abner.

"Where can speak privately?" Abner asked.

"Come with me," said Jurius.

Jurius had an unassuming office across the hall where numerous business deals had been forged. The office was as modest as the man. Jurius had a profound dislike for pretentious airs and he had no place for the symbols of wealth and power that were desired by so many businessmen less successful than he. The simpler the better and if simple was to be had at the best price, then he liked it all the more.

The room was small, but well ordered. The dark wood paneling gave it a business-like atmosphere but without the loss of comfort. Two large windows faced the Ramsgate. From there Jurius could watch the traffic of goods that were the source of his livelihood. It was here he hung his hat, and here where he found his purpose in life. Jurius entered the room, drew the drapes over the large windows, and then immediately lit the oil lamps. Their warm amber glow slowly filled the room.

"Please, Abner, sit here, be comfortable, and let us speak together."

"Have there been any strange happenings in Brantford lately?" Abner inquired.

"Yes, strange things indeed. There are two houseguests staying with us who are quite strange and they're acting very suspiciously!" Jurius responded.

"Hmm, as I feared, he suspects something. No doubt they are his Ganza spies, sent here to gather intelligence. We encountered the Sharokhan in the Great Forest, and as far as the Rapids of Noor. Have you seen them?" Abner asked.

"No, but there have been rumors of strange things afoot. Some folks deny it, while others say that it is paranoia and imagination. But the people are seeing something, of that I have no doubt," Jurius said with a sigh.

"It's the Artrax that is what they are seeing. They are his chosen ones, half bat and half man. They are the eyes and ears of the enemy. They are always afoot when war is imminent. They are his advance guard, and they never risk appearing in plain sight until the Ganza has worked their deception on the masses. Then the trap is set!" Abner exclaimed.

Jurius could no longer restrain his curiosity. Changing the subject, he boldly addressed Abner. "What is it that you want me to know? What are the things that have been withheld from me for my protection?" Jurius inquired.

"Jurius, your son and daughter-in-law did not perish in the Great War as you believed. They were rescued by the Rangers after the fall and razing of Esteria and were taken north to Aletheia for their protection. They are part of the Great King Sa'lem's ward, and they must remain so until the fullness of time."

"My son and his wife are alive?" he gasped.

"Yes, they are alive and well. You see, Jurius, the Great War merely set the stage for the enemy's ultimate plan, as a means to a greater end, as it were. He knows that he cannot conquer Urbania so long as the One who is promised lives. He was trying to kill the hope of the entire Middle Kingdom. He fears the coming One, and he seeks what he alone possesses," Abner said, while drawing a deep breath.

"Yes, and what ...?" Jurius began to probe once again impatiently.

"Daylin is the One foretold in the Ancient Scrolls," Abner said.

"Daylin, Daylin is the One? I knew this involved him somehow. But this cannot be! He is only a boy of twelve, and he is so immature. You can't be serious. No, no, haven't we lost enough?" Jurius pleaded.

"I know this all comes as a shock to you, but Daylin is the reason why the Great King Sa'lem arranged for you and Molly to live in Brantford these years. I know that you think it was the Brotherhood that made the provision for your new life, but your benefactor is the Great King Sa'lem. In his wisdom he knew that Brantford was a safe place for you to raise the boy and with so many orphaned after the Great War. The Great King knew that Daylin's situation would not draw undue attention. But he also knew that it would only be a matter of time before the enemy discovered him. I fear it is already too late.

"Jurius, I suspect that you already know much of what I am about to tell you. Your father, Cyrus Hanner, was instrumental in rescuing the Jasper Stone from the great temple in Urbanus during Nergal-Anshar's invasion. He and a group of men faithful to King Sa'lem secretly carried the precious stone out of the city before it fell to Nergal-Anshar and his pitiless hordes. They then made a pact to hide the stone, and they hid it in an unknown location. It is said that their secret died with them, but it did not. Urbanus may have been rebuilt, and restored to her former glory, but not the Great Temple. It has not and cannot be restored without the Jasper Stone. This is why so many desire to possess it; however, there is only one who can posses it, and he is yet to be revealed.

"For far too long, Urbanus has placed its hope in things that cannot deliver them from what they fear the most. Cyrus went to his grave without ever revealing the location of the treasure or the Jasper Stone. Alas, there are many who covet the sacred Stone, because without it they cannot rebuild the temple. The Brotherhood knows this, as does the Emir of the Southern Kingdom, Sanballat. Both are consumed with their lust for the power and prestige that such a sacred treasure will bring them."

"Now old friend, be truthful with me, do you have it?" Abner demanded.

Jurius paused and looked away. He wanted to deny it, but he knew that it was fruitless to attempt to deceive Abner, who could see through the motives of men like peering through a perfect pane of glass. Jurius was cornered; honest confession seemed like the best course of action.

"Yes, old friend, I have it! You knew that I did, so why test me?" Jurius retorted.

"A little testing is good every now and then. It keeps the conscience keen. Such secrets and mysteries have a way of twisting the strongest character. It is a burden that you have borne for too long a time. It is needed now. Where is it hidden?" Abner asked.

Jurius approached the chestnut paneled wall behind his writing desk and pushed on the panel. A secret compartment opened and a dusty cloth-covered box appeared. Jurius carefully opened it. Inside was the most exquisite pear-shaped crystalline jasper gemstone affixed to a silver chain. In the dim light of the candle-lit room, it reflected and refracted the light in a dazzling array of colors that seemed to dance off the walls and ceiling like shimmering lightning bugs on a bright summer's night.

"Do you know the history of this stone, Jurius?" Abner entreated.

"I think so, but please tell me what you know about it," he humbly asked.

"The Great King Sa'lem made your father, Cyrus, the steward of this precious stone. It is the sign, seal and symbol of the Northern Kingdom. It is the key to the twelve thrones and twelve gates of the city of the Great King. King Sa'lem authorized and commissioned Cyrus to hide the temple treasures and to keep the Jasper Stone of the temple from falling into the wrong hands. Cyrus and his posterity were to keep it in trust until the time it was called for, and that time is at hand. Only the One who is called may wear it without fear of being consumed by it. It is precious and beautiful beyond comparison, but it will consume any and all that desire it to satisfy their selfish ambition by possessing it."

Abner paused for moment gazing at the Jasper stone with a sense of awe mixed with apprehension. He then nodded his head in solemn approval and said, "It is time that Daylin knows."

Abner left Jurius in his office and retired for the evening. Though he slept, his thoughts remained troubled wondering what the morrow would bring.

****

"Good morning Jurius," Abner said.

"Your strange house guests, where are they?" asked Abner.

"I don't know. They appear to have left two days ago without paying their bill. One choked Daylin and threw him to the ground and we haven't seen them since," Jurius explained.

"They are the Ganza, and they're still here. I can sense their presence. There are eyes fixed on this house. I doubt that we entered here undetected. Can you trust Romona?" asked Abner.

"Yes, she is very trustworthy; she would say nothing," Jurius said confidently.

"Good, but we must now speak with all involved. Bring Molly to the great room, and I will share the whole plan with you, Molly and my companions," said Abner.

"The Rangers don't know why you're here?" Jurius asked in disbelief.

"No, it was too dangerous. The risk was far too great. A captured man, even a Ranger, would break under the enemy's cruel and crafty interrogation. His spells are far too powerful. These Rangers are good and faithful men, but it is now time for them to know the nature of their mission."

****

This was the first official trip to Urbanus that Ursus had ever taken. For reasons of security, he seldom left his home city of Hupsoma. He was coming to Urbanus at the invitation of Solon, the prince of Urbanus. Solon had invited the princes of the nine cites to attend a peace and unity conference. Ursus had many things on his mind but peace and unity were not among them. He was a focused man with only one passion, acquiring and maintaining power. Ursus was not a prince, but he coveted the position. He had deposed the prince of Hupsoma and assumed the illustrious title of "Strategos" or field commander of the Thema and Tagmata. Since he was not of royal blood, he had to console himself with these lesser titles, greater titles would be forthcoming if he had his way.

Since the Great War, Urbania was a house divided. Political factions, cults, and spiritual sects filled the ten cities. The lack of unity and the resulting social turmoil provided a tempting opportunity for an ambitious man of vision. Ursus recognized an opportunity when he saw one, and he had set a course to quench his lust for power and recognition.

Ursus sat tall in the saddle. Urbanus was just coming into view. It appeared slowly on the horizon like a mirage on the sands of the great desert. Raising his hand, he brought his entourage of five hundred to an abrupt halt. These were Hupsoma's elite soldiers, the Thema, and they weren't going to Urbanus with peace and unity in mind. This was a force large enough to accomplish his ends, but small enough not to cause alarm. Ursus was cunning, and he was always seeking an advantage. Savoring the moment, he sat studying the object of his lust, the gem that he longed to possess, and one more beautiful than any woman he had ever seen or possessed, Urbanus!

"What a sight my Lord, isn't she grand?" said Gordo, the captain of the Thema.

"Yes, a fine sight, but she lacks one thing, Gordo, a master who can give her order and purpose. Her people are intoxicated with their notions of peace and security. They need restraint, and I offer them just that," he said with a sarcastic smile. "Solon has made her a place of many voices and many visions, but freedom unrestrained leads to chaos. It is our duty to deliver Urbanus from this epidemic, don't you agree?"

"Yes, Lord Ursus. I see what you mean and, after all, this is a mission of unity and peace!"

"We shall unify them, Gordo, and there will be peace in Urbania, but it will be done in our way. First Urbanus and then the others, they will fall like rotting trees in a storm."

"The two men laughed in hearty agreement. Solon was a fool to give them such an opportunity. The disorder of the city made it a prime candidate for Ursus' hypnotic oratory. He knew that he could sway the masses of Urbanus to his point of view if given the opportunity. If Prince Solon only knew his true intentions! The more he thought on it, the harder he laughed.

****

The Hanner home had never witnessed such a collection of guests. Over the years, Jurius and Molly had provided hospitality to many a traveler, but there was nothing to compare to the assembly that filled their great room on this dark night. Molly had fashioned a semi-circle with the chairs from the dining room table, and everyone sat down with the exception of Abner who stood before the group.

"It is time that you know the nature of the mission that we have undertaken on behalf of the Great King Sa'lem. We have come to Brantford on an urgent mission." Abner explained in detail everything that he had shared with Jurius. They listened intently, and then he dropped the rock of revelation upon them.

"We have come to Brantford to seek the One foretold in the Ancient Scrolls," he said.

The room erupted in unison, "What, what did he say? The One, he is here, here in this forsaken place?"

Molly had barely recovered from the revelation that her son and daughter-in-law were alive and well, when Abner dropped this on her!

"Where is he? Does he live in Brantford? And what name does he go by?" she asked.

"His name is Daylin Hanner, and he lives in this house," Abner answered.

Molly fell off her chair in a dead faint. The revelation was too much for her to bear. The men of Invar tended to Molly as Abner demanded, "Where is the boy? The enemy wants him and will stop at nothing until he kills him. He knows who he is and what he possesses. Go and bring him here at once!"

Wain and his Rangers followed Jurius up the stairs, down the hall and straight into Daylin's room. The fate of Urbania now rested on his small shoulders, but you would never have known it judging by how soundly Daylin slept.

Daylin loved cold snowy nights. Grandma Molly's goose down comforter and his soft bed made sleeping more of an escape than a necessity. Life was good. But his young life was about to be rudely interrupted by reality. A cold bony hand rubbed his blond hair and shattered an otherwise perfectly fine dream. Abner spoke softly to him and said, "Wakeup, wakeup sleepy one, it is time for you to know what destiny has chosen for you!"

Daylin's tired eyes open slowly; it was a difficult choice to make. Should he return to the dream that he just left, or accept the invitation to this new one? He must be dreaming, after all, these were Rangers. And the old man ... what a strange old man. He must be a seer or a magician. But there was good news, too! At last someone recognized that he was special. He had always known that destiny had marked him for something special, and it wasn't to die of life-long boredom in Brantford.. This dream was too good to be true. But this time it was not a dream.

Hull's huge arms carried Daylin like a baby down the stairs. They brought Daylin into the great room. Grandma Molly was responding well to a cold compress and glass of water. The sight of Daylin caused her to forget her earlier swoon and she took Daylin by the arms and gently shook him. "Daylin, listen to me. These men are here on a very important mission. You must listen to them, child. Some things may be difficult for you to understand, but you must listen, nonetheless. Daylin, child, so much depends on you, please wake up!"

Daylin awoke at the sound of Grandma Molly's voice. He could never ignore that voice. To do so would mean a trip to the woodshed, and, oh, how he hated that woodshed. She had his full attention. This was no dream; these men were real.

Abner asked, "May I speak with him alone?"

"Yes, of course, come let us leave them. Come with me to the kitchen. Molly will prepare some food and drink," Jurius said.

Molly's kitchen proved to be a fine distraction for the Rangers. Fresh baked bread, potato and cheese casserole, hard cheddar cheese, smoked salmon and venison, pickled herring and pitchers of ale eased the tensions of an otherwise tumultuous evening.

"The woman works magic at the stove. This is her domain gentleman and there is no finer cook in all Urbania!" Jurius boasted.

"None will contest it sir," answered Hull, who was never known to turn down a free meal. The food and the fellowship were as intoxicating as the ale. They ate and drank until their hunger and thirst were but memories. Relaxation can put a person more at ease than weary minds and bodies; but too much food and drink does the same thing to sound judgment. Poor Hull was flustered; his leggings had come apart, he needed to repair his lacing, but he couldn't find his Noraxe.

"What are you looking for; what do you need, Hull?" asked Lothair.

"My knife, I can't find my Noraxe!"

"No problem, Hull, use this one!"

Without hesitation, Lothair reached under his leather vest, pulled another knife from its sheath, and handed it to Hull. Hull reached for the knife and began to cut his broken laces, when he noticed that the knife wasn't a Ranger's blade at all.

"Where did you get this, Lothair? Where is it from? I've never seen anything quite like it!" Hull said.

"I found it when I was scouting the shoreline at the Noor. I don't know where it came from, but it's a handsome blade. It doesn't belong to the Sharokhan. Perhaps a boatman lost it!"

"I doubt that boatmen would own a blade like that; look at the markings on it. Those are military insignias!" Hull exclaimed.

Lothair was growing impatient with Hull's questions and he abruptly cut him off, "Do you want to use this knife or not?" Lothair demanded.

While the Rangers ate and drank, Abner spoke with Daylin. Time was short, and the boy needed to know everything. There were so many things to say, and the boy had so many questions, but in the end he understood. Abner explained that this honor also placed him in grave danger. Now the strange happenings in Brantford made sense. The enemy was intent on finding him. What next?

"You must go to Urbanus."

"But, why?" asked Daylin.

"That will become clear to you in due time," Abner said.

"Until the remnant is united, the King of the North cannot return. The Ancient Scrolls need to be fulfilled. You must unite the Brotherhood, and then the armies of the Northern Kingdom can enter Urbania and destroy the works of the enemy. Their eyes are blinded. They are divided. They are more concerned with their opinions and their reputations than they are with preserving the kingdom of Urbania. The enemy and his agents have deceived all the mortal men of Urbania. The Brotherhood claims to see, but they are as blind as bats. The others are blind and deaf, to boot, and even brag about it. There is too much at stake: the fate of the Toon, the people, and all creatures of the Great Forest. They will all perish if the enemy succeeds in killing you and subduing the ten cities. The fate of Urbania rests on your shoulders, Daylin."

"There is one more thing!" Abner reached into his bag and drew out the jasper stone fixed to a silver necklace. He stooped down and placed it over Daylin's head and around his neck. This cannot be removed from you. It is permanent; no man can remove it. Wear it well and never remove it! It will guide your path and be a light and lamp in the darkest of times. Listen to what it reveals, and in due time you will understand."

Daylin was completely bewildered by all of this. It was overwhelming, almost beyond belief.

"We will leave in the morning. It's best that you sleep now, for you may not sleep again for a very long time," Abner said in deadly earnest.

But sleep was the last thing Daylin's on mind. His thoughts swirled like a dust-devil on the high plains of Lamburg. How could he sleep at a time like this? He was overwhelmed with the matters that Abner had revealed to him. It was true that he was a dreamer, but dreams and imagination were nothing compared to what Abner had just shared. Perhaps he should ask Grandmother Molly for a glass of warm milk and attempt to sleep. Perhaps the morning's light would prove that all this was just a dream. But he knew in the deepest recesses of his soul that this was no dream. This was all too real, and it begged the question: "What would become of him?"

Episode II
The Narrow Gate

THOSE THAT BEND

Daylin awoke confused and disoriented. Where was he? He struggled to focus his eyes and to gather his thoughts. Was it morning? The sun's rays had not yet penetrated his room, and Grandma Molly's familiar pleas to get out of bed and start the day were not to be heard. Rubbing his eyes, he reassured himself that this was no dream. Suddenly, a tall figure appeared and placed a hand over Daylin's mouth and then placed his index finger over Daylin's lips, making a sign that Daylin was to remain quiet. The man's strong arms picked him up, cradling him like a doll. In one fell swoop the tall figure leapt out the window and made straight for the apple orchard. The moonless night was cold and Daylin couldn't see a thing. The cold wind slapped his face, ending the memory of the comfort and warmth of his bed. The tall figure's long pounding strides hit the ground in quick succession, propelling him toward the unknown. Daylin's dream was about to become a nightmare.

The tall figure suddenly stopped, and as he did, two men emerged from the orchard. Although it was dark, he recognized them. Daylin could feel their presence. He knew them, especially the taller of the two. He was the man who had choked him on the porch steps. Something was very wrong. Daylin struggled, but it was all in vain. The tall figure's strength was far too much for a boy to resist.

"You have done well Lothair," the tall man hissed.

"Yes, our master, will reward you handsomely for this act of service," the short man said enthusiastically.

"The deed is done, get going before they suspect something," Lothair said franticly.

The tall man grabbed Daylin, grasped him by the throat and slowly choked him.

"I would choke the life out of this little maggot right now and end his miserable existence if I had my way. It is too bad that our master wants him as the center piece of his victory parade in Urbanus. When he's done with him, I hope he will reward me with the honor of gutting the little pig," sneered the tall man in disgust.

The short man laughed with glee and with a motion of his hand he gestured that they make for the Ramsgate where a black ship silently waited for them. As the oars of the ship cut through the water of the Ramsgate, Daylin knew that each stroke of the oar meant that he was one stroke farther from home. All this is in the span of one night. He now regretted that he had ever wanted to be part of a great adventure. "Old Blandford," as he called it, began to look better and better to him. In truth, anything was better than his present circumstances, for he lay bound and gagged on the cold wet deck of the black ship surrounded by the Sharokhan.

****

There are two things that even the strongest of men cannot accept: the first is broken expectations, and the second is the circumstances they bring. Wain was no exception. While the others searched the house and the property, he knew the truth. Their river boats were gone; Daylin was missing, and Lothair was nowhere to be found. The others, including Abner, refused to speak of the unthinkable, but it was true, nonetheless. Lothair had betrayed them.

Wain sat down and accepted the sick aching feeling that gripped his stomach, the companion of grief. But Wain had no time for grief. He loved Lothair. He was more than a brother to him; he was his best friend, or so he thought. Somehow, some way, he had to resist the temptation to surrender to his emotions and quit. He had to go on, but this time the call of duty would not propel him over this wall as it had so many times before. In his heart of hearts, Wain knew the truth, but he could not accept it. Something was buried deep within him from that very moment that no one could see. Deep in the recesses of his heart, Wain buried Lothair, and from that time on chose not to speak of him. But yeast cannot be hidden in a lump of dough.

His realization that the other Rangers had come to the same conclusion was heralded by Hull, "The filthy scoundrel. That vile snake! I'll rip his heart out with my bare hands!" he screamed.

The men of Invar encouraged his rage with their own assessment of the circumstances. Every flaw and failure of Lothair's life was now fair game, and the hunters showed no mercy. For an hour they vented their rage on Lothair's memory and, like vultures feasting on a corpse, they left nothing on the carcass of his reputation. Wain's ears were as closed as his heart; it was as though Lothair had never existed. He vowed that he would never allow Lothair or the memory of him to hurt him again.

The feeding frenzy continued unabated until Abner could bear it no longer.

"Silence, silence, hasn't there been enough wrong done here tonight? Must you now crucify Lothair before you know the facts? Making up what you don't know will not lead to the truth. This will accomplish nothing."

Quill angrily retorted. "The facts speak for themselves! He has betrayed us all, and he's sold the boy to the enemy. We are finished, and so is Urbania. Spare us your wisdom, old man! It is plain to see what's happened here!"

"Yes, perhaps you're right but the facts need interpreting! You are looking at this situation through a lens of self-preservation and wounded pride. What shall we do? Shall we surrender? Shall we ask for a truce? No, we must go on and we will go on, or we die; and if we die, everything dies with us.

One man has possibly failed; shall we follow him down the path of least persistence to eternal shame? Not I! Decide amongst yourselves what your course of action will be, but I must go to Urbanus. So long as the boy lives, hope lives. The enemy cannot take his life. Daylin is under the watch and care of the Great King Sa'lem. The enemy must turn him. Daylin must surrender to the will of the enemy by his own volition. Until then and only then is all hope lost."

The Rangers gathered together to consider their options. Wain remained aloof; he refused to speak. While the others argued, Wain packed his gear and prepared to travel. They all wanted to know the answer to the question. Swain finally summoned the courage and asked, "Where are you going, Wain?"

"Where am I going? We are going after the boy! Are you through with your deliberations? Good! Now do something useful and pack your gear; they already have a day's head start. We'll have to ride through the night to catch the ship and even then, it will take a miracle to locate them. There's nothing else we can do. Abner's right, we can't just sit here and wait for the inevitable. Let's make a move!"

It was what they were waiting for, a committed course of action. They knew to a man that it is sometimes better to be committed than to be right. Jurius provided them with horses and supplies, and after calculating the direction and trail that the enemy might take, they set out to find Daylin. Abner chose to stay with Jurius because he would only slow them down. Moreover, they reasoned that safe passage to Urbanus could be arranged for him from Brantford. It was agreed that Wain and the others would meet Jurius and Abner in Urbanus.

****

Mara the Magnificent

The lands of the Southern Kingdom were comprised of vast stretches of parched, lifeless tracts of arid land, punctuated by an occasional pale oasis dotted with palm trees. Outside of nomadic desert tribes, the greater portion of this formidable wasteland was uninhabited. It was a virtual wilderness, the deadly haunt of Jackals, wild dogs, scorpions and snakes. It was scarcely a place where men would choose to live, if given the choice. All these factors combined to give it an intimidating aura of invincibility. The kingdom was as inhospitable and unwelcoming as its climate. Its relentless dryness and heat stood in stark contrast to the verdant forests and deep, clear life-giving rivers of Urbania.

Strangers and wayfarers were not welcome anywhere on the Southern Kingdom's treacherous landscape. Here the indomitable camel was the preferred form of efficient transportation. There was scant need of trusty river boats with their proud broad oars on this vast ocean of sand and rock.

That is not to say that there was no life at all within the boundaries of the Southern Kingdom. There was, in fact, one place where a form of life did, indeed, exist in abundance. It was a place where the inhabitants did enjoy the benefit of one great river, the Amar, on the eastern border. To the west, the El-Bashir escarpment towered high above the desert. A natural fortification against invasion, it also prevented the moisture-laden winds of the eastern ocean from bringing thirst-quenching rains to the parched landscape.

Mara camped on the Amar; it was there that the vast majority of the inhabitants of the Southern Kingdom congregated taking advantage of the river's bounty.

"Mara the Magnificent" as she was called, occupied the eastern and western banks of the Amar. Here the populace found water in abundance, and the seasonal flooding produced fertile farm land that was exploited to its fullest. Mara rose arrogantly above the river with its white limestone buildings. Sanballat's palace was situated at its center and dominated the landscape, as if to boast of its prominence. The common folk lived in adobe-style dwellings made of mud bricks, baked in the torrid heat of the relentless sun.

Mara was nearly impregnable to invasion. Her walls rose to the height of 100 dextars and were wide enough for four teams of chariots to ride abreast of each other and circle her walls according to legend, took a full day. The Amar gave the city life, and that life needed defending since the mighty river ran through the center of the city. To prevent a siege that would cut off the water supply, massive iron gates were constructed, making sailing the river impossible unless the gates were raised. Great stone silos held vast stores of grain and the city could stand a siege of two years if need be. Mara's wealth, power, and strategic defenses defined her as a force to be reckoned with.

Despite her place of power and wealth, Mara's appetite had proven insatiable. She had long envied the wealth, power and prestige of her northern neighbor, Urbania, and its crown jewel, "Urbanus the Great." Over the centuries, Mara had invaded Urbania on four separate occasions, but on each occasion, the invaders failed to complete the conquest. These repeated failures did little, however, to deter the Southern Kingdom's strategic goal of conquering Urbanus and rebuilding the great temple. The population had always believed that conquering and ruling Urbanus was their birthright and that they were the rightful heirs to Urbania. Every Emir of Mara embraced this timeless belief and adopted it as his own personal vision. And Sanballat was no exception.

What news do you have to report?" the tall swarthy figure demanded with an impatient snarl.

Sanballat, Emir of Mara, rhythmically tapped his bony fingers on the arms of his throne, waiting for an answer, but no one dared answer him. Nothing could be heard except the deep rhythmic chanting of a group of Arche who formed a circle around an immense, imposing image of El' Shay'tan the Great Red Dragon.

A voice suddenly thundered above their incantations and demanded: "Where is Abner? Did we manage to turn Lothair and take the boy? Why haven't I received reports from Ursus?"

His deep voice penetrated every crevasse of the incense-filled chamber. His probing eyes searched the crowd with a cold, suspicious detachment. As he studied them, they cringed in fear, cowering like guilty children caught in their mischief. His patience was wearing thin. There had been no news for days, and he was frustrated and growing angry. The fear in the hall was so thick that all could taste it.

"Master, an Artrax has returned from Urbania. He brings news!" said a Sharokhan.

"Bring him to me, immediately!"

The Artrax entered the hall and spread his wings over his head as he bowed in homage to his master.

"Great Sanballat, master, I bring you good news. Lothair has done as he pledged. The boy, Daylin, has been captured and is now on his way to Hupsoma. Ursus is in Urbanus and awaits the arrival of Abner and the Rangers. The Brotherhood is prepared to receive Abner as you instructed. They will all be in one place, just as you desire. Those who serve you are eager to act. We await your command."

"Praise to the Great One! El' Shay'tan, the Most Excellent! Good news at last. Well done. Well done indeed! At least I have one faithful servant in my realm who seeks to please me."

With that rebuke the entire hall erupted in a rage of jealousy like Hyenas deprived of a share of the kill. They cursed and pointed their bony fingers at one another in accusation. Failure wasn't tolerated in this court, and the fast track to acquiring power and position was to blame another scoundrel for one's own failures. They grumbled and quarreled with each other until the Emir brought an end to the frenzy.

"Enough, there are plenty of scraps to go around, you sorry pack of jackals. Assemble my counselors. The rest of you get out of here. Clear my chambers, now!"

The massive throne was centered in the middle of the chamber, towering above everything in it. Nothing in the room approached its height or compared to its imposing features. Everything about it spoke of power and strength. The pale white stone from which it was carved gave it the pallor of a corpse. More than a symbol, it was a statement. The one who sat upon this throne considered himself the supreme sovereign of the world and all its kingdoms. A hallway half a dextor in length preceded the entrance to the chamber. Those summoned to the throne had to walk the entire length of the hallway, across the floor of the chamber, while the throne loomed ominously before their eyes the entire time. It was calculated to affect the one summoned, leaving them intimidated and feeling insignificant.

The Arche, who were the Emir's counselors, assembled around the throne and waited for him to speak. From the throne a deep voice demanded, "In the name of the Great One, is the darkness advancing?"

"Yes, master, as we speak. Thanks to Ursus, we have a stronghold in Hupsoma and a foothold in several other cities as well, and from there the darkness will spread throughout the Western Province. Phase one is complete, master," answered an Arche.

Purring like a blood-hungry Tiger over a fresh kill, Sanballat touched the ends of his fingers together and weighed the Arche's answer.

"Praise to the name of the Great One—The Most Excellent, El' Shay'tan. Ursus is such a pleasure. He's so compliant, and his naked ambition is so sublime. Nothing will stop him from getting what he wants; if only I had more like him. Ah, such unabashed ambition in the men of Urbania is rare, yet, it is a beautiful thing to behold. His help will prove to be the missing link in rebuilding the temple in Urbanus. It is rightfully mine and I mean to possess it!"

"Alas, let us not undervalue the Brotherhood, for it is they who will ultimately deliver Urbania into our hands. Indeed, there is nothing as valuable to our cause as a zealot who dogmatically defends his position at the expense of unity. The passion of self-righteousness is so intoxicating. It pleases me so when they destroy each other in defense of their perception of the truth and never experience a pang of conscience. They cannot see beyond their own misguided passion."

"In the past, many a zealot has removed a stone from my shoe. But it's their fatalism that's their greatest contribution to my cause because it allows me to infiltrate Urbania without opposition. They actually rejoice when I advance my dominion."

After all, he sneered with contempt and cold mockery, "It's all foretold in their precious scrolls. The superstitious fools! I could never have gained the advantage that I enjoy without them. Praise to the Great One the Most Excellent El' Shay'tan!"

The Arche surrounding the throne applauded and cheered at their master's cynical evaluation of the situation. They may have hated each other, but they hated the men of Urbania even more, so when Sanballat boasted of his plans to enslave them, they could not restrain their excitement. There would be enough slaves for all when his plan was consummated. Besides it was politically astute to pander to his egomania. They knew his addiction to flattery and praise, and they willingly indulged him, but he was correct, nonetheless.

"The boy must be neutralized. I cannot directly kill him since he is under the protection of my arch-enemy, Sa'lem. Our only recourse is to corrupt him. I trust that you are treating him properly and encouraging him to respond in the right way? This matter must be handled very delicately!"

"Yes, master, the Artrax report that the boy is filled with fear and confusion. Our goal is to make him blame himself for what has happened. He probably knows that he is the "One" and that all this trouble is his doing. We are seeking to create a lens of false guilt for him. This is the first step in the process. He won't be making any leaps of faith so long as he's weighed down with that burden. We have isolated him, and what communication he has, is always discouraging. He has been deprived of food and water. His condition is weak, and he is very vulnerable. His spirit is nearly broken. Your two Ganza agents in Brantford have taken a special interest in him. They are encouraging him to respond in bitterness and hatred. He will turn; it is only a matter of time," said another Arche.

"Excellent, excellent, I knew that I made a good choice in sending those two Ganza rodents to Brantford. Ah, the men of Urbania are so predictable, are they not? Take away what they hold dear and they must blame someone. In their rush to make sense of life they need straw men to burn when they think life is unfair. Fair! Fair is a place where hogs compete for ribbons! At their core, they are self-centered and egotistical. They really believe that life owes them something! They love to moralize about love and forgiveness, but let them taste betrayal or injustice and they respond like cornered rats. Oh, they'll cloak their bitterness in the rags of hypocrisy and rationalization, but in the end, they burn with hate. They've deceived themselves into thinking that they can drink a cup of poison while watching the other man die. Yes, 'to err may be human, but to forgive ...,' well, that's just a line."

The chambers erupted with cynical laughter and delight. Sanballat was a genius when it came to understanding human nature. He was correct. Forgiveness for humanity was more of a theory than a practice. For these henchmen and their subordinates carrying out these designs was pure sport.

They had been successfully infiltrating Urbania for decades, disguised in the familiar roles of society. They had infected and influenced every facet of life in Urbania. How they loved to destroy homes, marriages, friendships, and business relationships. Their toxic tongues and tactics spread gossip, slander and bitterness. But their ultimate goal was the corruption of the morals and ethics of Urbania.

Once the men of Urbania thought and reasoned like the Southern Kingdom, they would sooner or later imitate its behavior. They knew that ultimately selfish ambition divides humanity into irreconcilable sects and factions, making unity and agreement impossible. The culture of Urbania was now theirs for the taking. Nothing prevented them from complete dominion, nothing except the unlikely intervention of the Great King of the North, King Sa'lem.

Sanballat shifted his focus to Wain and said, "I can only imagine what Wain is experiencing at this very moment. It gives me such pleasure to know that I was responsible for destroying his relationship with his brother. The Rangers are crumbling in disunity as I speak. I have no fear of their reconciling because the more righteous their cause, the deeper their bitterness. Wain's disappointment is too deep and he's no doubt thinking that if he forgives Lothair and reconciles with him, he would be condoning his betrayal. Perhaps he thinks that it would undermine his moral authority and encourage others to betray him. He'd be compromising with the enemy, so to speak. But then, forgiving and restoring fallen leaders isn't one of the Rangers' strengths.

Lothair is finished! The Rangers will never take him back. He has served our purposes well. I venture to say that Wain is in complete denial and that's very good for me because unexpressed grief is as effective as cancer. He's dying on the inside. This is something he can't handle alone, but he'll try. Mark my words! The captain of the Rangers is now vulnerable. We can pick him like a ripe fig, and the time of picking is mine to choose. Once I deal with old Abner, that blind seer, I have something very special in mind for our Ranger."

The Arche applauded the Emir's insight. Filled with pride and smug self-satisfaction, he encouraged their worship, basking in their adoration. This is what he craved; this was the vintage wine that he savored. He was convinced that he deserved it, and he was on the verge of delivering everything that he had promised them.

****

Sunrise greeted Daylin with a swift kick in the ribs. The leather strips that bound his hands were shrinking and cutting into his wrists. As his blood tricked down his wrists and onto his hands, pain seared up his arms to the pleasure of his tall tormentor.

"Did my little maggot sleep well? Did you miss your Grandma, poor dear? She must be heartbroken at the very thought that her little boy has been taken captive. Ahh... The poor thing! He must be hungry," he snarled sarcastically.

He then spat in Daylin's face, kicked him again for good measure and walked away. The Ghouls that stood by watching this cruel affair displayed no interest in the events. They offered no visible signs of life, while the short man howled with satisfaction. The Artrax snickered and quietly laughed with approval.

The tall Ganza was not yet done with his fun. Looking down his crooked boney nose though narrow deep set eyes, he caught the glint of the silver necklace around Daylin's neck. Grabbing Daylin by the throat he inquired, "What have we here little maggot?"

Tearing Daylin's shirt, he uncovered the jasper gem-stone and grasped it in a vicious swipe as he let Daylin fall from his grasp. To his surprise the stone refused to leave the silver chain. It remained around Daylin's neck just as Abner said it would, despite the herculean effort of the vile brute to dislodge it.

Adding injury to insult, the stone emitted a blinding light that sent Daylin's tormentors reeling backward in fear. The tall man screamed in agony as his hand, still attached to the stone, became intensely hot. The smell of burning flesh filled the air, and the brute begged to be released from the stone. Daylin, unscathed by any of this, brushed the tall man's hand aside and seized the stone, marveling at what he was seeing. Fear gripped his captors; and they now realized that they had bargained for far more than they anticipated. The tall Ganza thrust his hand into a bucket of water hoping for relief from his pain, but as for his disgrace, he found no support among his companions, who relished his humiliation and chided him for his stupidity.

The oars of the black ship continued to slice through the waters of the Ramsgate. The enemy was growing very confident, believing that they were safe from detection. The beating of the drum now set the pace for the wretched galley slaves. Daylin could hear their groans and screams between the cracks of the beaters' whips, but he could not see them.

The slaves spent their lives below the waterline, never seeing the light of day. Their cries of anguish were almost too much to bear. Daylin took comfort in the fact that someone on this miserable ship was worse off than he was.

****

There was a growing frustration among the Rangers. Following a trail on land is one thing, but on the water it is quite another matter. The Ramsgate had many oxbows and tributaries that made playing hide and seek a game that they could not hope to win.

"Wain, this is no good! We can't hope to find them this way. We've been riding for an hour and I have a bad feeling about this," said Quill.

Wain replied, "True, this is going to prove more difficult than I thought. There's one thing for sure, they wouldn't sail for Urbanus. They set a course up river. The question is where will they start their journey overland and then turn south to Mara?"

"Allow me," said Lon, reaching into his pack, producing an excellent map of the Western province. "I thought that we might need this. Jurius has a fine collection of maps, so I asked him for one. I think that we can discern their intentions by carefully studying this map."

"But a map of the Western Province will do us no good if they're east bound!" said Hull.

The Rangers dismounted, tied their horses to nearby trees and gathered together to discuss their next move. Lon spread the map out on the ground, and they carefully assessed their options. Kneeling down, Lon pointed to the map and said, "Here's Brantford, they no doubt traveled east, up the Ramsgate that much we know, but … wait, wait, we have it all wrong, they're not going east, they are going west!"

"That can't be, they will be risking detection traveling down the Ramsgate in the light of day, and you know how they hate the light of day. True, but the days are growing shorter in the east as they extended their dominion. There they move freely, but in the west, the loss of light is just beginning," Swain argued.

"True enough, but what if the enemy has allies in the west? What if one of the ten cities has already struck an alliance with him? What if they have provided him with a base for his incursions into the west?" Lon retorted.

"How about Teleios, it's a likely place. No, too open, too many travelers journey there. There would be no way to prevent word from leaking out. You know what they say, 'it's easier to prevent water from leaking into your boat than to prevent a secret from leaking out,'" Quill said.

They all laughed. They desperately needed a little comic relief. Lothair's betrayal had sickened their spirits and what they needed was a distraction. Their need to find Daylin was the tonic the doctor ordered. Wain was still thinking about Quill's statement, when he said, "Quill, you're right about secrets, what secrets have been leaking out lately? Think on it."

Hull spoke up and said, "You know, something has been gnawing at me for days. Do you remember when we were gathered around the camp fire the night we came through the rapids? I believe that Lothair was signaling something, sending us a message in song! Do you remember what it was?"

"Something about, 'unyielding virtue blinding a man, and those that bend are those that stand.'"

"Was that it?" asked Swain.

"Yes, that's it, and he was sending us a message, perhaps without even realizing it. He had to have been planning this for some time. He couldn't have done this without a plan or without help! Who did he have contact with?" asked Quill.

"No one, we haven't been out of each other's sight since this mission began," Lon said.

"Yes, we have, for a very brief time, but Lothair was alone. Just before we entered the Noor, we hid along the eastern shore of the Ramsgate. Lothair went scouting by himself. He said it was safer that way. Better to lose one man, than several. We agreed and he returned in about an hour. There was no sign of the enemy, so we set out to find you," said Egbert.

The men of Invar all nodded in agreement.

That's where he said he found it!" Hull roared.

"Found what?" Quill asked.

"The knife had an insignia on it. I needed a knife and he let me use the knife that he said he found along the banks of the Ramsgate just before they entered the Noor. Found it, my eye! He made a pact with the owner of that knife. He exchanged his knife for the one with the insignia on it!" Hull said, in deadly seriousness.

"Yes, but who's the owner?" asked Lon.

"The answer to that question lies in the insignia. What was the insignia?" asked Wain.

"It was a bear standing on its hind legs atop a mountain peak," Hull replied.

"Ursus, the knife belongs to Ursus. They are headed for Hupsoma," Wain explained.

All bears leave tracks, and all criminals leave clues. Lothair had unwittingly revealed the contents of his heart and the details of the enemy's plan with his song in a careless, guilt-riddled moment. They now knew where Daylin was to be taken, but as to how they were going to rescue him, they didn't have a clue.

****

The Black Ship cruised through the waters of the Ramsgate as a fair wind filled her large black single sail. The wind which was placing even more distance between Daylin and the Rangers was ironically providing a welcome rest for the ship's galley slaves. The unfurled sail brought a welcome respite to the incessant beating of the drum and the screams of men under the agony of the whip.

On the aft of the ship stood the tall Ganza and three Artrax, and they appeared to be arguing. Something was causing a heated disagreement between them.

"I don't trust Ursus," said the tall man. "You should have escorted the boy east through the Great Forest. This is a major mistake in bringing him west to Hupsoma."

The largest Artrax met his criticism and screamed at the tall man. "You dare question the wisdom of our master? He is sealing his alliance with Ursus by entrusting the boy to him. There is no possible escape for the boy. Your concern is noted and so is your impertinence. The next time you dare to question our master, I will kill you where you stand."

The tall man was not easily intimidated, but the Artrax made the tall man's limbs go numb with fear! There was no other option for him except to apologize and assume the position of a defeated dog. "I am sorry; I did not know that it was the master's desire to send the boy west, I thought …"

"You thought what? You Ganza dog! You thought that if it was my plan, it was open to your insolent criticism?" roared the Artrax.

With a lightning-fast strike the Artrax reached for the tall man and with his massive hands, he grasped the tall man by the throat sinking his talons into his flesh. The tall Ganza was instantly brought to his knees gasping for breath.

Daylin was convinced that the villain was about to meet his well-deserved end when the Artrax suddenly relented. "Get up, you parasite, and never, ever criticize me or my master again, or next time I will finish the job, do hear me?"

"Yes, yes, I hear you," the tall Ganza whimpered.

Daylin refused to make eye contact with either of them; he knew that he was the likely target for any unexpressed anger. He pretended to be asleep, but in reality, he was wide awake with fear.

The Artrax signaled to the helmsmen to turn the ship hard to starboard and head down the tributary of the Ramsgate known as the Telos. The Artrax ordered full sail and with all the speed that the ship could muster, they set their course straight for Hupsominia.

****

"Teleios and Hupsoma are west of here. Let's make a move, there's not much light left in this day," said Wain.

They rode hard through the open country. They saw no one; more importantly, they hoped that no one had seen them. As night fell, they approached the river Telos and made camp. They couldn't risk a fire, so cold food and an extra blanket would have to suffice. That night they slept with one eye open. Each Ranger took a turn on guard duty, allowing them all equal sleep. The night was cold, starless and still. The darkness was palpable; it was more than the absence of light. It was something they could feel. It had a personality. It was if it was alive.

The morning sun strained to break through the clouds. They all agreed it was darker than it should have been at six o'clock. If they had doubts about Ursus making an alliance with Sanballat, those doubts were now erased in the morning's twilight. The unmistakable mark of the enemy's dominion was on this land: deep pervading darkness. With the darkness came the inevitable: death. Life was slowly being sapped from all living things. Beauty was retreating before their eyes, giving way to the rot of decay. Such evil is hard to comprehend; but then, evil doesn't need to be understood; it needs to be confronted and resisted.

The Rangers made their way along the Telos, hoping to catch a glimpse of the black ship. The Telos was becoming narrower by the dextor. Soon the Black Ship would have to dock and rendezvous with their allies from Hupsoma. Wain gave orders that Lon and Hull scout ahead while the others kept their eyes peeled for any signs of the enemy. Lon and Hull soon returned.

"Good news. They're docked just over that hill. The river here is too shallow for them to go any farther," said Lon.

Cautiously, the Rangers made their way up the hill, and then carefully assessed their position. It was obvious that the black ship was waiting to deliver Daylin into the custody of Ursus' Salisians. They could not hope to attack the ship; it was far too risky. Daylin could be killed in the ensuing battle. What if reinforcements were to prematurely arrive from Hupsoma? They would have to wait.

Teleios was no more than a dextor from the docking area. In a matter of minutes the road that wound its way to the docks was filled with a detachment of twenty-five Salisian soldiers. The tall man could be seen grabbing Daylin by his hair and throwing him down to ground. As soon as Daylin was delivered into their custody by the two Ganza dressed in black, the soldiers and their prisoner began their march back to the city. The Black Ship immediately set sail for the Ramsgate.

The Rangers made haste down the road, while seeking an ideal place for an ambush. They knew that surprise and deadly accuracy was their only hope for victory. They took their positions on a rocky overhang above the road and waited for the detachment to round the bend. Their aim would have to be perfect. The first volley had to take out the soldiers closest to Daylin. There would be no margin for error.

There is a unique sound that a perfectly tuned arrow makes as it cuts through the air; it was the last sound that the soldiers ever heard. Each Ranger readied three arrows. One was notched in his bowstring, and the other two were held deftly between the grips of their pulling hand. There were twenty-five soldiers and twelve rangers. It was understood that each Ranger would choose two enemy targets, while the last man standing would be the target of the Ranger with the best available shot.

The arrows hissed and screamed like birds of prey. In unison, the soldiers fell dead, each volley on the heels of the other. Some were shot through the heart, others through the throat. The last soldier wisely turned to run, but twelve well-aimed arrows put an end to his retreat. The tall man, who had delighted in tormenting Daylin, was quickly surrounded by the Rangers and Derek, who, without hesitation, grasped his Francesca and threw it, splitting the man's skull into two. The short man made a pitiful attempt to escape, but Doran and Jergen let loose several arrows that brought an end to his ill-fated escape. It was over in seconds.

Daylin had been standing there the whole time. He was in shock and he could not move a muscle.

"Are you all right boy?" Swain asked with deep concern in his voice.

"Yes, sir, I am fine. The tall one kicked me a lot, and I haven't had anything to eat or drink, but I'm …"

Daylin collapsed from fatigue and dehydration.

The Rangers quickly tended to him and then made a hasty retreat back to their horses. It would only be a short time before the soldiers were missed.

"Drag their bodies into that gully and cover them over with brush, then throw dirt on the blood spilt in the road. They'll be found soon enough, but perhaps we can buy a few extra dextors before they begin to track us," Wain commanded.

****

URBANUS THE GREAT

The ancient city of Urbanus was the crown jewel in the legendary Kingdom of Urbania, and worthy of much note. A constant gentle breeze blew over the land. Lush verdant plains encompassed its exquisitely smooth, friendly borders, exhibiting an extraordinary beauty, so rich and fertile that they yielded abundant grass and produced splendid grain. The mighty Ramsgate, pleasant to the eye and sweet to taste, sent its course along its northern bank. A multitude of fish teemed in its depths, furnishing an abundant fresh flow of food for the people there. Indeed, the mighty Ramsgate provided such abundance for all that food was never lacking.

Viewed from the Ramsgate, her numerous wharfs and docks on the waterfront greeted the traveler with a beehive of commerce. All the goods and produce of Urbania eventually arrived here. From there wide busy avenues, like staves on a wagon wheel, carried the goods and produce traversing the quarters of the thriving commercial metropolis into the hub of the city. From the waterfront the city's elevation rose gently from the Ramsgate to its highest point on mount Regius where its crescendo was marked by the Great Assembly Hall, the palace of the prince, and the homes of the privileged. From this vantage point one could see the gentle waters of the Oria flowing from Lake Hudor caressing the northwest border of the city.

Aqueducts carried its life-sustaining waters into the city's reservoirs and public fountains. Urbanus had long ago learned the value of sanitation in order to avoid the diseases and plagues that constantly threatened urban life. A vast system of sewers carried the city's waste to strategically placed leech fields far from the city's center. On the northeast border the mysterious and foreboding ruins of Beth Craven silently proclaimed a warning of dread and danger to any inquisitive souls. The towns of Pontus to the south and Nela to the northwest were places favored by the wealthy of Urbanus. It was here that they found hospitality and relaxation that stood in stark contrast to the frenzied pace of life in Urbanus.

To the untrained eye, the changes were architectural and superficial, but for those possessing the ability to see beyond the burgeoning landscape, Urbanus had now become a mere shadow of the values and vision that had been the bedrock of her foundation. On the surface she was splendid to behold, but the devastation of the Great War had exacted a greater, deeper toll than the eye could discern.

Urbanus was a city of many voices and visions. Her political evolution was unique in the annals of the history of Urbania. Originally established as a democratic republic based on the Ancient Laws and Covenants of Kronia, Urbanus had undergone a gradual but potentially fatal transformation. Though remnants of the republic's foundations remained intact, she was, at this point in time, a dictatorship ruled by a class of privileged elites.

The balance of power had slowly shifted from the Senators of the Great Assembly to the Prince. The Prince was appointed by senators who were chosen by the people. This subtle change had created an illusion of democracy, but in reality it fostered intense internal struggle for political advantage. The people's voice became an item for sale to the highest bidder. Principles of conscience and the rule of law had surrendered to political pragmatics. Ruthless and cunning princes ensnared the senators in a dragnet of greed and a lust for power. This was combined with a clever erosion of the people's voice through a two-fold strategy of social and economic dependency and the promise of peace and security.

Prince Solon, ruler of the city, like his predecessors, was a cold, calculating politician who desired peace and the security of the status quo above all. He would have gladly traded his conscience for political tranquility. He was often described by his peers and foes alike as one who watched the wind more than his ways. On every occasion he sought the refuge of delegation, choosing to lead from the shadows and to watch while others failed, rather than to expose his own foibles and failures to the light of public scrutiny and sanction. Like a man with his feet planted firmly in the middle of the air, all things were negotiable, and little was certain. For Solon, gray was his primary color.

The Patrikos comprised the ruling class and shared the same spirit and philosophy as Prince Solon. The senators of the Great Assembly came from their ranks. While the Senators were elected by the people, they were all members of the Patrikos and each candidate was hand-picked by Solon. This created the illusion that the people had a voice in the politics of Urbanus, but it was just an illusion.

The relationship between Solon and the Patrikos was at best symbiotic, and at worst tempestuous. They shared a singular belief, namely, that man was the master of his own destiny. They had no need for the shackles of faith and the restraints of religion. They believed that religion was nothing but a dangerous deception, an idealistic superstition, and the chief obstacle to progress in Urbania. They held the other social classes in contempt and referred to them as mud. *"You don't build a city on sand do you?"* they would say. However, expediency was their governing principle and they would, when necessary, curry and court the favor of any group to bolster one of their self-serving grabs for power.

For the Patrikos, the acquisition of power and interest in the name of progress was their reason for being. Nothing else mattered. Everything in their world was permanent, if but for the moment. Reason, and reason alone, was their guiding compass. They saw the road to power defined in the control and acquisition of property. They extolled the virtue that all wealth and property should be held in the common trust of all citizens in Urbanus, but the reality was that they alone determined how property was used and exchanged. This placed them in firm control, and, despite their lofty talk of freedom and all things held in common for the greater good, their grip on the power and control of the city's wealth was never released. They preached tolerance and the acceptance of all ideas as long those ideas fit their agenda.

All factions require a spokesman and the Patrikos found theirs in Meander. He was from an influential and affluent family that was highly educated, and renowned for their patronage of the arts and public works. The family name was inscribed everywhere that the eye could see, and was synonymous with philanthropy. Meander fashioned himself as an intellectual and a public speaker, and was often found on the public forum preaching the values and vision of the Patrikos.

Though fewer in number than their counterparts, the Patrikos were, at this time in the history of Urbanus, the far greater political influence. This influence Meander exploited to its fullest. Anyone who desired to advance in Urbanus, whether friend or foe, went to Meander for his endorsement and blessing.

All societies are governed by an economy, and at the center of these economies are the bankers or money changers. Wealth needs a manager and a custodian; such men are often the true power behind any kingdom. In Urbanus they were known as the Trapezites. They financed the rebuilding of the city after the Great War along with its massive public works projects. And they provided the funding for the ever-increasing commerce that defined Urbanus as the wealthiest of the Ten Cities of Urbania.

It is said that politicians spend the money they raise for political interests, but the Trapezites had but one goal and that was to acquire all of the wealth of the Ten Cities through debt. By enticing the people to borrow, they could force them into bondage through the law of compound interest. Once the people had drunk from the cup of greed, they would succumb to the slow-acting poison of debt. The only antidote for this poison of greed and self-indulgence was self-control, and the citizens of Urbanus displayed no interest in it.

The Trapezites encouraged the borrowing of money through low interest rates. This proved to be an irresistible temptation for the citizens of Urbanus, who sought personal peace and comfort as retreats from the horrific memories of the Great War. The Trapezites were driven by the reality that the borrower is, indeed, a slave to the lender.

It is for politicians and patriots to define and to defend boundaries; bankers are not encumbered by such restraints. They do business wherever their business takes them; and, the business of the Trapezites took them to Mara, the capital of the Southern Kingdom where wealth knew no limits. In Mara, unbeknownst to the majority of its citizens of Urbanus, the Trapezites found a limitless supply of the poison that defined their stock and trade. It was there that money was loaned to the Trapezites, who in turn loaned it to the citizens of Urbanus. In time, link by link, and loan by loan, this practice forged the chains of bondage that one day would be called to account.

At the bottom of the social strata of Urbanus were the common folk: tradesmen, fishermen, craftsmen, packmen, cooks, servants, dock workers and farmers, known as the Rasputitsa. Though they were held in low regard, they were, in truth, the backbone of this once great city. In the opinion of the majority, the city was still great and powerful. Urbanus was, indeed, wealthy and teeming with trade and commerce. However, this commercial vitality was a mirage, a house of colorful and cleverly dealt cards, for Urbanus had long forsaken the foundation of values that had built such a grand house.

But that same house was now showing signs of stress under the weight of a burden that the foundation was never designed to bear. As they say, "It takes money to make money."

Since the Great War, Urbanus had been short on capital, and all public works require capital as their life's blood. So, the Rasputitsa demanded goods and services, and Prince Solon was obliged to feed their growing appetite. Safety and security were the watch words of the hour. Freedom had once been prized as the gem of Urbanus, but freedom was now out of fashion, giving way to personal peace and prosperity, all in the name of security and safety. Of course, it was Solon and the Patrikos that now defined peace and prosperity for the people.

Meander, for his part, saw the advantage in placating their lust of things with sympathetic oratory and social programs. It would wed their mutual interests in a pact of assured destruction of the Rasputitsa. It was a tenuous alliance that could only be held together so long as there was enough money to pay for it. Urbanus was dying from a terminal disease of debt.

Despite this looming reality, the culture of Urbanus was outwardly rich and affluent; science and technology also flourished. Of utmost importance was the tradition of public discourse and debate. Philosophical and theological discourses were important in public life; all classes and professions took part. The debates kept knowledge and the admiration for the city's philosophical, theological and scientific heritage alive. Tolerance of divergent views had been a core value, but alas, the growing darkness was suppressing this virtue. Some voices now echoed louder than others in their quest for capturing the mind and heart of the great city.

Directly opposite to the Patrikos stood the religious sects and whatever the issue embraced by the Patrikos the religious sects stood in fixed opposition to it. Fiercely independent, the various sects had no faith in the ultimate good of mankind. They scoffed at the efforts of the Patrikos to engineer a utopian society. They had little regard for the government, and ridiculed the notion that the practical was of equal importance to the spiritual. Their lens of perception was the wisdom of the ancient scrolls. Revelation, not reason, was their authority, and everything was subordinate to it.

There were many religious voices in Urbanus, but among these voices, one stood above all the rest and that was the voice of Lemler. Lemler was a teacher; not an ordinary teacher but a guardian and teacher of the ancient scrolls. Huge crowds came to hear his insights and interpretations of the scrolls.

Lemler was convinced that the coming of the "One" foretold in the scrolls was imminent. Those who agreed with his vision hung on his every word. He lived to see the day when the great temple of Urbanus would be rebuilt. He believed that until this task was accomplished, the new age prophesied in the scrolls could not be realized. His books and teachings were read and quoted more than any other. He was the consummate voice in Urbanus. While his message was spiritual in nature, it had profound political implications for Urbanus and the whole of Urbania.

The order to which Lemler belonged was named the Brotherhood, which was by no means large in terms of numbers; but the influence of the Brotherhood was felt in every facet of life in Urbania. Solon, the prince of Urbanus, tolerated the members of the Brotherhood socially and politically, but was contemptuous of their self-righteous separatism. Solon understood that they were, nonetheless, a force to be reckoned with.

The Brotherhood's influence wasn't seen in what they promoted, but in what they opposed. If the Brotherhood opposed something, its fate was sealed in the court of public opinion. In the northwest quarter of the city, the Brotherhood occupied one hundred square hextors[3] of land. These beautifully manicured grounds were the repository of more than fifty splendid buildings housing a growing community of scribes, Preceptors (teachers,) and students. This was Lemler's world. From here his influence was shed abroad like a lighthouse beacon against a black sea. His vision was infectious. Overnight, numerous schools sponsored by the Brotherhood arose in the other provinces and Urbania. Lemler now possessed the status and the means that accompanied it, all with a view to shaping public opinion and the rebuilding of the temple.

It was difficult to pinpoint what made Lemler popular with the common people. He was not a scholar in the classical sense, nor was he a great speaker. He was not a gifted administrator or political tactician. Lemler was a plain, uncomplicated man of average stature and intelligence. Perhaps his gift was his ability to make the complex simple. Few citizens of Urbania could make sense of the rapid changes that threatened to engulf them, but Lemler offered them an easy to understand explanation of the present and the future. He understood the common man and he offered him a straightforward, uncomplicated vision. He offered them an opportunity to embrace something greater than themselves. "Nothing to die for, nothing to live for," he would declare.

---

[3] A hextor was the equivalent of 1.25 acres.

Lemler had a pulse on the heart-beat of the Kingdom. But while Lemler correctly diagnosed the disease, his cure had proven lethal. His teachings had encouraged the Brotherhood to withdraw from society; it was after all a sinking ship. Lemler had declared that they were living in the last days of Urbania, and that their hope rested on the coming of the "One" foretold in the ancient scrolls. So the Brotherhood hunkered down and waited. As the darkness encroached, their hopes soared. Lemler's vision, though appealing, fostered a pessimistic form of paralysis.

****

Prince Solon paced back and forth pensively peering from his window; he was overcome by the reality that Ursus was entering the city with five hundred soldiers. No ordinary troops were these, but they were the handpicked elite from the Thema of Hupsominia, and Ursus was their Strategos. The sight caused Solon's stomach to churn and his knees to knock. He saw himself as an optimist, but this sight required more faith than he possessed. He had lobbied hard at the Great Assembly and among the Ten Cities for Ursus's attendance, but was the risk worth the reward?

Prince Solon was a man who believed that every problem had a reasonable solution. He was committed to his convictions, and confident in his powers of persuasion. If he could only bring Ursus into his confidence, reason would prevail. Surely Ursus understood that in war, there are no winners, just losers. Bringing Ursus to Urbanus was in keeping with his convictions, but as the Toon are fond of saying, "When one fights with a skunk, it matters little whether one wins or loses!"

****

DELICATE MATTERS

Amenuus, Solon's scribe, peered out the window and then with hesitation spoke softly. "Ursus is approaching the assembly, my Prince. Shall I go out to meet him, or shall I send a welcome committee to escort him to your chambers?"

It was a very delicate matter. If he went out to greet him it would appear that he was hailing him as a conquering general, but if he did not, it could be taken as an insult. As strange as it may sound, Prince Solon, who was usually a man of detailed planning, had avoided making this decision, hoping that circumstances would conspire to relieve him from having to make a choice. But they hadn't.

Reality always prevails. Ursus was more than the pseudo prince of Hupsoma. He was the prototype of a new model of leadership in Urbania. He was a tyrant who used the power of his military to impose his will on the people. Solon had suspected that Ursus was doing something that had never been done before; he was conspiring with the Southern Kingdom, hoping to make alliances with hostile foreign forces. Ursus posed a real and present danger to the peace and security of Urbania.

"Sir, what shall we do," asked Amenuus, Solon's scribe?

Solon knew that he would regret his decision, no matter what course of action he chose.

But in a moment of inspiration, he devised an alternative. "Send Chancellor Doulos and the some of the prominent senators out to greet him, and then escort him here to my chambers."

"Yes, sir," said Amenuus.

He was now committed. Perhaps his personal charm and diplomatic skills would build a bridge of understanding with Ursus. He was well known for arbitrating conflicts, but this was the greatest challenge that he had ever faced.

****

"Ursus is here, Ursus of Hupsoma is here. He has entered the city with five hundred soldiers!" the panting boy reported to Lemler.

Lemler, who was preparing to teach a class at the academy, paused and took note that this news would dovetail very nicely into his afternoon lecture. News of this kind was a tasty morsel that the Brotherhood relished. Mounting political tensions were a sign of the end. How could war possibly be avoided now? The war drums of the Southern Kingdom resounded in his imagination.

Lemler took his customary place behind the lectern, arranged his notes and slipped his reading glasses down his nose. Looking out at the students, he paused for what seemed like an eternity. Then he theatrically clapped his hands together and confidently declared, "Brothers, we live in the most exciting times imaginable; we are the generation that will see the dawning of a new age!"

The class sat spell bound as Lemler shared the news of Ursus's entrance into the city. They knew the seriousness of its implications. As he interpreted the news for his students, he provided proof texts for his interpretation with numerous quotations from the ancient scrolls, while at the same time punctuating the "evidence" with large doses of personal speculation.

The excitement and interest reached a crescendo that was spell-binding. It was all taking place before their very eyes. They were the generation that would see the fulfillment of all things predicted. They felt vindicated and superior. Their sacrifice had been worth it after all. They had endured rejection and subtle persecution of every stripe. Their friends and family had ridiculed their faith, calling them socially irresponsible escape artists and doomsayers. They had been mocked and scorned by the mainstream of society as irrelevant, but they were now on the verge of vindication. Their critics were about to justly reap what they had sown. They were confident that they were a privileged remnant whose faith was about to be rewarded with rescue.

****

A quiet desperation was overcoming Solon. Ursus was moments away from entering his chambers, and the realization that he had no allies in Urbania was becoming too much to bear. It was true that with the exception of Ursus, none had pledged peace with Urbanus. They were as secure and stable as chaff in the wind. Solon needed an ally who shared his vision for peace and progress; he needed a man of Urbanus who would endorse him and his efforts. More importantly, he needed the appeal of an idea bigger than all the players in the game. He had to be a man of the people. He did not want a prince; a pauper would do if he could he could touch the hearts and change the minds of the people. The only man he could think of was Lemler. It was a decision borne of desperation, but he had already stooped down to lick the boots of Ursus. What would one more act of humiliation matter?

The sound of leather boots marching down the wooden floors of the Chancellery heralded Ursus's arrival. The door opened and Chancellor Doulos entered the room with Ursus, who was accompanied by his captain of the guard, Gordo. "Prince Solon, Ursus, ruler of Hupsoma," Chancellor Doulos said diplomatically.

"Greetings Ursus, we welcome you to Urbanus. It is a pleasure to have you visits our fair city at long last," said Prince Solon.

"How long has it been since we were together?" Ursus asked, although he knew the answer.

The two men carefully assessed the other, waiting for an opening to addresses the real issues of the day. Prince Solon exchanged small talk with Ursus until he sensed an opening, and then he changed the direction of their conversation.

"Are your men comfortable; do they have need of room and board? How may we serve you?"

Prince Solon had no idea that Ursus was bringing five hundred of his personal guard into the city. Solon was not prepared to deal with the logistics of housing and feeding so many men, nor the threat that they posed but better that he provide for them and keep a close watch on their every move.

"Chancellor Doulos, make arrangements for the men of Ursus," ordered Prince Solon.

"Yes, my Prince."

But just then, the tension of the moment was broken by the excitement of a soft and delicate voice that was as beautiful to behold as it was to hear. Her long blond hair followed her like the train of a wedding gown, and her turquoise blue eyes radiated like gem stones as she seemed to dance across the floor towards Prince Solon. Though uninvited she entered the room without hesitation or fear and, making her way straight to Solon. "Father, Father, what a wondrous sight. Did you see them? There are so many, and they look so impressive. Who are they?" she asked.

Ursus was totally taken aback by her boldness and beauty. Solon could not refuse her; he did not rebuke her, nor even act surprised at her entrance. She was always welcome in his chambers. It mattered little who was seeking an audience, or how important the business at hand was. Charitée was always welcome, along with his wife of course. One thing was clear. Solon ruled Urbanus, but this girl ruled his heart.

"Lord Ursus, may I introduce my daughter, Charitée."

"I am pleased to meet you. You are as bold as you are beautiful; a family trait I am sure," Ursus said half jokingly.

Chariteé responded by bowing gracefully and commenting on the impressive appearance of Ursus's entourage.

Solon took her in his arms and kissed her. "My child, business beckons me please go to your mother and wait for me there. We shall dine together tonight with Lord Ursus. I am sure he will answer all your questions and satisfy your curiosity then."

****

"Children are so infectious are they not? They may be small and helpless creatures, but they possess more power than an army when it comes to conquering the hearts of men," Solon said, making an excuse for Chariteé's irresistible impropriety.

The interlude gave Ursus an opportunity to study the real Solon and he did not allow it slip through his fingers. Ursus sat down and peered into Solon's eyes like a hawk sizing up a dove. He was growing more confident every moment. His hunger was about to be satisfied. He knew that Solon was hopeful, if not desperate, of reaching an understanding with him. He would act the part, but Ursus would not be touched by Solon's charm and diplomacy.

The meeting was brief and when it concluded, Solon was more convinced than ever that his base of support needed to be broadened. Perhaps Ursus would think twice about aggression, if Urbanus presented him with a united front, or perhaps the wisdom of the conference would finally convert him. Perhaps but the unthinkable had become the thinkable. Solon sent a messenger to Lemler requesting that he come to the palace at once.

Lemler came as requested, though the hour was later than he liked, but he could not imagine what Prince Solon wanted. Solon wasted no time, but immediately came to the point.

"Sir, I would like to appeal to you for support. I need your endorsement for my plans to succeed. The peace and unity conference cannot succeed if Urbanus refuses to practice what she preaches. I am requesting your visible and vocal support. Moreover, I am requesting that you do so when I address my appeal for support to the Brotherhood," said the prince.

Lemler appeared stunned. Solon was asking him for help? It went contrary to all reason and everything that Lemler believed. If he endorsed Solon's peace and unity conference he would be rejecting everything he believed and taught. His disciples would reject him as a compromiser, worse than an apostate! If he refused to support Solon, he would be seen as a traitor to his city and to his class. Lemler's straightforward, uncomplicated vision of the future was becoming more twisted and complicated by the minute. In a moment of inspiration, he appealed to Solon.

"Yes, my prince, I will stand at your side when you address the Brotherhood. But it will be far more effective for you to present your proposal to them personally. I could never do it justice. You have the passion for this vision of peace and unity; it is you my who should take full credit for it. I will make the arrangements and request that the Brethren gather from the four provinces and come to Urbanus. I believe that in three days you may address them."

The conference would start in one week's time and could not be delayed. As Solon saw it, he had to address the Brotherhood; he was in a sinkhole up to his waist without a rope and yet it was what it was. He had to accept the reality of the situation.

Lemler had taken his neck out the nose for the moment by indirectly avoiding Solon's request for personal support and deferring the final verdict to the Brotherhood. He knew that Solon's appeal would fall on deaf ears; he also anticipated that the Brotherhood would bear the blame for rejecting Solon's request for support. When the dust settled Lemler could offer his services as a peacemaker between the two parties. It was classic Lemler, playing two sides against the middle.

A strong cold wind blew down the river that morning. The rigging of the old grain ship groaned under the wind's unrelenting pressure. Large waves pounded the hull like a large fist, pushing the vessel into its moorings, preventing the crew from weighing anchor. The Ramsgate ruled, and it appeared to dare Abner to travel its waters to

Urbanus. He could not bear the thought of taking Jurius with him after all that had happened. He would go alone to Urbanus.

With that final thought, Abner resolutely looked west, peering beyond the white caps that punctuated the horizon. In defiance, he turned his back to Brantford walking up the gangway to the ship. As he boarded the ship, Jurius met him on the deck and, raising his hand to Abner's mouth, hushed the old man before he could protest. Jurius spoke with an air of quiet but stubborn determination.

"You cannot go alone old friend. Whatever lies before us we will face together; this matter is becoming too complicated for any one of us. You need me now more than ever; we must see this affair to the end," said Jurius.

Abner knew that it was fruitless to argue with Jurius, but he could not resist one final appeal, Jurius's love for Molly.

"What will Molly do without you? Stay with her; she must be devastated by the loss of Daylin." Abner pleaded.

"What will Urbania do if Daylin is not found? Besides, I have made this trip hundreds of times on business. My presence in Urbanus will not create suspicion. You need me to provide you with a reason for being in the city; it was part of the plan from the start."

Jurius was right. It was not a time to be thinking of personal interest. Great personal sacrifices would have to be made if Urbania were to survive. Jurius could, indeed, provide Abner with a perfect alibi, and introductions to the most influential people in Urbanus. He was Brantford's most respected merchant. Abner conceded as he embraced his old friend while anxious thoughts gripped his heart. Was he inviting Jurius to join him, or was this their final good bye?

****

It took three days to assemble the Brotherhood. They came from every province, hamlet, town, village and city. Their numbers swelled the grounds of the compound. The great meeting hall seemed bloated and ready to burst onto the grounds with their excessive numbers. They stood in the back and along the walls, some even sat on the floor while others stood outside. Solon looked out from the platform to assess their mood in order to forecast the fate of his appeal, but there were no tell-tale signs to be read. Their faces were blank and their mood was quiet, but serious.

Solon was bewildered by the Brotherhood's dress and mannerisms; was he in Urbanus? Their language was almost foreign to him; they used words in strange ways that were familiar only to them. Their culture was altogether foreign to him. He had never witnessed such a sight. This was his city and these were his subjects, but they were aliens to him all the same. No one greeted him or addressed him. He was a stranger in his own realm. Inwardly he felt insulted and slighted but his dignity would have to wait; he needed their help. It was discretion, not decorum that was called for.

Lemler had finally made his entrance into the meeting hall, but rather than enter from the side entrance by the platform, he chose to enter from the front and pass through the middle of the teeming crowd. He wanted to be seen and acknowledged. None could resist touching him, greeting him, and shaking his hand. He was their champion and spoke their language; Lemler articulated their vision. Slowly he made his way through the crowd and onto the platform where he greeted Solon, bowing in respect to him. With a gesture of his hand the crowd hushed, silently awaiting Solon's words.

Prince Solon approached the podium and surveyed his audience. He had prepared his thoughts, but he had decided not to use notes or a prepared text. He thought a sincere appeal to these men would be the best thing; he wanted their hearts, not their heads.

****

Citizens of Urbanus and the provinces of Urbania, I greet you today with a hope and a desire that we find a path for peace. I must address the clear and present danger to our fair Kingdom. This is a dangerous hour for us all. It is an hour for sober thought and decisive action. There is an enemy that threatens our very existence; it is subverting our foundations and dividing us into factions. There is only one antidote for this poisonous, selfish individuality and that is unity. We must stand together against these forces. We must bring the Ten Cities of Urbania and their provinces together in unity. We must preach, promote and practice unity and, above all, we must defend it.

As I speak, seditious forces are working to undermine our provinces and usurp the authority of their rightful princes. We may differ as to the particulars of our vision for the future, but what we have in common is greater than our differences. I appeal to you as good men. Join me in this quest for unity, and vocally and visibly support the Peace and Unity Conference. Work with me to unite the Ten Cities and form a league that will stand against those would divide us. Work with me for peace and unity in Urbania. Do not succumb to the failed ideas of the past, but work with me to build a new order, an order that will bring stability, peace and prosperity to Urbania for the common good.

The crowd had sat in silence through his short but passionate speech; he now returned to his seat and awaited their verdict. The Brotherhood murmured, and spoke to each other, but they offered no signs of approval or resistance to Solon's address. In the end, all eyes looked to Lemler. What was his opinion? Lemler stood to his feet and, as he approached the podium, the murmuring slowly ebbed. All the while, the Brotherhood awaited his opinion.

Brethren, I am honored to be your teacher and counselor in all matters spiritual, but I will not presume to dictate the course of your conscience in this matter. The decision is yours. What is your will in this matter?

No sooner had the words left Lemler's lips than a stout swarthy man sitting in the front row rose to his feet and shouted, "The ancient scrolls have prophesied that Urbania must fall to the evil one, resistance is hopeless. Urbania is doomed. Let the peace lovers cry for peace, but there will be no peace until the consummation. As foretold a new age will emerge from the ashes of the old one. I say that this conference is a vain imagination of desperate men who have ignored spiritual things for far too long!"

The Brotherhood rose to their feet and cheered in agreement. A wry smile slowly etched its way across Lemler's face. He had known the outcome from the moment he had left Solon's palace. The Brotherhood was saturated with his vision their response was conditioned; they had acted true to form. It was now Lemler's role to play the peacemaker and sooth Solon's dashed expectations.

"They have their convictions, my Prince. While they will not support you, neither will they oppose you; they are neutral on this matter. They remain your loyal subjects, but they cannot grant you your request. They will, however, pray for you and your Kingdom. I will try to work on your behalf and see what I can do to help you in this matter, but it will take time."

Prince Solon was cunning; he understood Lemler and the true meaning of his words. He could not help comparing and contrasting Ursus and Lemler. Which was the bigger scoundrel, he wondered? Both were deceptive, but at least Ursus was naked in his designs; he did not need pretense or hypocrisy to achieve his ends. But Lemler wore a thousand masks; not even he knew when he was being sincere. Solon shook his head in disbelief. These men were fatalists to the core. They were hardly neutral in the matter. Their rejection of his appeal was, in fact, undermining him. Loyal subjects, yes, but whose? He knew the answer. He would have to find another door of access into the heart of the Brotherhood. Experience had taught him that every idealist has his price.

"Phase one is complete. We are in Urbanus. The Thema are poised and awaiting the arrival of the Tagmata (professional army regiments) once inside the city we must consolidate our gains. What do my sources reveal, Gordo? What do the street urchins and the spies inside the city quarters tell us?"

"As you surmised, my Lord, Solon is confident that the conference will sway the dissenters into joining the League. He is unaware of your strength and the Emir's infiltration of Hupsoma. They have their suspicions but nothing concrete. We have word that the Brotherhood has rejected Solon's appeal for support, just as you predicted. It appears that Solon will have to appeal to the other cities without the help of the Brotherhood. Tragic, is it not? We await your orders."

"Hmmm, very good! The conference begins in four days. We have just four days to set the trap. In warfare there is nothing better than an unseen advantage. We are within Urbanus, and the Emir attacks from without. Victory is ours; how can we fail? Get word to him. Let him know that all is in readiness for his final assault on Urbania. We shall rule with him, for we have served him well," Ursus mused.

****

"Give the guard free reign in the city; they have earned a bit of pleasure and respite. You lead them and have a good time too. Let them have some enjoyment; let them freely indulge their pleasures. There will be enough hard work for them in the days ahead, for now let them wench and wine for a bit. Tomorrow is another day," Ursus said confidently.

****

DRUMS OF WAR

Day and night the city of Mara echoed with the resonance of drums. The monotonous marching sound of heavy leather sandals clattered against the walls of buildings in cadence with the drums, while the sound of steel on steel clanged and chimed in unison. Legions of the Sharokhan marched through the streets to the cheers of Ghouls, Artrax, and Salisian Regulars, while the populace looked on, as if seized by deadly paralysis. Each regiment took its turn in marshalling their numbers and displaying their weaponry. Huge black, red and silver banners were unfurled bearing the insignia of El' Shay'tan, while the frenzied blast of trumpets marshaled their cries for war. The hellish hordes of Mara were assembling for invasion.

Deep in the Sanballat's palace was a room adjacent to the great white throne. None dare enter there without being summoned. The room was simply known as "the chamber." Its vaulted ceiling and circular design made it appear more like a temple than a conference room. It was there that the plans for the final invasion of Urbania were being laid. In this inner sanctum Sanballat listened to the counsel of his Arche, while the generals of the Sharokhan laid detailed plans for the invasion. It was like a beehive in the spring swarming with activity.

It is said that armies march on their stomachs, but without a forge to fashion its weapons they are like a toothless tiger. But the giant forge of Mara worked non-stop to the cadence of the drums and marching boots. Swords, knives, spears, and battleaxes of Wootz steel were polished, honed, and stropped to razor sharp edges; shields and arrows were fashioned by the tens of thousands—the forge never rested. All the while the Artrax flew high above the city keeping an ever-vigilant eye, while the Ganza (secret police) patrolled the streets and the arid countryside. All this was done as a precaution lest some daring souls might venture into the Southern Kingdom in order to spy on its preparations. Sanballat was leaving no stone unturned.

****

Daylin was slowly recovering from his ordeal. He was safe for the time being. A good night's sleep and the Rangers' provisions had restored his spirits. He could travel, but he wanted to rest. Wain would hear none of it; they must leave the region of Hupsominia, maybe there was a village or a town nearby that would help them.

Once again Lon and Hull scouted ahead while the others kept their eyes peeled for any signs of the enemy. But Lon and Hull did not return for over two hours, and Wain was growing impatient. He was ready to dispatch Owen and Thrace to find them when they suddenly came into view with two gaunt looking souls, a man and a woman.

The couple looked like they hadn't eaten in months, yet there was a fire in their eyes that a flood of adversity couldn't quench. The woman's name was Ildikko, and her companion was Sandor. They were from a nearby town called Huiedien. The Rangers offered them food and made them as comfortable as possible. While they ate, they shared their story. It was a ghastly tale of subversion, betrayal and savage conquest. What they heard was almost beyond belief. Lon and Hull verified their story, but the Rangers had to hear it and see it with their own eyes.

Huiedien was a day's march from where they were camped. Since it was in the direction of Urbanus, they decided to go there and see the situation for themselves. The journey was dark and foreboding. The once rich farmland was now bleak, barren, and devoid of life. A force unfamiliar to them had ravaged the landscape, and it had been scorched by fire. Darkness now hung over the land like a morbid funeral shroud. Huiedien had once been a happy farming community filled with the laughter of children. It was now a ghost town encircled by rough-hewn wooden stakes topped with over a thousand human heads. In the middle of the village square laid the half eaten corpses of the beheaded victims piled high like mounds of hay. Sandor explained that Ursus had given these victims to the enemy. Anyone not fit for slavery or the army became food for the Ghouls.

"Poor wretched souls," Hull lamented.

"Yes, but they are the fortunate ones," added Ildikko. They are dead. The adults that were fit for the enemy's purposes are not so fortunate. The women become concubines and the men soldiers or slaves. They are forced to either renounce their citizenship and allegiance to Urbania or suffer the same fate as the others. As for the children, they become his slaves. It is as if their very souls have been taken from them. They have become the property of Sanballat. They were once our friends and relatives; they are now the enemy's servants," Ildikko said, while holding back strong, bitter tears.

Ildikko was slight in stature, but her eyes signaled an indomitable inner strength. She was slight of figure and lithe. Her sun-baked limbs were strong and not unaccustomed to hard work. She moved quietly and spoke rarely, but her hands, like her will, were strong and resolute. She had worked in the fields from daybreak to dusk for as long as she could remember. As a young girl, she had helped her father and brothers roam the rugged hills and dense glades of Huiedien with small bows and sharpened spears, in search of wild game and water fowl. She knew every season and scent, every plant and herb, and every hidden haunt of the roebuck, wild boar and badger.

Ildikko was, indeed, a force to be reckoned with. Those closest to her knew full well that she could dress a deer with the same skill as she could decorate a supper table. She was as unassuming as she was fearless. But the darkness and danger of recent events had made her equally cautious and vigilant. She carried little with her except for one small item that never left her. This she kept it from the wandering eyes of others. The neck knife that hung from a leather necklace and concealed within her vest had been forged and tempered by her father's own hand, and had a lethal, razor-sharp edge.

Ildikko gently reached for it and felt the familiar steel form against her chest as she soberly (but with a hidden surge of anger) bowed her head and grasped its handle while surveying the surrounding carnage.

The scene they witnessed was a living horror; even the battle-hardened Rangers had not seen anything like this before. This scene of slaughter was not a mere act of revenge, nor was it the work of a single madman. This cold calculated plan of extermination. They were now realizing that this would be the ultimate fate of Urbania. Every living thing was in peril, whether it grew or drew a breath. Macoot and the Toon, Bjorn and the men of the Great Forest and the people of Urbania were all slated for destruction. The darkness was descending like a fog over Urbania. Urbanus had to be warned.

"We must leave here at once; the enemy cannot be far away. Come with us; there is nothing left for you here," Wain said.

Sandor and Ildikko agreed to join them and guide them through the ravaged countryside to the nearest docking area on the Ramsgate. They knew the province well and they knew how to avoid the patrols of Salisian soldiers that were guarding every road and bridge between Huiedien and the Ramsgate. It was midday and despite the fact that the enemy could easily see them in the light of day, they thought it best to make haste towards the Ramsgate. If they made it there, they could secure passage on one of the riverboats bound for Urbanus.

With only twelve horses and fifteen riders, they had to make some adjustments; but at least they were riding, and not walking through this barren waste. The poor beasts had nothing to eat, and water was scarce. Time was growing short for man and beast; they needed to press on. So onward they rode, hoping that they would not be detected, and praying that their mounts would last the journey. By nightfall, the horses, now mad with thirst, could smell the river; with what little energy they had left, the horses carried the desperate travelers to the banks of the Ramsgate. There was a full moon visible on the other side of the river, but in Hupsoma there was no moonlight. The darkness was intensifying; they were escaping in the nick of time.

"Set the horses free. We cannot take them with us; they will have to fetch for themselves!" ordered Wain.

So they freed their faithful mounts and made camp by the river's edge. They would wait there until a ship bound for Urbanus would give them passage, or until someone less hospitable came along and discovered them.

****

It was a three days' journey down the Ramsgate from Brantford to Urbanus. Time was an enemy for which they had no defense. Time, like the Ramsgate, ran its course and they would have to flow with it, like it or not.

The accommodations on the old grain ship were anything but luxurious, yet Abner was glad to be heading for Urbanus. These sturdy river ships were built by the merchants of Urbanus for carrying the bounty of the eastern provinces back to Urbanus and points beyond. Passengers were always welcome, if there was room, and there was always room for Jurius Hanner and his ability to turn a business deal.

Abner's thoughts were troubled as he pondered the whereabouts of the Rangers, young Daylin, and the fate of Lothair. Deep in his heart he knew that the boy was safe. He wondered could he say to Jurius, who was racked with concern. Abner did his best to conceal his thoughts and defer the subject to more positive things, but Daylin and the Rangers were never more than a sigh away from his consciousness.

"A good day to sail is it not Jurius? The current is strong and the winds are fair. We will make good progress today," Abner said.

The river men say that time passes more slowly on the river than on land. The leisurely pace of the ship afforded the two old friends much time to reminisce, and reminisce they did. The stories of the good ole days took their minds off the troubled times that engulfed them. They laughed and talked all day; somehow they knew that this would be the last time that they would ever have together. It had been a good day, and now the grains of sand in the day's glass were slowly dissipating. They had scarcely noticed the time when the ship's first mate called them to dinner. No sooner had they stood up to go to the galley than one the sailors called out, alerting the captain that on the port side of the ship there were people waving from the riverbank. It was a common practice for those seeking passage to Urbanus to wait along the riverbank in order to signal a passing ship. Prices were always negotiable, and it was the fastest way to reach Urbanus.

"Shall we eat old friend?" Abner asked.

"After you old man; all this talk has given me quite an appetite. Molly's food it isn't, but I am so hungry right now that almost anything will do," Jurius said.

"Almost anything will have to do, indeed, old friend, "Abner replied.

The captain ordered the ship to turn towards the shore; once he was satisfied that it was safe, he ordered the crew to weigh anchor and dispatch a dingy to pick up the passengers. At the same time that Abner and Jurius were sitting down to eat in the galley, the crew was scurrying to assist a company of fifteen people onto the deck of the ship.

They were a worn and weary band, and the crew marveled at the twelve strangers, all of whom were men who could obviously take care of themselves in any situation. But the twelve men did not travel alone. The man, woman and young boy who traveled with the men were assumed to be family. The captain was at first apprehensive to permit armed men aboard his vessel, but his instincts told him that these travelers would offer him no problems. In fact, they might afford him protection from the rumored Black Ships said to be in these parts; moreover, they appeared to have more than enough problems of their own.

Wain thanked the captain for allowing them to board. He then negotiated the price of their passage, as the others made their way below deck to their quarters. They were too exhausted to eat. It was sleep that they craved. The moment their heads touched their makeshift pillows, they were all fast asleep.

There is a sound that sailing vessel makes as it cuts through the water, driven only by the forces of nature and skilled hands that manage and manipulate the rudder and the rigging. It is a sound that only sailors know and love, and it is a sound now consigned to ages past, but it was that distinct sound that greeted Wain that morning. Though the ship was round and robust and hardly a streamlined vessel, it cut its way through the river like the fin of a shark on the hunt. The smell of the water and the wind created an intoxicating potion that filled his nose and lungs like a tonic. The spray from the waves licked his face creating a pleasant contrast to the stifling atmosphere of Huiedien. No sooner had Wain begun to wonder about old Abner when he heard a gasp followed by,

"In the Name of the Great King Sa'lem," it is you, well and alive and…, and… did you find him?" Abner stammered.

Both men stood speechless for a brief moment, not believing their eyes, while at the same time wanting to scream with joy over this triumphal moment; good fortune was smiling on them, at last they were sensing that good would finally come out of this crisis.

"Where are the others? Are they all safe? And how is the boy?" Abner asked enthusiastically.

"They are all below. They are all safe and well. Daylin is well, too! They were hard on him, but he is fine. We also have two refugees with us. You need to talk with them; they have much to tell. They are eyewitnesses to the enemy's deeds and plans. Solon must hear what they have to say," Wain insisted.

"Excellent. I will get Jurius and meet you in the galley; quick, bring the others," demanded Abner.

The reunion was a joyful one indeed. For a brief moment, Lothair's betrayal was overshadowed by their joy to be reunited. Jurius held Daylin in his arms and wept; he knew how fortunate they were to be together again. Even Abner, who seldom showed his feelings in a demonstrable way, embraced Hull, Quill and Lon; the men of Invar danced about the galley and sang. No one seemed to care that they were behaving in such a strange manner. Sandor and Ildikko watched the festivities with a mixture of bewilderment and admiration. It had been a long time since they had heard the sounds of such happiness.

But their joyful mood eventually ebbed, giving way to the serious matters that lay before them. It would be two days before they docked in Urbanus, and they needed to formulate a plan of action. There were many preparations to make, but none as important as hearing Sandor and Ildikko's story.

Wain asked Lon to take Lothair's place as second in command and join him in the meeting with Abner and Jurius. Lon was the unanimous choice to replace Lothair, although none of the Rangers dared mention the word replacement. He had to be replaced nonetheless. Lothair was gone. Lon was a brilliant tactician, possessing keen insight into human behavior, and the task at hand called for more brains than brawn.

Abner looked straight into Sandor's eyes; his discernment reassured him that Sandor and his wife were not about to tell him lies. Suffering paints a portrait on the face of man that nothing can hide. The enemy was fond of using double agents and disinformation to confuse his opposition, but Sandor and Ildikko were not his pawns, they were his victims. Abner asked him to start at the very beginning.

"It is an honor to meet you sir," Sandor began. "Please allow me to help you understand our circumstances. Hupsoma and the province of Hupsominia are inhabited by two different groups of people. Ildikko and I are Crosians. The Crosian people are the largest group in Hupsoma. We are well known for farming and crafts; many merchants purchase our goods and bring them to Urbanus. Our people have lived there for generations; we love Hupsominia."

And then Sandor stopped, visibly distraught by having to recall the pain memories of his recent past. Abner and the others listened intently and gestured to Sandor to slow down and recompose himself. Wain offered him water. After a few moments, he resumed his story.

We first noticed subtle changes in Hupsominia. Rumors of strange emissaries from the far Eastern provinces and the South were seen in the palace of Ursus. Ursus is not Crosian; he is Salisian. The Salisian people are the second largest group in Hupsominia, and we have lived in peace for centuries. They are the rulers and warrior class; we are the workers, but we have lived in peace for generations. The appearance of strangers in the city became more frequent; no one gave it much thought, but then they began to appear in the villages with various officials from Hupsoma. Prince Tomas, our ruler, was good and kind to the Crosian people, but he died in very strange circumstances. Rumors circulated that Ursus had him assassinated. No one knows the truth of the matter, but everything changed when Ursus assumed power. He is not the rightful heir, but there is no one strong enough to oppose him.

Not all the Salisians agreed with his new policies, and those that opposed him were removed. It is rumored that they were murdered, but no one knows for certain. Hupsoma's council of advisors were silenced and replaced with cronies handpicked by Ursus. It was all so gradual. So long as the changes did not affect the Crosian people directly, there was no cause for alarm; it was a Salisian problem, but things changed. Our rights and privileges were slowly being lost. New restrictions were placed on Crosians.

Village life changed overnight. Everything was regulated; new laws were passed forbidding the buying or selling of goods without official permission. Other laws were passed preventing us from owning weapons. What weapons we owned were confiscated; the school became the voice for the new regime. Children were ordered to report any criticism of Ursus to their teachers. Dissenters disappeared and were never seen again. Huiedien was once a peaceful village, people trusted one another, and families lived and died there for generations.

But then another strange thing happened. The length of our days grew shorter and shorter; the daylight fled as darkness gripped Hupsominia. Fear, mistrust and bitterness soon replaced everything that was good. Trust was gone; love for your neighbor evaporated. Once we were divided from our families and our friends, we were defenseless.

Again Sandor paused to gather himself, but Ildikko grasped his hand and began to speak.

"I will never forget the day that the Sharokhan, accompanied by Ghouls and Salisian soldiers, marched into Huiedien. Without warning, they gathered the men in the village square and began to separate them into smaller groups. They carefully inspected them and formed them into still smaller groups. The older men, the sick, and the frail, were beheaded on the spot. I can still here their screams as they awaited they fate. The Ghouls then feasted on their bodies as the Sharokhan watched in silence. The women were brutally ravished, and then sorted into groups like the men. Those considered unfit met the same fate as the men. The children were taken south and never seen again."

"How did you escape?" Lon asked.

"Ildikko and I had decided that we needed to prepare for the worse. We could not convince the others to fight. We are not warriors. We had no weapons, and what weapons we owned before were confiscated. All we had is what we used to protect our flocks and herds. It was impossible to resist the Salisians. Few of us believed that they really meant us no harm.

We had lived in peace for so long, but I knew that it was only a matter of time before they came. During the night time we dug a tunnel under our house. The tunnel led to the fields. We filled it with what few provisions we had. We told no one of it, not even our parents; we could trust no one. It took weeks. It was finished just two days before they came. They appeared like a mist and descended on the village. Fortunately, we were in our house and were able to make our way into the tunnel. From there we ran for cover; once we were clear and hidden in the hedgerows, we could see what they did."

"When we met you in Huiedien, you spoke of the 'living dead,' what are they/" Asked Wain.

"They are people without souls, they are lifeless bodies that are now the possession of the enemy; they are now his servants and soldiers," said Sandor.

"Ghouls, that is what they are, Ghouls," Abner said in disgust.

"They are beyond hope; no one can help them. They are dead, but they are possessed and animated by demonic spirits," Abner said with compassion.

"Go and rest, the both of you; you have shared enough for now. We will talk more tomorrow," said Abner.

Jurius looked at Abner and said, "It is worse than I could have imagined. The enemy has occupied Hupsominia, Urbanus and the other cities have no idea of the peril that they are in. The enemy has a toehold; we must now find his foothold. He seldom attacks on one front. No doubt he is already working in Urbanus."

"No doubt he is keeping them occupied with distractions and diversions from the south, while the real threat is from within Urbanus," said Wain.

"What shall we do?" Asked Jurius.

"I must approach the Brotherhood and appeal to them and I must do something that I did not want to do, I must …," Abner said apprehensively.

"You must do what," asked Jurius?

"I can say nothing more for now, it is best for you not to know until the time is right. All in due time," said Abner.

They knew it was pointless to press Abner any further. He would not tell them. The old man had more secrets than the glaciers of Mithras had crevasses. Abner stood up signaling that the meeting was over. There was enough to ponder. All they knew was that were going to accompany Abner to Urbanus; Abner alone knew what they were going to do when they arrived there.

A House Divided

There was great anticipation aboard the ship that morning. On the horizon a spectacular sight emerged, Urbanus! The sun's rays glimmered off her whitewashed buildings and copper roofs like the facets of a diamond. The waterfront was a fury of activity resembling an ant colony collecting winter stores. Ships were loading, unloading and docking, while others waited to catch the tide and take their cargoes to unknown destinations. Huge quantities of grain, lumber and fresh produce were off-loaded as herds of livestock were led down gangplanks, producing a cacophonous roar, while workers competed with their dirge by singing working songs to lessen their loads. Wagons and teams of horses eagerly waited at the docks to buy and then load the precious goods for Urbanus's central market place.

Daylin had never seen the likes of this. It was more than he had dreamed; it was overwhelming his senses. Daylin stood spellbound watching every detail, and he would have stood there for the entire day had not Jurius broken his trance.

"Come boy, we must go. There is much to do and see. This is but the beginning; there is much more to come," said Abner.

Jurius had wanted to bring Daylin to Urbanus for his thirteenth birthday. It was meant to be a surprise, but his plans had changed; the beast laid plans always surrender to reality. He was saddened that he had not been able to give him the gift that he had planned for so long. Daylin was in Urbanus for reasons he could not fully understand; Abner alone knew the why of the matter.

In the meantime, Jurius inquired with his merchant friends and learned that Prince Solon's unity and peace conference was already underway. The city was filled with contingents from the Nine Cities, and everyone was gossiping about Ursus and the presence his army. The atmosphere was a balance of tension and optimism. Abner informed them that they should go straight to the Brotherhood's compound; Jurius hailed a large coach and together they embarked for their trip across the city to their final destination. Their progress was slow as they carefully weaved their way through the stifling traffic.

Packmen dressed in their long black hooded robes were everywhere leading their horses laden with firewood. Despite their number and the vast quantities of wood that they supplied, they could never satisfy the city's appetite for fuel. The air was filled with the foul odor of ammonia that emanated from vessels used as toilets that were commonly referred to as "piss-pots" by the locals. While the pots proved to be a convenience, the urine was a vital ingredient used by the tanners in creating the renowned leather goods for which Urbanus was famous.

****

"Shut your filthy mouth you vile gutter scum. I should have sold you at birth before you had a chance to cause me all this trouble," the old woman said.

"What do you mean that you only have five gold pieces to show for a full morning's work? Are you holding out on me again you beggar trash of a leach? I should cut that ugly nose off your face. Maybe then the girls would find you more attractive; you are so ugly you make blind men weep," she crackled in disdain.

Yes, it was sad, but true that Raymaris was ugly. Though he was of average stature, his slumped shoulders made him appear shorter than he actually was. He was round about the middle, and his arms and legs were thick. Upon this portly body sat a large head which housed an enormous gapping mouth that was seldom closed. His ears, by contrast, seemed too small, and his large flat nose and flared nostrils all conspired to create a grotesque sight. But his ugliness penetrated far deeper than his physical features. He was a street urchin of the vilest sort. Mother and child were bound together in a relationship that brought the worse out in each other.

They hated and loathed each other, but neither one dared to think of parting each other's company. Raymaris had become deaf to his mother's toxic tongue years ago, just as she had become blind to his ugliness. Karola needed Raymaris, and he needed her. It was a partnership of tragic convenience. Raymaris lied, manipulated and stole anything and everything that Urbanus had to offer. His mother protected and defended him from his accusers and critics, and above all anyone who would dare to offer help to the boy. Raymaris and his mother were leeches living off the life's blood of the city. They lived a low life, but it served the higher purposes of those with sinister plans for Urbania.

The clip-clop of the horse's hooves on the cobblestone street announced the coming of the coach that carried Abner and his friends. Wain and the Rangers felt very uncomfortable riding in a coach. It all seemed too soft for the Rangers, but they were, after all, in Urbanus. Sandor and Ildikko had never ridden in such a fine vehicle, and the sights of the city overwhelmed their senses. Daylin still lingered under the intoxicating effects of the entire experience. Jurius and Abner were amused by their companions' reactions and took the whole thing in stride.

As the coaches made their way towards the Brotherhood's compound, a boy darted out from an alley and straight into the horses' path. The coachman tried to bring the horses to a halt, but it was too late; the boy was hit broadside and fell unconscious beneath the horses. The coach stopped with an abrupt halt in the middle of the street.

"What happened? What was that?" cried Jurius.

Wain and the Rangers instinctively drew their swords, but were waved off by Abner. Jurius and Wain jumped from the coach along with the coachman to behold the boy lying unconscious on the cobblestone.

"My son, my son, what have you done? My poor son," cried the woman.

With reckless abandon she reached down and scooped him into her arms and tried to resuscitate him. As she wept over him and wailed with a volume that could be heard for a dextor, a crowd of curious onlookers encircled them. Eventually the boy's eyes gradually open and he softly moaned the word "Mother."

"He is a live and no thanks to you. Just because you ride in a fine coach and have money does not mean that you can do as you please!" she snarled with contempt.

The Rangers gathered around the boy, took him from his mother's arms, and gently lifted him into the coach. Jurius asked the coachman to call for a doctor. Everyone was absorbed with the excitement of the moment, with the exception of Abner, who stood with his back to the wall of nearby building pondering the situation. His spirit was growing more troubled by the minute as he reflected upon the accident. It was all too contrived, too convenient. But this was neither the time nor the place to accuse the mother and child of a scam.

Meanwhile, a new situation erupted from the alley adjacent to the street where their coach was stopped; a young girl surrounded by a band of Salisian soldiers was trying to free herself. She struggled violently, but each one pawed and groped her in turn, tormenting her for their amusement. Clearly, their leader was intent on having his way the girl. It was more than Wain and the Rangers could endure; without hesitation, they left the coach and ran to the girl's aid.

"Stop it, stop it now!" Wain commanded.

But the soldiers paid no attention to him and, like hounds on the trail of a fox. They continued their pursuit of the girl. Their captain grabbed her by neck and threw her to the ground. His intentions were perfectly clear to all who were watching. With one fell swoop, Wain placed a swift blow to the back of his neck that sent him reeling for the moment. But he retaliated with a kick that landed squarely in Wain's midsection followed by a blow to his chin. The Captain grabbed Wain by his throat and was about to choke the life out of him when Wain responded with a well-placed knee to his groin. The girl seeing an opportunity to escape, fled from her unconscious attacker and ran down the alley.

Several soldiers under the command of their fallen captain immediately met Wain with drawn swords; they commanded Wain to yield. Unfortunately for them, Hull and Quill were behind them. Without so much as a word, they drew their swords and jettisoned the soldiers' swords from their hands. The others thought it best to retreat than to risk a fight with the Rangers.

"Who among you wants to die this day?" roared Hull.

His request was met by stone-cold silence and a mad dash for safety as they ran down the alley faster than the girl, whom they were pursuing, leaving their unconscious Captain to fend for himself. The Rangers viewed the sorry scene with utter contempt.

While Wain and the Rangers were occupied with the matter at hand several Salisian soldiers approached the carriage and separated Sandor and Ildikko from Jurius and Abner. Ildikko immediately recognized one of their numbers; he was there in Huiedien on that fateful day when her family and friends were massacred. She would never forget that swarthy face, the goatee and those remorseless black eyes. He was as cold and detached as a viper. A chill went up her spine as the ghastly images of suffering torment flew past her mind's eye in recollection of the horror. In sharp contrast to her vulnerable mental state, her blood ran hot in anticipation of confronting the vile figure that had destroyed everything that she loved.

"Zestor, look what we have here! Ah, a sweet morsel for our dessert!!" another soldier said.

But Zestor had long since been watching Illdikko closely. When the moment was ripe, he gave the signal to surround the carriage and separate Sandor and Ildikko from their friends. Sandor would be no problem.

While Jurius and Abner were distracted by Karola's ruse, Zestor then left Sandor with his men, and hoisting Ildikko over his shoulder like a burlap sack of potatoes, whisked her away down an alley, where he was bent on having his way with her. Glancing from one side to the other to be sure that no one was in pursuit, he threw Ildikko rudely to the ground.

Ildikko was terrified, but she was no stranger to danger. The disgust of being violated by this filthy beast had come and gone. But as Zestor pressed his victim to the ground, Ildikko's body suddenly went limp. Without warning, she calmly reached for Zestor's head, so as to invite his advances. She gently stroked his face. "Yes," she whispered.

The utter shock and delight of her invitation took Zestor by surprise. In the same moment, Ildikko slowly slid her hands to her face. Her fingers grasped the hilt of her neck knife. In one expert stroke, she unsheathed the blade and plunged it into his pulsing jugular.

Before Zestor realized his fate, the blade had met its mark. Zestor released his fevered grip on Ildikko; his trembling hands reached for the hilt of her knife, but his body recoiled in pain. It was too late; her attacker, unable to either speak or to cry out, slumped and rolled to one side, drowning face-down in his own blood, leaving Ildikko untouched.

Ildikko quickly gathered her composure, and her skirt, rolled Zestor's limp body to an obscure corner of the alley, and quietly sauntered back through the narrow alley to the main road where the carriage was still parked. In the meantime, the Rangers had returned from their confrontation with the Salisians and had rescued Sandor. Zestor's companions were quickly dispatched and fled for their lives.

Sandor had resigned himself to his wife's fate at the hands of her assailant, but he was not entirely surprised when she came walking toward them; she appeared to be unshaken from her ordeal.

"Where did you go, Ildikko? Where did he take you? How did you get away?" Sandor asked a barrage of similar questions while Jurius and the Rangers watched in bewilderment. Wain remained silent, keeping his wise suspicions to himself. He was a wise and worthy friend.

With that, she glanced at Wain, whose eyes slightly narrowed, betraying a slight smile of approval She then nonchalantly took Sandor's arm, leading him forward as if on a summer stroll.

"There's something about that woman," Wain said to the Rangers. "I'm not sure what it is, but something tells me that she's the kind of woman I would want watching my back. Well, only behind Hull and Quill and the other Rangers, of course." But his point had been well taken and silently agreed.

"Yeah, I suppose you're right, Wain," volunteered Hull, "*It's too bad she's just a woman, or she could be one of us,*" he snickered, followed by a subdued wave of guarded laughter from the Rangers.

As they walked back to the coach to rejoin their companions, they could hear the mother of the boy bartering with Jurius and Abner who had joined him.

"Well, one hundred gold pieces might cover his medical expenses, but I think one hundred and fifty to be more like it; after all, you are one who caused this. I am sure that with the sheriff's help we could arrive at a fair agreement. Jurius and Abner both knew that a master con-artist was scamming them.

But time was short and they could not afford an investigation. After stepping into the alley to consider their options and what they should give the woman, they decided that expediency was better than thrift. So pay they did and no sooner were the coins jingling in her purse than Raymaris stood up and declared that he was capable of walking.

"Money is powerful medicine is it not?" Jurius said sarcastically.

"Indeed it is, and we may have bought more than we bargained for," Abner said cynically.

All the enemy's agents were now aware of their presence in the city. Abner was right. In a matter of minutes, the grapevine buzzed with the news that Daylin was in Urbanus accompanied by Abner and the Rangers. The stage was being set for the final act.

****

The Brotherhood's compound, which they called Eirene, was now in sight; it stood in stark contrast to the sophistication and pace of Urbanus. Like an oasis in the middle of a desert it beckoned the travelers to its serenity and refreshment. Travelers who entered its gates were transported to another dimension, befitting its name; it was a place of peace.

"This is but the second time I have been here; how it has grown under Lemler's leadership. I never imagined that the Brotherhood could have grown by such leaps and bounds," said Abner.

"Yes, I have come here often Abner. There was a time when Urbanus ignored the Brotherhood as an antiquated sect, but no longer. They are an influence and a force to be reckoned with. They see themselves as the conscience of Urbania. It is the Brotherhood, not the city states and the provinces, that are the people's first allegiance," Jurius replied.

"True." said Abner, but they are misguided in their convictions. If only they had the right understanding of the times and could harness their resources for constructive ends." The old seer was beginning to preach an old and familiar sermon, one that they had heard too many times. As Abner began, and as if a signal had been given, the Rangers politely tuned him out and dispersed. Abner was totally transfixed on his thoughts and was more than content to offer a soliloquy. Over the years he had acquired a lifetime of pent-up frustration with the Brotherhood. It was his time to vent. He would have his hearing, but whether they had ears to hear remained to be seen.

The Brothers were warm and cordial, and Abner was accorded the greatest respect. He was legendary among the Brotherhood; though he never officially joined their ranks, they considered him one of their own. He was in many ways a prophet for his times, but his disdain for titles and religiosity was well known. Abner was a complex man, but he was honest and sincere to the core. While men accorded him respect, they walked on eggshells around him; if he detected any hero-worship on their part, a swift rebuke was their reward. In an age of heroes, Abner stood apart; the truth held the highest priority for him, not systems and organizations. Wherever the truth took him, there he stood; popularity was never his mistress. He courted no man's favor, not even the favor of princes.

The news of Abner's arrival spread like a prairie fire in a drought. Lemler halted his biggest lecture of the day in the middle of a sentence and left the podium post haste to greet him. The spontaneous greeting grew to massive numbers as all came to greet Abner. Even Abner was slightly impressed with the zeal of their welcome.

"Greetings, Brother Abner! What an honor and an unexpected surprise to have you visit us. We had heard that you were in Urbania, but we could only hope that you would come here and honor us with your presence. Our prayers have been answered; welcome to you and your friends."

Lemler turned his gaze towards Daylin and stroked his hair with a fatherly gesture but for a moment one could suspect that his eyes were betraying that he knew more than he wanted his guests to know."

"This must be the brothers Fairn and the men of Invar and, of course, our old friend dear Brother Jurius. Please introduce us to your friends. Are you from Hupsoma? We greet you all. Please enter our humble dwellings, eat and rest. You will address the meeting tonight, will you not Brother Abner?" said Lemler.

"I must speak to you alone before that can happen. May we retire and discuss the matter?" asked Abner.

"At once," Lemler responded.

Abner accompanied Lemler to his office while the others retired to the kitchen of the main dormitory. The smell of fresh baked bread permeated the air like perfume. The cooks of the Brotherhood were perpetually busy preparing food for their brethren and their labors filled Eirene with wonderful aromas.

Abner came right to the point.

"I must address the Council of Elders tonight. It is imperative that I do so; there is no time to waste," Abner said emphatically.

"Why the haste, brother, what could be so important? Before I can convene the Council of Elders, I must have more information," Lemler rejoined.

"Information, yes, of course I will give you all the information that you require. You will get more facts than you can digest. The husband and wife who are traveling with us are from the village of Huiedien in the province of Hupsominia. They are living proof that Ursus has allied himself with the enemy. Hupsominia is already in the enemy's possession.

Ursus is not attending the Unity Conference in order to decide which side he will support; he is here to aid the Enemy in his conquest of Urbanus, and ultimately of Urbania. As goes Urbanus, so goes Urbania. There are Black Ships on the Ramsgate and Sharokhan in the Forest of the Toon. The Artrax and the Ganza roam about the eastern provinces at will. To the South, the largest army and naval force ever assembled is ready to launch an invasion of Urbania; and all the while, Urbanus is being probed, prodded and spied upon from within. Sanballat has more eyes and ears in the city than can be counted. Urbanus has but days to decide her fate. It may be too late."

"Brother, you are weary from your journey. Tomorrow will bring you a new perspective. A perspective, perhaps that is more optimistic. Do not the scrolls say that, 'Anxiety is for the night season, but joy is the gift of the morning'" Lemler responded?

Abner could bear no more of Lemler's condescension; in a manner uncharacteristic of him, he slammed his fist on the desk and screamed, "Listen you pompous ass! Listen to me! I'm telling you the unvarnished truth; this city and Urbania are in the gravest peril. Convene the Council Elders and let them decide the matter."

Lemler was taken aback by Abner's outburst; no one dare speak to him as Abner did. He swallowed hard and absorbed the rebuke, but inwardly he fumed with anger. For now he had no other choice but to acquiesce to Abner's request, but he would bide his time in order to settle the score.

"As you wish Brother, I will convene the Council of Elders tonight; by all means, share with them the things you have just told me."

After their lunch and a long afternoon nap, Wain and the Rangers were ready to venture into the city. Abner decided against their attending the meeting with the Council of Elders. He believed that their presence would only complicate matters. So with mixed emotions, the Rangers set off for a night in the city. Urbanus had many fine inns and taverns, and they decided that their first trip to the city should be a memorable one.

Urbanus was renowned for its beef. The aroma of steaks, ribs and assorted cuts of meat filled the night air as outdoor fires roasted the bounty of the eastern prairie to perfection. An endless stream of customers came and went through their doors as waiters maneuvered between the rows of tables carrying food and drink to their patrons like mother birds feeding hungry chicks. Hull licked his lips with anticipation. Before Wain could chose a suitable location, Hull was through the door of an inn named "The Open Arms" and immediately summoned a waiter, sat down and placed an order for twelve; the others did not know that Hull was only ordering for himself...

"And one bowl of boiled cabbage; make that two, and vinegar for the cabbage. Make haste lad! I'm so hungry that I could roast a Ghoul."

Lon quipped, "Looks like an ill wind will blow tonight men, and Hull sleeps alone."

Even Wain broke into laughter at Lon's wit. Hull did everything in a grand fashion and eating was no exception, not to mention the after effects of his meals. The Rangers hastily sat down beside Hull and, after gathering their senses, all agreed that Hull had made a good but impetuous choice in the Open Arms. In no time, they relaxed and ordered large glasses of Toon cider and the house specialty, roast prime rib. And what a feast it was! They could hardly believe that they were experiencing such a time as this while the world that they knew hung in the balance.

For a few brief moments they sat in silence. There was an unspoken understanding amongst them that night; they would not talk about their mission: they had agreed to occupy themselves only with their food and drink. They were coveting every moment of this night; they were going to enjoy themselves, and enjoy themselves they did. When they had finished, they all agreed that this had been one of the finest meals that they had ever had.

Sensing that the time was growing late, Wain called for their waiter, but there was no response. Again he signaled but again there was no response. Puzzled by the lack of service, he left the table and summoned the owner of the inn, but before he could speak with the owner, a familiar face intercepted him and bowed courteously.

"Kind sir, do you remember me? I am the boy who was hit by your coach today; I have something for you."

Wain composed himself, and said,

"How could I forget you; I will never forget that performance as long as I live. What do you want?"

"My Lord, I have a letter for you, it is from the girl whose honor and virtue you so bravely defended. She is very grateful to you for what you did and she asked me to give you this."

Raymaris handed Wain the letter and then he scampered out the door as quickly as he appeared. Wain looked at the letter and then placed it unopened is his vest pocket. He may as well have placed a hot coal on his chest, for from that moment on he could think of nothing else.

****

DIVIDED WE FALL

Abner's request to address the Council of Elders had been granted. The Council of Elders consisted of twelve of the most respected teachers of the Brotherhood. They lived at Eirene and taught the students in the academy known as the School of the Seers. The Elders set the tone and direction for the Brotherhood in all matters of faith and policy. If Abner could influence them, he could utilize their influence and deliver to Prince Solon what he desired and what Urbania so desperately needed, unity.

The Council of Elders convened in a large dark paneled room; its high white cathedral ceiling and gray marbled floor gave it an imposing air of authority. At the front of the room was an elevated massive oak bench that was almost as wide as the room itself and behind it sat the Council of Elders. It looked more like a courtroom than a council chamber; how fitting, because in reality Abner was on trial. The Brotherhood needed to know the truth and once they knew it, Abner hoped that the truth would set them free from their dogmatism and permit them to act in the best interests of Urbania.

A new chairman was selected annually to preside over the Council of Elders. He was chosen from the twelve standing members of the council. This year the chairman was Brother Echidna. He was a tall handsome man whose head of wavy gray hair housed a keen intellect, a resonant voice, and an unequalled power of persuasion. All of these attributes conspired to make Echidna simultaneously admired and feared by all who knew him. But it was his serpentine cunning that set him apart from his peers. Few men dared to challenge him; those who had, had paid dearly. Echidna was the consummate politician; he never allowed his scruples to influence or interfere with his goals.

Abner understood the situation and slowly bowed his head looking at the floor. His heart sank. This was not an auspicious beginning; Echidna's differences with Abner were well known. Abner drew a deep breath and slowly raised his head, making eye contact with each of the twelve elders.

"Welcome Brother Abner; you honor Eirene with your presence. We have unanimously decided to grant you your petition to address this council; we understand that it is a matter of extreme urgency. Therefore, we will forego our normal formalities and proceed immediately to your concerns. Please state your case. Please begin," Echidna said without a hint of emotion.

The scene was set and, while the situation was not to Abner's advantage, he was far from intimidated by it; he had waited for this day. He was about to seize the moment and speak his mind regardless of the outcome. Abner rose from his chair and faced the Elders who sat perched on a raised platform three dextars above the floor. The room was filled to capacity with the senior members of the Brotherhood.

Jurius, Daylin, Sandor and Ildikko sat directly behind Abner. He quickly glanced back at them, cleared his throat and prepared to speak. Abner's small frame and physical frailty stood in stark contrast to the carefully choreographed room. Echidna and his colleagues loomed above him, like predatory birds of prey, their eyes giving careful scrutiny to Abner's every move. Meeting their challenge, Abner slowly moved towards the platform and fixed his gaze upon Echidna. With a ballet like pivot of his feet, he turned his back to the elders and began his address to the audience.

> People of Urbania, there has always been a harmony among all living things in Urbania. That harmony is fragile; it is delicate and it is precious. It is a gift bestowed upon you by the Great King Sa'lem. That gift is also your stewardship; it must be guarded and preserved. It is essential to the very

preservation of all the things that we love and hold dear. For countless generations mortal men and the Toon lived in peace and harmony; there was room and resources for all. The forests knew no limit; the waters ran freely, and the fertile land was endless. All the creatures of Urbania lived in security and contentment. But this has all changed. How did it change, you ask? The change was subtle and invisible to the naked eye; it was a slow gradual change that affected the hearts of mortal men. The delicate balance that had long sustained Urbania was slowly upset, and with it the hearts of mortal men were corrupted. Darkness has encroached upon the borders of Urbania and leached into the very fabric of its collective soul.

And what was the response of the leaders of Urbania to this crisis? They formed alliances with the enemy, alliances forbidden by the Great King Sa'lem. These are the same alliances that have created a corrupt competition for power and interest among you. The peace that once ruled Urbania for millennia ended and spawned endless series of wars. You all know the outcome—Urbanus and her allies may have declared themselves the victor, but I tell you that there was no victor. Countless lives were lost, cities were destroyed and the landscape laid waste; the harmony of all living things was destroyed. In truth, the Great War vanquished all the creatures of Urbania.

However, this was not the work of mortal men alone. Behind the scenes of this great drama were two personalities, two forces, yes, two kings. Each had a different agenda for Urbania. Each had a direct and active role in the Great War. Neither its beginning, nor its end was the result of chance or the devices of mortal men but the carefully laid plans of these two kings. Who are they, you ask? They are none other than my Lord and King, the Sovereign of the Northern Kingdom, His majesty King Sa'lem; and the second is his arch enemy, Sanballat, the Emir of the Southern Kingdom.

No, the Great War produced no victors and worse—the war did not end. Those mortal men who have eyes to see and ears to hear know that the war continues to this very hour It has changed fronts, and its combatants have adopted new tactics, but the strategic goal remains the same, the conquest of Urbania. You are the prize and you are also participants. It is you who will decide your fate; it is you who must chose who will become your conqueror and your eternal sovereign.

Years ago as the violence of the Great War ebbed, King Sa'lem made a crucial decision; he appointed a spokesman to Urbania, a spokesman who would be his voice in the realm, and one who would turn the hearts of mortal men to the truth and thus restore the balance of harmony. He endowed these mortals with wisdom and wealth. He opened doors of influence for them and he gave them favor with the Princes of the Ten Cities. He gave them prominence and position in Urbania.

And what was their response to His graciousness kindness? They took all that he gave and squandered it on their own selfish interests. They perverted his message of triumph and hope into one of inevitable defeat and pessimism. They preached the futility of resisting evil based upon the very scrolls that were entrusted to them. And when King Sa'lem sent messengers of correction, they scorned them and they refused to listen to them. They rejected his counsel and used their position as spokesmen as though it were theirs by right. As their numbers swelled, so did their heads. As the darkness advanced, they celebrated the fulfillment of their predictions. They opposed all efforts at making peace between the Ten Cities, and they condemned those who tried accusing them of compromise and heresy. No other group has contributed so much to the destruction of Urbania as they. In them, the enemy has a true friend and a co-conspirator. And you know better than any, of those of whom I speak!"

Yes! Hear me! They do not bear the burden of this guilt alone. The Patrikos have seduced you with their crooked vision; they have promised you security and peace, but at what cost? You boast of your wealth and position and claim to be free men, but you have sold your birthright for a bowl of gruel. You may be free from some of the minor pains of life, but you are not free to decide your future. You do not possess liberty. They decide the manner in which you use your land and they decided when it can be sold and to whom. They decide if you are worthy to keep what you own, and whether your personal interests outweigh the common good, which they alone decide. Free men indeed …; a bondservant in King Sa'lem's house has more freedom than you!

As for the Trapezites, they enslave every living man, woman and child and those yet unborn with the shackles of debt. They encourage greed, covetousness, discontent and theft. I ask you, was it gold that made Urbanus great, or goodness? You are sick and do not know it! You think yourselves rich, yet you are poor! Alas, while you revel in wealth and well-being, the blind woman in your midst, whom you ignore, she alone understands and sees your nakedness.

There is a plague, an unseen but ruthless pestilence, rampant in the land, not borne of vermin of the animal kind, but rather of deep darkness. It infects good men with evil thoughts, words and deeds and causes their hearts to grow cold and indifferent; it threatens to extinguish goodness and truth from Urbania. Even now the Enemy is at the gates; you have become the objects of his desire. There are debts to be paid. He aims to collect; he will seize Urbanus as collateral and you as his slaves.

Abner paused and turned around to face the Elders seated high upon their perch, gruesome and with gapping, ghoulish mouths, like vultures anticipating the death of their helpless, hapless prey. How fitting it seemed for these white-wash tombs to sit so high and mighty above the people. The tension in the room mounted and intensified like an overly tightened violin string, yet the room was so quiet that a mouse could be heard breathing. Indeed, it seemed as though the breath had been sucked from them all, leaving them suffocating with guilt and shame. The faces of the Elders strained until the veins in their faces appeared to burst. Their eyes betrayed their intense hatred of Abner and though silent, it was evident to all. They did not interrupt him. They displayed remarkable restraint under his scathing attack, for they knew that they would have the last word. Their soulless eyes betrayed their true state. They were consumed and corrupted by jealousy and greed, desperate to satiate and advance their own twisted ambition. Abner (so they believed) was building his own gallows, much to their misguided delight. But Abner continued.

> Lest you think that I only speak in metaphors, be advised that at this very hour the forces of the enemy are poised to invade Urbania. Hupsominia has already fallen into the Enemy's hands. Ursus is attending the Unity Conference in order to aid the enemy in his conquest of Urbanus. There are Black Ships on the Ramsgate and a fleet assembling at the mouth of the Ramsgate on the Western Sea. The Sharokhan roam the Forest of the Toon; the Artrax and the Ganza move about the eastern provinces at will.
>
> To the South the largest army ever assembled is ready to launch the final invasion of Urbania. The enemy lies within and without. You must change your course and direction. You possess the means to turn the hearts of the mortal men before it is too late. You claim to be students of the future, and your looking-glass is the ancient scrolls, but your eyes are clouded you see only what you want to see. You are looking through the wrong end of a spy glass.
>
> You see a far different vision of the future than I. You see the triumph of evil before a new age of peace and prosperity. I see the hope of the coming of a new man, the dawn of a new day, and the triumph of goodness over evil. I see the Promised One leading the combined armies of Urbania and the Northern Kingdom into battle and crushing the enemy once and for all.
>
> You must choose this day whether you will blindly follow these other blind guides down a path to destruction, or whether you will listen to my words, words which I have received and speak on behalf of the Great King Sa'lem.

Echidna looked down at Abner and without a hint of emotion said, "We shall consider your case carefully brother Abner; this meeting will resume tomorrow at the second hour past midday. It is then that we shall render our verdict."

Abner turned to his friends and then sat down beside Daylin, who found it difficult to digest all that Abner had said. Who was the "One" he had referred to? Why was he here? It was all overwhelming him. He thought to himself, "What was I thinking when I said Brantford was so boring?"

Abner's criticisms and warnings of impending doom seemed to be ignored by the Elders, but Jurius knew that Abner was in serious trouble. How could they listen to Abner's firsthand knowledge of the impending invasion and not even speak one word? Echidna's carefully chosen words echoed in his mind. "It is then that we shall render our *verdict*." It was all beginning to sound more like a criminal case rather than a plea for a decision or a change of policy by the Brotherhood. Jurius wondered, *was all this going according to plan or was the whole thing out of control?*

"He's gone too far. We must rid ourselves of him once and for all," Echidna said forcefully.

"You are right. He is a threat to the Brotherhood. He defies our authority as ruling elders, and he undermines and opposes our doctrine. He is a cancer, creating dissension and disorder throughout the congregations of Urbania," said Elder Lache.

"I totally agree. He must be dealt with. He is not one of us. How dare he claim to speak for King Sa'lem? He is a compromiser and a heretic. He charges us with heresy and openly advocates making alliances with secular government," snarled Elder Fierte.

"Did you hear what he said, 'No other group has contributed so much to the destruction of Urbania as they have? In them the Enemy has a true friend and a co-conspirator,' what other proof do we need?" demanded Elder Commerage.

"What we need is something more substantial than a charge of heresy. Urbanus cares nothing about our doctrinal differences with Abner. That is our problem. But if it can be proven that Abner is a clear and present danger to Urbanus, well that would be a different matter, would it not?" Echidna said with cool aloofness.

"Indeed it would, but you are speaking of treason, Brother, and not mere heresy. The penalty for treason is death and that is far different thing than excommunication," said Elder Menteur.

"That bothers you, brother? Does the loss of everything that we have worked for bother you? Allowing Abner to turn the hearts of the people against us and become the leader of the Brotherhood. Doesn't *that* bother you? If someone and something is going to die, it might as well be Abner and his inane cause," retorted Echidna, like the skilled debater that he was.

"What do you propose?" asked Menteur.

"We must meet with Solon and Meander tonight and offer Solon what he desires most—our support. In exchange for charging Abner with treason, we will endorse the peace and unity conference. We will instruct our teachers to tell their assemblies that this not a change in our doctrine or policy. After all, the scrolls command us to love our leaders and to support them. We will make a clear distinction between supporting peace as an ideal and our belief that it cannot change what has been predicted by the scrolls. After all, Solon only needs the illusion of unity to keep his enemies at bay. A united Urbanus along with the support our assemblies throughout Urbania gives him more political currency than he can spend, and the real bonus is that we get rid of Abner once and for all," said Echidna.

"But how are we going to convince Solon that Abner is a traitor?" asked Elder Lache.

"We need to secure witnesses who have firsthand knowledge of his conspiring with the enemy. It is clearly evident that he is under the enemy's influence. He is deranged and that no one can hold such a view of the future and be in their right mind. He is a menace to the public good and a corrupter of sound teaching. Listen to me, once he is charged and convicted of conspiracy with the enemy, his support of Solon and his peace efforts will mean nothing. He will be discredited in the eyes of everyone; they will demand his execution. His heresy will die with him and, more importantly, the Brotherhood will live on. In my mind it is a very workable solution to a delicate problem," Echidna responded.

The others nodded pensively and in unanimous agreement. A messenger was immediately dispatched to Solon's palace requesting a meeting of extreme urgency. The plan was hatched.

A weary Solon, accompanied by Chancellor Doulos and Meander, were to meet Echidna and the Elders in his private chambers. Solon gave strict orders that no one was to speak of the meeting. It was to be held in the strictest of confidence. The risks and implications of the meeting held at this hour were enormous. Solon knew that desperate men take desperate measures when what they love most is in jeopardy.

"My Lord Prince, we thank you for graciously granting us this audience at such an inconvenient hour, but we assure you that this matter it is of the gravest importance. You must hear us, for the very existence of Urbanus is at stake. We know of no other way to state this than to come out and confess that one of our own brothers is a traitor to Urbanus and, is as we speak, conspiring with the Enemy to invade the city and Urbania as a whole. He has come to Urbanus under the guise of raising support for your peace and unity conference, but he is spreading strife and dissension among the Brotherhood and he is, in reality, a spy and a traitor," said Echidna with an air uncharacteristic passion.

"Who is it? Do you have conclusive proof of this?" Solon asked.

"Yes, we do, my Prince, and I am ashamed to say that the traitor's name is Abner."

"Abner, I know that name. He is an old and renowned seer from the North is he not?"

"Yes my Prince; he is, and that makes the matter all the more serious. Abner has influence in all the Ten Cities and their provinces. The people love and respect him; but under the guise of supporting your peace efforts, he is plotting against you," said Elder Menteur.

Solon drank in all that they shared, but he was not a gullible fool. He understood what Lemler had done to him earlier. Now the

Brotherhood was acting like beggars knocking on his door and courting his favor. He couldn't resist the temptation to throw the matter back in their pasty faces.

"Plotting against me or against you? I know of no element in the Brotherhood that supports my peace and unity conference. Treason is a serious charge and you know that it carries the death penalty. It sounds like the Brotherhood has a rather large stone in its shoe."

"My Prince, I assure you that there is ample and conclusive proof of his guilt and, while it is true that he is causing us serious problems we have mutual interests here," said Echidna.

"Mutual interests, what interests do I share with you? Please enlighten me. As I recall, Brother Lemler made it quite clear that the Brotherhood was neutral when it came to matters of state. I deduced that he could not endorse the conference without turning his back on his teachings. I also recall that one of your Brothers received a standing ovation at the expenses of my dignity when he said something to the affect that the ancient scrolls have prophesied that Urbania must fall to the evil one and that resistance is hopeless. The opinion was also stated and agreed to by the audience that Urbania is doomed, and those who hope for peace are deceived because there will be no peace until the consummation. The same individual said that the conference is a vain imagination of desperate men who have ignored spiritual things for far too long! Correct me if I am wrong, but these are the sentiments and teachings of the Brotherhood, are they not?"

Echidna replied, "He spoke rashly under the passion of the moment. He is correct in what he said as far as our position is concerned, but he failed to clarify that we are men of peace and we support you in your efforts to seek and maintain peace. We believe that the use of force in resisting evil is futile, but we do not oppose the seeking of peace. We see no contradiction in that. We take comfort in that the future has been revealed to us while we know the inevitable outcome, we must act responsibly in the present, and that is why we are here," said Echidna.

Solon knew that they were arguing from desperation. He had his comeuppance in making them raise their ragged skirts of hypocrisy as they waded through their troubled waters. However, he could not afford to turn down this opportunity to gain their support and if they were right about Abner, he must act and act now. He conferred with Chancellor Doulos for a moment in private and then spoke.

"Abner will be arrested immediately and his fate will be decided tomorrow. As loyal subjects of Urbanus please accept my thanks for bringing this matter to light, there is, however, something that you can do for me in demonstrating your gratitude. It would be very beneficial to the cause of peace and unity if the Brotherhood would openly endorse the peace and unity conference."

"We will endorse the conference and send word to all our teachers and their assemblies to promote it and to encourage their participation in it. You have our whole-hearted blessing in this endeavor my Prince," Echidna promised.

After they had exchanged final greetings Chancellor Doulos turned to Solon and mused, "These men are quite confident of the future are they not? Such confidence is usually reserved for those who wager on horses when they already know the outcome of the race."

"True, Chancellor, but we dare not risk the fate Urbanus in wagering against them. What if Abner is guilty? They are desperate to resolve this matter. The question is why? We shall see what the morrow brings."

Solon was a consummate politician. If necessity and the "greater good" demanded that he falsely accuse an innocent man of treason, so be it. He would be party to it for reasons of political expediency. He consoled himself with the fact that the real guilt belonged to the noble Brotherhood. He had no other course of action. If Abner was innocent, surely the facts of the case would exonerate him and if not, then a Prince must find the good in every situation. When circumstances alone dictate your choices, the Toon are fond of saying, "The tail is wagging the dragon."

****

Like a child nestled in its bed for the night, Eirene lay fast asleep but the serenity of the moment was shattered by the stomping of marching boots on her cobblestones. A detachment of Solon's Eagle Legion marched straight to the door of the dormitory where Abner and his companions lay fast asleep. For reasons of security they slept in the same room with the exception of Sandor and Illdikko.

The butt end of a sword hammering on the oak door rudely awakened them. The Captain of the Guard barked, "Open the door in the name of Prince Solon, and deliver, Abner the Seer, into our custody!"

In an instant, the Rangers jumped from their beds fully dressed with swords in hand. They were prepared to defend Abner to the last man as they formed a human shield around him. Abner looked Wain in the eyes and slowly motioned that they put down their weapons. "This is not a time for swords, but for words," he said softly. Abner made his way through his protectors to the door and opened it. "You seek me?" he asked.

"Are you, Abner the Seer?" the Tribune demanded.

"I am, and why do you come for me at this untimely hour?"

"You have been charged with treason against Urbanus and her Prince. You are to come with me. You are under arrest!"

Abner was shackled hand and foot, to the protest of his companions, and led away by the soldiers.

"Be careful you cowards! He needs more than shackles. He's stronger than ten men, you're going to need another dozen of your kind to subdue him," Quill said mocking them.

As the soldiers marched into the night, the dimming flicker of their torches seemed a fitting picture of the Rangers' hopes. The light was slowly being absorbed by the darkness. To surrender Abner without a fight was too much to bear. They just stood there and watched as he was taken to the palace dungeon.

****

The dawn of the next day brought with it a cold rain. A dense fog silenced the normal clamor of the harbor's traffic. The rain beat down upon the streets with a steady cadence as the people of the city peered out their windows hoping for a respite in the weather and the opportunity to resume their business, but commerce would have to wait. Urbanus had more important business to attend today on this day.

Heralds had been announcing Abner's trial since dawn and the word spread through the city like the fog that enshrouded it. The weather only complicated matters, making travel difficult. Wain and his companions made their way by coach to Solon's palace where Abner was to stand trial. Crowds had already gathered around the palace and were standing in the pouring rain anticipating a verdict. Wain and his companions assessed the situation and Lon summed up their plight when he broke the silence and said, "How are we going to get into the palace?"

He was right. It was painfully obvious. They were not invited to the proceedings. They could not break in and petition the guards. What good would that do? They just stood there staring at the white marble of the palace wondering what was to become of Abner. Their mood was growing as somber as the weather.

From a window high above their coach, an unseen hand brushed aside a drapery and peered down at them. A signal was given to a trusted steward who understood what was desired of him. Making his way through the palace to the main gate, he approached the coach and asked, "Are you the companions of Abner the Seer?"

"We are," Jurius said answering him.

"Leave here at once. You are in the gravest peril. Abner, the Seer, has little chance of being declared innocent. His enemies are conspiring at this very moment to ensure his fate. Do not return to the Brotherhood's compound. Take these instructions and go to this address written on this parchment and wait there for further instructions. Trust no one and speak to no one of this matter. Make haste before you are recognized and arrested."

Without further hesitation they ordered the coachman to leave. Wain knew that this had to be prearranged, but by whom? Why weren't they arrested along with Abner and held for questioning? Someone was protecting them, but who and why?

****

Abner entered the large white marble room and was escorted to the platform by two legionnaires. Solon was seated in the center of the platform on a high-backed gilded chair. Chancellor Doulos sat beside him and behind a table strewn with parchment and writing instruments. A dozen stairs covered with red velvet and sectioned by four large marble columns accessed the platform. Abner stood directly in front of Prince Solon. Given the gravity of the circumstances, he appeared calm and collected. Solon would be the judge and jury of these proceedings. He and he alone, would decide Abner's fate.

Chancellor Doulos introduced Solon to the audience according to the protocol of Urbanus. Chancellor Doulos then read the list of charges against Abner and asked, "Who makes these charges against this man?"

"On behalf of the people of Urbanus, we do," said Echidna.

"Who are you and for whom do you speak?" asked Chancellor Doulos.

"I am Echidna of Urbanus, Chief Elder of the Brotherhood speaking on behalf of its membership and its board of Elders."

"What proof do you offer to substantiate these charges of treason?" asked Chancellor Doulos.

"We have two witnesses to prove beyond a shadow of doubt that Abner, the Seer, is in league with Sanballat and has conspired against the City of Urbanus and the province of Vestland," Echidna answered.

A wave of murmuring made its way through the crowd and reached a crescendo until Prince Solon tapped his scepter on the marble floor of the platform calling for order. As the murmuring ceased, all eyes turned to Abner. Was it possible? Could these charges be true? Could Abner's problems with the Brotherhood turn him into a tool of the Enemy? Had the old seer become perverse and twisted by bitterness and self-interest?

"Call your first witness," Chancellor Doulos ordered.

Echidna signaled to his brethren and from the crowd emerged two familiar figures, Raymaris and his mother, Karola. They approached the platform and waited to be summoned. Chancellor Doulos asked them to identify themselves, their occupations and where they lived. After charging both to tell the truth, he warned them that lying to the Prince carried the penalty of death. Raymaris and his mother answered all his questions and made it clear that they fully understood the responsibilities that they assumed. Chancellor Doulos then commanded them to share their testimony

"It was three days ago, my Prince, that I was walking the street with my mother when a coach carrying this man and his companions ran me down. I was nearly killed by their speeding and recklessness," Raymaris said. He then turned to his mother and she continued the tale.

"I ran to his side and he was unconscious lying in the street as this man looked on with his friends, cold hearted they are. They showed no concern at all for my poor boy. I was ready to call for the sheriff when one of his friends offered me ten denari for my troubles but that would not buy bandages, much less further care for my boy, if he needed it. We argued back and forth about the money when a commotion started in the alley across the street. A young wench was flirting with some soldiers and getting what she deserved when the old man's friends ran to her rescue and attacked the soldiers."

Chancellor Doulos was growing impatient. "What does this have to do with the charge of treason, woman?"

"I beg your indulgence, my Lord, but you shall see what it has to do with it. Please allow me to continue."

Reluctantly Chancellor Doulos ordered her to continue her testimony but he ordered her to come straight to the point.

"Yes Sir, I will, promise I will. While the fighting was going on the old man and his companion went into the alley to discuss the sum that they were going to give me. Anyway, they returned and gave me one hundred denari, the cheapskates. Then they drove off, but my son, bless his heart isn't the most honest of lads. I've told him many times not to take what wasn't his ...but, but, forgive me Sir, they had just cheated me and I felt that he deserved it, if you know what I mean! You know—sowing and reaping so to speak. So ... my son trying to right the score picked the pocket of the other gentleman. You know the one who looked like a business man. But, I am very glad that he did because it may save this city. Sir, you can plainly see that it is addressed to "My faithful servant, Jurius Hanner." It speaks of a mission and the invasion of Urbanus and Urbania. Look here, it has the royal seal of Mara, plain as day, it does."

"What did you do with the letter after you stole it?" asked Chancellor Doulos.

"I immediately showed it to several of the men who were there; after all I didn't want to be caught with it in my possession. Several of them were soldiers and one of them was a member of that Brotherhood and he said that we should bring to Elder Echidna. He would know what to do with it. We decided that we should take it to him."

Raymaris echoed her testimony with, "It is as exactly as my mother says, Lord."

Prince Solon demanded to see the letter and he gave it careful scrutiny. The audience once again was moved to murmuring by it all, which again brought an immediate response from Prince Solon to restore order to the room.

Chancellor Doulos asked, "Besides your son, who can testify that you are telling the truth?"

On command several men marched to the stage as though the whole affair was a well-rehearsed play. Argent, one of Urbanus's most respected businessmen accompanied by a hard drinking sailor named Lutteur and Apprenti, a student from the Brotherhood's Academy, who coincidentally was Lemler's understudy and heir apparent. Each claimed to be an eyewitness of the event in question and each verified every detail of the testimony. They sang their tune of false witness in perfect harmony.

Chancellor Doulos dismissed the two scoundrels and ordered Echidna to the platform.

"Elder Echidna, come forward and explain your involvement in this matter!" Chancellor Doulos demanded.

Echidna approached the platform as commanded and facing Prince Solon he said, "Lord, it was two days ago that the woman Karola brought me the letter in question. I have carefully examined all the facts and the witnesses in this case, and I believe that the letter is authentic. Moreover, I believe that the witnesses are telling the truth; therefore, I am forced to conclude that Abner, the Seer, and Jurius Hanner are guilty of conspiring with the Sanballat against you! Furthermore, it is my conviction that their companions are co-conspirators. Prince Solon, where are they? If they are innocent, why are they not here to testify on this man's behalf and their own? Though all the evidence presented is circumstantial, it is in my opinion that it is conclusive."

"Thank you for your opinion, Elder Echidna, but opinion is never out of season. Facts are stubborn things, and they are not the same. This court deals in facts," Chancellor Doulos responded.

Turning to Abner, Chancellor Doulos said, "You have heard the charges that your accusers have presented to this court against you; do you wish to speak in your defense?"

"I do, Sir," answered Abner.

"Please tell this court what you know of this letter?" Chancellor Doulos demanded.

"Lord Chancellor, Prince Solon, the letter in question was never in my possession. The truth of the matter is I did not know of its existence until this day."

"The letter in question is addressed to Jurius Hanner; however, it contains statements concerning you that if true, are highly incriminating. To be specific, it mentions your opposition to the Brotherhood and their positions. As such, it encourages Jurius Hanner to utilize your opposition to create dissent and division among the people of Urbanus and it encourages open rebellion against Prince Solon. What do you have to say in your defense?" Chancellor Doulos asked.

"I am not now, nor I have ever been an agent of Sanballat, and I fear that I am the victim of false accusation by desperate men who are motivated by jealousy and selfish ambition. They have set their own interests above those of Urbanus and Urbania. The woman is telling the truth, in so far as the accident is concerned, but she is lying about the letter being in the possession of Jurius Hanner. I came to Urbanus to address the Brotherhood, to give them a message from the Great King Sa'lem and to bring you, Lord Solon, proof of an imminent invasion of Urbanus. That is why I am here today, because I dared to tell them the truth and hold them accountable for their gross irresponsibility done in the name of prophecy. *They shovel fog and peddle it as revelation; they are prophetic panhandlers,*" Abner answered.

Unmoved by Abner's passionate indictment of the Brotherhood, Prince Solon intervened and demanded: "What proof do you offer us of this impending invasion?"

"My companions and I are eyewitnesses of the enemy's plans and preparations. Jurius Hanner is a well-respected businessman from Brantford of Lamburg. He is not an agent of Sanballat. He will testify to the truth of these things. Wain and his fellow Rangers have traversed the Eastern Provinces and the Province of Hupsominia in assisting me in my mission. They have rescued the grandson of Jurius Hanner, who was kidnapped by Sanballat's agents. They have seen firsthand that Hupsominia has been given over to the Enemy. They rescued a husband and a wife from a village in Hupsominia, and they will tell you of the atrocities committed there. Prince Solon, I believe that my reputation as a man of truth and honor precedes me; please allow my companions to testify on my behalf."

"Make it so," Prince Solon ordered. "Bring these witnesses before me." A silence filled the room as they waited for the witnesses to emerge from the audience, but no one approached the platform.

"Search the city and find them and bring them here as soon as possible," Prince Solon ordered.

Prince Solon and Chancellor Doulos conferred for a few moments and made their decision to adjourn the trial until the next day. Witnesses or no witnesses, tomorrow was all the time that Abner had. Chancellor Doulos stood to his feet and said, "We shall adjourn this trial until tomorrow at the same hour."

****

The Old Quarter of the city was a place that decent folk did not venture. It was situated behind the wharfs of the harbor and it had a well-deserved sordid reputation. Few men dared to walk its streets at night unarmed. The vilest sort of criminals lived and hid there, making a mockery of the sheriff's best efforts to apprehend them. Once they found cover in its baffling maze of shoddy tenements and run down hovels, they seemed to evaporate like the harbor mist meeting the rising sun. The Old Quarter was an affront to the eyes and an assault on the nose. The stench of refuse filled the air as waste trickled its way down the trenches dug along the side the buildings. In order to cope with the odor, the residents ignited pitch pots, which filled the air with a black acrid smoke that burned the eyes. It was here that Abner's companions found their hiding place.

The day's hard rain had provided some welcome cover for them as the city's traffic was greatly reduced. No one seemed to notice their arrival at the tenement house. They were just another group of odd-looking characters that filled the nooks and crannies of the Old Quarter.

Lon cautiously looked out the window from the cramped tenement apartment that now served as their refuge. "I don't like it the place is a fire trap. There is only one way out of this place. Worse, it faces the street. We are cornered with our backs to the wall," he said apprehensively.

"What troubles me is, 'why are we here?' If a friend arranged this, then we are safe for the moment, but if not, then we are in serious danger!" Wain said in agreement.

"We can do nothing but wait. Whoever arranged this will be communicating with us in one way or another," Jurius added.

"Grandfather, I'm hungry, is there anything to eat?" Daylin asked.

"As soon as it gets dark I will venture out, get food and take a look around. Daylin you must be strong, we are in serious trouble," Wain said.

"I'll go with you," Lon offered. "So will I!" said Hull. But, Wain thought it was too dangerous for more than one of them to be seen together. He was in charge and he would take the risk. Lon could handle matters in his absence.

They all agreed that they had better get some rest. They did not know when they would have another opportunity. Wain stood guard facing the street as the others one by one fell asleep. He leaned back against the wall and slid down its cracked plaster until he was sitting on the dirty floor. He felt an impulse to reach into his vest pocket. A memory of the message given to him by Raymaris danced through his thoughts. He had not had time to read it, but now was as good a time as any. Reaching his hand into vest pocket, his body went numb with a sudden pang of caution. A hollow sinking feeling gripped his stomach as he sat motionless starring across the room. The Northern folk are fond of saying that emotions are as trustworthy as the weather. Such was the case for Wain as his thoughts drifted back to the note handed to him by Raymaris. He thought it strange that he was so fixed on it when he first received it but the events of the past two days had erased it from his memory. He opened it and slowly folded back the parchment.

Kind Sir,

I cannot thank you and your companions enough for coming to my aid. I do not know what would have become of me had you not intervened. I am eternally grateful to you. I would like to speak with you at your convenience. I believe that I can be of help to you and your friends in the days ahead. You may call on me at number 6, Ox Road. My home is above the Inn de Fosse.

Your Grateful Servant,

Lady Vixeena

The rain had finally stopped as the sun set over the Old Quarter. The dreariness of the rain now surrendered to the cover of darkness. The sounds of people about their business could be heard in the street below. Wain emptied his pack and prepared his weapons. The others were now waking from their nap. It seemed like a good time to set out and get food and do some reconnaissance. Putting his tunic over his head, he carefully opened the door and walked out into the street. Down the alley and over a fence, he made his way to the main street of the Old Quarter. Avoiding eye contact and keeping close to the buildings, he tried to look as unassuming as possible.

Finding food at this hour was going to be a challenge, but, the smell of bread baking seemed like a good omen. His nose located the stone building where the wonderful aroma originated and, to his surprise, the proprietors sold a modest sampling of other goods as well. He was able to purchase bread, cheese and wine from the shop. It would have to do, and it would have to last. One out of two he thought, the food is taken care of. Now for some equally fresh information, he thought.

Ox road was a dead end street in the Old Quarter. It was the home of countless inns and pubs. Only the strongest survived in this place. No mercy was shown to the weak and none was expected. It was not uncommon to find an occasional body in the alleyways, losers in the continual struggle for dominance. It was like playing king of the mountain on a dung heap, but in the Old Quarter you played or you died.

Wain slipped through the crowds and kept a sharp eye for any place that might offer him cover and the possibility of gathering information. And then there it was, appearing almost out of nowhere—the Inn de Fosse. He pondered the situation, thinking the better of it, but he needed information on Abner. He needed information, any information, from the grapevine of the Old Quarter and anything else that might be of use. Whether it was desperation or lack of discretion that propelled him through the doors of the Inn de Fosse, he could not tell. He only knew that he was now committed to a course of action that he hoped he would not regret. He surveyed the inn, but he could not see an entrance to any apartment or living quarters. He decided to approach the proprietor of the inn and make an inquiry.

"Inn keeper does the Lady Vixeena reside in this building?"

"The lady?" he asked with a hint of sarcasm. "Yes, the *Lady* Vixeena is upstairs. Go through that door over there and up the stairway. She's in; I saw her go up there just a while ago," the innkeeper's eyes analyzed everything about Wain. "Lady, Lady indeed," he scoffed!

"You're not from Urbanus are you; been here long?" he probed.

"Long enough," Wain said with a serious tone.

"Where did you say you were from?" the innkeeper inquired?

"I didn't; thank you for your help," Wain said curtly, cutting off further interrogation.

The walk up the stairs reminded him of a man going to the gallows. Ironic that there were thirteen stairs on the staircase; the comparison unnerved him. Upon reaching the top of the landing, he almost decided not to go on with the visit, but what choice did he have? He had nowhere to turn.

There was no solid door to her dwelling, just some worn drapes covering the entrance to her room. He cautiously peered into the room as though reconnoitering an ambush. She stood at the window as if anticipating his presence. Two jade green eyes peered into his, framed by long auburn hair undulating over her shoulders and down her white silk dress. Her form was delicate and lithe. She moved with an effortless compelling grace. The long and intense stare that penetrated Wain's personal space was followed by a broad and inviting smile. She sighed gently, "Oh, I'm so glad that you have come," she said winsomely. "They're looking for you and your friends you know. The old man is on trial and they want you and the others to testify. There is talk on the streets of the Old Quarter that the whole affair is an evil plot hatched by the Sanballat's agents and traitors from within Urbanus. I don't know, I mean, all this drama is far too much for me. I cannot understand these things. They are so complicated. All I know is that if you had not been there to rescue me ... there's no telling what might have happened. She reached out and softly caressed his hand. You and your friends had better stay out of sight. You took a great risk in coming here tonight."

"I know," he said, "but I had no other choice. In your letter, you said that you could help us." She continued her gentle caress of his hand while closing the space between them. She motioned towards her couch as she bid to him to sit down. "Enough talk, sit down. Some wine perhaps?" Reaching for a goblet perched on a table beside the couch, she offered it to him, "Drink this and relax; there is plenty of time to talk."

As Wain sat down on the couch and sipped the wine from the silver goblet a strange sensation overcame him. The more he sipped the more intense the sensation became. It was one completely foreign to him. He had never known anything like it. His face felt flushed with fever and he could barely breathe. As Vixeena gently rubbed his arm, he could sense something take control of his mind and body. He did not know its source but he knew that resistance was nigh impossible. It seemed as though he was falling into a deep well that had no bottom. His customary self-control and restraint were being slowly eroded. Before he knew it, he was in her arms and kissing her. Every fiber of his being convulsed in a losing struggle for the control of his will.

As Wain lay upon her bed starring at the ceiling, wondering how this could have happened to him, the bedroom drapes opened and in came two huge, well-armed goons. They were on Wain in an instant and strategically placed their swords on his body. One of them growled, "Get dressed Ranger, you're coming with us. There's someone who wants to talk with you. One dumb move and we'll cut your throat and dress you out like the pig that you are."

As he dressed himself, his heart sank into a quicksand of guilt and despair. He had never experienced such humiliation. He was a Ranger; he had taken vows of chastity, honor, and duty. Everything that he believed in and held dear had now been violated. He loathed himself. He had never felt so unclean. The decades of faithful service to King Sa'lem evaporated like rain on molten lava. He dressed himself, but he still felt naked. The sewers of the Old Quarter seemed pristine by comparison. Invisible chords of his own making now bound him, making the leather thongs that cut deep into his wrists seem like ribbons.

As he left the room, he glanced back at Vixeena, but her focus was on a purse of coins given to her by the one of the goons. "Count it again; it's all there wench. Count it once more if you like, but Le Parrain would never cheat you. You're one of his best ponies. He knew that you'd come through for him. Ha, ha, ha, and come through you did. " Despite his depressed and disorientated state, Wain was beginning to realize what had happened to him. It had been a cleverly designed trap.

****

Souteneur was a parasite of the lowest sort. He was fond of calling himself the King of the Old Quarter, but those who worked for him, simply referred to him as Le Parrain. There was no deal that he considered beneath him. If the money was right, Souteneur was involved. As he was fond of saying, "Money never smells, no matter the sewer it is fished from." In his realm this fat self-assured potentate of the Old Quarter possessed power and authority equal to Prince Solon's. If you wanted something, anything, Souteneur could get it for you, but you would pay, and pay dearly. Those who made deals with him never got the best of him and worse, they were never free of him. Prostitution, blackmail, extortion, gambling and theft were his stock and trade. He drew the line at assassination of public figures because it drew unwanted attention and that was bad for business. Besides, corrupt Patrikos and Trapezites were the web that this spider used to trap his prey. An occasional murder now and then was hardly problematic because it kept all his customers in line, fearing the long arm of his retribution. But he preferred the power of persuasion to the persuasion of power because as he said, "Live men pay, dead men don't."

Souteneur was deviously clever and he was always one step ahead of the competition. Wain was about to be unceremoniously introduced to Le Parrain, King of the Old Quarter.

****

"Get up you pig. Did you enjoy her? She has pleased so many before you. Charm you did she? Fool! What were you thinking? I expected more from a Ranger, but then, a man is a man." Souteneur said with contempt.

A bucket of cold water hit Wain squarely in the face before he could think of forming a response. This produced a good laugh for Souteneur and his thugs. Wain reeled under the shock. But, he quickly gathered himself and mustering what little dignity he had left and then asked a profoundly stupid question, "Who are you?"

"Who am I? Who am I, you ask? I am Souteneur, the King of the Old Quarter. I own these streets. Nothing happens here without my say so. I am the man who holds your life in his hands, Ranger! I decide if you live or die or better still, if Sanballat gets your worthless carcass." Turning to Carty, his number one lieutenant, he growled, "Get out of here, all of you! Now! I want to be alone. All of you get out!"

"Well, it's good thing I found you first, Ranger. They paid me well to trap you, and trap you, I did, yes?" Think you got problems, do you? Yes, you do, and plenty of them, but if Prince Solon's guard had caught you, trust me, you wouldn't have made it to the palace alive. Oh they would have said that you tried to escape or something like that, but they'd kill you dead, Ranger. You know too much. Abner and Jurius are done for. There is nothing you can do to help Abner. Souteneur knows, trust me. I am about to do you a favor. What favor you ask? I am going to help you and your friends get out of Urbanus alive."

"Why would you do that after tonight?" Wain asked.

"Oh, never confuse making a little money on the side with my ultimate personal interests. I had to wet my beak a little in the deal!" he said smugly.

"But, I have no use for Sanballat and his plans. If he conquers Urbanus, there goes Souteneur's business. No, no, I can't have that. You'll recover. I've done far worse to better men than you, and I never helped them out of their pit. You see, it's like this, wars are bad for business. I'm not an arms dealer you know. I sell happiness to the highest bidder and I need peace and tranquility in order to do that. Do you think that if Urbanus falls to the Sanballat and his hordes that there will be room for me and my ilk? No, not a chance! There's no free enterprise when he's in town. If Urbanus falls, I am done for," Souteneur said, loving the sound of his own voice, restated his twisted rational for helping Wain and the others one more time.

"They came to me and asked for my help. I had to help them a little for appearances sake. But, I've got no use for them. Don't get me wrong, I didn't mind turning a few denari in hook'en you up with Vixeena but that's where I draw the line. I don't want to see you dead, Ranger, and I certainly don't want any invasion of Urbanus. Listen to Souteneur. They had this planned before you entered the city. The accident with the coach and your brave rescue of Vixeena was all a setup. All of them are work'en together. That letter, the one that the slug and his fat cow of a mother supposedly pick-pocketed from the old man ... all a scam, pure lies. They're accusing the old man of treason and they're using the letter as proof. Ah, it does bear Sanballat's seal; but, it came to Urbanus by way of Ursus, that Salisian scum.

The old boy has some very powerful enemies, eh? As for Abner, he never could keep his mouth shut. A man with a conscience is more dangerous than a rabid dog. He has condemned himself with his own words. They cut him off from you and the others and now …, any way, they saw to it that you couldn't testify. Even if you could, they would never believe you. Your little tryst is going to get you dead. Vixeena is going to testify against you tomorrow. She's been bought and paid for. I can't risk trusting her in this matter. She's playing her role for them and the less she knows the better. It has to play out like this. You will be convicted of rape and condemned to death. Without my help you're a dead man, Ranger. Strange is it not, but, I am the only man you can trust?" Patting his fat belly with one hand while stroking his beard with the other, he chided Wain and asked, 'Tell Souteneur, just how desperate are you?'"

"Please, let me go back to my friends. I must get back to them. They need food and drink and so long as they're left where they are, they're in danger!" Wain pleaded.

"Tell Souteneur something that he doesn't know. No worry, no worry, Souteneur has everything in control. They are on their way here as we speak. I'm not the King of the Old Quarter for noth'en. You'd be under arrest or be dead by dawn, if I left you in that rat hole. Why do think they brought you there? Maybe you had no choice, but it was dumb of you to go there. *And I know something else; it's the boy they really want. Some of them aren't convinced that he's the One, but I am. I know who he is and I won't wager against him. I've had contact with King Sa'lem's agents too and, as I live, the boy will live. King Sa'lem has guaranteed it. The Enemy fears that boy. He is special to be sure. Souteneur will take good care of him, heh?*"

Just as Souteneur promised, Wain's companions came through the doors of his lair, hungry and weary from the day's tensions. Wain was glad to see them, but his shame was all too obvious to discerning eyes. Lon knew that something was very wrong with Wain.

"How did you get here?" Wain, Lon asked.

"It's complicated, really complicated, Lon, I'll explain it all later."

"We were contacted by one of Souteneur's men. He told us that we weren't safe where we were and he presented us with your sword as proof that they held you here. We debated among ourselves for a while, but in the end, we decided to trust him. We felt we had no choice. Well, here we are what next?" Quill asked.

"What's next?" Wain put his arm around Daylin and said, "I think it's time that we eat and drink. Souteneur has much to share with us about our situation."

****

The courtroom was filled to overflowing. The elite of Urbanus took their seats of honor, along with the Princes of the Nine Cities and their entourage. The gathering was a cross section of the assorted layers of the Urbania's social classes. Rank has it privilege, and the lower their rank the farther they were seated from Prince Solon. The lowest in rank stood in the back of the courtroom straining for a glimpse of the impending trial. Prince Solon called the proceedings to order and Chancellor Doulos summoned Abner to stand before him.

"A search of the city has not produced your companions. You have no witnesses to testify on your behalf and you offer this court no concrete proof of your innocence. Honorable citizens of Urbanus have accused you of the crime of high treason against Urbanus and the welfare of Urbania. You have conspired with Sanballat and his allies to invade Urbanus and Urbania. This court has no other choice but to declare you guilty of these charges. Do you have anything to say before your sentence is rendered?"

With a dignity and calm reserved for a man being honored by his King, Abner answered, "Yes Sir, I do!"

> Prince Solon, Lords of the Nine Cites, honorable Chancellor, people of Urbanus and Urbania, I will not repeat my testimony from yesterday, nor plead for your mercy. Instead, I chose to share with you a revelation hidden from ages past and now made known to you by the kindness of the Great King Sa'lem. It is true that there is a conspiracy to conquer this fair city and Urbania. As I speak the forces of the Enemy are preparing to invade Urbania.

Hupsoma has already fallen into the enemy's hands. Ursus, you are the servant of Sanballat. You are a traitor and your province has been given over to the encroaching darkness that threatens the whole of Urbania. I have seen with my own eyes the Enemy's Sharokhan in the Forest of the Toon, and Black Ships on the Ramsgate. I have experienced the sinister schemes of the Artrax and the Ganza, who have spied upon and infiltrated all of Urbania. I have witnessed the atrocities committed by the Salisians and their demonic allies in the villages of Hupsominia. And as I speak, to the South, the largest army and naval force ever assembled is being readied in preparation for an invasion of Vestland.

I am not your enemy. It would be a simple and equally tempting solution to accuse Lord Ursus, Elder Echidna, his fellow elders, and their hired false witnesses of being the true enemy here, but I will not succumb to it. Yes, their hands are stained with guilt and blood, but they are mere pawns. The real enemy lies within. Not within the walls of the city, but within your hearts. The harmony that once ruled Urbania and gave her peace has been corrupted. The hearts of the people of Urbania are filled with darkness, and it is the darkness within them that conspires with the Enemy. Open your eyes. Who among you can say that what is done here today is just? You have eyes, but you do not see what is set plainly before them. You have ears, but you cannot hear the words of truth. You have hearts of stone incapable of love or mercy,—that is the true enemy.

That is the lock, but I now share with you the key. A key fashioned like no other. A key that has the power to open the eyes of the blind, give hearing to the deaf and soften the hardest heart. The ancient scrolls predicted such a key and King Sa'lem has purposed to make it known to you. The key is the One foretold and promised in the ancient scrolls and he is among you this very moment. On his shoulders rests the robes of wisdom and peace. In due season he will be revealed to you with the power to restore your hearts and harmony to Urbania.

My companions and I were sent to Urbania by The Great King Sa'lem to deliver him from the evil plans of the

Enemy. He is your hope of victory. He will lead you in harmony and peace, triumphing over the forces of darkness. He will point the way. Hear him, listen to him. I adjure you; do not harden your hearts. Open them and listen to the message that he will bring!

The courtroom erupted into a furor of rage and protest. Members of the Brotherhood hissed and jeered. The common folk screamed curses as the Princes and dignitaries looked on with mocking scorn. Many of those standing charged the platform intent on killing Abner with their bare hands. The palace guards responded to the situation by placing a human shield around Abner and sealing off the platform. Prince Solon stood to his feet and demanded that order be restored or there would be arrests forthcoming. The crowd slowly dissolved under Prince Solon's threats and order was restored to the courtroom.

"I will not tolerate another outburst in these chambers. Anyone who challenges the authority of this court will be immediately jailed and flogged. Do I make myself clear?" Prince Solon thundered.

A hush of acknowledgment swept over the enraged crowd. Solon may have restrained their actions, but their intentions were crystal clear; it was Abner's head that they wanted. Clinched fists and snarling lips temporarily yielded to the persuasion of power. Prince Solon then commanded Abner to proceed with his final words.

> Thank you Prince Solon. Seldom does a prophet have the privilege of seeing his words fulfilled as he speaks them. People of Urbania, hear me, the "Promised One" is coming. Receive him. Listen to him. Follow him. He prepares the way. He has the blessing and endorsement of the Great King Sa'lem. There is hope for Urbanus and Urbania. King Sa'lem has not forgotten you in your hour of need. Give heed to my words.

Cries of "liar, fraud and madman," filled the courtroom as the crowd once again convulsed in rage. They shook their fists and spit at Abner. Prince Solon made a pragmatic decision to momentarily abdicate his powers of judge and jury to the would-be mob. For several minutes he allowed them to indulge their thirst for blood, responding only when he sensed that it was either act now or lose complete control of the situation. "Silence, silence in the court!" he demanded.

"Abner, in view of the fact that you have failed to produce witnesses before this court who could exonerate you of the charge of high treason against Urbanus and her Prince. In view of the fact that you have failed to offer any form of acceptable proof of your innocence, it is the verdict of this court that you be found guilty as charged. Furthermore, the sentence of this court is death by stoning. Tomorrow at three hours past dawn, you shall be taken to the *Place de la Mort* and there stoned by the citizens of Urbanus until you are dead. Your body shall then be delivered to the pit of Komodus the dragon and your name shall forever be erased from the records of the city in any and all forms, be they written or spoken. So be it. Take the prisoner away!"

****

While Abner stood trial before Prince Solon, Wain stood before his fellow Rangers seeking forgiveness and healing from his self-inflicted wound. To a man, they knew that something was amiss, but not even the intuitive Lon could anticipate what Wain was about to confess.

A broken and disheveled Wain stood before the private gathering. The battle for the control of his thoughts proved more intense than any skirmish with a physical enemy. He struggled to find an appropriate way to broach the subject that tormented him. It was clear that the night had not granted him respite from his anxiety. The normally confident, take charge leader was completely disoriented. With a voice weakened by exhaustion, he began to speak.

"I want to explain to you how I came to fall into Souteneur's hands," Wain said, looking at the floor. "After I left you, I set out to purchase food and to gain some information concerning Abner. I proceeded down the main road of the Old Quarter and looked for a likely meeting place but nothing appeared safe. I then went to an inn named the Inn de Fosse. I did not go there by chance, but by invitation. The night that we gathered at the "Open Arms," the boy who had that convenient accident with our coach gave me a letter. The letter was from the girl whom, you will recall, was the object of the soldier's desire. She thanked me for helping her and she offered to help us. I debated what I should do, but I finally decided that there was no other option open to me."

Not one of the Rangers took their eyes off Wain and not one spoke a word. Though their minds denied it, in their hearts they already knew what he was about to say.

"I went to her apartment and we talked. She offered me wine and … I, I, I don't know what happened. Something came over me. I don't think that I was drugged or poisoned, but it had a similar affect upon me. As we sat and talked, I fell deeper into this trance-like state. I could barely breathe and then …, we kissed. I lost all self-control. For the first time in my life, I was in the arms of a woman. I will spare you what happened next," he said, with his head in his hands. "I have violated my vows to King Sa'lem, to you and to myself. I have failed you all. I am no longer worthy to be your Captain or a Ranger."

Heartbreak spread over their faces like the ripples made by a stone cast into a pond. Men, who had never wept before, broke down and fell into one another's arms, lamenting their fallen captain. His death would have produced no less mourning than his confession.

Lon spoke for them all when he asked, "How could you? You were always the strong one. We looked to you for strength. You carried us on your shoulders when we were weak and weary. Your wisdom sustained us when we faced challenges that pushed us to our limits. I would have died a dozen times before now, had you not been there for me. I would have believed that the sky could have fallen, but not you. Wain, how could you?"

Hull could not speak. All he could do was weep at volume that made everyone in Souteneur's compound take notice. This giant of man, who was given to extremes, stayed true to form. Even Souteneur was moved by this display of passion. For a brief moment, his calloused heart opened, admiring their intense concern for one another. There was nothing like it among his kind.

Wain deeply respected the Brothers Fairn and the men of Invar, but now he had a greater fear of their rejection. Looking directly into their eyes, he begged, "Please forgive me for breaking my vows and failing you."

Thrace, who seldom spoke a single word in a day, waxed more eloquent than Abner on this occasion. Walking straight to Wain, he placed his massive arms around him and said with tender mercy, "I forgive you and I release you from any debt that you feel that you owe me. You are my friend and I will always love you, my captain. May you find mercy in the eyes of the Great King Sa'lem." Thrace was not the timid mute that they had taken him for. Clearly he was a man who had saved his words for a season when words were scarce.

One by one they approached their wounded captain and communicated the same message to him. They embraced him and consoled him. Their forgiveness and acceptance bathed him like a mountain stream and refreshed his broken spirit. Wain would never be the same after this. His failure had paralyzed him like a surprised drunk who wakes up the next morning with a new tattoo. Wain would forever bear the marks of his indiscretion but the forgiveness extended to him by his friends gained him insight that would serve him well in the days ahead.

****

The young woman stood before the congregation and wept. Lemler gently placed his hand upon her shoulder and encouraged her to confess her wrongs to the audience. He said that it would clear her conscience and assure her entrance into the Brotherhood. "I have lived a loose life," she said. "I have known many men, but I now wish to confess my wrongs and live a good life as a member of the Brotherhood. That is, if you will have me. I cannot live with what I have done. I was rescued from a band of Salisian soldiers by a man, his name is Wain. He is the Captain of the Rangers. I sent a letter of thanks to him and invited him to my home to personally thank him and there he raped me. At the time I did not know that he was a fugitive sought by the authorities. I am so sorry. He had helped me and … She sobbed uncontrollably.

No herald in all the land could have spread the news of Wain's failure more effectively than Vixeena. She deftly played her audience like a fiddle while singing their requests. They swooned to her confession, granting her absolution, while sealing Wain's fate. In the eyes of all he was a traitor to Urbanus and to King Sa'lem. Lemler called for a resolution declaring Wain an apostate and forbidding any contact or communication with him by the Brotherhood. Echidna made the resolution. It received a second by Menteur and it was adopted unanimously. They all agreed that it was done in order maintain the Brotherhood's high standards of ethical integrity. It was a theatrical masterpiece of hypocrisy and deception. It had an immediate visible affect on all present. The sheriff was contacted and a warrant for Wain's arrest was issued, just as Souteneur had predicted.

****

The dungeon doors creaked and groaned as they opened. The old man emerged from his confinement with a look of fresh determination. "Are you ready for today's sport?" he asked his bewildered captors. If they were expecting fear or pleading from him they were mistaken. Abner was ready to play his part. He had known all along that this was his last mission. Abner was a Seer, and on occasion, seers have insight into their own lives.

The streets of Urbanus were lined with a throng that resembled a victory parade for a conquering general. The macabre spectacle had a carnival atmosphere. Merchants and vendors filled the streets opportunistically taking advantage of the crowds. People jostled for position along the way, they filled the open windows and doorways of buildings, and they even climbed trees in order to get a glimpse of Abner. The palace guard led him down the streets by a long chain distancing themselves from any flying objects that might precede the stoning. Taunts and curses pelted his ears, as garbage and sewage cascaded down upon him from the rooftops and windows that lined the streets of the procession.

Through it all Abner kept his dignity. His composure only fanned the flames of the crowd's hatred. They did all they could to solicit a response in kind from him, but he would not indulge them. Abner was man at peace with himself. Death could not intimidate him.

The Place de la Mort was the final solution for those individuals deemed a threat to the safety and well being of Urbanus. However, the intellectuals had an ongoing debate concerning the barbarity of public executions and the unwholesome effects produced by them. Urbanus was a place of culture and refinement. Such a practice seemed incompatible with her status as the most enlightened city in Urbania. Not even the critics raised a challenge to Abner's execution. It seemed that even the most zealous opponents of public executions could find at least one exception to their best arguments against it.

Abner was led into a small arena whose center was below street level. Seated high above the circular opening were grandstands made of marble where Solon, his quests and the officials of the city sat with an unobstructed view. In front of the grandstands were massive steps surrounding the circular depression, allowing several thousand stone throwing participants a clear shot at the helpless victim. In the name of fairness, only commoners participated in the stoning, and they were selected by lottery. Each participant was given a single white stone the size of an apple.

The *Place de la Mort* had one other distinguishing feature. It was the home of Komodus the dragon. In the center of the arena was a large iron grate that covered a pit. The pit was the entrance to a series of caves that honeycombed the foundation of the arena. The founders of Urbanus had never succeeded in eliminating old Komodus. They decided to keep him trapped in the caves beneath the city. But Komodus was an unusually resourceful dragon, and he managed to survive despite being caged. One enterprising individual decided that if you can't free a dragon, feed a dragon; and thus was born a very practical solution to one of Urbanus's most serious problems. Urbanus had an overpopulation of criminals. It was a simple solution to a complex problem. And feed him they did. Komodus grew fat and content on a regular diet of criminals.

The day was unusually warm for that time of year as the cloudless sky exposed the crowd to the sun. A fair wind blew in off the sea and up the mouth of Ramsgate. It was all in stark contrast to what was about to unfold. *Abner stood chained to the iron grate in the center of the arena* patiently awaiting Prince Solon's order. It was customary to grant the dying man a few final words. Reluctantly, Solon conceded and allowed Abner to speak. He feared a riot would ensue, but he relented, pointed to Abner and commanded him to speak his final words.

Abner's eyes panned the crowd, suspending the mob's anger and hatred for a brief respite. He then fixed his gaze on the Brotherhood and their compliant prince and said: "I will die today, but I will not die alone. While many a guilty man has met his well-deserved fate in this place, to your shame, you have shed the blood of untold numbers of innocent souls. Their blood cries out from the earth and their bones demand recompense. The day will come when the bones of the innocent dead will march through the streets of Urbanus, mount its walls, and do what you could never do—Stand in defense of the truth and administer swift and impartial justice!"

No sooner had the words left his lips than thousands of stones cascaded down on the old Seer. It was over before it had begun, leaving a grisly heap of scattered blood-stained stones around his battered corpse. Solon then ordered the guards to release his body into the pit. Immediately two guards gingerly made their way over the stones to Abner's body, unchained it and released the iron grate. The scent of blood had not gone unnoticed by Komodus. As the guards released Abner's lifeless body into the gaping throat of the pit, the open jaws of the dragon were ready to greet him.

With two lightening swift bites Abner's lifeless remains were reduced to appetizers for the beast. The crowd retracted in terror, fearing that Komodus, in a fit of uncontrolled rage and hunger just a few meters below the grid, would spring loose through the now suspended, unprotected opening. But Komodus was content to remain caged so long as his hunger was satisfied. The dragon quickly snatched his prey and escaped into the caves below. Abner was gone!

Episode III

The Promise of Redemption

STRANGE BEDFELLOWS

The grapevine of the Old Quarter had no competition when it came to speed and accuracy. The news of Abner's show trial and execution predictably made its way through the streets and haunts of the Old Quarter like a flash-flood. While Abner's death had been a foregone conclusion for Souteneur, he knew that it would be another setback for the Rangers. They, too, understood that the outcome was inevitable, but when you love someone, foreknowledge is no defense against the pain of loss.

A throbbing realization kept pounding in Wain's head—Abner was gone. Abner, dear old Abner, was dead. What were they going to do? Like a ship without a rudder, they were thrown to and fro by every wind of anxiety that swirled around them. They were adrift in a foreign city, and their last hope of rescue rested on the word of the most notorious criminal in Urbanus.

"Mmmm, I'm very sorry my friends, what can I say? He is gone. You have lost a dear friend. When you have such powerful enemies it is very difficult to defend yourself, is it not?"

Comforting those in mourning wasn't Souteneur's specialty, but he was doing his best to show the Rangers some compassion and understanding. He had as much at stake as they did, even if they didn't recognize it. It was clear that they needed to trust one another and the sooner the better. While Souteneur lacked any semblance of social grace, he had no equal when it came to political gamesmanship. He was in his element and he relished the chance to play the game of power politics when so much was at stake. At last Souteneur was competing toe to toe with the powerbrokers of Urbanus and he was as dizzy as a schoolgirl with anticipation.

"Listen to me my friends," said Souteneur; "there is not much time. They will not cease searching the city until they find you. This matter has gone beyond the powers of the Sheriff, who, by the way, is on my payroll. Solon has ordered his legions to search the Old Quarter. That, my friends, is not good for Souteneur's business. They will burn it down, if they have to. They will leave no secret place unsearched; even the sewer rats are not safe. It is better that you leave today. I must arrange a little ruse for them, so that they will know for sure that you are out of the city. Mind you, under normal circumstances you are more than welcome here, but I cannot afford the Eagle Legions of Urbanus marching through the Old Quarter. It is very bad for business."

"He's right. We have to leave Urbanus. They really don't want us. They want Daylin. For his sake we must leave as soon as possible Parrain," Wain said, as a sign of respect. "Make the arrangements and we will leave as soon as it's dark."

****

"Are things proceeding according to plan? Well, it's about time that my strategic genius has borne some tangible fruit," Sanballat chuckled with sinister delight.

"All Praise to the Great One, The Most Excellent, El' Shay'tan! The reports from Urbanus are most encouraging! Abner is dead at last and Wain has fallen into my little trap and disgraced himself. The boy is in hiding somewhere in the city, like a ripe plum ready for the picking. Our agents and spies are doing a splendid job."

Pausing for a moment, Sanballat looked down with a hawk-like gaze while stroking his beard. "I wonder how I shall reward them. Hmmm, how delicious! I have just a few loose ends to attend to, and then the invasion will be launched. How I love the sound of that word—invasion, it has finally come. I have waited so long for this day. Pity the creature that fails me or gets in my way," Sanballat said to himself.

"Master, there is news from Urbanus. Based on the reports, I believe that the boy is being protected by Souteneur in the Old Quarter of the city," an Artrax said reverently.

"Fool! Where else would he be? Of course Souteneur has him! Who else is shrewd enough to hide him when so many eyes are looking for him? Moron! Imbecile! You vile scum! You dare insult my genius by stating the obvious? I don't need analysis. I need action. Every minute he remains hidden in Urbanus is time that they have to plan an escape. I cannot endure such incompetence. Why do I let scum like you breath?"

The room was filled with Artrax and select agents of the Ganza. These were Sanballat's most trusted counselors; but past performance was no guarantee of a long life in Mara. Turning to the Artrax, Sanballat pointed his long bony finger in his face and in a rage screamed, "Die you must, you maggot!"

Drawing his sword he took off the head of the Artrax and with one lightning stroke. The creature's headless corpse fell to the floor at Sanballat's feet draped in its black wings. Paralyzed with fear the room went silent. Sanballat's mood instantly changed and he nonchalantly continued his instructions as if nothing had happened.

"Next time, show a little initiative!" he said, stepping over the Artrax while walking toward a large map. He pointed to Urbanus and said, "Urbanus is no longer safe for them. They must leave the city. We nearly had them, but that cunning Souteneur, curse him!"

Slamming his fists on the map table he hissed like a coiled snake. "I will deal with him myself. Keep him alive for my personal pleasure. Alert my Salisian Thema on the south bank of the Ramsgate to stay vigilant! That is their only route of escape. They cannot go north or east. There are too many eyes and ears that would detect them. No, they have to cross the Ramsgate and proceed south to the Moors of Fange.

I will give the city of Urbanus to the creature that brings me the boy. Moreover, I will give Teleios to the creature that brings me Wain's head on a pole. There will be rewards for success," and pointing to the lifeless remains on the floor, he threatened, "And I will deal severely with anyone or anything that fails me."

****

As the Rangers waited for nightfall, they began to form a plan for leaving the city. What they needed to do was clear but it was not clear how they were going to do it.

"I am sorry, but I don't see it. How are we going to get out of the city without being detected?" Swain asked.

"They are sure to watch every street, and every harbor wharf will be guarded. The main gates of the city are sure to be closed and everyone going in or out of the city will be interrogated and searched. We can't wait till morning, as Le Parrain said, tomorrow they will surely call out the Eagle Legions and search the Old Quarter," Wain responded.

"You've come to respect that old weasel haven't you?" Lon observed.

"Yes, I have, indeed, now if I can only learn to trust him!" Wain said.

"We need a plan. We need to do something that they won't expect, something bold and creative," Quill added.

"Thank you, Quill, for that wonderful insight; I trust you didn't lose too much sleep coming up with that one," Hull quipped.

"Enough," said Wain.

Souteneur entered the room and immediately, sensing their frustration, while ignoring the obvious, he asked, "Ready to leave Urbanus?"

"How will we do that?" Swain asked.

"How you ask? How indeed! How, is why I am Souteneur and you are not! No offense my friend, but that is why you are who you are," he said to Swain condescendingly. "Ah, yes, yes, I am so good. Sometimes I even amaze myself. And now let us have a little wine. Let us drink to your safe and prosperous journey."

"First explain how!" Lon demanded.

"Alright, I think you will appreciate the utter beauty of this; then we will drink, yes?"

As you know, there is no way out the city. In truth, there is no way out of this hideout. Therefore, we must make you blend into the surroundings so that Prince Solon himself would not stop and question you." He then clapped his hands and rubbed them together enthusiastically while two of his men entered the room carrying some familiar uniforms. "Nice tailoring, eh?" Souteneur joked.

"Those are the uniforms of the Eagle Legion. How did you get them?" Wain asked.

"I have friends in high places, and so do you it appears. Quick, time is short, put these on. The boy and his grandfather and the couple will dress in disguise as members of the delegation from Arnos. No one will recognize them from such a backwater as Arnos. They don't even recognize each other in that backwater," he laughed. "No worry, my friend. They have brought two more divisions of the Eagle Legion into the city from the north. They are expecting trouble of some kind. All who see you will consider you just a new face. The real problem was getting that one a uniform as he pointed to Hull. Making it fit was a challenge even for my tailor. Ah, but here is the best part. We have a coach. Not just any coach but one that no one would dare to stop. Oh, this is so beautiful."

Souteneur laughed until he cried. He had outdone himself this time. This scam would make up for all he insults and backstabbing he had endured at the hands of the high and mighty elites of Urbanus.

"Everyone get dressed and give me what you are wearing now. Ah, but wait! First we drink." One of his men brought a platter filled with goblets of fine Esterian wine. Souteneur's confidence was infectious, so they did as he asked and each of them, including Daylin, took a glass and raised it high. "To King Sa'lem, Kingdom, Glory, Dominion." To the success of his servants and long live Urbania," Souteneur said in raising a toast.

"So be it" was echoed by all in the room.

****

His fellow Rangers laughed until their sides hurt. Hull was a sight to behold. Never had they seen anything like it. "Is he a member of the Eagle Legion, or is *he* the Eagle Legion?" Swain scoffed. "He's the northern division," Quill howled. Hull didn't find any humor in the situation. He was dressed like a stuffed turkey. "They sure have a flair for modesty," Hull said, breaking the room into uproarious laughter.

"What have you done with our clothes?" Wain asked Souteneur.

"They are being put to some very good use as we speak," He said with smug satisfaction. You will get them back in due time, but for now be content with these. We must go now your coach is waiting. Follow my men! They will take you to it. Obey their instructions to the letter. I hope to see you again in better times my friends."

"Thank you Parrain. You have rendered a great service to King Sa'lem; may he reward you in kind," Wain said warmly.

This pleased Souteneur more than his current scam. To have the respect and gratitude of the Rangers was like receiving an honor from King Sa'lem himself. What an irony, Wain thought. The vilest criminal in Urbanus was displaying more integrity than all its so-called "good men." He shook their hands and showed them to the door. They were now on their way out of the city and into the unknown under the guiding hand of Carty, Souteneur's right hand man.

"Let's make a move," Wain ordered, as one by one they filed out the backdoor of Souteneur's hide out and into the back alley. From there they made their way into an old tenement building and up to its rooftop. Numerous ropes joined each rooftop, creating makeshift unseen walkways. It was an ingenious rooftop highway that led them out of the Old Quarter.

"There it is! Look, your coach! It's down there in front of the market place," Carty said. Souteneur was right. It wasn't just any coach; it was Chancellor Doulos's coach. The royal insignia of Urbanus was clearly displayed on its doors. It could seat twenty, and was driven by five teams of black steeds. The driver sat patiently waiting for his passengers to arrive. Down the stairs and into the street they went. They did their best to act dignified, but it took every ounce of restraint that they could find in order not to run to the coach.

Jurius opened the door of the coach, peered inside, and was shocked to see Chancellor Doulos waiting for them.

"The time is short. Hurry, inside, quickly! Two of you ride on top with the driver; he's one of Souteneur's men," he said.

Off they went and, just as Souteneur had said, no patrols stopped them. Once they saw the royal insignia of Urbanus on the coach, they let them pass untouched. After all, no scoundrel would be so bold as to highjack a royal coach, unless, of course, that scoundrel was named Souteneur.

Chancellor Doulos was sacrificing more than the use of his carriage. If he were found out, he would meet the same fate as Abner. But Chancellor Doulos was a man of principal. He knew that Abner's fate was unjust and that his message from King Sa'lem was genuine. Even now, he believed that he was acting in Prince Solon's best interests. He was doing his part. For Urbanus and Urbania to survive, more good men would have to follow his example and risk everything.

"I am taking you to the harbor where you will board my personal ship. The crew is made up of loyal navy regulars and marines, plus a few of Souteneur's men. The regular crew was given a three-day leave. They know nothing of our plan. It is not safe for you to go east or to journey north. The Eagle Legions are looking for you and anticipating that you will venture there. There is only one place for you to go—the Moors of Fange. You can find refuge there. It's dangerous, but it's the lesser of many evils right now."

Slowly shaking his head with a look of anxiety, he said, "I will try to send word to you in the days ahead but that depends on the Enemy's movements. If he attacks Urbanus, you are on your own. However, if by chance the invasion does not take, I will arrange safe passage for you to the eastern provinces. From there you can make your way north. May the Great King Sa'lem guide you!"

No sooner had Chancellor Doulos finished his instructions than the coach came to an abrupt halt. After thanking Chancellor Doulos for his help, they boarded the ship and set sail for the south bank of the Ramsgate. Little did they know that their welcome was already being prepared.

****

"Stop or we will launch our arrows! Drop your weapons and surrender or suffer the consequences!" the Tribune ordered. On command, the Eagle Legion closed in and surrounded their quarry. As ordered, the suspects dropped their weapons and raised their hands. "Who are you and what are you doing here?" the Tribune demanded.

"We're just out for a walk in the city, sir! We are practicing for a play. We are actors, good sir. These are but costumes. We mean no harm."

"Search them!" the Tribune ordered in disgust. And search them they did, but they found nothing. What a coincidence that the actors bore an uncanny resemblance to Wain and his companions. But they were, as they claimed, actors from a local drama troupe. In fact, they were Prince Solon's favorite. Little did they know that their newfound patron of the arts was none other than Souteneur, Le Parrain of the Old Quarter!

****

"How could they have escaped? Someone must have helped them, but whom?" Pausing for a moment he said, "Curse that Souteneur, I'll wager my realm that he's behind this!"

"My Prince, we do not know for sure. There is no proof of his involvement," Chancellor Doulos answered.

"What proof do we need? The stench of his vile hands is all over this. That scoundrel is behind every crime in Urbanus. Nothing happens without his involvement. He did this right under our noses. I'll wager that he's gloating over his wine at this very moment. I will skin him alive and stretch his rotten hide over the main gates of the city before this affair is over. He has aided and abetted traitors. It will be my distinct pleasure to personally feed his skinned carcass to Komodus."

Prince Solon raged on, while the perceptive eyes and ears of a scribe, without the benefit of ink, recorded every detail.

****

THE MOORS OF FANGE

The Moors of Fange occupied the southern bank of the Ramsgate opposite Urbanus and stretched over ten thousand square dextors. It was here that the band of pilgrims would land seeking refuge. The Moors of Fange were desolate and dangerous by day, but by night they were believed to be the haunt of creatures from the underworld. Given that they were useless for farming or husbandry, the people of Kronia seldom visited them. Sinkholes, quicksand, fog as thick as lentil soup and giant Dire Wolves were enough to dissuade potential travelers. The Moors of Fange provided the people of Urbanus with endless tales of horror. Whether the tales were true or not, mattered little, everyone justifiably feared them.

"It's about three hours before dawn," Quill observed.

"That's about right. We will need to go ashore and find a fit place to make camp. No fires, it's too risky," Wain warned. "See if there are any extra blankets on the ship. Bring all the water you can hold and bring those Eagle Legions' shields. Jurius, Daylin, Sandor and Ildikko will need protection if we encounter the enemy. At first light we'll scout the area and find a permanent place to camp," There was no moon that night and the wind was still. The Moors most distinctive feature, the fog, was about to become both their friend and foe. "Do not lose sight of each other!" Wain ordered, his voice becoming increasingly tense. "Be quiet and stay together!"

The Moors appeared to be utterly desolate and void of life. The landscaped was dotted with undulating drumlins that linked its countless peat bogs into a spider web of death traps. Watching your step in The Moors of Fange was more than good advice. They wondered for a moment if they were being too cautious, after all, who could live in such a place?

As the fog grew thicker, they did their utmost to stay together. At first they held hands, but with each uneasy step their only final recourse was to tether themselves to one another. While the tether restricted their movement, it prevented them from falling into a bog. The damp cold penetrated their clothes and numbed their flesh. The thick, suffocating blanket of darkness left them blind as moles and made their pace agonizingly slow. They were the definition of prey. They knew that they must find higher ground and soon.

The Rangers carefully felt their way using their bows as staffs. At last, they found a high drumlin. As they made their way to the top, their visibility improved and they could now faintly see each other. The night grew colder and colder.

Wain knew that they had to risk making a fire. Upon the drumlin lay dead trees, and peat was plentiful. As always, Hull was the resourceful fire maker. He was always prepared for times like these and in no time, he had a blaze roaring that warmed their flesh and comforted their very souls. The fire was a source of warmth, but it was also a signal of their location.

Suddenly Daylin noticed that the Jasper Stone that was concealed beneath his tunic was intermittently glowing. He cautiously grasped the chain and removed it and placed it his hand. As he stood there marveling at its glowing light, the night was punctuated by an ominous serenade. A chilling, "Ow, ow..., ow, ow, ow," broke the silence of the Moors.

First one, and then another blood-curdling cry penetrated the fog. Soon it was coming from all directions. Closer and closer it came, growing in volume and in number. "Dire Wolves, and too many of them to count," Lon said. The wolves were closing in on an easy meal.

"Stay near the fire Hull" Wain commanded. "Stoke it as hot and high as you can. Rangers string your bows and prepare to fire at will. Daylin and Ildikko, get behind me. Jurius and Sandor get a sword and strike to kill anything that gets by our arrows."

Deep growls filled the night as gnashing teeth and raised hackles indicated the wolves' eagerness to satisfy their blood lust. Up the drumlin they came in a feverish lunge, leaping and bounding directly at them. "Fire at will," Wain ordered. Volleys of arrows hissed like vipers toward their gapping mouths. Two and three arrows would hit the same wolf, but still they came. Some fell dead at their feet, while others retreated for a moment and then resumed their attack. It was difficult keeping enough arrows in the air to keep the wolves at bay.

Just then, without warning, one giant of a wolf broke through and, as if he understood the chain of command, made a beeline for Wain. Wain hit the ground hard, and before he could make a move, the wolf was poised to finish him with a bite to his neck. But before the salivating fangs could do their work, and without a second's hesitation, Sandor jumped on the giant's back, and with two hands thrust his sword into the wolf's spine. The wolf shrieked in agony, whimpered and immediately fell dead. The other wolves watched their leader go down, and with him their courage to continue the fight gradually faded. They gave up the attack and retreated into the fog.

"Is anyone hurt?" Wain asked.

"No, we're all fine. Apparently you got the worst of it, Wain" Jurius answered.

"I'm alright. I just got the wind knocked out of me. Whew, did you see the size of that beast? It has to be seven dextars long and four dextars high! Thank you Sandor, that was extremely brave of you. What did you say, the Crosian people aren't warriors?"

Wain's remark offered the pilgrims some welcome laughter, and Ildikko a long overdue opportunity to admire her husband. He was, indeed, a brave man, and Urbania needed every brave man that could be found in such a desperate hour.

In time the amber glow of dawn appeared in the eastern sky as the sun wrestled the fog for control of the Moors. Weary from the night's adventure, the small bands decided to rest and eat before venturing any farther into the unknown.

"What now? Where are we going? " Daylin asked his grandfather.

"I don't know, but I am sure that the Rangers have a plan," Jurius answered confidently. Although the others knew that he was just trying to calm Daylin's fears.

The Rangers gathered around the fire and assessed their situation. They could not stay at the edge of the shore where they would easily be spotted by passing ships. They had to move inland. Daylin's questions needed answering, "What now? Where are we going?"

"We will proceed south. If they know that we're here, they won't expect us to march towards them. If we remain unseen, we will have a chance to escape." Wain said.

"How will Chancellor Doulos get word to us?" Lon asked apprehensively.

"One challenge at a time," Wain answered deliberately.

****

The terrain was difficult and it offered them little encouragement. The wretched landscape was monotonous, one dextor after another. Drumlin after drumlin and bog after bog, they wondered how anything could survive in such an inhospitable place? But things not only survived in the Moors! They thrived there, as they would soon find out.

Two large drumlins separated by a large bog appeared straight ahead. It was the highest ground that they had seen thus far and it seemed like an ideal place to build a camp.

"Look, that high ground looks promising for a camp site." Lon said.

"Or, a perfect ambush!" Quill replied.

"Both, I fear! String your bows and ready your swords," Wain ordered. "Jurius take Daylin and Ildikko to the rear and look for cover at the first sign of danger."

Wain signaled with his hands that they would not talk from this point on. Slowly they advanced toward the two large drumlins. They could not see anything or anyone, but their advance came to an abrupt halt as an arrow hissed into their ranks and found its mark, glancing Egbert's thigh. The air was at once filled with volleys of arrows and javelins. Quickly they scurried for cover and returned fire. They were vastly outnumbered. If they did not act immediately, they would soon be surrounded.

Wain decided that they could not hold their present position. The enemy would soon outflank them.

"Lon, take half of our force and circle around from the left. We have to take the risk and try to outflank them. Make every shot count." Wain ordered.

Wain signaled to Jurius to take Daylin and look for an opening in the enemy's ranks. Thrace, Derek, Sandor and Ildikko joined them as they departed. The air was filled with the hiss of arrows and the thud of javelins striking the ground all around them. The Rangers returned fire, trying to give them cover as they departed. Well-aimed arrows dropped those of the enemy who dared show themselves.

Lon did as he was ordered and the Rangers responded by firing their arrows with deadly accuracy, pinning their foe to the drumlins. Like a snake carefully looking for an opening to strike, Lon and his comrades made their way around the left flank and up the Drumlin. The over-confident enemy never knew what hit them. Well-placed volleys brought an end to their assault. Those that were not taken out by the Rangers' arrows fled in retreat into the bogs only to meet their end in the mire of the sinkholes.

Daylin tried to crawl to safety, but he was frozen with fear. He wanted to move but his legs refused to respond.

"Hurry lad, come on, come on!" his grandfather exhorted, but Daylin couldn't move. Derek sensed the boy's fright and crawled back to him. With one hand, he grabbed him by the collar and dragged him to safety behind a large rock that was out of the enemy's range. Thrace surveyed the landscape and decided that they had better keep moving away from the battle. He wanted to join his fellow Rangers, but Daylin's safety was paramount.

"Daylin, stay by my side. Let's make a move." Thrace ordered. Where they were going and what awaited them, they did not know. All they hoped for was escape. Following Thrace's lead, they ran as fast as they could from the cover of the rock and toward the Ramsgate. The soft footing made every stride difficult, but they ran with all their might toward the river. Jurius was about to stop when the ground beneath their feet seemed to vanish. One moment they were running in full stride, and the next they were free-falling down a dark shaft into an abyss. Their brief tumble ended in a rude thud on the soft earth below. Jurius was stunned and almost unconscious, while Daylin and the Rangers tried to adjust to the darkness. Deep groans and grunts filled the darkness accompanied by the sounds of stomping of boots. Ghouls carrying torches led by the Sharokhan entered the shaft and quickly surrounded them.

****

In the meantime, a solitary figure ambled along the river's edge, stumbling and stammering with each step. The wretched soul tripped over the debris strewn along the bank while righting him against the saplings that protruded from the water's edge. His beard was tangled and matted and his hair resembled a patch of briars. His filthy tattered clothing revealed that he had spent more time on his belly than his feet but despite his exhaustion and delirium, yet he kept moving. He was being constrained by an unknown force.

The only sound that he could hear was the voice of regret that filled his mind every moment of very day. Tortuous accusations swirled around him like a caldron until they overflowed with a crescendo of screams that sent the local wildlife in search for cover. Gasping for his next breath like a hunted beast, his wild eyes paned the horizon revealing a soul where fear and dread ruled. He was alone.

He could not last much longer in this condition. His westward trek through the now desolate Province of Petrosia had brought him to the edge of the Moors of Fange. Winter was fast approaching and he had no chance of surviving it.

Fortunately, he was oblivious to his peril. Onward he went, step by deliberate step, falling and then getting up once again. Nothing could prevent him from moving ahead until at last he approached a large hedge rock that blocked the otherwise accessible trail provided by the riverbank. He could not go around it. To the left the brush was too thick to negotiate and to the right meant a swim in the frigid waters of the Ramsgate. The hedge rock had to be climbed, but how he wondered?

Driven by instinct, he approached the rock and attempted to scale its face, but the soft shale crumbled in his hands and broke away beneath his feet sending him tumbling to the ground. Stunned and flat on his back, he gazed upward only to be blinded by a light so intense that it was painful to behold. A voice called to him from the center of the light. "Lothair," the voice called. "Lothair, why do you roam the land like a madman? Why are you running, and where are you going?" The voice inquired. The intensity of the light slowly subsided and a figure began to emerge from it. He could see a man small in stature, with a face furrowed with wrinkles, covered by a long white beard. His hands were gnarled and bony but despite his frailty, he possessed an authority that was commanding. The old man pointed his bony finger at Lothair and said, "A traitor's burden is heavy, is it not? Far too heavy a load for you, I fear! Alas, what shall I do for you?"

For the first time in weeks Lothair's thoughts were lucid and unfettered by the torment of his guilt. He recognized the voice, but was it a dream or one of the Enemy's schemes? It was difficult to tell if he was awake or in a dreamstate. Anticipating his bewilderment the voice said, "You are not dreaming, Lothair; this is all real. Do you recognize me? It is I, Abner, your old friend."

"Where am I?" Lothair asked. "You look so different! What has happened to you?" Lothair demanded. Abner's appearance had brought back his last clear memories. He remembered that he had been in Brantford and that he had abducted Daylin. He now remembered everything in minute detail. The knowledge of his deeds caused Lothair to collapse in tears of grief. He sobbed and sobbed, all the while begging Abner's forgiveness.

"King Sa'lem has sent me to you. He offers you mercy, not judgment. He offers you life and a place at his table." Abner said.

"How can this be? How can he forgive me after all that I have done? I have conspired against Him and sabotaged the mission to save Urbania. I have given Daylin over to the enemy. Tell me, how can he show me mercy? How can I hope to be forgiven and restored?" Lothair pleaded.

Abner pointed to the crack in the side of the hedge rock where a trickle of water reddish brown in color flowed gently downward. "Be released from the curse that oppresses you! Look up and live," Abner commanded.

Lothair approached the crack in the rock and peered into the crevasse. An object slowly emerged from the mist that shrouded its full image. It was as if it was attempting to reveal itself, yet was veiled by an invisible force that masked its full form. Like the tide of the Western Sea the object advanced and then receded, coming in and out of sight. "What is it?" he asked?

"It is the source of all that you seek. It is death to that which oppresses you and life and liberty to that which it beckons. It is revealed and yet it remains hidden until the appointed time. It is majesty cloaked in a crown of shame. It will make you wealthier than all the gold of Urbania, but it makes of a pauper of the rich and proud. It beckons you Lothair. What is your response?"

Lothair could not find the words to respond in his broken state. His sorrow was far deeper than the sorrow of regret. The Toon say that it is easier for a hunchback to lose his hump than a guilty man to lose his regret. Yet somehow he knew that his remorse was not an endless cycle of torment. It was culminating in a new understanding of his motives that led to his failure. It was as if his mind were renewed. He was seeing things more clearly than ever.

Abner had told him on many an occasion that the things you look at never change until you change the way you look at things. Change had indeed come. Deep within his being he realized that this offer of forgiveness was real. It apprehended him, before he comprehended it. It was no false hope. He knew that his failures were more than forgiven; he had found an inner strength to start his life anew.

"There is nothing as profound and so often misunderstood as mercy and forgiveness," said Abner. "It is more precious than gold and rarer than rubies. It is something unearned and undeserved, but it is nonetheless free. King Sa'lem extends mercy to you, Lothair. He is a King like no other. He knows you better than you know yourself. His judgments are sure and just. Receive it!" Abner commanded.

Abner waved his hand over Lothair and spoke words that were unfamiliar to him. He then commanded that the curse placed on him by the Enemy be broken. At that instant the hedge rock rumbled, creaked and groaned and then split open. From the top of the rock a crevasse emerged and a vine growing out of it. Downward it descended until it touched the riverbank.

"This is your way of escape, Lothair, but it must wait until morning. Provision has been made for you for the night. Rest here and wait for the morning's light, and then resume your journey" Abner instructed.

"There is more for you to do, Lothair; be patient and be confident. He who shows you mercy is with you. Rest now, yes rest!" Abner pleaded. At that instant, just as he had come, Abner seemed to dissolve into the rock and disappear before his eyes. Lothair hastily called out.

"Wait Abner, what of the others? Where are they?" Lothair pleaded. But, Abner had disappeared like the mist, and Lothair was alone once again on the river bank. Lothair was beginning to understand that something had happened to Abner. It was Abner whom he had seen, but in many ways he was different than the Abner he had known. Before he could finish his thoughts, the air was filled with the flapping of wings.

Downward they swooshed diving around him and circling closer and closer until they landed at his feet. Six large ravens alighted on the ground before him, each carrying roasted meat, small loaves of barley bread, and a flask of wine. They set their gifts upon a flat flint rock and then set off into the twilight of the evening.

Lothair ate and drank these choice morsels with a profound sense of gratitude. The voices in his head were gone; his mind was now clear. He was beginning to feel strong once again. Despite his weariness, he gathered pine branches and made a bed at the base of the hedge rock. There he fell into a blissful state of unconsciousness, free from the pain of the past.

****

The Mark of Maturity

Daylin swallowed hard and looked with horror at the dark figures rushing toward him. They seemed to have eyes only for him; they would deal with his friends later. He immediately recognized them. How could he possibly forget their last encounter? Stampeding like a herd of feral hogs, they grunted and hissed making hideous sounds that sent a numbing fear through him. Waving their torches in one hand and their swords and battle-axes in the other, they created a parade of grotesque silhouettes on the tunnel's walls.

A Sharokhan targeted Daylin and came straight at him on a dead run and with an out stretched arm. He opened his enormous hand grabbing Daylin by the throat. But the iron grip clamped down on his windpipe and then suddenly went loose. The hand that reached for him was now falling to the ground severed from the attacker's arm.

Just as abruptly, the walls of the tunnel closed in around them, engulfing the Sharokhan and the Ghouls. The stone became as pliable as putty as it singled out its victims, crushing the life out of them, while at the same time creating protective enclaves around Daylin and his friends. Another tunnel suddenly emerged before Daylin and a voice ordered, "Move on, move on, do not delay!"

Daylin listened and obeyed; running as fast as he could. Suddenly the tunnel came to an abrupt halt ending in a large cavern whose walls were lit by glowing quartz crystals. It was the most beautiful thing Daylin had ever seen. "Sit down little one. You are safe for now," a deep voice said softly.

A trembling Daylin gathered himself while staring at the beautiful aura that filled the cavern.

"You have come far, for such a little one. You must, no doubt, be very tired and perhaps a little afraid of what you see. But you are among friends. We cannot offer you food, but water is plentiful here."

In the center of the cavern a depression appeared and immediately filled with crystal clear water that was illuminated by the glowing quartz. It was a dazzling sight, but the anticipation of the cool waters quenching his burning thirst appealed to Daylin more than its beauty. He plunged his hands into the water and scooped the honey liquid in wild abandonment drinking and washing his face all in one motion.

Looking around the cavern for someone to talk to he asked, "Who are you, and where is my grandfather? What of the others? Why am I here?" Daylin demanded.

A soft-spoken, but authoritative voice responded, "If you please, we are the Silca. We are the most common of things and what are most taken for granted in this world. We are the rocks that men walk upon, throw and use as they will for their projects. We are quarried and mined, piled and broken, valued and discarded with equal passion. We are the rocks, stones, minerals and gemstones that fill your world. Like you, we have many relatives, many kinds and types; but we are all brethren and we stand as one in this present crisis. No greater danger has ever been posed against the earth than now. We fear we shall all die if we do not aid King Sa'lem to thwart the advancing darkness. It grows day by day, and soon there will be no communication with our kind."

The voice spoke with a calm dignity and with a sadness that instantly won Daylin's heart. In many ways he sensed that these rocks were very much like him, threatened, hunted and alone.

"Why don't you fight the darkness? There are so many of your kind. Can't you do something to stop the advance of the darkness?" Daylin pleaded.

"The darkness binds us. It affects the life-force of the stone! Where the darkness rules there is no harmony and there are no vibrations in the rock for us to communicate. The land is deaf and dumb. We are the very foundation of Urbania. We are a living chronicle and we are being destroyed as we speak. When our kind perishes the earth will be a different place, and I fear that everything will perish with us too!" the Silca said.

"But the earth is filled with stones and rocks of all kinds, how can this be?" Daylin asked.

"You don't understand, little one. Not all stone is alike. Some are living stones and they sing in harmony with the spirit of life. We resonate with the life around us. We amplify it. We communicate it. We shelter and record it. We provide everything necessary for life and peace. We are part and parcel of this wonderful mystery called life. We have been created for this purpose, to support the world you know and to help sustain life.

The Enemy knows this and he has attacked the very foundations of Urbania. He has chosen only the finest living stones for Mara. His throne and all his evil works are made of what were, from ancient times, my brethren. But now we are quarried nearly to extinction. Those of us who remain are losing their "unser-atem." We cannot communicate. We are losing our memory and our history. Something must be done, but we do not know what to do," the Silca said sadly.

No sooner had the Silca finished his sorrowful tale than the earth beneath Daylin's feet began to writhe in agony and shake so violently that Daylin fell backwards against the cavern wall. The opposite wall of the cavern began to crack like a mirror and as if in a convulsion. Molten lava poured in on to the cavern's floor, rushing towards Daylin. Immediately the Silca responded by shielding Daylin from the poisonous gas and molten rock.

"We beg your indulgence little one. At times the grief is more than we can bear. We often erupt when contemplating our predicament and the fate that awaits us. You are safe for now, but time is of the essence. I must tell what awaits you."

"What of my grandfather, Sandor, and Ildikko and the Rangers?" Daylin asked.

"They are safe! They were rescued as you were but they could not come with you on your journey. It is yours alone.

Daylin pondered these words; they made no sense. How did the rocks know anything about him, much less his future? *"I have truly brought all this on myself,"* he said to himself.

****

The gold and purple pennants of Urbanus waved majestically in the strong winds of the Ramsgate. The ship cut through the waters, making a course upriver for the southern bank of the Ramsgate. The Moors of Fange lay on the Southern horizon and the captain gave orders to head up river and then come about at the nearest oxbow. The crew was keeping a keen eye on the southern shore looking for someone or something. "Easy as she goes." the captain ordered. The imperial ship obeyed and all eyes were fixed upon the southern shore.

"Captain, we must not fail in this quest," Chancellor Doulos said pensively.

"Yes, Sir, I know, but we can only do what we can do," the Captain replied.

"All hands to battle stations, to arms men! Archers, prepare your bows. Ready the longboats and prepare to launch at my command," ordered the captain.

"We are nearly at the spot where we left them. Poor souls, I hope they survived the elements and whatever else lurks in the Moors of Fange these days," Chancellor Doulos said apprehensively.

"Look, there's a man on the river bank, running for cover," the watchman called from the crow's nest! "He's seen us but I have him in full view. He's got nowhere to go except into the Moors."

"Launch the longboats and bring that man to me alive!" the captain ordered.

Six boats made their way to the shore. Three sought to land upstream of their quarry while the remainder went downstream hoping to head him off. The man looked to the left and to the right and then did the most extraordinary thing. To their astonishment, he sat down on the riverbank and waited for his pursuers to come to him.

"There he is. Take him alive," ordered the First Mate. With swift precision the marines encircled their quarry and apprehended him. "Your name?" demanded the First Mate.

"I am Lothair of Lair. I am a Northern Ranger in the service of King Sa'lem."

The soldiers looked at one another in bewilderment. What a strange sight this wretched creature was. Since childhood they had heard stories of the Northern Rangers, but the reality they beheld was unlike anything that they had imagined. The First Mate broke the silence of their bewilderment and ordered: "Take him to the ship, do him no harm, unless he resists."

Immediately the soldiers obeyed and escorted Lothair to the ship. The remaining boats patrolled the shores of the Ramsgate searching for Wain and his comrades.

Chancellor Doulos watched the events from the deck of the ship. His looking glass was trained on the shoreline hoping against hope that Wain and his pilgrim band had survived. "I fear the worse," he said apprehensively.

"If anyone can survive the Moors of Fange and its dangers they can, Sir," the captain replied.

Chancellor Doulos grasped the rail of the ship staring pensively at the shore. "I hope so, so much depends on them," he said with a sigh.

****

Daylin's weary eyes slowly opened. He struggled to focus. It was as though lead weights were attached to his eyelids. The more he tried to open them, the more they recoiled at the intruding shards of light that caused him to squint. As he regained his faculties, he remembered where he was and how he had arrived in this strange place. To his surprise, he had been sleeping on the stone floor of the cavern. The stone was warm and unexpectedly comfortable. Or was he too numb to take notice of his condition? A sharp pain stabbed his stomach causing him to double over. It was that old and familiar enemy that constantly harasses a growing boy—hunger. He was so hungry that even his shoes looked appealing.

"I see you are awake, little one. Sleep is such a strange thing. My brethren were watching you closely while you slept. We have no need of sleep or food, but you appear to need both. We regret that we have no food here, but soon you shall have it in abundance, but beware, not all that you will see will be fit to eat. Eat nothing until you come to the honeycomb. Drink from the pool and listen carefully to my instructions," the Silca said.

Daylin drank and drank. He was quenching his thirst, but filling his stomach with water seemed to ease the gnawing hunger pains that refused to release him from its grip. As he drank the Silca began to give him parting instructions.

"Little one, you must leave here now. The Enemy knows where you are and will make every effort to find you. The wall in front of you will soon open, giving you entrance into a tunnel. Follow it to its end and make haste and do not turn back. There will be nothing for you here. You must press onward."

No sooner had the Silca finished his words than the wall of the cavern opened revealing a tunnel illuminated by glowing gemstones. Daylin gathered himself and walked slowly toward the opening. He looked down its long expanse, but there was no end in sight. Daylin stepped into the tunnel and as he did, he began to realize that this journey was more than an escape. This was a rite of passage. Where he was going, he did not know, but he sensed that he belonged here and that this entire adventure had a greater purpose than he could now understand.

Each step demanded more strength than he possessed, but he pressed onward. Somehow he knew that the words of the Silca were all too true. There was nothing for him back where he had begun this trek. He knew that whatever lay ahead of him was all that remained. Daylin had never felt so alone. In his delirium, his thoughts drifted back to Brantford and the times when he lay upon his bed longing for adventure. His daydreams now seemed liked self-fulfilled prophecies. He now longed for the comfort and safety of his home and the routine of going to school with his friends.

"What a fool I am," he thought. *"Sometimes you get what you want only to find that what you want is something that you are not prepared for."* Home, Grandma Molly, Vim and Doron did they ever exist? Was this a dream, or was it real? But one thing was real enough. His hunger was real. Whether it was the push of pain or pull of hope that compelled him to press on, he did not know, but he refused to surrender. He had come too far.

The words of Grandfather Jurius echoed in his mind: *"Diligence Daylin, diligence, it's the philosopher's stone. It turns to gold whatever it touches!"* Remembering these words doubled his resolve, and he pressed onward. *"Due diligence, due diligence, do it when you don't feel like it, and tomorrow you will be twice as good,"* he said to himself.

As his thoughts swirled around in his head, a rushing sounding began to emerge from the far end of the tunnel. Each step heightened its intensity until his eyes confirmed what his ears had told him. It was a river of foaming white water cutting its way through the rock. The tunnel and his journey ended abruptly at the river's edge. The spray of the foaming torrent caressed his parched lips bringing relief to his thirst, but the water also signaled that he could go no farther.

Daylin stood staring at the cavern wall on the other side of the raging river. He did not dare to swim these rapids. The current was too strong and the distance too great. All he could do was stand staring at the far wall of the tunnel's end. He wondered, was this the end?

His weary eyes struggled to focus on the obstacles facing him; was it fatigue or was the cavern wall on the opposite side of the river moving toward him? Daylin steadied himself as though he had lost his equilibrium, but the wall was indeed moving towards him forming a bridge across the foaming river. It was a full arm's span wide and three dextars deep.

Cautiously, Daylin placed a foot on it, testing its strength. It was stone to be sure. Without further hesitation, he rushed across it, forgetting, for the moment, that his destination was the stone wall on the opposite side of the river. Nothing made sense in this place. He was acting on impulse alone. His rational senses seemed all but useless in this realm.

As Daylin took his last step across the stone bridge and approached the cavern wall, a large section of the rock wall began to dissolve. The rock separated into two portions producing a breach in the wall that opened into the most enchanting sight that Daylin had ever witnessed. It was like gazing into a looking glass that allowed you to see into another dimension. Everything under its azure sky and golden sun was beautiful beyond description. The jade green leaves of the trees shimmered with intensity, while the fruit that hung heavily upon their branches begged to be picked and eaten. The air was crystal clear and perfumed with the scent of flowers and the sweet song of birds filled the air.

Until this moment, fear and desperation had ruled him, but the sights and aromas of this place displaced them. He would now satisfy his hunger and rest. He did not know whether he was walking or floating as he took his first steps into the undulating grass of the field.

Mesmerized by the wonders that filled his senses, he had scarcely noticed that the stone wall behind him fused itself closed. The scent of the orchards seemed to call his name. He had never smelled such a sweet fragrance. His eyes bulged at the spectacle of the huge apples and pears that awaited him.

As he reached for a succulent pear that hung at eye level form a pregnant branch, the words of the Silca echoed in his mind, *"Eat nothing until you come to the honeycomb."* The Jasper stone around his neck began to pulsate with light. What did it matter if he ate? He was starving, and the fruit was obviously free for the taking, but the

Jasper Stone and the voice within once again echoed its command, *"Eat nothing until you come to the honeycomb."*

Daylin reluctantly relented and released the pear from his grasp while looking about to see if any bees had made their hive in one of the trees, but he was immediately disappointed. There were no bees of any kind. In fact, he did not see or hear any insects. How strange, he thought, honey without bees? What kind of a place was this?

Just then, a soft warm breeze arose, feathering his hair, reminding him of what Grandpa Jurius used to say to the sailors at the Ramsgate before they set sail for Urbanus. *"May the wind always be at your back!"* And it was, so he decided to proceed straight ahead until he came upon something that would give him a clue as to why he was in this mysterious place.

The walking was far easier than the monotony of the caverns. He may not have known where he was going, but the beauty of the scenery made the journey far easier to bear. The Jasper Stone had gone dim. He concluded that when it glowed in intervals that he would pay close attention. There was only one lingering problem—hunger. He had to eat. He was now beginning to chide himself for not eating the fruit that he had declined. The hunger pangs were becoming unbearable.

Daylin walked and walked until he came to an outcropping of rock in the middle of the grassy field. It stood like a sentinel and it seemed to beckon him. It was a peculiar sight, completely out of place with the pristine surroundings. In fact, at first sight it appeared as a huge ugly rock in the middle of a giant meadow. He approached it slowly, almost reverently and to his amazement it became an awesome sight. Daylin could not imagine what purpose or power had placed this giant structure in the middle of such a beautiful place.

As he walked around it, he felt energy emanate from it. This was no ordinary rock. It was almost alive! As he examined it, he noticed a deep cleft in the middle of its right side, and as he approached it, an unmistakable sweet aroma filled his nostrils. Honey! It was as the Silca had said, honey! Throwing caution to the wind, he charged straight into the cleft and into the biggest honeycomb that he had ever seen.

There were no bees, just limitless honey. Thrusting both hands into the honeycomb he grabbed the golden treasure and stuffed his face with the bounty of the rock. As he gorged his hunger on the nectar, he felt a surge of energy and strength flow into him. It was more than food. It was life to his very soul.

****

Wain and his companions fought bravely, buying time for the others, but they were waging a hopeless battle against overwhelming odds. For every one of the enemy they killed, ten seemed to emerge and take their place. The ground seemed to open up pouring out legions of the enemy burrowed like army ants. Thousands of Ghouls and Sharokhan accompanied by the Ganza spewed out of camouflaged tunnels. Wayne knew what awaited them if they hesitated and he ordered that they make a run for the river. It was a desperate act. The river would not spare them from the inevitable. The enemy rained down a torrent of arrows, some of which fell far from their mark, but others were too close for comfort.

It was here that the shields of the Eagle Legion were put to use as cover for their four companions. Wain ordered that they be locked in the tortoise formation, creating a shell of protection around them and keeping them safe from the enemy's arrows. The Rangers moved with lightening speed, dodging the deadly volleys and returning fire at the same time. They ran towards the river and through the foul smelling oil slicks that festooned the shallow pools of black sulfur water. The stench of sulfur and oil filled the air, choking them as they tried to breath. Beyond these foul pools laid the Ramsgate and a strategically placed drumlin that blocked their view of the river.

Just then Wain had a revelation. If they could get to that drumlin before the enemy could catch them exposed in the open then these fetid pools offered a chance for escape. "Hurry, men, make haste, make for that drumlin! Hull, strike a flint and set some arrows ablaze." Like deer fleeing hunters, they charged through the pools and up the drumlin. Hull did as Wain commanded. In short order, several arrows were blazing and notched upon bowstrings. "Prepare to fire on my command into the pools!"

The enemy was descending through the Moors and into the pools like a flash flood. The roar of their numbers was deafening. The ground shook under the Rangers, but they held their line nonetheless.

"Steady men, steady." Wain waited until the main body of the enemy's numbers was fully exposed in the middle of the pools. The enemy was supremely confident that they held the advantage. They made no attempt to outflank the Rangers or to send a scouting party to reconnoiter the situation. Headlong they plunged towards their prey, drunk with the desire for blood. Wain raised his arm and dropped it with an air of determination. The Rangers' arrows arched high into the sky and then made their homeward turn toward the earth. The flaming missiles landed in the pools and ignited.

Screams of torment thundered through the Moors and could be heard for a dextor. The fire danced like an evil apparition over the pools, engulfing its victims. Struggling to escape the flames, they trampled each other in a desperate state of confusion. Writhing and convulsing in agony, their skin melted from their bodies as they fell. The intense heat forced the Rangers to cover themselves with their tunics and face the ground. The flames would burn for days, being fed by an almost endless supply of fuel. The screams of its victims slowly ebbed into soft moans and blackened, smoldering remains.

The remainder of the enemy dejectedly retreated back to their underground stronghold. The stench of burning flesh filled The Moors of Fange as the flames created a pillar of black acrid smoke that ascended high into the sky, visible to any eyes that were searching the landscape.

****

THE CAVE OF BITTER WATERS

Daylin was very tired but he had a full stomach, something he had not enjoyed since Brantford. That was so long ago, he mused. The pressure and rapid pace of the previous days had caused him to forget the familiar things of normal life. He was now focused on surviving this ordeal. He was numb with exhaustion, and he could no longer resist the temptation to close his weary eyes. Sleep was a welcome respite, and sleep he did.

When he awoke, he noticed that he had not moved a muscle. He was in the same position than when he had succumbed to his fatigue. He could not remember the last time that he had never slept like that. It was as if he had fallen down a deep well, and he was just now climbing back to the top. Opening his eyes was proving to be a daunting task. His mind was hazy and he needed to regain his powers of concentration as soon as possible. *"Is this real?"* he wondered. *"It must be, because this place is just as I remember it before I fell asleep."*

Grasping a nearby sapling, he pulled himself upward. His legs felt like the egg noodles that Grandma Molly used to make for her soups. Gathering himself, he forced himself to stand and surveyed the landscape. In the distance, by the edge of the meadow, a rock wall protruded into the grass. "How strange," he thought. He hadn't noticed it earlier. *"Perhaps I was too hungry,"* he thought to himself. *"Anyway, it needs to be investigated because it might be a way out of this fantastic place."*

As he approached the protruding rock, he noticed that there was an opening. It was the mouth of a cave. The Jasper Stone began to glow intermittently. The closer he came to the opening of the cave, the faster and the more intensely the stone glowed. It was as if it was trying to communicate with him.

Daylin surveyed the meadow. There appeared to be no end to its borders. It was more like a vast plain than a meadow. The rolling fields of grass looked like an ocean of green punctuated with flowers. It was beautiful and serene, but it was lonely. The cave was the solitary landmark that offered the possibility of finding his way back to the surface. He felt a strong compulsion to leave this magical realm. He longed to be reunited with his family and friends.

Cautiously, he approached the opening and peered into the gaping jaws of the unknown. One stride beckoned another as he entered the dark interior of the rock. He was now committed to the journey. The only light he had to guide him emanated from the Jasper Stone. It provided enough illumination for a single step, and no more. This made his progress painfully slow and added the fear of the unseen to his concerns.

Onward he marched until he came to a slight bend in the cave which abruptly veered to the left from the main path of the tunnel. Just beyond the bend emerged a shadowy figure of a woman. She was dressed in a long, sheer gown of black silk trimmed in silver. Her waist-length straight hair was as black as a raven's plumage. Her eyes were shaped like two azure almonds set in an angular face, punctuated by sharp and distinct cheekbones. Her skin resembled ivory and all of her features conspired to make a statement of compelling beauty, framed in a stunning necklace of rubies and diamonds that adorned her neck.

"Daylin, you have come far. You must be so tired and confused," she said sympathetically.

She knew his name, but how, he wondered? What was she doing here? He had so many questions crowding his thoughts and competing for his attention. Yet, he was well schooled in polite manners and so he responded to the lady with respect cloaked in apprehension.

"Yes, my lady, I have indeed come far and I am very confused. Where am I, and what is this place?" he asked politely. "May I have your name, my lady?"

"I am Aphrodinia, guardian of this path," she said softly. "I am here to guide you and to help you in your quest."

"What path is this, and what quest are you referring to?" he asked inquisitively.

"The path is the path of wisdom, and wisdom is what you seek, is it not? It is what you will need if you are going to fulfill your destiny," she said.

"I am just a boy from Brantford of Lamburg, and I have been kidnapped by strangers and taken far from my home. I am lost and looking for a way out of this place," he said nervously. "Can you help me?"

"That is why you are here, Daylin. I have been summoned to instruct and to help you. All is well, trust me. Your heart's desires will be granted all in good time, Daylin."

Hope was what he needed, and hope is what the Lady Aphrodinia offered. His desire for encouragement and the possibility of escape caused him to deny what his eyes were clearly telling him: The Jasper Stone pulsated and glowed with rapid intensity.

"That stone you are wearing is quite interesting. Where did you acquire it? You will not need it beyond this point," she said.

Reaching into her pocket, she presented a large triangular black stone of onyx, fastened to a gold chain.

"It is time for you to exchange your stone for this one. It is essential that you do so, for this stone will allow you to see the future. This knowledge that this remarkable stone offers is beyond the one which you bear and will make you the equal of all your enemies. You will need no man to instruct you or to help you. You will be the One."

Daylin wanted to please her and comply with her demands, but he remembered the words of Abner "Wear it well and never remove it!"

Lady Aphrodinia was determined to take the Jasper Stone from Daylin and before he could make a reply she closed in to make the exchange.

"It is very beautiful, and such a heavy weight for a small boy, please allow me to help you."

Lady Aphrodinia reached for the Jasper Stone and grasped it. The stone began to glow intensely, sending a current of energy flowing through her body, dropping her to the ground. Her hand writhed in pain forcing her to release the stone.

Gathering her composure, she stood up and demanded. "Give me the stone!"

Daylin remained resolute. He could not give it to her. Abner was right. No one could take it from him. He felt a sense of duty that demanded he resist all her cunning ploys.

Swiftly changing her front of attack she said, "In time Daylin, in time. You will see that what I am saying is for your good. You will grow to trust me because I have your welfare in mind, unlike those who have lied to you. If they love you, why are you here? Why are you all alone in this place? Friends, friends indeed! You need more enemies if these are your friends!"

With a graceful wave of her hand, the cave was lit with a soft light that reminded him of dusk on the Rill of the Ramsgate. Everything was visible, yet cloaked in shadows. It was as she said, he no longer had to rely on the Japer Stone alone for light.

"Your eyes will adjust to the light, and then you will understand," she said confidently.

Before Daylin could answer her questions, he was ushered into the tunnel and to a circular pool of water.

"You must be thirsty. Yes, come drink and rest," she said invitingly.

Daylin squinted to adjust his eyes to the veil of twilight that hung like a mist over the pool. He was thirsty, but the Jasper Stone pulsated rapidly, temporarily breaking the hypnotic state that drew him to the water.

"Drink and you will find the clarity of mind that you seek. Wisdom and understanding will be imparted to you. Drink!" she exhorted.

Daylin approached the pool and looked into the inviting water. His face reflected off the surface like an opaque mirror. As he gazed into the pool, his image merged mysteriously with that of the tall stranger who had treated him with such cruelty. He could still feel the stranger's fingers grasping his throat and choking the breath out of him. He could also feel the imprint of his boot smashing into his ribs, followed by a torrent of insults. Resentment turned to anger, and his anger, slowly simmered, waiting for expression.

Then, just as quickly, the stranger's image dissipated, and the image of Doron, the school bully, emerged. Doron's ridicule and harassment had caused Daylin more embarrassment and insecurity than anyone knew. He had buried Doron's sarcasm and taunting in the recesses of his heart and mind. The more he suppressed them, the more he was reminded of them.

On a number of occasions, he would have relished the opportunity to place his fist in Doron's big mouth, but grandfather Jurius would not stand for it. "You mustn't fight evil with evil," he would say. Daylin was forced to tackle the bully in his imagination, but the end result of these fictional conflicts was always the same, *"I should have... The next time I'm going to ..."* But his wounds had never healed, leaving him vulnerable to further infection.

"What are you feeling right now, Daylin?" Lady Aphrodinia asked, probing for an opening.

"Feeling? Oh nothing. Just thirsty," he answered.

"Come to me, young one, tell me what bothers you," she said softly.

He had not heard such soft, compassionate and inviting words since Brantford. Perhaps she really did care about him and that was something that he had missed. He felt so alone. Sensing his vulnerability, she gently stroked his face and ran her fingers through his hair. It was all very intoxicating. "Tell me, Daylin, what are you feeling right now?"

"Well, my Lady, I just had the strangest experience. I saw the faces of two people whom I know and, well, they aren't two of my favorites, if you know what I mean," he said.

"Go on. Explain how you feel about them. Do you feel that they have wronged you? Some wounds never heal until we have satisfied our hunger to settle the score, you know. Would you like to settle the score?"

Her words were carrying him in a direction that he knew better not to pursue. He had been raised to believe that life was the great equalizer. That the long term harvest reaped by the bad behavior of an offender was always a fate far worse than any short term revenge that he could hope to inflict. However, her touch and her comforting words were very compelling.

"Drink, Daylin. Drink and then you will see," she promised.

Daylin stooped down and with his hands he attempted to scoop the water into his parched mouth while the Jasper Stone flashed its silent warning.

"Stop!" a voice rang out. "Do not drink from that pool!" the voice commanded.

Daylin looked up. To his astonishment, another woman appeared. She, too, was beautiful to behold, but in a manner different than Lady Aphrodinia. Her beauty seemed more inward, and radiated outward. She was dressed in a gown of white, and her face was covered with a sheer sky blue veil of silk. A sash of crimson girded her waist, and on her feet she wore silver slippers. She held a branch in her right hand as she moved towards Daylin with a grace that appeared more like a dance than a gait.

"What are you doing here, Agatha?" Lady Aphrodinia snarled.

"I am here preventing you from deceiving and destroying what King Sa'lem has intended for the good of many!" she said with an uncommon authority.

"Daylin, have you drunk from the pool?" she asked with deep concern.

"No, no, no, I haven't!" he said fearfully.

"Good," she said. She then took the branch and stirred the waters of the pool until a whirlpool appeared and swirled like a tornado on the high plains of Lamburg.

"You can drink now, Daylin. The waters are now safe to drink," she explained.

At the sound of these words, Lady Aphrodinia went into a rage. Her delicate features distorted into a vile ugliness, and with one sinister swoop she reached for Daylin and attempted to stop him from drinking. But Lady Agatha intervened and reached forth her hand, forbidding her to touch Daylin. It was as if Lady Aphrodinia had slammed headlong into the wall of the cave. She was no match for the power that now confronted her. In an instant she vanished into thin air taking the shadowy twilight with her.

The Jasper Stone ceased to pulsate and glow and Daylin was now beginning to understand the importance of this strange stone that Abner had placed upon his neck.

"I am Lady Agatha, and you are Daylin. The Silca have sent word of your coming," She said.

****

Sanballat anxiously paced back and forth as his Artrax, generals and Salisian spies all gathered in the war-room complete with a floor size map of Urbania. The room was furnished with a full scale model of Urbanus which was surrounded by armies, ships, and siege equipment that were strategically placed. This was the great invasion plan, and it was now being revealed under Sanballat's watchful eye.

"So, the plan is to invade on two fronts! The first front will be in the west from our fleet that will sail the Western Sea and attack the Vestland from Camesa. The second front will be from the south. First our forces will conquer Naxosis and then cross the Ramsgate landing in Hupsominia." Sanballat said.

An Artrax answered and said, "Yes, Master, all is prepared! Our western fleet is ready to sail at your command. And as we speak we have enough ships docked in Telos on the Ramsgate to transport our forces across the Ramsgate. With the help of Hupsominian ships it will prove no difficulty!" he boasted.

"Then you will march through Zunderland and attack Vestland from the East?" Sanballat asked pressing them for details.

"Yes master. We will divide the forces on that front. Half of our forces will sail down the Ramsgate and land in eastern Vestland, cutting off Zunderland at the Verfall pass. The Salisians will take care of Zunderland. The other half will sail down the Ramsgate and attack Urbanus from the river and cut off all escape routes. Our forces will concentrate on Urbanus; only then will we attack the other provinces," a general answered.

Sanballat trusted no one. He fancied himself as a great military tactician. His opinion, however, was not shared by his Artrax or his generals. However deluded Sanballat was, none dared to express their opinion. For those fond of living it was best to keep one's opinion to themselves. There was a saying that circulated among Sanballat's advisors: *"There is no law against unexpressed stupidity"* To disagree with Sanballat was to become food for the Ghouls, and the Ghouls seldom went hungry.

"And the remainder of the fleet, what is their role?" he demanded.

An Artrax faced Sanballat and spoke, "Master, two fleets each consisting of three thousand Black Ships will sail from our southern base on the Great Western Sea. One will sail up the Ramsgate and assault Urbanus from the water's edge. The other will sail north and land our forces on the western coast of Vestland. As already stated, our third fleet is being prepared in Hupsominia and will sail from the east.

"We will then cover the western flank," he continued. We have a secret base in Kronia and tunnels under the Moors of Fange. It is our plan to breach the walls of the city on four fronts. Urbanus will be surrounded and cutoff. Victory is all but assured, Master!" an Artrax explained.

A general stepped forward and added: "Last but not least, we have Ursus and his Salisian forces inside the city preparing to sabotage their communications, assassinate key individuals and open the gates at the appropriate moment."

"What is the time frame for the launch of the invasion force?" Sanballat asked.

"A fortnight Master, from the moment you give the command," they replied.

Sanballat grinned, and declared, "Praise to the Great One, El' Shay'tan, who has blessed us with wisdom and the will to crush his enemies. He has granted us this opportunity to build his temple in Urbanus and realize the dream so long deferred," he shouted triumphantly.

****

"Daylin, follow me and listen careful to my instructions. I will be your guide during this portion of your quest," Agatha said, gazing into his eyes seeking affirmation.

"I have so many questions," Daylin queried. "Who was the other beautiful lady, and why was the water dangerous? Was it poisoned?"

"I will answer these questions for you, but no more after these, Daylin. She, the Lady Aphrodinia, is the woman who beguiles the foolish and leads them to her house of destruction. She entices and enslaves the foolish with what they bring her, the contents of their hearts. If there is some secret hidden within, she will draw it out and with it forge the chains that will bind them. The water in the pool was not poisoned, it was far more deadly. It was filled with the slowest acting deadly toxin known—bitterness. You saw several faces in the pool didn't you? They were only a very few of the faces of many toward whom you are embittered."

"Bitter? No, I mean, I don't like them. They are cruel and they have no use for me. But I'm not bitter."

"Daylin," she responded compassionately, "The path that Lady Aphrodinia was leading you down was not the path of wisdom as she said. It was the path of perdition, and it is paved with denials, lies, and deceit. The water in the pool is, indeed, the water of bitterness. If you had drunk it, it would have forever changed you and made you a slave of those you hate. It would have locked you in a prison of your own making."

"But I don't hate them!" he argued.

"Daylin, can you forgive them? Can you let them go and release them from your standard of judgment?" she asked.

Her words penetrated deep into his heart. She was correct. He had not forgiven them. And it was just as she said. Whenever a similar situation arose it would remind him of the cruel stranger and the bully Doron. He would then imagine getting even with them. After all, it was only natural to right a wrong. Yes, it was natural, but he knew that it was wrong. Grandpa Jurius was right, "You can't fight evil with evil."

"I do now forgive them," he said, finally. "I will not take prisoners in the future; they are too expensive to feed," he said jokingly.

"Be careful, Daylin," Agatha cautioned. "Forgiveness is more than word to be professed. Take heed, Daylin. Your words will be tested in short order. Beware of sacrifices that cost you nothing. Say what you mean, and mean what you say, and no more," she exhorted.

"It is time, Daylin, for you to proceed with your journey. The most difficult part of your quest is yet to come, but you are now prepared for what lies ahead. Be strong and courageous. Remember, a pure heart conquers all. To virtue belongs the victory!"

Lady Agatha then led him back to the main path of the cave, and there she prepared to bid him farewell with further words of instruction.

"The Jasper Stone will guide you from here. Pay close attention to it. Do not stray from the main path. Remember, watch where you walk and be careful where you stand. Do not sit down until you come to the appointed place. There will be many voices along the path that will be contending for your ear and for your heart, but pay no attention to them. Do you understand?" she exhorted.

****

Daylin took a step down the path and, with a sigh of regret, looked back, but she was gone. Lady Agatha had returned to where she had come from. Once again Daylin was alone.

With resolve, he peered down the hall of the cave, but he could see very little. He knew that his mind would cause him to see what he wanted to see, so caution was the word. He had just experienced enough sleight of hand to last a lifetime. The Jasper Stone was once again his only source of light, but as before, it only provided enough light for a single step. Onward he marched and very soon the spot where he had begun his journey was but a memory. The cave grew narrower as he marched on and he could sense that its walls were closing in making him very uncomfortable.

"Come lad take the turn on the right. It's a short cut," a voice said reverberating off the walls of the cave. Suddenly an opening appeared on the right, ambling downward toward what appeared to be a distant chamber filled with voices. He could not make out what they were saying, but there were people there!

He did his best to fight the irresistible temptation to find the source of these voices but remembering the words of Lady Agatha, he forced himself to march on. The voices grew in number and pleaded with him to join them. "Be reasonable, or this will not come to a good end.

Who counseled you to walk this path alone? Would *they*? Walk lad. Walk down the path..." But he resisted.

Pushing onward, the voices slowly ebbed. Ironically, he felt a peace come over him when they finally ceased. Loneliness is not the worst fate that a man can suffer. Being in the wrong place at the wrong time could prove far worse. It was impossible to keep track of the time in this place. He had only his thoughts to occupy him, and they were occupied with taking control of his fragile emotions. He was vacillating between the noble courage of a warrior and the fearful tears of boy.

"Stop, who goes there?" an unseen voice demanded.

"What do you want in this place?" it growled.

"Quick, state your business! Stand there and don't move!"

He was afraid, but somehow he mustered the courage to defy the command. Keeping his eyes fixed on the path ahead, he paid no attention to the unseen inquisitor.

Again the voice, like the ones before, slowly faded as he made progress down the path of the cave, but the passageway grew steadily narrower. The only reality he knew was beginning to invade that private space that keeps one safe from the intrusions of life. It was becoming more difficult to breath as the narrow confines of the cave and the darkness conspired to stifle him.

As he walked on in the darkness, the walls of the cave began to morph into the faces of men. They would come into full view and then recede as though they were taunting him. Their faces were etched with pain and sorrow, like a tapestry betraying lives lived on their own terms, but meeting with tragic ends. Despite their wretched state, their knees were not bowed. They had long ago made their choice and were doomed to this eternal state of darkness, but they relished the chance to scoff at anyone who yet possessed the very hope that they had forfeited.

"Ah," echoed another voice from the walls, "there is nothing as pitiful as a fool's errand! Thinks he has a way out of here does he? Take our counsel lad and leave this path and join us. Sit here and listen to us. We know what you seek, and it will only trouble you. What advantage does a good life offer except the denial of pleasure and the delight of going your own way? We had our day and we wouldn't trade it for your situation."

Laughter then turned to ridicule followed by insults that pummeled him from all directions. "He's lost the little fool is lost. He will never get out of here. He has the eyesight of a mole and the brains of an earthworm he does. There's no hope for him. He will never make out of here. Sit down lad and surrender! Come with us or you will die in your own arms!"

He recalled the old saying from the schoolyard in Brantford when someone was taunted, "Sticks and stones can break my bones, but words can never hurt me." *What village idiot had concocted those words,* he wondered. No doubt they had never experienced what he was going through. The wounds of a weapon may leave visible scars but they eventually heal. However, the unseen wounds of toxic words can paralyze a soul for a lifetime. These words were slowly eroding the only confidence that remained—hope.

The wretched souls of the rock walls scoffed at him with a volley of lies and deception, but one thing was sure, they were correct in that there was no way out of this place. And then the path abruptly ended. Daylin had come to a dead end.

Mocking laughter filled the cave and became deafening to his ears. Daylin's knees began to knock together and tears streamed down his face. Fear filled the cave as thick as gravy, and he could taste it.

Suddenly, from the wall of the cave where the path had ended a face emerged unlike the others. The white hair and the furrowed but kindly face was very familiar, but also very different in many ways. He looked intently and the listened as the taunting voices were silenced by the words of the old man.

"Daylin, you have come far and done well. The path of wisdom is fraught with many trials and snares, but it is the only one that leads to life, success and happiness. I see you still wear the Jasper Stone. Well done, when so many covet it, but it is for you alone to bear. There remains one more test. Your strength and heart have been tested and they have passed the tests appointed for you, but this test will test your mind. It is a riddle. A saying of the wise, which, as the ancients say, is like a well-driven nail. Are you ready for this test?"

Daylin was a bruised reed shaken by the winds of the storm, but he was not broken. Drawing a deep breath, he said, "Yes, I am ready."

At that instant, a hand appeared and began to inscribe the words of the riddle on the wall were the old man's face had been. Letter by letter and line by line it was etched on the wall as Daylin stood pondering its meaning.

> Though Ponderous, still unweighed...
> Powerless in form, impervious to the sharpest blade
> Strong against the fiercest flame,
> And gentle foe to all consuming fame...
> Though weaponless, red rage disarming;
> While living still, still left for dying...
> Strong through weakening; a victor seen declining...
> Thought dead at last, yet ever death-defying...
> Who am I?

****

THE ULTIMATE POWER

"There, on the starboard side, smoke! There's' smoke, captain!" the first mate yelled excitedly. "Hard to starboard and prepare to launch three landing parties," ordered the captain. The ship's crew acted in unison as they responded to the captain's orders. The longboats were readied and lowered over the side of the ship. In swift succession they descended into the waters of the Ramsgate and headed for the beacon of black smoke. On the distant shoreline stood a weary band of pilgrims huddled together in obvious difficulty. The looking glass revealed several warriors, an elderly man, and a younger man with a woman. They were not what the sailors and marines were expecting, but they were in distress and they were obviously involved in the unfolding events. One of the boats headed directly for them while the other two boats made haste towards the pillar of smoke.

After assessing the battlefield, the landing parties returned to the ship with the band of pilgrims. And they were a miserable sight to behold, but they were alive and well. Their clothes were now tattered and soiled by the elements and by the fires that they had lit to fend off the enemy. The captain greeted them and inquired as to their health.

It was food and water that they craved and the captain ordered that they be given whatever they required. Water never tasted so good. The acrid waters of the Moors were hardly drinkable and they would have soon perished of thirst had the timing of their rescue been delayed.

The captain was a wise and discerning man. Instantly, he sensed that broaching the subject of his other passenger need to be handled delicately, if what he suspected was true.

"We have another passenger on board who is currently enjoying the hospitality of the ship's brig. We found him upriver walking about on Petrosian land. He claims to be a Northern Ranger," he said frankly.

The Rangers, already slightly delirious from the ordeal of the Moors, scarcely could believe what they were hearing. Wain could not summon the strength or the will to ask the question that loomed liked an ignored dragon in the room.

Lon finally posed the question: "What is his name?"

The captain said, "He calls himself Lothair of Lair. Do you know him? Is he one of yours?"

"He is my brother," Wain replied slowly.

The others waited for Wain's lead; however, they were torn. They wanted to restore the Rangers and their relationship with Lothair, but he was a traitor. He had not merely failed them; he had betrayed King Sa'lem and every one of them. They had loved him and trusted him. But, Wain was his brother, and it was for Wain to set the tone and direction of this dubious reunion.

"Bring the man here at once," ordered the captain.

Lothair emerged from the brig and was led to face his old comrades by two Marines. The captain then gave orders to free him from his restraints and allow him to join his fellow Rangers. Lothair was granted temporary freedom under the watchful eyes of the marines.

Wain's eyes met Lothair's in a long still silence. The rules of warfare dictate that he who holds the high ground holds the keys to victory. However, unbeknownst to Lothair, there was no high ground to be held by Wain.

"Brother, how did you get here?" Wain asked.

Lothair paused, trying to find the right words. "My so-called friends abandoned me after I delivered Daylin to them. They paid me, took me with them, and then sailed down the southern shore of the Ramsgate leaving me in Petrosia without food, water or protection. You might say that I harvested what I planted. The guilt and shame of my treason weighed me down in torment, and if I could have, I would have ended my life. I wandered the wilderness for days, knowing that I was losing my sanity."

"Abner is dead. He was charged with treason and convicted in a show trial, and then executed. Abner is gone," Wain said regretfully.

"I saw Abner! At least I think it was Abner … no, no, it *was* Abner. He was very different. It was no dream or vision. I know he was there. He said that he had a message for me from King Sa'lem. He said that I was forgiven. He said, 'King Sa'lem shows you mercy, not judgment. He offers you life and a place at his table.'"

"Is he here with you? Where is he?" asked Lothair.

Lothair could scarcely believe Wain's words. His face contorted expressing an inner anguish still buried deep within and his eyes filled with tears of sorrow and regret. Lothair shared in the guilt of Abner's death. Mercy may triumph over judgment, but the consequences of a man's failure remain.

Attempting to regain his composure and taking a deep breath, he said with great apprehension, "Then he left me and the most incredible thing happened … unbelievable, just unbelievable."

These words broke Wain's normally resolute composure and he collapsed in his brother's arms and held him to his chest and said: "I love you, forgive me," he said, as he choked his words through a torrent of tears.

"Forgive you," Lothair said! "I is I, who is in need of your forgiveness, brother?"

"No, Lothair, for I too have failed! My bitterness toward you consumed me. I lost my focus. It was as if I was locked in a prison cell and all I could think of was you. I hated you and yet I loved you. Over and over, I asked myself, 'How could he? Why, why? My bitterness would eventually blind me, bind me and grind me. Like a dumb ox, I went to slaughter and was led there by my own lust for revenge."

"Discretion and self-control were no longer my companions, and when I needed them the most they were nowhere to be found. I fell to temptation and broke my vows. I was judged by the very same standard that I set for you. It is true that in the end, we become just like the one we curse. You see, brother, I too have failed King Sa'lem. These brothers of ours have forgiven me, but I still have to face King Sa'lem. You are blessed to be relieved of your burden, but I still carry mine."

Words no longer sufficed. Both men broke down and wept uncontrollably. It was a compelling, yet peculiar sight to behold. Two great warriors who had for so long a time and had faithfully guarded the Northern Kingdom had been vanquished by an unseen enemy that took advantage of the one thing that they had failed to guard—their hearts.

The audience that surrounded them could not remain indifferent to all of this. Ildikko covered her face with her hands and fell to her knees sobbing. Sandor joined her as the Rangers rushed to Wain and Lothair and embraced them. Jurius stood transfixed, as did the captain and his crew. The hearts of these men were as hard as the steel of Lair. Even they could not restrain their emotions.

Wain and Lothair demonstrated that covenants can be broken with tragic consequences. But covenants can be restored and renewed when both parties seek reconciliation over revenge and retaliation. Such was the case with these two estranged brothers. Indeed, they had much to discuss in seeking the root of their mutual failures and separation, but that would have to wait. The fruit that they had harvested brought them both to the realization that bitterness blind s a person to the reality of sowing and reaping. Indeed there are no crop failures with this law of life. It is inviolate and impartial. But for Wain and Lothair the priority of the hour was restoration. They knew that where there is fruit, there is also a root, and the axe must be applied to it.

Each man grasped *the other's right hand* and knelt facing each other. They drew their knives and made an incision on their right wrist and then mingled their blood together. Wain said,

"May the blood that flows from our bodies mingle together and join us once again as brothers. I declare that your family is my family; your friends are my friends; your enemies are my enemies. I now pledge to you my loyalty and my resources until the end of my days. If you are ever in need and I fail to come to your aid, may I and my posterity be accursed."

Lothair repeated the oath and they were once again united as brothers. Their comrades stood as witnesses and affirmed their oaths with shouts of, "So be it, make it so!!"

EINHEIT

It was a time to rejoice and to celebrate what they had believed was lost to them forever, but time was not a thing to be grasped. The sands of time were slipping through the hour glass and no man could stop its march. Their happiness now turned to a sober assessment of their situation. They had to leave the Moors of Fange immediately. Sanballat's Black Ships posed a pressing and ominous danger. However, the captain was well prepared for this threat and he laid out the plan that he had devised for their escape.

"Set sail for the north shore. Then proceed north northeast to the Vertrauen, and then to Einheit of Zunderland," The captain explained.

The sailors snapped to, and in unison they manned their stations. The ship, like a well aimed arrow, made haste to the chosen spot. When all was set and the vessel was well underway the captain turned to the Rangers and explained the details of the escape plan.

"It has been arranged for you to find sanctuary in Einheit of Zunderland. You will be safe there. The people of Einheit are refugees and outcasts of Vestland. They were once prominent families in Urbanus, but they made the mistake of opposing the agenda of Solon, the Patrikos and the Trapezites. They defended the rights of the Rasputitsa and sought justice for the oppressed. Their enemies used their power and influence to drive them out of their homeland. They love Urbanus and wait for the day of their return. The man who will be your contact is named Samuel Alder and he leads a group of Loyalists. They are trustworthy people. You will remain there until, well, until the political winds are more favorable and you can return to your homeland."

The sun set quietly on the Ramsgate and the cover of darkness now afforded them some measure of protection from intruding eyes intent on their destruction. They sailed by the light of the half moon keeping as close to the shore line as safety would allow. Their pace was slow, but deliberate. The Ramsgate was once a safe place to travel, but in these perilous times travelers grew accustomed to the feeling of constantly being watched.

From the port side of the ship the silhouette of the Vertrauen slowly emerged against the backdrop of darkness. The winds were fair and what ripples there were created by the ships stern reflected off the water and glistened like diamonds. The beauty of this voyage stood in stark contrast to its dangers. Holding a steady course mid-river, they sought to avoid the lurking sandbars and shoals that would snare the unsuspecting sailor. Onward they sailed up the Vertrauen towards Einheit.

The fair winds exacted a high price for the tranquilly that they offered. Progress was painfully slow. The sun was now breaking through on the horizon sending out its probing rays demanding unconditional surrender from the night's grasp. A new day awaited them, but what would it bring?

As they approached the docks, several figures came into focus. The greeting party consisted of three men who were expecting the pilgrims, having prepared horses for them. The men greeted the captain, and for several minutes they spoke out of hearing of the others. Nodding their heads in agreement, they motioned that the pilgrims should mount up and proceed to the chosen spot.

The captain bid them farewell and a safe journey and then gave orders for the ship to embark for its return voyage to Urbanus. As quickly as they had landed, they departed and were off.

Einheit was a sleepy town surrounded by prosperous farms. The people lived securely and without concern for the things that obsessed those of Urbanus. They were a sober and serious folk who cared deeply for ideals and principles. They favored simplicity and avoided prideful displays that drew attention to oneself. They disdained small talk and frivolity, favoring discussion, debate and, afterward, a coming together to make decisions as a united community. There was a solidarity that permeated the atmosphere, modeled by their guides who seemed to move and think as one. Wain thought that he had not encountered men like these since they left Mattydale.

After an hour's ride, they came to a large estate surrounded by barns, stables, silos and fields. It was an impressive sight. This was no small enterprise and the level of energy exhibited by the workers provided ample testimony that these folk were not given to idleness. This was the Alderhaus and it would now be their refuge and home until circumstances would dictate otherwise.

"We are honored to have you stay with us. Allow me to introduce ourselves. My name is Samuel Alder and this is my home. These are my friends and bothers in the cause, Jonas Eberhardt and Hans Jurgen," he said with a quiet dignity and self-assurance.

Wain offered gratitude and thanks on behalf of the pilgrim band for the hospitality and refuge extended to them. It was more than kindness that they were bestowing on Samuel and his friends. It was a risk that could cost them their very lives.

Samuel invited them into the spacious Alderhaus, and they were immediately escorted to their rooms. Food and fellowship would have to wait. A hot bath and the prospect of sleep had made their demands upon them and they welcomed the offer after their recent voyage.

The Alderhaus was a large octagonal log structure, two stories high that resembled a fortress. It was surrounded by a log wall twenty dextars high on a foundation of stone six dextars high. Water was abundantly supplied by several artesian wells. The Alderhaus was built to withstand a siege and survive. Careful planning had gone into every facet of its design from the minds of men who expected no quarter to be given by the enemy. It reminded Jurius of the ranch houses on the high plains of Lamburg, but its parapets betrayed the fact that it was built to do more than house its inhabitants. It was designed to defend them.

****

Their tired bodies readily settled into their goose down beds. Jurius and the Rangers had not known the comfort of a bed since Brantford. Sandor and Ildikko could not recall the last time they enjoyed the pleasure. The smallest of things now seemed to be great luxuries, a bed and a bath of warm water.

Refreshed and revitalized they gathered in the grand dining room of the Alderhaus. The abundance of hot food and a steady supply of ale and cider were reckoned by all to be a feast fit for a prince. Their hunger muted their conversation, only the intermittent sounds of "mmm" and "good," punctuated by an occasional belch from Hull could be discerned. The food and beverage flowed until all were filled beyond capacity.

Samuel sensed the time was right to broach the subject of the hour. He surveyed the table pensively and knew that this was the opportune moment to engage his guests in what would become a pact of common concern.

"We are deeply saddened by the loss of Abner" Samuel said. Collectively they bowed their heads in resignation. Together they acknowledged the suppressed grief that the crisis of the previous days had denied them. They sighed, wept and offered fond remembrances of praise for their old friend whose wisdom and courage were needed now more than ever. Abner was gone. His passing needed to be accepted before they could move on, but move on they did. In unison, as if heeding a sacred, unspoken ritual, they raised their heads and placed their focus on Samuel.

"The news from Urbanus is not good. You have powerful but very vulnerable friends in Urbanus. It was they who arranged all of this for you in the event that you survived the Moors and the Ramsgate. I fear for their safety. They took a great risk in helping you. Solon will require blood vengeance for their faithfulness to King Sa'lem. Urbanus is filled with deceit and intrigue and the enemy has eyes and ears everywhere. Moreover, he has many bloody hands willing to do his bidding. They have been bought and paid for and sit within the city walls biding their time."

"We have reports of an impending invasion and the time is short. There is little hope for the Vestland and if she falls the other nine provinces will fall like leaves in an autumn gale. The situation is grave indeed," he said solemnly.

"We have waited and planned for the day that we will return to Urbanus and reclaim our birthright which was taken from us by political theft and the usury of robbers in the name of business and the common good. Zunderland is not our home and we pledge you our aid and support in our common cause to restore Urbania."

Jurius, who was normally reserved and business-like, uncharacteristically spoke first and said, "I cannot speak for my compatriots, but as for me, I believe the people of Lamburg will support any and all efforts to rid Urbania of the threat of Sanballat and the darkness that he would impose on us. This is not a matter to be negotiated; it is one to die for. It is liberty, or death, there remains no other option."

All heads around the great table nodded in approval accompanied by shouts of, "So be it! Kingdom, Glory, Dominion!"

"We are not alone in this conviction and commitment. Tomorrow we will gather with the Loyalists of Zunderland. There you will address them and share the plan for the future," Samuel said.

There is a connection that men have to the lands occupied by their ancestors. This land they define as their birthright. It is a connection that extends beyond the boundaries that mark it, be they natural or otherwise. It is a connection that extends beyond the legalities of property rights and title deeds. It is a spiritual connection. They and the land are inseparably one. To be uprooted from it is to be disconnected from who they are. Wherever they settle and make a life there remains an unrequited desire to be there, to be home.

Such would be the heartbeat of the gathering that they attended the next day. These people were refugees, aliens and strangers in

Zunderland. They were successful by any standard of measure and they should have been content with the prosperity that Zunderland had rewarded them for their diligence. Yet, they longed for the Vestland. For these Loyalists, the Vestland and Urbanus in particular were home. It was their birthright. Prosperity could not fill the void in their hearts for their homeland.

****

The next day dawned with a bright sky and a mild breeze wafting over the undulating fields of Zunderland. It was winter and the land lay fallow. Dairy cows could be heard mooing contentedly while grazing on what was left of the previous season's foliage and the mounds of feed left in uniform heaps by the farmers. Sheep and goats leisurely roamed about in large gated pastures secure from predators. Zunderland was indeed a fertile land.

In the center of Einheit stood a large meeting hall constructed of massive logs decorated with a facade of fieldstone. Its location signaled the importance that the Loyalists placed on public meetings. Its rustic character stood in sharp contrast to the sophistication of the business conducted there. In the main room a cathedral ceiling ascended thirty dextars, creating a reverberating quality to the oratory. It was here that any and every concern that affected the public welfare was discussed, debated and decided with a genuine attempt to find solutions pleasing to all parties without betraying their core values.

The years of banishment in Zunderland were not wasted in corrosive bitterness plotting the violent overthrow of Urbanus. Instead, the population had sought a cure to the disease that plagued Urbanus, the very disease that caused their banishment and placed them in this current crisis. They had used their days of separation wisely. They had constructed a bottom up model of government that would serve the people of the Vestland well upon their return. And they never spoke of "If," but *"when"* they would return. This was their conviction and it was wed to their organizing principle of life that all government begins with self-government. The fruit of self-government would build moral and ethical character, strong marriages, families, religious societies and civil government. They defined self-government as life viewed through the lens of King Salem's Law and whose fruit consisted of self-control, personal initiative, industry and independence.

Wain and Jurius were introduced as spokesmen. They were warmly greeted and an eager expectation permeated the room as the crowd awaited to hear words of encouragement and hope. Their longing eyes beckoned to Wain and Jurius indicating that they had placed a burden on them that they could not hope to bear. The news they brought them was not what they wanted to hear. Despite this harsh reality, they proceeded to brief the gathering of about five hundred men and women from the surrounding region.

Wain was the first to speak:

> Friends, as you know, Abner the Seer is dead, executed by the hands of short-sighted men whose greed is second only to their cowardice. His defense in the face of slander and false witness was courageous. Never did he sway from the mission for which the Great King Sa'lem had commissioned him. He faithfully delivered the message to Prince Solon, the other Nine Princes of Urbania, and to the Brotherhood. It is self-evident that they refused to heed his warning. Urbania is now the target of an impending invasion the likes of which have never been witnessed in your history. Sanballat has marshaled his armies and navies. His reconnaissance forces are already probing the eastern provinces and sail the Ramsgate unhindered.
>
> We are witness of these facts and worse. Two of our number lived in a village named Huiedien in Hupsominia whose people were massacred by Salisian forces allied with Sanballat. The crimes committed there are unmentionable. The same fate awaits every man, woman and child of Urbania. Darkness is advancing in the east and an evil transformation works in the Great Forest of the Toon and now probes Lamburg. Hupsominia on your eastern border has secretly forged an alliance with Sanballat. Ursus and his Thema are now within the city gates of Urbanus.

Jurius, taking his cue from Wain, followed him:

> My grandson, Daylin, was the purpose of Abner's mission. Friends, as you know there are many factions in Urbanus. Some swear allegiance to King Sa'lem, but many do not; they have made their alliances with Sanballat. King Sa'lem would intervene and support Urbanus against the coming threat, but until there is unity among his subjects, he cannot; therefore, he sent his faithful servant Abner to appeal to them to unite as one. They follow a different vision. Their hope rests in their understanding of the ancient scrolls; they believe that the temple must be rebuilt and then be destroyed once again. They believe that evil must triumph before the final victory and then King Sa'lem can return.

> My father, Cyrus Hanner was commissioned by King Sa'lem to rescue treasures from the great temple in Urbanus during the first invasion from the South. He and a group of confidants secretly carried the precious items out of the city before it fell, and they hid them. The Brotherhood is sincere in its interpretation of the ancient scrolls that the temple must be rebuilt, but they are wrong. Many of their leaders are wolves in sheep's clothing; this my father knew, and he did his utmost to keep the temple treasures and the Jasper Stone out their possession. They are not alone in this obsession; Sanballat also shares this vision, but for very different reasons.

> As my father's reward for his service to King Sa'lem, the Jasper Stone was placed in his possession. It was kept in my family's trust for safe keeping until Abner called for it. Abner placed the stone on Daylin's neck with instructions never to remove it. Daylin has been chosen to prepare the way for King Sa'lem's return. The enemy will not rest until they have destroyed him.

> Daylin was taken from us by enemy agents, the particulars of this incident you do not need to know. However, he was subsequently rescued and reunited with us. Unfortunately, we were once again separated while fighting enemy forces

in the Moors of Fange. Where he is now, we do not know. We wait for news and orders from King Sa'lem."

A hush of quiet despair greeted the words of Jurius. A thunder clap and lightning bolt would have had far less impact on the crowd. They stared at the Wain and Jurius mesmerized in a stupor of stunned disbelief that begged the question, "What will we do now?"

Samuel Alder was a man who had a reputation for knowing what to do when no one else did. He was both wise and courageous. His faith was coupled with works that put skin on his convictions. He was a leader who needed no title or position to persuade others to follow him. One could tell that he was a born leader because behind him there was always someone following his example. This was the moment that providence had prepared him for.

> Friends, words are powerful things are they not? With them our spirits rise and fall, ebb and flow with the tides of hope. What we have heard would break the will and confidence of the average man or woman, but we are far from average. From the ashes of despair in this foreign land we have rebuilt our lives and families, and forged a new vision of liberty and justice for all peoples. Our destiny has been, and remains to this day, to return to Urbanus. Yes, but we will do more than return! We shall bring reformation, and with it this new vision of equal justice and opportunity to the Vestland and all of Urbania. We will once and for all rid Urbanus of the greed and corruption that has possessed her and oppressed her people, making her vulnerable from within and without to the plans and designs of darkness.

> The answer to the question that is etched on your despondent faces is: "We will wait!" We will wait confidently and expectantly for a sign that what King Sa'lem has promised, He will deliver! This battle cannot be won by the sword alone; it must be won in the will! There is no need to despair, do not allow your imaginations to dictate the reality of the situation. Our cause is just and justice will conquer.

These folk were not given to outward displays of emotion. They preferred facts to feelings, but Samuel had skillfully married the two. The solemn assembly erupted in a display of faith and joyful persuasion. To their mind he was correct; fear would profit them nothing. They had faced adversity and dire circumstances before; it was a time for confidence and resolve. More was happening than mortal eyes alone could discern. A cosmic battle was unfolding; the temporal things of Urbania were slowly passing away, while the eternal realm of the unseen that remained was being birthed. A new order was arising, and a new day dawning; however, labor pains are the prelude to the blessed, agonizing joy of birth.

****

THE CRYSTAL CITY

Daylin's weary eyes were fixed on the wall of the cave. He never felt more helpless than he did at this moment. He felt like giving up. "What was the point of all of this? He was just a boy, why was he experiencing this test? Who was testing him? Couldn't they find a man suited for this? Why me?" he silently argued. These were good and honest questions, he thought, but the reality was that they were not going to be answered. The "why?" of the situation was in reality secondary to the "what?" What did the riddle mean? Slowly he gathered his concentration.

He was resolved to the reality that the riddle needed to be solved. He could hear grandfather Jurius say, as he often did, "Due diligence, due diligence, Daylin; it's the philosopher's stone that turns everything it touches to gold." And, he could also hear Grandmother Molly's familiar refrain, "Get on with it, Daylin, get on with it!"

And so he did. He could supply diligence and he was now committed, but he needed a plan of attack. "A plan ... a plan ..., I need a plan!" Had he learned anything in school? What did his teacher used to say about tackling a problem? "Stand back and look at the big picture and ask, who, what, how ... and then ask, "What is the problem that is trying to be solved, and why is this important to my situation?"

Though Ponderous, still unweighed...

Stand back Daylin, he said to himself; why are you here? This is a test, but a test of what? That's the answer, the thing being tested.

Powerless in form, impervious to the sharpest blade...

It's something that cannot be defeated. It is stands strong in a test, yet it is friendly?

Like my dog!

Strong against the fiercest flame

and gentle foe to all-consuming fame...

Who am I?

"Hmmm… what is that he pondered? Sounds like something I could say to shut Doron's big mouth but then I never did find anything I could say … hmmm… what did shut him up? Silence! He would tease me for being good and obeying my grandparents, but he could only mock me. I knew he was jealous of me and I think deep down he felt guilty, but he couldn't help himself."

Though weaponless, red rage disarming...

While living still, still left for dying...

It seems to be something that is not strong in appearance alone, mused Daylin.

Strong through weakening; a victor seen declining...

Thought dead at last, yet ever death-defying …

Who am I?"

This riddle must be a part of the bigger puzzle. What did the old man say?

'Your strength and heart have been tested and they have passed the tests appointed for you, but this test will test your mind.'

Hmmm … Strong through weakening; a victor seen declining … Could it be? Yes!

My heart… my heart … my heart… MY HEART! That's it! But what about it, how can that be true?

Pacing back and forth and muttering to himself, he repeated the word 'heart' over and over. He then remembered another principle that his teacher had taught him: Gather the facts, contrast, compare and analyze—and then predict.

What was different about his heart? All the hearts he had known on this path were cruel and deceptive, with the exception of Lady Agatha. She had been kind and wise. She had a good heart, he thought.

It's a test for my mind … my strength and my heart has been tested. Hmm… if my heart has been tested and it passed, how and why had it passed the test? Is my heart like Lady Agatha's? Could it be? If so, then I have a good heart! "That's it!" He shouted, "A good heart!"

His words echoed off the walls of the cave, and then, in a crescendo of thunder, they rumbled down the floor causing the very earth beneath his feet to tremble. The voices that had mocked him were now shrieking in terror and agony. His victory was their demise, "To virtue belongs the victory!" The cave convulsed and quaked. He now feared that the very walls would tumble down upon him. The riddle was being erased before his eyes as it crumbled and cascaded downward in a pile of dust and rubble. A pathway emerged where the dead end had stood blocking his progress. He could see a light beckoning him to walk toward it.

****

The Sharokhan with black veiled faces topped with gleaming steel helmets, adorned in uniforms of black linen and chainmail, goose-stepped as one to the hypnotic cadence of war drums echoing off the city the walls. Trumpet blasts ordered razor-sharp lances donned with red and black insignias of El Shay'tan to be thrust forward and back again into position. War hoops declared with pride that these were the indomitable Sharokhan. They gave no quarter, and expected none. They did not fight for personal glory, but for their Emir; surrender was not a word in their vocabulary. Tens of thousands strong, they marched west to Araba their port of embarkation. Untold thousands of Ghouls marched in deadly silence behind them in eager anticipation of the promised feast. Mara was preparing to launch its armada of destruction upon Urbania.

At the same time, six thousand Black Ships were fit and ready set sail at the port city of Araba. Sanballat and his entourage had made the trip from Mara to witness the spectacle. At last the death blow would be levied against Urbanus. He would then pluck the other cities like dates from his palm trees. "All praise to the Great One, El' Shay'tan!' All is prepared. May the seas prove calm and the winds fair," he said to his admirals.

Standing on a high platform overlooking the harbor, Sanballat raised a large banner and waved it back and forth, signaling that the order to embark had been given. Trumpet blasts, drum beats and the crack of whips encouraged the pitiful galley slaves to heave to and row. It was an awesome sight to behold.

****

Daylin did not know where he was going but the light offered him the hope of freedom and fresh air. The confinement of the cave was stifling. He wanted to see the sun, the stars, to breathe clean air. *"Oh' how I have taken such simple but wonderful things for granted,"* he said to himself.

He was once again on the surface of the Moors. After the experience of the cave, even the Moors seemed welcoming by contrast. The sunlight met his eyes like shards of glass and he winced trying to fend off their intrusive probes. Slowly but surely he opened his eyes, seeking to adjust them to his new surroundings. A familiar face appeared and this time, in the clear light of day, he knew who it was. It was Abner. He was different and he looked stronger. His face glowed.

"Abner, it is you, but you have changed. What happened to you?" He asked excitedly.

"That would require a very long explanation, and time is short; all in due time, lad," he said calmly.

"Daylin, King Sa'lem has sent me here to arrange your journey to Aletheia."

"Where?" he asked. "Where is this place?"

"It is in the distant north, very far from here. Its distance cannot be measured by time and space alone. Listen carefully, Daylin. You are being given the honor of an audience with King Sa'lem. This trial you have undergone, and the testing that you have endured and overcome was to measure you. You see, no man can stand in King Sa'lem's presence that has a hard stubborn heart that will not submit to His law. You have been weighed on the scales of truth and justice and found to be sincere. Your heart has been found to be pure. Therefore, King Sa'lem believes that you are fit for the task that He has for you. The fate of Urbania will be determined by its outcome."

This was far more than the mind of a twelve year old boy could fathom. This had to be one of his daydreams spiraling out of control. Maybe Doron was right after all. Daylin's fantasies had taken him to the brink this time. With the thumb and index finger of his right hand he pinched his left arm and, sure enough, what was happening was all too real.

"To everything there is a season, and this is the season. There is a time to every purpose. The time is now. The purpose will be revealed to you in Aletheia by the Great King Himself," Abner explained.

No sooner had Abner uttered his last word than a strong wind descended on Daylin. With a woossshhhhh and a single flap of its wings, he was caught up in air in the powerful talons of a massive eagle, and then gently nestled in the breast feathers under the mighty raptor's beak. Daylin grasped the plumage and held on for dear life. Upward, ever upward, they ascended until only the clouds below were visible. The eagle's huge wings flapped effortlessly as if dancing on the current of air that took it aloft. Daylin had often dreamt of flying, but not even his over-active imagination could have envisioned what he saw and felt at this moment. The air was frigid. In order to protect himself he burrowed deeper into the raptors soft breast feathers and closed his eyes.

****

"Is there any news of the fugitives?" Prince Solon demanded.

"None my Lord, we have searched the city where possible and there is no sign of them, my Prince," the nervous captain said.

"There is no sign because they are not in Urbanus and "where possible" means that you and your valiant Eagle Legion dare not venture into the Old Quarter for fear of your lives!" Prince Solon said angrily.

"They have had help in their escape. Not even Souteneur could perform this sleight of hand without help from those in high places. What of those actors, did they confess? Did they offer any information?"

"No, my Lord, they said that they had been paid by a stranger to wear the fugitives' clothes, and since they needed the money they obliged, my Prince."

"It is all too convenient. Arrest them and get the truth out of them. Use whatever means necessary, but acquire some useful information. Do you hear me?"

Prince Solon approached the captain in a rage and said: "I want them found and I want them in chains before the sun sets. Do you understand me?"

"Yes, my Prince!" the Tribune replied.

A steward entered the room and announced that Lord Ursus would like an audience with Prince Solon. The request broke the tension in the chamber returning Prince Solon to his usual calculating and dispassionate self.

Sensing a weakness in Solon's position, the opportunistic Ursus asked, "Is all well with you my Lord? You seem slightly distressed. May I be of service?"

Prince Solon, not to be out-maneuvered, decided to heed the old adage of, "Feed the fox and keep a close on eye on him." It seemed wiser to involve Ursus in the matter at hand rather than to alienate him. Perhaps it would reveal his true allegiance and, more importantly what he knew. Prince Solon chose to exploit the vanity and greed that Ursus could not conceal or control for his own ends.

"Perhaps, you can be of service, Lord Ursus. I'm sure that the recent events have not escaped your notice."

"You mean the execution of Abner and the sudden disappearance of his friends and co-conspirators?" Ursus said calculatingly.

"Exactly, they must be found and soon. There are rumors that their plot involves a boy who is supposedly the 'chosen one,' who is destined to restore Urbania and deliver it to King Sa'lem. While we both know that this is an old wives' tale fit for fools and simpletons like the ilk of the Brotherhood, it may prove to be a spark in a very dry and volatile political haystack. Lies topple Kingdoms more often truth. We cannot underestimate the gravity of this threat," he said pensively.

"Allow me to investigate the situation. I surmise that the fugitives received some aid and comfort from someone in the city sympathetic to their cause, am I correct? Someone with the means to get them out of the city undetected. The traitors must be found and made an example of," Ursus said.

"Agreed, use whatever means necessary to extinguish this spark before it consumes us," Prince Solon said.

"Are you sure of this 'using whatever means necessary'? That would require authorization that I do not possess," Ursus said true to form.

"Amenuus, come here, and write what I dictate," ordered Prince Solon:

> To all citizens of Urbanus:
>
> Be it known that this writ of inquiry and execution is duly authorized in the name of Prince Solon ruler of Urbanus and declares and empowers Lord Ursus of Hupsoma and his subordinates to conduct unrestricted searches and seizures and where necessary to incarcerate and interrogate anyone aiding and abetting the enemies of Urbanus. Let it

be known that any and all behavior deemed subversive that undermines the general peace and welfare of the city shall be considered treasonous. Interfering with the execution of this writ shall be deemed a capital offense punishable by death.

Prince Solon of Urbanus

Ursus slowly nodded his head in hearty agreement. A cat with a freshly caught mouse would have displayed no less satisfaction at the prospects of his good fortune.

****

Amidst the clouds emerged a mountain that ascended high into the heavens surrounded by a city that seemed to have no discernible end. The great eagle circled high around it and slowly descended to a large portico, depositing Daylin on its crystalline floor. The entire city was composed of pure crystal. Everything was transparent to the eye and was illuminated by a bright light whose source he could not determine. The city appeared to be carved from a single crystalline gem stone.

Daylin stood to his feet, amazed at the spectacle before him. Nothing in Urbania resembled this place; it was beyond words. Craning his neck upwards he could not see the limits of its height. Scanning the horizon to and fro, he could not see the limits of its width. It was as massive as it was beautiful. This was Aletheia.

He would have stood there all day if two men not broken the blissful trance that held him transfixed. They motioned that he should follow them; Daylin followed their lead and walked behind them. A short distance later they came to two crystalline gates. The men instructed him to enter, but the gates were locked and it appeared that was no way to open them. One man turned to Daylin and said: "The Great King Sa'lem calls upon you and requests your presence in His palace please enter here. They then walked away, leaving Daylin baffled and wondering what to do next.

Daylin examined the crystal gates carefully; he could not see handles with which to open the gates, nor any device to announce his presence. He slowly ran his fingers over the surface of the gates and something caught his eye. On the left side of the right gate there was an indentation with a very familiar shape. It looked strangely similar to the Jasper Stone! Immediately the Jasper Stone began to glow with intensity unlike anything he had seen previously. Daylin carefully placed the Jasper Stone in the indentation, and the great crystal gates silently swung open.

Entering the massive edifice, he slowly walked down the long corridor, peering through its sides into the clouds that surrounded it. It was like walking on air. At the end of the corridor stood a circular structure surrounded by twelve gates. Each gate had a golden throne on top embedded with gem stones of numerous kinds and multifaceted shapes. He wondered how would he enter, which was the correct gate?

Just then, to his right, a gate silently opened and a man emerged, bowed, and invited him to enter. Upon entering the chamber, he saw a large throne in the center and a figure sitting upon it bathed in the brightest light that he had ever seen. A rainbow encircled him and voices echoed throughout the chamber singing softly in a language that he did not know. Daylin placed his hands over his eyes to shield them from the light's intensity.

"Welcome to Aletheia, Daylin, my son. I am pleased that you have come. You have done well. I am King Sa'lem!"

****

Ursus wasted no time invoking his newly acquired authority. His Thema arbitrarily rounded up suspects in the Old Quarter where, after a brutal introduction, escorted the victims to holding pens where the persuasion of power and pain would produce confessions. People fled in all directions. No partiality was shown to rank or social class. The Thema's brutality spared no one in its search for those who had helped the fugitives to escape. When the sweep of the Old Quarter yielded no useful information, they turned their attention to the remainder of the city. A reign of terror descended on Urbanus. No one was safe.

Chancellor Doulos knew that he had taken a great risk in help the pilgrims escape the clutches of Prince Solon and the Brotherhood. Sitting at his desk, he pondered the situation. He knew that it would be just a matter of time before one of the sailors would turn and confess their guilt after a false offer of amnesty and safety for their families.

He was correct in predicting the outcome, as the march of boots and the ringing of tempered steel announced the arrival of the Thema to his office. Heavy boots kicked the doors open and without a word, the courageous chancellor stood up, faced his murderers, and was run through with a dozen swords. His blood gave solemn testimony to his belief that, "If a man has nothing to die for, he has nothing to live for."

Predictably, the captain of the ship, his crew, the marines and all their families were arrested, taken to the center of the city and crucified for their alleged treason. The men watched as their families preceded them and were nailed upon the crosses before their very eyes. The sight was horrific. The screams of the women and children writhing in agony echoed throughout the city. The captain and his valiant men followed their loved ones to the same fate. They paid the ultimate price for their roles in opposing tyranny. Urbanus was bathed in the blood of the innocent and it cried out for justice.

****

King Sa'lem stood up and pointed His silver scepter towards Daylin. The young lad instinctively fell to his knees and bowed his head before the majestic king who was attired in a white robe of seven dextars in length and trimmed in crimson. On his head sat a three-tiered crown of gold embedded with twelve different gem stones. On His right hand he wore a signet ring of gold encrusted with twelve precious gem stones. His feet were shod with golden shoes that reflected the light around it into a beautiful orb of dazzling colors that cascaded downward. As He stood before the throne, the voices that had sung in the unknown tongue came to a crescendo of honor and adulation for their king.

An undulating chorus of adulation flowed from a host of invisible voices and filled the temple courts. Daylin stood stunned in rapt silence, filled with an inexplicable peace.

High above Daylin sat King Sa'lem. As Daylin stood in silent awe, he sensed the power and majesty of the King's presence. Once again, Daylin heard what he thought were voices accompanying the glorious splendor and spectacle before him. Unseen voices sang, as if to introduce their ineffable Host.

"He is glorious and approachable;

"He is eternally just, and righteous;

"He is a pillar of strength, and his promises are sure;

"He is merciful to the faithful and a ruthless foe to those who rebel;

"His commands are gentle and gracious, and his covenant is everlasting;

"He is the sovereign King, Sa'lem."

As Daylin stood in a state of awe and reflection, a strong assuring voice emerged from the light, like the sound of rushing waters. As King Sa'lem spoke, a calm silence settled upon the great chamber as if on command.

"Daylin, do you know where you are?"

"Yes, King Sa'lem, I am in Aletheia!"

"That is correct, but do you know where you stand at this moment?" King Sa'lem asked.

"No, your majesty, I do not."

> You are in the temple! This is the eternal temple, not like the one made by men that stood in Urbanus. The first temple served its purpose as a reminder for the need of a more perfect and permanent one. I chose your forefather, Cyrus, as my steward to guard and to keep the treasures that were kept there from falling into the wrong hands.

There are many who seek to rebuild it, but it is a false hope and a vision that leads men astray. What they seek is not found in temples fashioned by the hands of man, but by the one fashioned by the power that is unseen and eternal. You must persuade them of this truth. It will be very difficult to do so when so many have invested so much in this error and have so much to lose.

Daylin, I have called you, and now I have chosen you. It is my desire to save Urbanus and all Urbania. I wish to restore it and to realize the purpose for which it was created. For too long a time the lust for power and self-interest has plunged Urbania into constant warfare. The darkness which has ebbed and flowed over the span of time is now advancing once again from the south and the east. The evil that animates it blinds the minds, enslaves the will, and captivates the hearts of men.

This conflict has been very costly. My servant Abner was faithful unto death, having proclaimed the message that I entrusted to him. His exhortation fell upon deaf ears and hardened hearts. His friends escaped and are safe for the moment. They have been given sanctuary by a remnant that remains in Urbania. The remnant awaits a spokesman and leader. The coming battle cannot be fought with swords and bows alone. The men of Urbania believe that power comes from the edge of a sword. However, victory will require a far more powerful weapon. You will be equipped with such a weapon, as will those who join you. You will liberate the captives and prisoners from the bondage of tyranny. You will triumph over the enemy. Virtue will be victorious!

Daylin listened to the words of King Sa'lem in surprise and utter disbelief. He was, after all, just a boy of twelve! A chosen leader and spokesman who had never led anything or anyone. How could this be?

And then King Sa'lem said, "Come here, Daylin, and stand before me!"

Daylin rose and obeyed. An attendant took the scepter from the King's hand, and King Sa'lem placed His right hand on Daylin's head.

Go in the power and authority of my name and kingdom. The words that you will speak will be my words. The deeds that you perform will be by my might, and the Jasper Stone that you carry will be the sign and seal of your commission. Those who serve me shall serve you. Let no one look down on your youth, for I have chosen you as my servant. The foolish things will confound the wise and the weak shall conquer the strong. So be it!

The voices once again reverberated throughout the chamber, growing louder and louder in celebration of Daylin's commission. His ears had never beheld singing like this. It was ethereal and flowed through him as if he were one with it.

You shall return in the same manner by which you came. My faithful servants, the great eagles of the northland, are my messengers and do my bidding. Not one of their kin falls to the ground without my notice and care. They will guard you and keep you until you reach Einheit. There you will be reunited with your grandfather and my servants. You will not return here until the end of your days. You will live long and prosper so long as you remain faithful to me as your Sovereign Lord and King. Go in peace and, in my name, assert my crown rights and extend my kingdom. That is all, my son. You may now leave as you came.

****

THE VALLEY OF VERFALL

The spectacle of a giant eagle circling high above Einheit was not a trifle to go unnoticed by the people of Zunderland. From every nook and cranny of their everyday routine of life a strange chorus of people seemed to suddenly appear. Men dropped their tools, women their laundry and mothers hid their children and students closed their school books and ran outside to the witness the sight. In unison they dropped their jaws in an arrested state of awe. Everyone gathered outside their dwellings craning their necks and pointing upward as they surveyed the sky, wondering what it was and what it meant. This was the stuff of myth, legend and bedtime stories told by grandfathers to their grandchildren.

It was, however, something very familiar to the Northern Rangers. This was the sign that they waited for. It was the signal that the final phase of their mission was about to begin. Hope was being realized on the wings of an eagle. These great raptors had come to their rescue many times before.

Slowly the great bird descended spreading panic and alarm to the gazing crowd. Men ran for their weapons fearing the worst for their children and livestock. Bows were strung and arrows pointed skyward taking careful aim. The great bird would have been an easy mark for the bowmen had providence not intervened.

Three blasts of a hunter's horn pierced the air and signaled the alarm for the people to assemble at the meeting hall. The people of Zunderland were well schooled in preparation for potential emergencies. Despite the irresistible urge to release their arrows at the descending eagle, they made haste to the meeting hall. Samuel Alder, along with his companions and the pilgrim band, stood waiting for them. It was a hard ride from the Alderhaus and they had arrived with no time to spare. Samuel ordered the people inside and asked Wain to explain the situation in order to calm their fears.

"People of Zunderland, calm yourselves. You do not need to be alarmed; there is no danger to you or to your livestock. As Northern Rangers we know these great eagles to be our friends and protectors. They are messengers sent by King Sa'lem. We will bring you news and inform you of what we learn. Stay here and wait for our return."

The Rangers, Jurius and Samuel Alder then left the meeting hall; but no sooner had they locked their eyes on the sky than the great eagle landed with a grace uncharacteristic of a bird its size. It carefully inspected the men with its penetrating eyes. Recognizing the Rangers it closed its wings and proceeded with a deft but gentle gesture of its beak and gently lifted Daylin, depositing him on his feet and face to face with the astonished observers.

"Daylin, you are alive and well!" grandfather Jurius said joyfully. "I can't believe my eyes. How did you … what happened to you when were separated in the Moors of Fange?"

"There is so much to explain; it is unbelievable, but I will try to explain it. I hope you can believe me," Daylin said apprehensively.

"Go on Daylin, tell us what happened to you," grandfather Jurius said.

Daylin then began the task of reconstructing his adventure from the time of his separation from the group in the Moors of Fange until the present. He told them of the help he had received from the Silca and of their plight. He described in detail the tempting but deadly fruit of the great meadow and the honeycomb. He recalled with fondness Lady Agatha, who had saved him from the evil designs of Lady Aphrodinia. He described his trial in the cave of bitter waters and how the Jasper Stone had been the faithful guide that Abner said it would be. Finally, he shared his journey to Aletheia, his audience with King Sa'lem and the great commission bestowed upon him.

Daylin's account of his fantastic journey was greeted with stunned faces and stone silence. Hull broke the silence with his usual lack of tact and rhetorically asked, "You mean we will be led by a boy?"

Abner had prepared them for this reality. He had informed them of King Sa'lem's desire to use Daylin as his messenger, but despite Abner's words they had not anticipated this revelation. Lothair gazed into Wain's eyes for a reaction to Daylin's account and he could discern none! Wain knew that Daylin was incapable of creating so tall a tale on his own. Daylin was telling truth. For Wain that was a given. His only concern was how they would accomplish this mission with the meager resources that they possessed?

Jurius had the benefit of his family's storied history and the fact that for generations they had enjoyed the provision and protection of King Sa'lem. He was, nonetheless, overwhelmed by the reality that Daylin was to be the one that would lead the forces loyal to King Sa'lem. He was, after all, just a boy of twelve.

Lothair, Lon, the brothers Fairn and the men of Invar were men of duty and honor. They were not given to questioning orders and this time would prove no different. They would carry out their orders and do their duty despite Hull's customary episode of speaking before thinking. Action preceded understanding when it came to duty.

Samuel Alder stood on faith alone and a vicarious faith at that. He would have to trust in the wisdom and experience of these men who had come so far and risked so much. What other choice was there for the Loyalists? The stage was set. It was now time for each man to play his part. There would be no turning back. And worse, there was no alternative to moving forward.

****

The assembly hall was filled to capacity and beyond. Scores of people stood around the room, and scores more waited outside for news. The room buzzed with an air of nervous tension similar to the proverbial "lull" before a thunderstorm. It was still and filled with the static electricity of expectation.

Samuel Alder stood on the platform of the assembly hall before the crowd and raised his arms to ask for their undivided attention.

"People of Zunderland, we bring you news that will affect us all. It is what we have hoped and planned for these many years. King Sa'lem is preparing to intervene on behalf of Urbania."

A murmur flowed through the crowd in the hall and reached those outside reacting to Samuel's statement. Again he raised his arms requesting their attention. The murmur slowly dissipated and he continued.

"The great eagle that appeared over our lands was, and is, as our esteemed guests told us, a messenger of King Sa'lem. Furthermore, there is another messenger from King Sa'lem, and I want to introduce him to you."

Daylin stepped forward. The crowd, reminiscent of the gophers that inhabited the farms of Zunderland, retreated to their holes in denial and disbelief, only to nervously reappear and venture a peek at the boy who stood before them. Expectations are indeed the beggars of life.

The Jasper Stone began to glow with the same intensity it had exhibited in Aletheia and Daylin drew confidence from its light. All that he had seen and heard was at this moment being realized.

> Good people, hear me! I have a message for you from King Sa'lem. This Jasper Stone which you now see is proof of my commission. It is the gem stone that was kept in the Great Temple of Urbanus, but its origin is the city of Aletheia. King Sa'lem desires to come to our aid and save Urbania from the evil which now threatens it. His intervention depends on one thing only, but it is something that even He cannot provide. This is our responsibility and ours alone. What He requires is our unity. We must stand as one, struggle as one and fight as one! For too long we asked Him, 'Whose side are you on?' That, good people, is the wrong question. The question is: 'Who is submitted to King Sa'lem?' We have been divided by the very things that should have united us.

The ancient scrolls given to us for guidance and instruction have become a battlefield. We have fought for status and position while ignoring the fact that love and humility are the marks of King Sa'lem's subjects, not knowledge and arrogance! We cannot allow pride and selfish ambition, or our petty interpretations of the ancient scrolls, to divide us into factions. We are a plum ripe for the Enemy's picking. The Great King calls us to unite before the hour arrives when unity will be impossible. Choose this day what course you will take, the one that leads to slavery and death, or the one that leads to life and liberty!"

As Daylin spoke, the crowd was carried along by an invisible current, moving as one from skepticism to the belief that his words were true and that they carried a weight of power and insight that no boy of twelve could possess on his own. His wisdom was far beyond his years. It was clear to all that these were the words of an authority that needed no qualification, correction or interpretation. His was, indeed, the word of the Great King!

One by one the people bowed their knees and, as was their custom, raised their right hand and responded as one, "So be it, in the name of the Great King Sa'lem!"

At once, as if by unseen command, a powerful presence filled the hall unlike anything that they had ever experienced. It filled them with the purpose and confidence that the words that had been spoken had emanated from an invisible source. Such words were life-giving and life-sustaining. Spontaneously they turned to one another, asking forgiveness for offenses given and taken, promising restitution for wrongs done, and offering help and assistance to those in need. The relationships of families, friends and foes alike were being restored and renewed. The normally reserved and independent Loyalists of Zunderland were succumbing to the one weapon for which there was no defense—unconditional love.

****

The axe of truth had been sharpened and honed to a razor's edge and it was now the moment to strike at the unseen root that had grown for so long a time in the souls of Wain and Lothair. The experience of the assembly hall had proven that no one was immune to the call of introspection and self-evaluation. It was a season of mercy triumphing over judgment, and it was a time to heal. For Lothair and Wain it meant that a long-ignored conversation concerning the roots of their failures had finally arrived. Wain cautiously but confidently turned to his brother and asked, "Lothair, what caused you to turn as you did?"

Lothair paused for a long moment and then answered: "Brother, from the time that we were boys, I always felt inferior to you, although we were never in direct competition. I felt that whatever we did, you were the one who always received the praise and glory. You were the one considered to be the best and brightest, and it was you to whom everyone looked for direction, advice and leadership. I did my best to imitate you, but no one seemed to notice. As we grew into men, our neglected boyhood conflicts only intensified. We walked arm in arm as Northern Rangers, but we were dextors apart as brothers.

During the Great War when Hupsominia was our ally, I formed a relationship with an ambitious captain named Ursus. He seemed to understand me and my need for recognition and affirmation. He very cunningly convinced me that you were deliberately taking credit for my accomplishments and that you had no regard or respect for me as a man. He was quick to tell me that your successes were at my expense. He told me that I was the reason for your success and that you had stolen the credit.

After the Great War we maintained communication. About a year ago I received word that he wanted my assistance in a matter. I listened because my will had long since passed the point of resistance. However, I do not blame Ursus. The blame is mine. It was I who planted the seed of bitterness. He watered it, and everyone shared in the harvest. My envy and jealousy brought me to my inevitable end," Lothair said contritely. "Can a man grasp burning coals with his hands and not be burned?" he asked.

"And you brother, what happened to you?"

Wain sighed, paused, and then began to speak in a slow but measured manner. "Brother, my failure was with a woman. I was blind to the danger and to the cunning trap that she laid for me. I thought that I was immune to the temptation that she presented. But I was far from immune. I was as vulnerable as a mouse toying with a cat. I can see now that I was filled with bitterness over your betrayal. I spent every waking moment filled with the desire for revenge. In the end, I was hung on the gallows that I built for you. Bitterness is what the ancient scrolls say it is: "Bitterness is a cup of poison a man drinks, all the while hoping that the man he hates will die.""

****

There is saying among the Toon that, "You do not need to advertise a fire." The word was spreading to the surrounding provinces that something extraordinary was happening in Einheit. The Alderhaus was a now a beehive of activity as messengers arrived from Verna, the capital city, and even the most remote corners of Zunderland. They came to investigate the reports of the recent events to see whether what they had heard was true. Einheit had undergone a transformation of spirit that could be felt and seen. The light was shining in Einheit in stark contrast to the growing darkness that encroached on the borders of Urbania, and men were being drawn to it. It would not be long before the news reached the ears of those who would not welcome it.

They gathered around the great dining table of the Alderhaus forming a plan of action. Daylin briefed the gathering and informed them that their goal was to march to Urbanus. The messengers would take the details of the plan to their towns and villages. It was agreed that the march to Urbanus would begin in three days time. The women and children would remain in Zunderland under the protection of a chosen rear guard, with the one exception of Ildikko who refused to be separated from Sandor. She had come far and had admirably demonstrated the strength and courage required. All able-bodied men who chose to march to Urbanus were welcome, but it was understood that this was a voluntary venture; no one was to be compelled to take part.

****

Prince Solon stood behind his massive ornate desk and demanded, "What information have you gleaned from your methods of persuasion? Did any of the traitors reveal the location of the fugitives?"

"Yes, my Prince," the captain said. After a long season of interrogation they revealed the truth. They said that they had brought the fugitives to Zunderland and that they have sought sanctuary among the Loyalists of Einheit. We believe that they are under the protection of Samuel Alder; however, I doubt that they will dare show themselves, my Prince!"

"Perhaps, perhaps, but while they are of no strategic threat to Urbanus, they are a political and moral cancer that could easily spread throughout Urbania. We must deal with this immediately by preparing a preemptive strike. I want to crush that Samuel Alder and his loyalist vermin once and for all. They have been a stone in my shoe since they were banished from Urbanus so many years ago. Their ideas are seditious. They are sowing seeds of rebellion. Their childish tune of individuality and independence is a threat to the common good. I would relish the opportunity to decorate the public square by hanging their bodies on crosses just as I have done with Doulos and those who have betrayed me!" Prince Solon snarled.

"Prepare an expeditionary force of modest size, say three legions, and attack Zunderland as soon as possible. Focus your attack on Einheit, and then take Verna. Raze Zunderland to the ground. Spare no one and leave nothing alive. Not even a goat! Do you hear me? Use our forces exclusively. No mercenaries and no Salisians. I want no other claim to the lands of Zunderland except my own. Zunderland will be ours at last. They have given me the perfect opportunity to strike by harboring these fugitives. You see, as Prince, I must possess the discernment to see the golden opportunity that every crisis provides. Even a pile of dung has a side which faces the sun," Prince Solon said cynically, while broadcasting a wry smile.

Cackling their approval like a pack of hyenas, they affirmed Prince Solon with boisterous laughter followed by equally insincere praise for the proposed plan to attack Zunderland. They knew the wisdom of stroking the vanity of their petulant prince. Like a viper, his senses were finely tuned to its environment, detecting the slightest scent of variance. While they laughed, he profiled their every move and facial expression. After all, survival is full time job for a tyrant. Only dead ones sleep soundly, he said to himself.

****

The three days of waiting for the volunteers to gather in Einheit had ended. Their preparations were now complete. A flurry of activity filled Einheit as men sharpened swords and lances, crafted arrows, and fine-tuned their bows in eager anticipation to begin their campaign. Despite the stark reality that engulfed them, they had no idea of what awaited them. Would the people of the Zunderland and the Vestland join their ranks, or would they oppose them? What would they do if and when they arrived at Urbanus? They could not besiege the city since they lacked siege equipment, and they were hopelessly out numbered. A Toon proverb says, "In life it is impossible to know all the answers, but any fool can know all the questions." Answers were indeed hard to find, and they had no shortage of unanswered questions.

The time to embark had finally come. Wain surveyed his motley militia comprised of four thousand light infantry. Each man was equipped with a circular shield, two swords, a composite bow and a kantos, which was a fourteen foot lance. A thousand mounted bowmen rounded out the militia, giving it mobility and fire power on the battlefield. The men of Zunderland were renowned horsemen and bowmen who had honed their skills from youth. This was not a fighting force that could hope to match the venerable Eagle Legions of Urbanus. However, what they lacked in fire power and numbers they compensated for with courage, will and the Rangers' martial experience. It was a curious spectacle. Five thousand strong, they set out from Einheit led by a boy twelve years old, a boy who had overnight become not only a man but also the hope of Urbania.

****

The expeditionary force of twelve thousand strong marched towards Zunderland under the command of Field Marshal Victus. Victus was a battle tested veteran who had steadily risen through the ranks despite his humble origins. He had proven himself to be an able soldier having served with valor and distinction on the eastern front of The Great War. His skill as a tactician was uncontested and his flair for the bold and daring defined him as legendary. He was Prince Solon's first choice for dealing with, "the stone in his shoe," Zunderland.

The morale of the Eagle Legion was high. They were supremely confident that whatever resistance that they would meet during this campaign would soon feel the edge of their swords. Their destination was Verfall. Verfall was by any political standard of measurement completely insignificant. However, Verfall was of great importance when calculating its strategic value. Verfall sat at the eastern end of a wide valley surrounded by rugged mountainous terrain. The valley floor proved to be the quickest and safest land route from the Vestland to Zunderland. Whoever held the valley controlled access to Zunderland. With the eye of the tiger, Victus was committed to controlling Verfall.

Samuel Alder's motley militia was composed of an evenly balanced number of native Zunderlandians and Loyalists. But it was Wain and the Northern Rangers who provided the leadership that they so desperately needed. The Zunderlandians were brave men who were no strangers to hard work and defending the homes and families from predators and occasional bands of Terrarinian raiders, but they were not professional soldiers of the kind that marched steadily toward them.

Nevertheless, they marched with surprising speed, having the advantage of a smaller more mobile force than the enemy. They also possessed the all important advantage that every indigenous force enjoys, an intimate knowledge of the land. They, too, set their sights on Verfall, knowing what was at stake.

High above the cloud cover of the western border of Zunderland a solitary sentinel circled undetected, its piercing eyes carefully assessed the situation below surveying every detail. Victus and his legions were unaware that they had been detected and that the advantage of surprise was now lost to them. Confidently they marched believing that victory was theirs for the taking.

****

The Jasper Stone flashed its light intermittently sounding its warning of imminent danger. Daylin knew that this could only mean one thing, the enemy was near. What form and number, he did not know, but his recent experience had taught him to heed its warnings. Daylin turned to Wain and said, "The enemy is near. We must be careful!"

Wain gave orders to pass the word that there was to be no talking and that all equipment should be tied down. Silence was the word. But the silence was soon broken as their old friend, the Great Eagle, swooshed to the ground halting their progress. Wain signaled that the entire force stand down and remain silent. "I've seen this before," he explained. "The Great Eagles do not land unless they are transporting someone or something or there is imminent danger ahead. I fear that it is the latter and we need to prepare. "Lon and Quill, scout ahead and bring us a report," Wain ordered. "Lothair, come with me; we need to devise a defense." Wain then ordered the remaining Rangers to walk the line and maintain discipline in the ranks.

Lon and Quill stealthily made their way down the valley with the skill that only years of combat experience can yield. Surveying the skyline for movement, they would from time to time place their ears to the valley floor listening for the tell tale vibrations that only a large force could produce. They did not know the identity of the threat that awaited them. They wondered whether it was the Sharokhan whom they had encountered in the Great Forest or the Salesians of Hupsominia since they shared the border with Zunderland. Both forces remained ignorant of the existence of the other and both were equally ignorant of the events that had conspired to bring their counterparts to this place in time.

Taking a position on a ledge high above the valley floor, Lon scanned the horizon with his looking glass. Slowly panning the valley entrance, in an instant he froze motionless and pointed to the west while gesturing to Quill that he had something significant in his lens. To his surprise, it was three Eagle Legions sporting nine thousand heavy infantry, accompanied by three thousand light calvary. They were outnumbered by more than two to one.

****

"They have not sent out scouting parties in advance of their main force, they are obviously very confident that there is no significant opposition ahead of them," Quill said.

"It appears to be the case, that is something that we will need to address," Wain said calculating the situation.

"This commander, whoever he is, appears to be bold to the point of reckless," Wain said with a hint of sarcasm.

"It seems to be the case, judging by the way they march, that they have little respect for the men of Zunderland," said Lon.

"That, too, is a deadly mistake that we will soon correct," said Samuel Alder.

"Many of my Loyalists served during the Great War. And as for the native Zunderlandians, these invaders will soon learn how skilled they are with a bow from the back of a horse. Their line of retreat will be marked by their dead all the way, to very gates of Urbanus," he said with resolve.

"Samuel, take five hundred of your bravest men and proceed west down the valley. I want you to attack and harass the main body of their forces as they enter the mouth of the valley. Draw the dragon to the bait. His blood lust will override his caution. This commander was sent to make short work of a group of rebels for whom he has little respect. We will use that to our advantage."

Wain paused and stared into Samuel's eyes and said, "This is the key, engage them, but do not linger and expose your men to their full force. If you do, they will over run you. You must fight as they expect you to. Fight like cowards and then retreat. Swain and Thrace will then lead our light cavalry and attack them. They will see this as your reinforcements. Swain and Thrace will then retreat as well and employ the 'poisoned arrow.' Our main force will be hidden in the rocks waiting for their full-scale pursuit."

"If they take the bait, it will work," Samuel said pensively. "But if they sense a trap, what then?" he asked.

"Then we fight were we stand," said Wain. "And may the Great King Sa'lem show us mercy."

As Lon and Quill departed, Wain turned to Samuel and asked, "Who do you believe is the commander of these Eagle Legions?"

"There is only one man, whose style fits this scenario, and he's the only commander whom Solon trusts and that would be Victus. You remember him from the Great War, don't you? He hasn't changed his tactics much over the years. Why tinker with success? The forced march and the lack of scouts fit his profile, but I don't know for sure."

Wain knew that one of the keys to victory depended on an extensive knowledge of his adversary. He needed to think like him, anticipating his every move, understanding his tendencies and weaknesses. He needed to know his family history and current lifestyle situation. Any and all information needed to be analyzed, synthesized and developed into a profile that could predict his adversary's plan of action. If this was Victus, he felt confident that the plan they had devised was a boot that was custom fit for their uninvited guest.

Wain gave orders that Illdikko, Daylin and Jurius be hidden under guard, high on the valley wall out of harm's way. Sandor was given the option of remaining with his wife, but she knew his heart. This was their struggle too, and he wanted to do his part. They kissed and warmly embraced as she bid him success with tears in her eyes.

Desperate Measures

Souteneur was growing impatient and increasingly disturbed by Solon's constant surveillance and the arrests of his employees. "I ask you, how can an enterprising businessman like myself make an honest living with the all this disruption and commotion going on? It's hard enough in the best times to turn a profit. Picket-pockets can't work and my ladies aren't safe with those Salisian pigs harassing them on every corner! There are too many prying eyes on the docks preventing me from lifting a trifle or two from those fat merchants and I cannot run my gambling houses without paying bribes to Solon's thieves," he said in disgust.

Adding insult to injury, he had to retreat to his hideout of last resort, affectionately known as the "Pit." It derived its name from its best known occupant, the old dragon Komodus. This was his home and the honeycomb of limestone tunnels made it a perfect lair for an old dragon. Here he could leisurely wait for a good meal. And good meals were never in short supply due to the efficiency of the city's executioners.

Souteneur's predecessors had long ago learned how to deal with old Komodus by constructing barriers of iron bars creating secure passage ways, but otherwise old Komodus was allowed to roam free. He was the "guard dog" that kept away unwanted visitors. Souteneur did not tolerate disloyalty or failure when it came to his business, and old Komodus regularly proved his usefulness in alleviating these irritations.

The Pit was a city within a city, or more accurately, a city under a city. There were numerous secret entrances and exits that were known only to the underground culture of Urbanus. The underground culture was fond of saying: "You might find your way in, but you would never find your way out."

It was indeed a remarkable place. There was no lack of resources in the Pit. Everything that was available in the upper city was available below. One could live safe and secure from the tyranny above. However, Souteneur preferred the charm of the Old Quarter because there he was closer to the pulse of Urbanus and the air was fresher. But for now the Pit was home. Although he was far below ground, his numerous eyes and ears were as universal and attentive as Prince Solon's and they probed the city looking and listening for anything that would help Souteneur to break the iron grip that was choking the life out of his business.

****

Lack of confidence is terrible thing as it robs a man of those precious few opportunities for success and worse still is over confidence. Victus was a supremely over-confident commander. Consequently, he committed the cardinal error of warfare. He had completely underestimated his adversary.

As the Eagle Legions boldly marched towards the valley of Verfall, Victus calculated his forces' imminent success. The day was bright and clear. The winds were light and at their backs. All this combined to build an optimistic mood that this campaign would be over quickly.

But then, just as quickly, the commander's mood of optimism was instantly shattered by an arrow that pierced the throat of the Eagle Legion's standard bearer. The standard bearer dropped face forward to the ground, sending out an immediate call to arms. On command, the Eagle Legions formed phalanxes, locking their shields together and thrusting their lances forward.

In immediate response, a force of five hundred men appeared at the entrance of the valley and began to assail the attacking force with volleys of arrows only a few of which hit the mark. They were not arrayed in any particular military formation and this reinforced Victus's conviction that the approaching rag-tag contingent was no more than an undisciplined mob.

Victus then ordered his infantry to advance on the enemy and they slowly retreated just as he anticipated. However, as they fled the field they were reinforced by charging horsemen that fired volleys of arrows upon the oncoming phalanxes. Victus then ordered his cavalry up from the rear to respond in kind. This sent the attackers in an all out retreat. The commander then ordered the phalanxes to follow the cavalry and wipe the field clean of the rebels.

The Eagle Legion immediately charged into the narrowing valley in hot pursuit. And their efforts were being rewarded as they rapidly closed the distance between themselves and the enemy.

But In a lightning-fast gesture, and in unison, the men of Zunderland who were in full retreat turned in their saddles while their horses continued at full gallop. At the same instant the horsemen turned, they released volley after of volley of arrows from their powerful composite bows. Very few arrows missed their mark.

The maneuver that they had perfected was the famed "poisoned arrow." It was a cunning and deadly ruse that had taken the lives of many over-confident foes. The Eagle Legion's cavalry was mowed down like fresh autumn wheat. The infantry which followed them panicked at the sight and before they could respond the rocks and hills above them erupted like a volcano. Volley after volley of arrows found their mark as the Eagle Legionnaires fell one by one.

Commander Victus bravely held the line, ordering his men onward, but an arrow that seemed destined by design found a crease in his armor sending him to the ground mortally wounded. With their commander fallen, the Legionnaires broke rank and retreated as every man sought to save his own life without concern for his comrades. The underestimated motley militia made short work of these once brave and over-confident warriors. Their swords and their kantos did not rest until the last legionnaire had fallen and was silenced. No quarter was given, and no prisoners were taken that day in the Valley of Verfall.

****

Samuel sent messengers to Einheit and Verna bearing news of their incredible victory. It would prove to have a powerful effect on Zunderland and the surrounding provinces. It had now become evident that the once proud Eagle Legions of Urbanus were not the invincible force that they had longed believed. The Toon say, "It only takes a spark to set a forest ablaze." The spark of Verfall now threatened to engulf the forests of tyranny.

Daylin witnessed the battle from his perch high above the valley. In his heart he knew that this victory was the sign and confirmation that was needed by all. The Enemy could no longer paralyze them with threats of intimidation and retaliation. He also remembered the words of King Sa'lem that this war could not be won by the sword alone. It would require weapons of a different kind.

The motley militia had no time to savor its victory. The supplies and wagons of the Eagle Legions would prove to be a necessary resource in the days ahead. The confiscated weapons of the battlefield would equip any new recruits who would choose to join their cause. Field Marshall Victus was buried with military honors, and the bodies of his men treated with the respect accorded a noble enemy.

That day the dead outnumbered the living and the loss of life would be felt by the victors and vanquished alike. While their own losses were minimal, there would still be families in Zunderland grieving the loss of their fallen heroes. In war, death is impartial and grief universal. The glory of war is for scribes to immortalize, for little boys to fantasize, and for the soldier to agonize. Victory in war is a myth embraced by those who have not paid the price for it.

****

As predicted, the news of the victory at Verfall spread like a prairie fire throughout the eastern and northern provinces. Within a day's time men from every occupation and persuasion set aside the tyranny of the mundane to join the cause. They came on foot, by horse and by water to join Daylin and the motley militia. There was no time to wait for their arrival. They would have to come running in order to join their ranks. Hope is as contagious as fear, and it was that wind of hope that now filled their sails as they set a course for Urbanus.

But time was not their ally, so Wain ordered his forces to embark after a day's rest. The endless stream of new recruits would have to be equipped and readied for what lay ahead without training. At the end of each day's march the Rangers would instruct the new recruits on their duties. The life's blood of this newly formed organization was communication. Priority was given to veterans of the Great War for leadership roles since they possessed the training and experience required. Wain then divided the militia into groups of fifty under the leadership of a captain, believing that no man could effectively lead more than fifty men at one time. He then organized the groups of fifty into ten groups, forming a single regiment under the command of a major. It was a simple but effective way of maintaining order and communication. Wain also gave orders that there would be silence on the battlefield. Communication would be by banners. They were to fight as one, not as individuals.

As they marched toward Urbanus, the crowds gathered in increasing numbers. People from every walk of life came to see the spectacle of an army of motley misfits led by a boy. Whenever the militia would come to a halt and rest, Daylin would take his stand on the highest available spot and would speak to the people. His message was in essence the same as the one he delivered in the assembly hall of Einheit. His words were simple and to the point, but they carried a weight that captivated the hearer and begged a response. Each time he spoke the effects were the same. He won their hearts and minds even as King Sa'lem had said he would. A weapon was being forged more formidable than any that Urbanus had ever encountered.

****

Northeast of Urbanus lay the ruins of an ancient city named Beth Craven. The monstrous creatures known as the Cannabis had occupied it for centuries, but they were only its most recent residents. There were many opinions and theories as to when the city had been constructed, by whom, and for what purpose. No one knew for sure. However, the lack of factual information did not prevent the people of Urbanus from engaging in their favorite past time defined by: "What people don't know, they make up."

Beth Craven was rich in myth and folk lore of the darkest kind. The people of Urbanus did agree on one thing though, Beth Craven was a place better off avoided. It was rumored that its high places were the chosen spot for the practice of the black arts and human sacrifice. On moonless nights unexplained apparitions roamed the ruins accompanied by the tormented voices of the dead. All of these strange and unexplained events conspired to define Beth Craven as a perpetual haunt of disembodied spirits. Whatever the truth, its reputation and situation served Souteneur well. A professional army could not have provided tighter security than the fear and superstition that surrounded Beth Craven.

Concealed deep in the recesses of the ruins laid several secret passage ways that created a direct line to the limestone labyrinth of Urbanus. The Pit's escape route was known only to Souteneur, Carty and a few of Souteneur's inner circle. Whenever Prince Solon would try to arrest Souteneur, he would retreat to the Pit and if he needed to travel undetected outside the city using the underground passages that led straight to Beth Craven. In this fashion, Souteneur came and went as he pleased.

****

There were no survivors at Verfall, but the news inevitably made its ways to Urbanus within a day's time. Bad news, like an illicit, affair cannot be kept secret for long. Perhaps it was the vultures circling over head anticipating a feast, or an opportunistic raider from the hill country who had witnessed the debacle. It is true that dead men tell no tales, but the vanquished army of Verfall was speaking volumes to the living.

Prince Solon sat at his desk paralyzed with depression, unable to move. With his head in his hands, he pondered the impossibility of three Eagle Legions under the command of Victus being decimated. How he wondered and by whom? There were no answers. He was now forced to calculate what he could not see. Solon sat in his chair transfixed as a numbing pain crept through him. Fear was now his constant companion, and paranoia his counselor.

As of late, Prince Solon preferred the privacy of his office to the splendor and formality of the throne room. While he could charm a crowd and play the role of host with panache to be envied, he was nonetheless a private man, who seldom revealed his true thoughts. Not even his wife and children knew him. Solon was a man in love with a mistress named power. His love for her exceeded his love for anything and everyone. Everything in this world was expendable except her. He would have her, no matter the cost.

As the sun set, he slowly emerged from his grave of depression. He had not eaten or drunk water since the moment he had heard the news. He arose and slowly opened the door to his office. His servants and advisors who had remained in the hallways lacking the courage to disturb him waited for him to speak. Solon, however, retired to his quarters without a word, leaving them as they were.

****

A sleepless night lent little clarity to the situation, but the new day put some distance between the numbing pain that he carried in his stomach and his ability to think. He had to carry on, there were no alternatives. The time for self-pity had come and gone and he had to banish it immediately, if he was to survive. There were too many political jackals and hyenas about with a keen sense of smell for weakness. Like all skilled politicians he had long ago mastered the art of hypocrisy. His face seldom betrayed his emotional state or his plans. He was fluent in the language of lies and deceit.

"Amenuus, Assemble my war council at once, bring Ursus here and find that messenger who brought the news," Prince Solon ordered.

Within an hour everyone was present as ordered. They too had heard the news of Verfall and an unsettling mood filled the room. The messenger was brought forward and debriefed, but he could add little to what they already knew. Victus was defeated, there had been no survivors; however, there were rumors of a spontaneous uprising. Crowds of people from the east were marching westward.

"What do you make of this?" Prince Solon demanded surveying their faces.

"I do not know?" said the messenger.

"And the rest of you?" he asked his with a sarcastic angry tone.

Field Marshall Ricimer stepped forward seizing the moment and said pompously, "Give me six legions and I will march east and meet the enemy. Victus was, no doubt, ambushed. There will be no such advantage for them this time."

"The enemy? What enemy? We don't even know who they are? This much is certain, I ordered Victus to crush the Loyalists and he failed. Victus was vanquished. What we do not know who they are. Is this the doing of Sanballat, or is this the work of those loyalist rebels? I smell something here reminiscent of the fugitives and their loyalist protectors. But this debacle is far beyond their talents and abilities. Until we know what we are facing, we had better wait before we take action," Prince Solon advised.

Ursus reinforced Prince Solon's counsel and said, "I agree, it would be wiser to confirm the rumors of the gathering crowds and learn their purpose and motivation. I advise sending out spies and let them mix with their numbers. Give them three days. In the meantime we can prepare our forces."

Ursus knew that time was not Solon's ally. His counsel was sound but self-serving. Nonetheless, it seemed to be the wiser course of action. So, forty spies were dispatched and instructed to glean whatever information they could. Prince Solon and his counselors were confident that the delay was to their advantage. But as they waited and prepared to face the unknown threat from the east, a storm was forming in the south the likes of which they could not imagine.

****

The culture of Urbanus was not dissimilar to any other large city. Those in power by day paraded themselves as patrons of the arts, protectors of the realm and pillars of society. By night they preyed upon the run-a-ways, castaways and castoffs of the city. Their appetites for the lewd and lascivious knew no bounds. It would require a unique man who could satisfy their insatiable appetites. And that man was Souteneur.

Nothing on Souteneur's exotic menu came cheaply and the real price far exceeded the asking price. Your business with Souteneur was never finished even after your bill was paid. He knew that the real worth of your business was not what you paid up front, but what you continued to pay him for the secrets that he held over your head. Blackmail was his stock and trade. The Trapezites may have brokered the deals of day-to-day finance, but they bowed in deference to Le Parrain of the Old Quarter. The Patrikos filled the Great Assembly with oratory and were venerated by the people of Urbanus, but it was the unseen and unspoken Souteneur who made the final decisions concerning those who rose and fell in the ranks of power. The Patrikos were seen as the head, but Souteneur was the neck that turned it. They were mere pawns on his chess board, enslaved by their appetites and victims of their passions.

****

As they marched toward Urbanus, the crowds swelled in number as new recruits eagerly joined their ranks. Weapons were now in short supply; whatever the men could muster was employed. Anything and everything was used, even farm tools, wooden spears and sling shots. They were now about a day's march from Urbanus. Wain and the Rangers met as often as they could with their majors and did their best to keep the men focused on their objective, while no one posed the question which was obvious to all, "What would they do when they arrived at Urbanus?"

In the mean time Solon's spies slowly worked their way through the crowds and the militia, feigning interest in the cause but all the while seeking answers to their subtly crafted questions. Many went undetected, but a few were less fortunate. Two were caught by the careful observations of the men of Zunderland, who saw through their façade and exposed their deceit with clever questions of their own. They were taken to Wain and Samuel Alder for further interrogation, but true to form, they revealed little, fearing Solon's wrath more than torture and death. Wain assured them that torture was not in their future, but they would remain his prisoners. Kindness can be a conspiracy all its own, and so they were kept in the custody of men who were instructed to treat them well and subtly undermine their convictions and confidence in Solon's tyranny. They understood that a man convinced against his will, is of the same opinion still.

"They're biding their time and gathering intelligence," Wain said apprehensively. "There are far more spies in our midst than those two that we caught. By now they are making their way back to Solon. He will soon know who we are, and our capabilities. Moreover and, more importantly he knows that we cannot hope to lay siege to Urbanus. We will need more than numbers to attack Urbanus. We need a solution and we will need it soon." Samuel agreed and they turned their attention to food and rest hoping that the morning would bring them better prospects.

****

The sun rose and lazily broke the horizon as the men of the militia scurried to prepare and eat a simple breakfast before the day's march. As Wain and the Rangers ate their bread and savored the little bacon that remained in their rations, a familiar face appeared, walking straight towards their tent through the camp.

"Any more of that?" he asked. "My word that smells really tempting. Hospitality seems to be in short supply around here," he said sarcastically.

Wain's eyes bulged and he did his best to recall the name behind the familiar voice. It was Carty! Wain was both perplexed and happy to see Carty's ugly face.

"Of course, sit and eat. What are you doing here?" Wain asked.

Carty savored the bacon and bread and made his hosts wait until he felt sufficiently satisfied before he fed them information. He was used to being in charge and he did not like being rushed, especially when it came to a meal. "Ah, that was good," he said rubbing fat belly.

"You are probably wondering why I am here, are you not? I suppose you are and well, it's like this ... Souteneur requires your assistance. He knows that you cannot hope to attack Urbanus. While he is no Field Marshall, he nevertheless understands your predicament, and he has a possible solution," he said with smug satisfaction.

"Got anymore of that bacon? And some bread, too, while you're at it, and a little ale. Tea can ruin a man you know, and it gives me gas!" Carty was relishing the drama of the moment and milking it to its fullest.

Wain was growing impatient. Hull was about to unceremoniously interrupt and teach Carty some manners, but Lon intervened and with a flat hand to his massive chest stopped him where he stood. Quill quickly fetched Carty's food and drink and set it in front of him and they resumed their vigil, waiting for Carty to finish.

Smacking his lips and savoring the last morsel. Carty wiped his mouth with his shirt sleeve, licked each of his fingers clean and then wiped them on his shirt. As a signal that he was finally finished with his breakfast he announced his satisfaction with a hearty belch that could be heard reverberating throughout the campsite.

"You were saying, a possible solution to our dilemma?" Wain inquired.

"O' that, yes, Souteneur wants Solon's boot off his neck. He's growing impossible to be around. Those Salisians are harassing us and business is terrible, and you know how he gets when business is bad," he explained.

"What's the solution?" Wain asked.

Gesturing to his hosts to follow him into the command tent away from prying eyes and ears, Carty spoke in a hushed tone.

"There's a secret passage into Urbanus known only by Souteneur, myself and two others. It leads straight under the city to the limestone tunnels called the Pit. There's another city down there and the people of Urbanus don't even know it. We come and go like ghosts and they never suspect anything. You can march your entire army under their noses and they would never know it until your swords are at their throats. Sounds good, eh?"

Wain looked at Samuel and the Rangers with wide eyes full of optimism. At last the missing piece of the puzzle was in their hands. It was time to formulate the last phase of their plan.

****

The spies returned and immediately reported to Prince Solon. They bore the news that he desperately wanted to hear. It was just as he surmised. It was the Loyalists behind the rebellion and the battle of Verfall had been led by the fugitives. He stood there, immersed in his own thoughts, calculating his options. As he pondered his enemy's strengths and weaknesses, he begrudgingly admired their battle tactics and the boldness that had cost him his favorite commander and three legions. He also concluded that despite their courage and numbers, they had no ability to attack the walls of Urbanus.

Solon was safe and secure within the city; therefore, he decided not to risk the loss of more legions and worsen his political position by another defeat. After all, it was winter. The winter weather and lack of food would send the mob back to their homes in short order. It was the Loyalists who were under siege not Urbanus. A well-planned spring campaign would solve the problem of Zunderland once and for all. Time, he believed, was his ally.

****

Carty explained the proposed plan to the Rangers, their appointed leaders and to Daylin. They would enter Urbanus using the secret passage ways of Beth Craven. Under cloak of darkness they would lead a minimal number of hand-picked men. The plan had to be kept secret for there were now too many men that had joined their ranks in recent days who were unproven as far as trustworthiness. They all agreed that only the original militia formed in Zunderland would go to Beth Craven. The remainder of their numbers would march to Urbanus creating the distraction needed. Jurius, Sandor and Illdikko would go with this group under the leadership of Jonas Eberhardt and Hans Jurgen. These were Samuel's most trusted comrades and they were given the task of occupying the city's attention while Wain and the militia followed Carty through the underground maze.

****

"I am very troubled by this," Jonas said to Hans. "Protecting our homes and families is our right and responsibility. Attacking Urbanus, where is our justification for this act? Where will it end? Will we kill the Prince and take the kingdom by force? The ancient scrolls condemn this. The Prince exists for our welfare and protection. Even if he is misguided at times, he is still our sovereign. We must not do this," he said passionately.

"You are correct. I doubt if the men will agree to this plan. If we plan to attack Urbanus then ..., well, they might return home. We have always believed that violence is a means of last resort, and we have no solid ground to stand on in arguing for it," Hans said in agreement.

Just then Samuel entered the tent. He had overheard their conversation and their faces were like those of children caught in mischief. They could not conceal the truth. Samuel knew that their conflict was one of conscience. He understood the consequences that would follow if these men abandoned the march to Urbanus. He had anticipated this and was prepared to address their concerns one by one.

"So, you are discussing the proposed plan to attack Urbanus?" he said succinctly.

"Yes, and we are not alone; there are many who share our concerns. Samuel, we are called Loyalists for good reason. We bear that name because the foundation of our convictions lies in the bedrock of loyalty to our Sovereign. We are commanded by King Sa'lem to faithfully support the rulers whom He has placed in power," Hans said.

Samuel folded his hands, paused, and responded with a carefully measured tone.

"You know that I have always agreed with what you have said, however, that being said, what you have said is incomplete. These are different times. What were we trying to accomplish? Were we hoping to negotiate a peace with Solon? I think not! It is true that the battle of Verfall was fought to protect our families and our homes, but you and I both know that there was more to it. Solon will not rest until he has destroyed us. Tell me, why are we marching to Urbanus?"

"When we were driven out of Vestland, we refused to strike back at those who wronged us. We chose to do the honorable thing and we left rather than to fight and instigate a rebellion. However, I now believe that we were wrong to do so. Why?

We were victimized by rulers who were mandated to provide for us and protect us. They were commanded by King Sa'lem to praise good behavior and punish the wrong doer. They chose instead to call what was good, evil, and what was evil, good. Rather than being our servants they usurped King Sa'lem's authority and became our masters. Our reward for obedience was oppression.

We received partiality in the place of justice, and scorn instead of honor. They conspired through corruption and greed to steal our land under the guise of the fair use of private property and taxes. Like sheep we paid these ever increasing taxes in the name of paying our fair share in the name of the common good and the result? We were smeared, and our reputations ruined, and then we were banished from our homeland."

"But we are commanded to pay taxes, how can we call ourselves loyal subjects and not pay them?" Jonas retorted.

"There is no question that we should pay our taxes. The question is whether the taxes we pay are just? When we are taxed and have no say in the matter by definition that is tyranny. When the few bear the burden of the many and the many pay no tax at all. How is that just and? The question isn't the tax but rather who is taxed and how they are taxed. If justice is to be equal, then taxes need to be levied equally. All should pay the same percentage.

The Ancient Scrolls declare that King Sa'lem abhors corrupt scales and dishonest weights and measures. Solon and the Patrikos punish hard work and honest labor and reward slothfulness. They create envy, jealousy and division among the people. They steal from those who earn and give what they have earned to those who sit on their hands while eating bread that they did not work for."

The Seventh Precept of the Laws of Kronia says:

> "Honor and befriend your neighbor;
> Work diligently;
> Share your wealth with the poor;
> Comfort, console and care for widows in their distress;
> Bind up the wounded and care for the sick;
> Be generous to all."

"We are commanded to do these things voluntarily, not under compulsion of law or the manipulation of tyranny. It is our conscience and compassion that compels us, not the fear of the fate that awaits us if we violate the laws and dictates of tyrants," Samuel said.

Jonas paced nervously back and forth pondering Samuel's words. He was torn between an angry rejection of Samuels' argument and surrendering to its compelling logic. Hans sat and listened intently and was drawn to Samuel's appeal for equal justice. This discussion was not new to them. Many a night they had discussed these issues over a pint of ale. Those were different times. It was now becoming a debate that demanded that they decide between taking up arms against tyranny or continue to defend themselves from its incessant advance.

Jonas reflected for a moment and then spoke. "I believe that it comes down to this. We must obey those in authority over us. We are obligated to do so. We may appeal, but take up arms? The ancient scrolls command us to submit and obey, as it is written in the Seventh Precept of the Laws of Kronia."

"Love, honor and respect the King above all others; Respect
the elders and appointed authorities of your clan; obey
them, for they are Appointed and invested with the King's
authority to exercise His sovereign will in all things and in
accordance with His just and righteous will."

"This is true, and I agree with you," responded Samuel. "However, the
truth lies not only in its interpretation but in its application. Shall we
surrender our common sense and our clear understanding of what is
right and wrong when we are ordered to do something that is contrary
to what we know to be right? Shall we violate the spirit of King
Sa'lem's Law when a tyrant demands obedience to his orders, while
quoting the letter of the very same text as justification for ordering
us to commit evil? Is our obedience blind or are there circumstances
when a higher law than 'obedience for the sake of obedience' is called
for? Shall we surrender innocent people to the sword in the name of
blind obedience to authority?" Samuel asked.

"It is not we alone who have an obligation to obey King Sa'lem's
Law, so does the Prince. When he fails to fulfill his sworn oath and
obligations to protect and to provide for his subjects, his subjects are
no longer obligated to obey him. Our allegiance is to King Sa'lem
and to the spirit of His Law, not the letter of man-made laws carrying
the weight of His name, and not a minex of His character." Samuel
retorted.

"We are not sheep that will be silently led to slaughter, bound by
wooden interpretations of ancient scrolls. Solon's throne has become a
throne of corruption, greed and the insatiable lust for power. It is built
on a foundation of sand. His sovereignty is a magician's illusion. He
is in debt to Sanballat and to the Trapezites, who will, in short order,
demand payment in full. I too believe in submission to authority, but
I do not believe in blind obedience to morally blind men, who twist
and distort our convictions and use them as chains to bind us. Evil will
always triumph where good men debate and do nothing. Soothe your
consciences if you must and embrace the myth that you must obey
the demands of tyranny even when they are evil but not me. You are
correct that violence is a means of last resort, but we have now come
to the last resort. It is not violence that I chose. I choose liberty and

liberty is not a last resort. Liberty is the first priority. Without it you are slaves on the plantation of tyranny."

With those words, Samuel stood up and walked out of the tent into the night.

****

Prince Solon was in dire need of some amusement and an enjoyable distraction. The solution was a grand dinner party in the ballroom of the palace. This would serve as a tension breaker and a diversion for his cadre of sycophants. He was buying time and keeping the political hounds at bay. In this setting he could charm them and take their political pulse. He knew that these normally reserved and discreet politicians were vulnerable to wine and beautiful women. He knew that they could find an opening where a cockroach could not.

Solon's palace was decorated and attired in resplendent opulence. Golden fountains flowed with the finest wines. Tables were filled to capacity with the choicest delicacies imported from the farthest reaches of Urbania. Silk drapes of exotic colors spanned the halls, backlit with candles, creating a mysterious aura. No expense had been spared and all agreed that this dinner party was more impressive than anyone could remember. Solon made certain that anyone of political and social importance was in attendance. Only Ursus and his Salisian captains lingered while planning to leave prematurely. The elite danced and dined while two determined and destructive forces took dead aim at the city.

****

The most difficult thing a man can do is change his mind. The words of Samuel Alder had pierced the defenses of Jonas and Hans. They had been long conditioned to defend their sovereign, but there was no defense against Samuel's argument. He was right, as he said; they offered an argument based on half a truth. Yes, they should obey established authority, but one cannot aid and abet evil by hiding behind the skirts of obedience and following orders. Samuel had offered a balanced argument. Truth is always a tenuous balance. They knew that Samuel was not a rebel at heart. He was persuaded that this was the only justifiable course of action left to them to restore liberty to Urbania.

The military counsel gathered in Wain's tent. The men of Zunderland were conspicuously absent. The silence in the tent was deadening. They could practically hear the blood running through their veins as their hearts pounded in anticipation. They were so near to their goal and now the missing piece to the puzzle was in their hands. Now they could do nothing but wait.

Through the flaps of the tent two sheepish looking men appeared. Jonas and Hans looked fearful anticipating the reception that might receive, but they were amazed and surprised when the tent broke out in applause, hugs and embraces. In short order they were accompanied by the remainder of the majors and captains from Zunderland. There they stood in agreement that the course that they now embarked upon was the only just and reasonable course left to them. There was no turning back, they were united in purpose.

Wain explained that their forces would be divided into two groups. Jonas and Hans would lead the main body to Urbanus. The Rangers, Loyalists and the men of Zunderland would follow Carty through the ignoble 'Pit' to Beth Craven. Secrecy and silence were the watch words, as the meeting closed they wished each other success and victory.

****

The gaiety of the dinner party was only surpassed by the opulence of the room. Wine and food flowed unabated, as did subtle political conversation and the unceasing flirting and posturing for an end-of-the-night conquest. Such was the life of the rich and powerful. Since the upper classes never looked servants directly in the eye, they seldom remembered their faces. This was an opportunity that Souteneur exploited to full advantage. The palace was full of servants that night and most were tied to Souteneur's purse strings.

Ursus displayed his usual low threshold for social gatherings by making excuses that he need to attend to the security of the city which he claimed was his highest priority. In reality this was a splendid opportunity to further assess the city's defenses while everyone of importance was distracted. Ursus approached Solon and politely asked permission to leave and to see to his Thema. Solon agreed and thought nothing of it. Besides, he thought Ursus and his Salisians were crude and unrefined. They had no place at his table. As Ursus left the party Solon rolled his eyes in contempt.

****

While the throng merrily dined and danced the night away, Carty led the motley militia through Beth Craven and the maze of passage ways that led to the Pit. Downward they descended into the limestone tunnels. They were nearly four thousand in number and while they were too large a force for such a delicate operation, they were too few in number to attempt to seize a city the size of Urbanus. They needed to strike the jugular of Urbanus if they were to have any hope of victory. Onward they marched until they came to a large open room surrounded by torch light. The door to the room was a massive iron gate locked with a large chain and a formidable padlock. Carty took the key that he wore around his neck and unlocked the door. After the last man passed through the doorway, the door was sealed from the inside. It had the look and feel of a prison cell and tomb all in one.

Down the tunnel they marched until a robust figure appeared and, with his customary bravado, bid them welcome. It was none other than the redoubtable Souteneur.

"I'm glad to see that you made it thus far Rangers and your friends as well. I see, ah, and you have brought the Nobel Warrior, Daylin, with you. Young man, I have heard much about you, but I warn you that Souteneur is immune to virtue … ha, ha, ha! You will need all of your number tonight to be sure, but I have prepared a little surprise for you that will make your work far easier."

Souteneur had instructed the servants on his payroll to gradually drug the food and wine offered at the grand dinner party. Over-indulgence was expected and when a guest would pass out, no one was especially surprised or took notice.

However, on this night things took a different turn. Slowly but surely everyone was succumbing to the effects of the potions placed in their refreshments. While they slowly surrendered to the demands of unconsciousness, the motley militia worked their way like termites through the labyrinth below into Solon's palace unnoticed and unopposed. Even the palace guards had been seduced into enjoying a little well deserved wine. The bloated plum was now ripe for the picking.

When the party was finally over, Solon awoke to the keen edge of Wain's sword pressing on his throat. The entire military counsel of Urbanus was under arrest. In one fell swoop, the city's elite had been corralled and neutralized; however, there were others who remained unaccounted for. Ursus, Gordo, and the Salisian captains were not among the captives. They needed to be located and dealt with.

Wain ordered Lothair and the men of Invar to find Ursus and the Salisians and take them dead or alive. Samuel and several Loyalists who were veterans of the Eagle Legions donned their uniforms and with several hundred militia men proceed to the legionaries' barracks. Being veterans of the Eagle Legion they were well known to them and to their surprise the coup was welcomed with celebration. Few legionaries had any love for Solon and they welcomed the news. Eager to play a role in the new order, they marched through the city informing the people of the changes that would bring a total transformation of Urbanus.

****

Ursus and his Salisian Thema walked the southern walls of Urbanus that defended the water. They took particular interest in its strategic preparations, taking careful note of every potential weakness and blind spot in the city's defenses. Sanballat would reward him well for such information, he thought. Gazing downward into the city center they noticed crowds gathering as the Eagle Legion sounded trumpets and herald's proclaimed the news that Solon had been deposed. Their bewilderment soon became fear as they realized the danger of their situation. Before they could devise a plan of escape or attempt one, they were out-flanked and cut off by Lothair and the men of Invar on the right and Eagle Legionaries on the left. Like cornered rats Ursus and his Salisians bared their fangs and in desperation launched an attack on their pursuers.

Lothair's eyes were fixed on Ursus. He could not see anyone else. Ursus drew his sword and ran straight for Lothair, intent on cleaving him in two. The men of Invar likewise drew their swords and rushed headlong towards Gordo and his companions. The clang of steel rang like bells sounding an alarm.

Gordo fought furiously and deftly deflected the thrusts of two attacking Eagle Legionnaires killing both of them in swift succession. Owen instinctively turned towards Gordo and engaged him; his reward for his efforts was a laceration on his left shoulder. Owen responded by spinning to his left, and in one fell swoop removed Gordo's head from his shoulders.

The Salisians fought furiously with no intention of surrender. The tide of action swung like a pendulum until the men of Invar closed in on their adversaries and ended the struggle with their swords and Francescas.

Like the final act of a tragic drama, Lothair and Ursus stood alone as all eyes now turned to witness the end game being played out between the two titans. Ursus was filled with demonic rage. His snake like eyes opened like windows in an empty house, betraying his barren soul for all to see. Pure hate emanated from the deepest recesses of the man. He was intent on dying but not before he had taken as many with him as he could.

Their swords chimed with the song of war, each demanding blood for their efforts. Both warriors were expert swordsmen and experienced in deflecting the blows of their opponents. The contest continued like a macabre opera while the audience was transfixed by the skill and tenacity of the contestants.

"It is time for you to die and venture north for the final time," Ursus said mockingly.

"It is my time, but you will have no say in when I depart. I will be the last thing you see when you depart for the bad lands of the south. You will never corrupt another servant of King Sa'lem," Lothair retorted.

Intent on making good his promise, Ursus, after feigning a thrust to Lothair's right side, thrust his sword towards Lothair's midsection. Lothair moved to avoid the thrust, but was cut on his right side causing blood to pour from the open wound. Lothair winched in pain and fell backwards against the wall. Ursus ran towards his reeling opponent, intent on finishing him with a two handed over the head strike, which the Salisians call the "falcon's swoop." But Lothair instantly ducked, turned to his left, and ran his sword through Ursus' stomach and out his back.

Ursus stared at Lothair with a blank face and the pallor of a corpse. At last he recognized that this was the end of his grandiose plans for glory and power. Clenching his fists and grinding his teeth together, he grimaced and fell straight forward. The audience stood gazing in silence harboring mixed reactions to the demise of this monster. In the end it was all for the sake of vanity. Ursus had destroyed countless innocent lives for personal gain. Like all men, he left with nothing but his legacy. This legacy was best defined as warning to others who would be driven by the same vain desires.

Without a word, the Eagle Legionnaires laid hold of his lifeless corpse and threw it unceremoniously over the city wall and into the Ramsgate while shouting, "Hail Lothair, hail Lothair!" Seldom does life provide men with an opportunity to conquer their demons, but as Abner promised him, "King Sa'lem offers you mercy, not judgment. He offers you life and a place at his table."

****

The gates of the Urbanus were opened to welcome Jonas, Hans and company. Their ranks were filled with people from all over Urbania who were drawn by the prospects of change. For Jurius, Sandor and Illdikko, who had endured the harrowing experiences of the previous days, the welcome was more like a dream. They had anticipated a violent struggle, but found a peaceful welcome instead.

But it was a far different story when it came to the Salisians. As a rule, they did not surrender. Their goal and purpose in the city as agents of Sanballat was to undermine the city's defenses. While they were only five hundred in number, these were fierce professionals. Defeating them would prove to be a daunting task.

The Salisians were quartered on the waterfront. Their tents were arranged in a traditional circular pattern defining them as them as the Thema of Hupsominia. They were at liberty that night and blissfully unaware of the looming events. Souteneur had graciously offered them the hospitality of his ladies of the night, and it was an offer that that they happily accepted.

The men of Zunderland had little love or respect for the Salisians who had for centuries raped and pillaged the farms and towns of Zunderland. It was a time for a reckoning. With the stealth of a leopard, the Zunderland contingent prowled and encircled the perimeter of the encampment. One of the Souteneur's ladies was abducted as she attempted to leave. They instructed her to return and warn her friends in order to escape the coming barrage of arrows.

When the last woman had left the camp, the signal was given to ignite arrows soaked in pitch. On command, they released their arrows high into the night's sky, ascending and then descending like a hellish meteor shower on the tents of the Salisians. Volley after volley was loosed; the screams of tormented men, writhing in pain, reverberated off the walls of the warehouses and anchored ships of the waterfront. Flames flickered off their burning flesh, illuminating the darkness like grotesque candles. The Salisian threat was swiftly neutralized and a reckoning had been rendered.

****

The Brotherhood lay blissfully unaware, fast asleep in the isolation of Eirene, undisturbed by the momentous events of that night. Until the very end, its occupants had remained detached and aloof from the world around them, dwelling in an imaginary dream state. Urbanus had fallen, though their world unbeknownst to them, had forever changed.

They had believed that the world around them was shaped by their interpretations of prophecy. Sadly, their system lacked any means of self-correction and examination. Error was recycled as truth and if their predictions failed, well … good intentions do cover a multitude of sins. In truth, their "prophetic" world was built on the sands of speculation. The new world which was birthed that night was to prove to be a world not only foreign, but hostile to them. It was a realty to which few of them would adapt and survive.

Their once fluid, fluctuating interpretations of the timeless, ancient scrolls had long ago solidified into the rock of dogma. They would tragically learn that dogma does not shape the world. Dogma merely forms the lens through which men view it. What a man believes may not be true, and what is true he may not be capable of believing.

The echo of the legionnaires' marching boots that once visited Eirene at the request of Lemler and Menteur to arrest Abner and his companions now came for them. The hypocritical cover of their religious rags was now lifted exposing their naked ambition. The Brotherhood's harvest was ripe and they would now have to answer for their crimes and hypocrisy. They had chosen to shed innocent blood in order to protect their power and position, all of which had now evaporated under the scorching scrutiny of the sun. All that remained was the innocent blood of Abner that cried out for justice.

Lemler and Menteur were roused from their beds, unceremoniously arrested, and taken in chains to Solon's palace to join the ranks of the deposed elites. The forest of tyranny which had grown and expanded unchecked, was now in ashes. A single righteous spark had forever ignited the unquenchable fires of liberty.

The grand dinner dance had come to a sudden and unexpected ending. The clouded minds and eyes of the guests slowly opened to the realization that they now wore the chains that they had forged for others. There were over two hundred captives under arrest and awaiting their fate. They had defined themselves as the refined and sophisticated elite of society, but the evil legacy that they bequeathed to the citizens of Vestland defined them as monsters.

Virtue, honor and loyalty were relics of the past in their value system. Their standard was cold hard pragmatism; everything was judged politically. The traditional values of Urbanus that had made it the envy of Urbania had long since been replaced by the new order. The state was supreme and no other allegiance mattered. Personal convictions were trampled, ancient property rights were ignored, diluted and placed under the control of those who "knew best."

Every phase of life was under control of Solon's hand-picked planners, who concocted a witch's brew of stifling regulations. The elites had grown fat and powerful while hiding behind the façade of public service and compassion. Their paternalistic arrogance knew no limits as they attempted to redefine the culture after their own image and likeness. This was a day that they never imagined would come, but come it did.

Their proud faces betrayed more than fear. Their arrogant eyes oozed contempt for their captors. Tyrants love to invoke the power of the law when it suits them and all too often use it to mask their tyranny. Solon, ever true to form, would now defend himself by hiding behind the legal principles that he held in utter contempt. Solon's defense was summed up in the question: "By what authority do you commit this travesty of justice?"

The reality was that the authority of their captors was in principle only. It had yet to be realized in position and practice. It is one thing to depose a Prince and it is another to anoint one. The hard and stubborn fact was that there was no government. It was clear to all that if they acted in the name of justice, without a government recognized by the people, they were acting as a self-appointed mob and setting a terrible precedent for the future of Vestland.

Jurius, Samuel and their loyalist contingent, the men of Zunderland and the Rangers were resolved to finding an amicable solution to this matter. It was essential that a prince be appointed. The key government posts in the city and province were in desperate need of honest public servants. They gathered in Solon's office and began the arduous process of discussing, debating and deciding. Morning morphed into afternoon and daylight was now being absorbed by the approach of evening. They all agreed that this battle was more difficult than Verfall. Pride and selfish ambition can be a deadlier foe than the sword.

Samuel Alder was keenly aware that his Loyalists had long harbored the dream to be reinstated in their original positions of power, and that Samuel Alder would lead them. The men of Zunderland had deep reservations on this issue. When the Loyalists were banished from Urbanus the men of Zunderland had welcomed them.

They had enjoyed a prosperous relationship as equals, but Samuel's becoming prince of Vestland would radically change everything. On the surface, it appeared to strengthen the bond between Zunderland and Vestland, but power has a way of changing men. In truth, fear and suspicion now emerged that had been long hidden by a mutually beneficial relationship.

Moreover, whatever they decided had to be ratified by the good will of the people of Urbanus. While their political voice had been slowly silenced over the years, few doubted that they would tolerate more of the same. They had been skillfully manipulated into trading their freedom for the promise of security. Bread, clean water and public housing had been used to keep the Rasputitsa pacified. They were now like the drunkards of the Old Quarter, willing to do anything for another drink of Solon's compassion. Political expediency also demanded the loyalty of the Eagle Legions who would not endure another tyrant like Solon. The challenge before them was to lead all the citizens back to their roots of self-determination, minus the coercion to which they had become accustomed. The foundations needed to be reclaimed.

Jurius had an opinion, but he thought the better of sharing it, fearing that his family was already too heavily invested in the outcome given their storied history. He had the solution to their impasse, but it would have to come from a neutral source in order for its merit to be seen without appearing prejudiced. He did not have long to wait.

Illdikko had earned the right to attend this seminal gathering by virtue of her bravery and support for the cause. Her quiet, gentle demeanor and kindness all too often left her dismissed as just another woman. But Illdikko was far from just another woman, as the Toon say: "The quiet waters of the Ramsgate run the deepest." She had sat for the day observing the men, studying their mannerisms as they conversed, politely avoiding the key issue for fear of giving offense and creating deeper factions than already existed. She had listened and observed for hours, and now she could tolerate no more.

"Brothers, may I speak? You know that Sandor and I are of Hupsominia. We have no direct stake or part in the decisions that you may reach. However, what you decide will not only affect Vestland but all of Urbania. The question that must be answered is, 'Who will be the next prince of Vestland?' There has been enough talk he today to fill the Ramsgate, and still you have no answer. The answer to your questions sits in that corner before you."

Illdikko pointed to the large window in the office facing the public square. There sat a twelve year old boy slouching in his chair, laying with his head on the window sill sound asleep. He slept as contentedly as a well-fed dog before a fire, oblivious to their discussion.

One by one they slowly turned their heads towards Daylin, giving recognition to the obvious. Samuel stood up and said, "Illdikko is correct. King Sa'lem commissioned Daylin had he not; we would not be here discussing this matter as of this moment. His courage, endurance and spirit has made all this possible. The King's mantle rests on his shoulders. I agree that he should be our prince."

The Loyalists recognized the implications of Samuel's words. He was renouncing all claims to the office and freeing the conscience of his compatriots to do what was best for all. His support for Daylin was critical, and this act of humility and honesty spoke volumes about his integrity. Samuel Alder's stature and reputation became legendary that day. He may not have been declared prince of Vestland, but in the eyes of all, he was a prince among men.

****

On the next day the crowds gathered in the center of the city filling the great square beyond capacity. There they stood in anxious anticipation of the news that a new prince would ascend the throne. On the platform stood Samuel and Jurius surrounded by the Rangers while silver trumpets echoed off the city walls and through the square heralding that the moment had arrived. The Eagle Legion placed itself between the people and the crowds as a precaution.

Jurius stepped forward, raised his arms above his head calming the crowds and spoke.

> As I speak, that threat looms on the horizon. It is a force that you cannot face alone. To survive you must have the support of King Sa'lem, and in order to have His support you must make great changes and reforms in Vestland. Abner defined the disease that that is killing this once great city and province. Tyranny, animated by greed, lust for power and cruelty has twisted the minds and souls of your rulers. King Sa'lem cannot and will not ally Himself with such evil cloaked in the guise of authority.
>
> Your choice is between King Sa'lem's law and your own. Ultimately, it is between liberty and tyranny. The essence of this tyranny lies in the reality that there is no just and impartial law in Urbanus. Your laws are written and enforced by those who are exempt from them. They use the law to further their corrupt and unjust ways. They are above the law and you are under its yoke. They have bribed you with a bowl of gruel and defrauded you of your liberty by offering you security at the expense of freedom. You have traded your independence for serfdom on their public plantation. If you do not take a stand and submit to King Sa'lem you will soon have neither freedom nor security.

While you slept and took your ease, Sanballat infiltrated
every facet of life in Urbania. His armada is at the gates.

Jurius bowed and waved his hand towards Samuel Alder. Samuel
deliberately stepped forward and said:

> As a citizen of Urbanus, this city is my home. I love this
> city and province, and I have been away from it far too
> long. My heart's desire is to return here to live out my days,
> but I want to live my life as I choose, not as some self-
> appointed lords wish me to. I want the fruits of my labor
> to be spent as I choose, and not to be compelled to pay for
> the slothfulness of others. Nor do I wish to be robbed in
> the name of taxes. I want the right to spend, invest and give
> my hard-earned wealth as I see fit and not in the name of
> the public good and paying my fair share. Graft, greed and
> corruption are the hallmarks of those who demand that I
> do so while growing fat off the labor of the honest man.
> I want to live in a city where all men are equal under the
> law. I want to live in a city where the law is administered
> in a just and equal fashion. I want to live in a city that
> recognizes the dignity and worth of every citizen and their
> right to choose their own path. For this to be a reality, I
> must have a prince who is of the same heart and mind.
> He must recognize that submission to the law is not only
> required of the citizen, but of the prince as well. He must
> be a prince who will promote these values and protect them
> from enemies within and without. King Sa'lem's choice for
> prince of Urbanus is also my choice; allow me to introduce
> him to you.

As Daylin stepped forward a hush swept over the massive crowd.
Necks craned, eyes squinted and children were lifted in the arms
of their parents as the people jockeyed for a better look at their new
prince. Daylin raised his hands and with a calm dignity he began his
address.

> Citizens, I come to you with a message from King Sa'lem.
> He said to me, "Daylin, I have called you, and now I have
> chosen you. It is my desire to save Urbanus and all Urbania.
> I wish to restore it and realize the purpose for which it was

created. For too long a time the lust for power and interest has plunged Urbania into constant warfare. The darkness which has ebbed and flowed over the span of time is now advancing once again from the south and the east. The evil that animates it blinds the minds, enslaves the will, and captivates the hearts of men.

"The coming battle cannot be fought with swords and bows alone. The men of Urbania have believed that power comes from the edge of a sword; but victory will require a far more powerful weapon. You will be equipped with such a weapon, as will those who join you. You will liberate the captives and prisoners from the bondage of tyranny. You will triumph over the enemy. Virtue will be victorious!"

Then He said to me, "Go in the power and authority of My name and kingdom. The words that you will speak will be my words; the deeds that you perform will be by my might, and the Jasper Stone that you carry will be the sign and seal of your commission. Those who serve Me shall serve you. Let no one look down on your youth, for I have chosen you as my servant. The foolish things will confound the wise and the weak shall conquer the strong." So be it!

Daylin then raised the Jasper Stone as high above his head as he could and waved it back and forth. The stone's light shone like the sun, sending out its rays to the farthest reaches of the crowd. It was a dazzling white light that bathed the crowd in its aura and dazzling warmth. It was as though the clouds had opened and were raining diamonds. A calm and serene atmosphere fell upon the crowd that spontaneously produced shouts of, "All hail Prince Daylin." The shouts continued for what seemed like an eternity, as they celebrated what they hoped was a new era of liberty and prosperity.

****

The celebration continued throughout the day and into the night. Urbanus was experiencing the hope of peace and security that it had not known in decades. The same wondrous effects experienced in Zunderland were now experienced in Urbanus as torn relationships were being mended. Trust was being re-established between the people and their rulers. The light was penetrating the darkness and hearts and minds were being changed. A new spirit emerged in the city as the yoke of tyranny was lifted and sullen faces devoid of hope were exchanged for expressions of joyful optimism.

Daylin retreated to the palace and began the essential and critical task that all leaders must undertake. He needed to appoint faithful men and women to assume the leadership roles left empty by the coup. The mantel of power needed to be delegated to begin the task of ruling Vestland.

Samuel Alder was the obvious choice for Chancellor. Daylin would allow him to appoint the most qualified Loyalists to the key offices of the chancellery. His grandfather, Jurius Hanner, would organize the legal system. It would be based on King Sa'lem's Law, and the entire judicial system would be reformed. The men of Zunderland would be offered positions in the military, if they chose to remain in Urbanus and, if not, they were free to return to their native Zunderland with his blessing.

However, two important questions remained unanswered. Who would fill the office of Minister of Finance, and what was to be done with Solon and his ilk?

MATTERS OF THE HEART

Souteneur was at a crossroads. He had plotted the overthrow of a Kingdom built on corruption and that corruption was the very lifeblood of his business. It was, indeed, ironic that Souteneur had effectively destroyed his business career in order to insure his personal survival. If Solon had been bad for Souteneur's seedy business, how would a virtuous Urbanus affect him? He was rapidly becoming a man without a country. If he couldn't survive under tyrants, what would he do surrounded by good men? Pride does come before a fall, and Le Parrain, it would seem, had masterfully engineered his own downfall.

Daylin sent word to Souteneur that he would like to meet with him. Like a cautious coyote, Souteneur put his nose to the wind and agreed; he was however, perplexed as to the purpose of the meeting. He had played as large a role as anyone in securing the victory over Solon's tyranny. But, as he saw it, he was neither a hero nor a villain. He was just another man faced with the daunting realties that change inevitably brings.

"Welcome, Souteneur, I'm glad that you decided to accept my invitation and come to the palace. It was, after all, a request and not a summons. I want you to feel free to enter the palace whenever you desire," Daylin said kindly.

Souteneur was astounded at how mature and dignified the boy of twelve appeared. He sounded like a mature man and a seasoned statesman. He was both perplexed and at the same drawn to this precocious youth.

"The people of Urbanus and all of Urbania owe you a debt of gratitude. There are great changes taking place and I would be pleased if you were to take part in them. You are a man of business and you possess great insight," Daylin said graciously.

"You are most kind, and I am flattered by what you say. However, I am not the kind of man that you require. I am of another breed. King Sa'lem has no use or need of me; I am a liar, a cheat and a thief. I am no better than those I pulled down. I may not suffer from their delusions of grandeur and superiority but, I know who I am," he said as a matter of factly.

"You are correct!" Daylin said, knocking Souteneur off guard by being so quick to agree with his self-effacing, if not self-serving, assessment of his character.

"However, you are also honest when it comes to your limitations! You are not defending yourself, which tells me that you have lived this life of crime because you see no other alternative," Daylin said.

"Alternative, what alternative did I have? From the time I was a boy this was my chosen life," Souteneur responded.

"Chosen, or chosen for you?" Daylin continued. "The coin that you hide in your vest pocket—you know the one that no one has ever seen; what does it represent?"

Souteneur could hardly believe his ears. Daylin had revealed a secret known only to him. "The coin, ah, well it is nothing important, only a keepsake," he said.

Daylin looked into his eyes and said, "No, it is a piece of your life's story. Will you tell me, or must I tell you the story behind it?"

Souteneur's face turned ashen. The normally strong and self-assured man was helpless before the prophetic insight of this boy prince. He decided that telling the truth was the wiser course. Lying to someone who could reveal the secrets of his heart was all but futile.

"When I was a young boy, like you, but younger, my drunkard of a father decided that he could not afford to feed me any longer. My mother had just died from a long illness and I was too young to maintain the house. I wasn't useful in his eyes and so, on one dark cold night in a drunken rage, he tossed me in the street. I walked the city knocking on doors looking for a place to find shelter, but there was none.

I continued to walk until I came to the Old Quarter and ducked into an inn. The drunks were stumbling in and out of the cold, and the coins in their pockets were so inviting. So, I decided to ease their burden and remove their heavy load. What easy targets for a cold and starving boy. I did what I had to do to survive.

This coin is the first coin that I snatched. I made a vow that night that I would never lack one again. I must have snatched three or four more, anyway, enough to buy bread and soup. I begged the innkeeper to let me sweep his floor, if he would only allow me sleep in his store room. He agreed and because I served him well, he took me in and taught me my trade. I called him Pappy, and he was more of a father to me than that drunk ever was.

He was a business man, but he was also a master thief. Through greed and guile he was connected to all the important people of the city. I learned quickly. After he died, I rose through the ranks of is group until I stood alone at the top. You know, I have never told this story to anyone including Carty," he said.

"You have an important decision to make. Will you continue down this path to destruction, or will you turn your life around and accept King Sa'lem's offer to start anew? Souteneur, true and lasting change is unseen. It begins in the recesses of the mind, the will and the emotions. But it is a decision that must ultimately take place in the heart. It is a decision that you, and you alone, must make, and it answers this question: Will you submit to King Sa'lem's Law, or will you continue to live by your own?"

Souteneur was in no position to argue. His cunning, charm and force of personality offered no defense against the truth. Either way, he was faced with the destruction of the old life that he knew, either by recompense or repentance.

"What will you choose, the push of pain or the pull of hope? You must release your father from the chains of bitterness that binds you to him. You are in a prison cell of your own making. Forgive him. Release him, or you will die having become just like him."

"I have never feared anyone or anything, but I have to admit that this terrifies me! I know nothing of the life that you offer. In these things you are the elder and I am the younger. I have experienced enough and caused too much pain for a life time. I choose hope; I will forgive him."

Souteneur bowed his knees before Daylin, who placed his right hand on his head and said, "So be it!" With these words the Jasper Stone illuminated the room with a blinding light causing Souteneur to lie prostrate on the floor covering his eyes.

The light slowly ebbed in its intensity as Souteneur slowly rose to his feet. Daylin looked intently at him and immediately recognized the transformation. Souteneur was no longer the rebel bent on self destruction. For the first time in his life he was free of the demons that had tormented him.

"I am choosing you to be my Chief Minister of Finance for Vestland" Daylin said.

****

THE HARVEST

Bringing tyrants to justice would appear to be an easy task. They have, after all, left a trail of human misery that a blind man could track. However, tyrants cannot rise to power without the consent of the people who were willingly seduced by their short term solutions to complex problems. All too often the sugar coated poison is the promise of prosperity minus pain.

The people of Urbanus had willingly eaten the crumbs from Solon's table and, so long as there were sufficient crumbs, they tolerated his tyranny. The system of dependency that he had built drew upon and was sustained by the worst elements of human nature. Bread, clean water and inexpensive housing were offered in trade for personal freedom and opportunity.

After the misery of the Great War, this exchange was welcomed without critical consideration. The people's addiction to Solon's system of dependency had been seen to be complete and had been praised as the final solution to all that ailed Urbanus. The enemy had been redefined as anyone who challenged this scheme and offered a solution based upon individual initiative and liberty. Variance to Solon's vision had been considered as treason and sedition.

This erroneous belief had fueled the fate of Samuel Alder and his Loyalist companions. Their passive opposition proved fatal as they had fled for their lives. They lost everything in their flight from Urbanus.

When former customers bring the drug lord to trial it carries the stench of hypocrisy. Thus, the people of Urbanus lacked the moral authority to pass judgment on Solon and his ilk. Solon knew this. He would now skillfully play the role of the victim, who until recently had been the benefactor of his current accusers. Like people, like tyrant. However, it was Jurius and the Loyalists representing Daylin and King Sa'lem who would now provide the needed moral authority.

Now that a legitimate government had been formed and officers appointed to the numerous posts, the task of prosecuting those accused of crimes against the citizens of Urbanus could now proceed. Jurius was given the responsibility of organizing and conducting a tribunal consisting of himself, as the presiding judge, and Samuel, Jonas, and Hans as justices. Souteneur, for his part, was tasked to employ his network to find those who had testified against Abner. The defendants would be responsible for their own defense and for answering the charges levied against them based on personal testimony, circumstantial evidence and character witnesses. They would also be allowed to question the tribunal on any subject pertinent to their defense.

****

Solon refused the bailiff's instructions to stand as the judges entered the chamber. He was making it clear that he did not recognize their authority over him. Ursus, Menteur, Lemler and Meander stood to their feet, but their cold resolute faces betrayed their contempt for the proceedings. These five were chosen for trial, the remainder of those arrested would have the choice between banishment and old Komodus. They made their choice without delay.

There was no desire for revenge in these proceedings. It was justice that was sought. Men who habitually treat their fellow man with cruelty seldom recognize mercy when it is extended to them. To their jaded eyes, it appeared as weakness and such was the case with the six that stood before the tribunal.

The gavel rang throughout the chamber commencing the proceedings. "Bailiff, read the charges brought against the six defendants," Judge Jurius ordered.

"Let it be known, that the following persons: Solon, Meander, Menteur, Echidna, and Lemler of Urbanus are hereby charged with the crimes of: murder in the first degree, conspiracy to commit murder, bearing false witness, sedition, treason and perjury.

"How do the accused plead?" Judge Jurius asked.

Solon remained defiant, refusing to stand or plead. The remainder of the accused spoke in unison and pleaded, "Not guilty!"

And so the tribunal began. Solon was the first to be called in his own defense.

"What defense do you offer against the charges levied against you?" Judge Jurius asked.

"None," Solon replied. "I have no need of a defense because you have no authority over me. This tribunal, as you call it, is a sham and a charade. I am by right the only man in this room with the legal claim to the office of prince of Urbanus. I am the only recognized authority in this chamber. You are all rebels and usurpers. Your charges against me are a tissue of lies and a fabrication of your imagination, built on your jealousy and selfish ambition. It is *you* who should be standing here in my place. It is *you* (he hissed) who should be on trial for treason, not I!" Solon said in the heat of anger.

"Your authority as prince is not based on your right," Samuel Alder retorted. It is based on your faithfulness to execute your responsibilities. Your authority is derived from your relationship to King Sa'lem. You were qualified to exercise that authority as long as you remained under King Sa'lem's authority. Your authority ceased when your submission to your Sovereign Lord and King ceased. The citizens of Vestland are not slaves to your whim and will. You were charged to protect and to serve them as their servant, not as their lord. This privilege was yours so long as you fulfilled your obligations, but you have chosen to serve your own interests. You are a petty tyrant, not a prince!"

"That is your opinion," Solon said contemptuously. "And it is an opinion based on folk tales and superstition. These are dangerous times, and such times require a strong leader. Authority is based on the strength of will, and power comes from the edge of a sword. I possess the will and the sword, and I use it as I see fit for the common good. I need no authorization from mythical sources. I possess the office and I possess the power. I and I alone, define what is good for Vestland. One man's tyrant is another man's prince. You are not fit to lick my boots when it comes to matters of state."

"Your rejection of this tribunal's authority is duly noted, but it must also be said that a rejection is not a refutation. The fact remains— it is you who are on trial here, and not this tribunal. We represent King Sa'lem and Prince Daylin, The focus of these proceedings is your alleged crimes, chief among which was the murder of Abner, the Seer, and Chancellor Doulos. What defense do you offer against the charge of first degree murder?" Jonas demanded.

Solon recoiled and pivoted in place. His face contorted and his rage could no longer be restrained. To his mind, the indignity of this legal travesty was more than he could endure. The final straw was the title, "Prince Daylin." This launched him into a fit of uncontrollable rage. He attacked the guards to his left and right, throwing punches and kicks while spitting in the direction of the judges. It took four guards to finally restrain him by binding him to his chair and gagging him. This made it impossible for the trial to continue on its present course. Judge Jurius then called another defendant to answer the same charge of first degree murder.

"Lemler of Urbanus, what defense do you offer on your behalf against the charge of first degree murder?" asked Judge Jurius.

Lemler sought a different tactic than Solon's. He was a master of manipulation and he hoped that a soft approach would appeal to the judges. They were, after all, rational men. Perhaps they would see the wisdom in his pragmatic approach to solving the problem that Abner presented.

Looking directly into the eyes of the judges, Lemler said, "Abner addressed the Brotherhood and shared what he believed was a message from King Sa'lem. The elders of the Brotherhood took his words under consideration. Our conclusion was that Abner was a heretic.

While we could abide slight variances in doctrine, the so-called 'seer' was threatening the peace and tranquility of Vestland with his outrageous claims of infiltration from the east and an impending invasion from the south. We believed that it was our duty to report his seditious claims and ideas to Prince Solon. The evidence against Abner was beyond a shadow of doubt. He stood trial and was condemned for his treason and sedition. It was our sincere belief that it was more expedient for one man to die for Vestland, than for Vestland to die because of one man."

"You mentioned 'slight variances' in doctrine, could you be more specific?" Judge Jurius asked.

"The Brotherhood believes that according to the Ancient Scrolls, Urbania will be conquered by the forces of darkness, thus ending the Age of Consummation. Any attempts to prevent the demise of Urbania are thus futile according to the ancient prophecies. A New Age will dawn after King Sa'lem's defeat of the powers of darkness. Abner believed that the 'Age of Consummation' would not end with the destruction of Urbania but with King Sa'lem's intervention by defeating the powers of darkness and heralding a new age. We are right; he was wrong," Lemler said smugly.

"And this is what you refer to as a 'slight variance in doctrine?' So, are you suggesting that you did not view your decision as a threat to your popularity, power or position? Were you not concerned that Abner's views and powers of persuasion would cause dissension in your ranks?" Judge Jurius asked intently.

"We are a very tolerant society. Abner's views were his own, and he was free to express them. However, we could not reconcile his interpretation of the Ancient Scrolls with his claim that he was sent to us by King Sa'lem. He was old and perhaps a bit senile. Our real concern was his seditious ideas and the harm that such ideas would create if spread in the name of sound religion. Moreover, our fears were justified when the correspondence between Abner and Sanballat was produced in court," Lemler said.

"What proof do you offer of the validity of this correspondence?" Hans asked.

"The document was sealed with the seal of Mara. What other proof do you require?" Lemler replied.

"Something more concrete, perhaps a personal confession or the confession of co-conspirators. The justification for your position is all too circumstantial. What if the document was a forgery, or what if it was planted and false witnesses were paid to implicate an innocent man?" Samuel asked.

Echidna and Menteur were then asked the same questions and, in turn, gave similar testimony. They all agreed that Abner had been, indeed, guilty as charged, but they could not offer any proof of his guilt other than their mutually shared opinion.

Meander denied any knowledge of the matter. He said that he had not been involved in any of the deliberations concerning Abner before or after his addressing the Brotherhood. Meander, true to form, intended to survive by any means possible. The truth was a luxury that he could not afford.

The tribunal was interrupted by a messenger who signaled his presence to Judge Jurius, momentarily halting the proceedings. A cohort of Eagle Legionaries entered the chamber accompanied by two very curious, but very familiar individuals. A woman and a young man bound in chains were escorted before the bench and placed before the judges. Judge Jurius immediately recognized the pair and asked, "Why are these two individuals brought before this tribunal?"

The Tribune answered and said, "They both testified against Abner the Seer and produced the document bearing the seal of Mara, Sir!"

"Is this true? Did you testify against Abner the Seer, and did you produce the document in question?" he demanded.

"Yes Sir, we did," the woman answered meekly.

The seeds that they had planted in secret were now beginning to produce a harvest of fruit in broad daylight. The duo then openly testified as a last resort, hoping to save their lives in exchange for cooperating with the tribunal. Judge Jurius asked for their names and they answered Karola and Raymaris.

The eyes of Lemler, Echidna, Menteur and Meander locked onto Karola and Raymaris, frozen in the fearful realization that their carefully crafted web of lies was about to be exposed.

Judge Jurius asked the two to sum up the testimony that they gave under oath against Abner. To their horror, they now realized that the man whom they claimed that Raymaris had pick-pocketed was the presiding judge of the tribunal who would determine their fate. They were trapped. No lie, no matter how eloquent could save their flea-bitten hides.

The presiding judge, Jurius Hanner, was one and the same with the man falsely accused of treason. The letter was a fabrication given to Karola and Raymaris by Ursus, and they now confessed. They had knowingly perjured themselves, and it carried the death penalty. They sought from the court the one redeeming element that they had refused to extend to Abner and all the innocents who perished because of their lies and deceit—mercy.

The accused were given one last chance to produce further evidence in their defense, but they refused to speak. The rest bowed their heads in recognition that their conspiracy and lies had been unmasked. The respectable public image that they had so carefully created was exposed for what it was—a maggot infested corpse of hypocrisy.

A short recess was taken while the judges deliberated the obvious. The verdict was not the question before them, but the fate of the accused. They were painfully aware that justice is as much perception as it is reality. They agreed that they render their verdict in the name of King

Sa'lem and that the sentence be based upon His law. A precedent for justice needed to be established in Urbanus. The city's history of partiality and arbitrary enforcement of the law had to end if the city was to heal.

"All rise," said the Bailiff. The six defendants remained seated, resolute to the end. Karola and Raymaris stood with heads bowed hoping that their gesture of respect would curry favor in the eyes of the judges.

"It is the verdict of this tribunal that the defendants: Solon, Menteur, Meander, Lemler, Karola, Raymaris, Echidna of Urbanus be found guilty of first degree murder, conspiracy to commit murder, perjury, and bearing false witness in the case of Abner, the Seer, and Chancellor Doulos. The tribunal has seen fit to dismiss the additional charges against the defendants given the gravity of the crimes already stated. It is our judgment that the defendants forfeit their lives as penalty for taking the life of another. We render this sentence in the name of the Great King Sa'lem and according to the principle of His law that states: 'All men bear in the image of the King. The one who takes a life must pay for it by forfeiting his.' So be it."

The tribunal recognizes the cooperation of Karola and Raymaris of Urbanus in these proceedings. Their appeal for mercy has been given due consideration, but it is the opinion of this tribunal that their request for mercy be denied. It was their premeditated plan to conspire against Abner, the Seer, and to bear false witness against him. Their false witness was instrumental in his unjust death and the deaths of Chancellor Doulos and his associates. Furthermore, the defendants gave testimony under oath with full and complete understanding that perjury and false witness carried the death sentence. Therefore, the defendants are found guilty and sentenced to death in the name of the Great King Sa'lem.

"The sentence is to be carried out tomorrow at high noon. The defendants will be taken to the Pit and incarcerated there without hope of escape. So be it!"

****

The news of the tribunal's verdict and sentencing of the five defendants spread throughout the city like an early morning fog off the Ramsgate. Prince Daylin and his entourage would be present at the proceedings. Prince Daylin desired to use this opportunity to create a much needed object lesson for the citizens of Urbanus. Solon and his ilk had created a standard of judgment by which they themselves were now being judged. However, a different standard was desperately needed, and this required a new and different attitude towards law and justice.

The people of Urbanus had been conditioned by tyranny and oppression. Solon had used the law as his chosen instrument to persecute his enemies under the guise of the administration of "justice." This practice had been no more than an opportunity for revenge and reprisal.

Prince Daylin desired a new attitude and understanding of justice in Urbana. No one would be above the law, and law and justice would be administered equally. There would be no favoritism or partiality shown to those who had violated the law due to social rank or privilege. Mercy would be extended to those who had shown mercy, and the full measure of the justice of the law to those who had not.

****

It seemed as though the entire city was in attendance that day, although the stadium held but a fraction of the city's population. Men, women and children from every walk of life appeared not knowing what to expect from this new order of things. Prince Daylin stood on the great platform that had witnessed untold numbers of such spectacles and, raising his hands above his head, addressed the people.

> Citizens of Urbanus, a new day and a new order are dawning in this great city. It is a day in which the light of truth will restore the meaning of things that have been twisted and distorted by and for the privileged elite. From this day forward, law and justice will no longer be words synonymous with tyranny. No man shall be deemed above the law, and no one shall be deprived of justice. Urbanus will be ruled by King Sa'lem's law. It is a law which is

universal, just and absolute. As your prince, I am submitted to that law. It is my privilege and responsibility to serve and to protect you. I am not your lord; I am your servant.

We come here today to witness the administration of justice for crimes against the people of this city, against the servant of King Sa'lem and on behalf of the innocents who suffered from them. We take no pleasure in these events, and I command that there be no ridicule of the accused and no celebrations of their fate. I am saying this for two reasons: one, it is with regret and not revenge that we administered the ultimate penalty for the crimes committed. There are no victors when the law is broken; there are only victims. Secondly, these men and this woman go to their deserved fates, but they are not the only guilty parties here today. The citizens of this city are equally guilty. So long as you benefited from the injustice and oppression of your former prince, you also tolerated his tyranny. And when the innocent were condemned and paraded through the streets, you gladly cheered and participated in the evil which you yourselves had condoned. Like sheep led by a wolf to slaughter, you closed your eyes and opened your mouths for the crumbs that fell from his table.

Today, I declare a new order in Urbanus. It will bring the needed reforms to restore liberty and justice to Vestland and to all Urbania. The weak and the least among us will not be ignored by us in our haste to make right the wrongs of the past. We will help bear the burden of the weak, but the weak will also bear their own load. No partiality will be shown to anyone when it comes to access to good food, clean water and safe housing. We will help those who cannot help themselves, but the able-bodied will work or they will not eat. The Patrikos will no longer lord it over you and treat you as serfs on their estates. Many of which were gained by the usury of the Trapezites. These properties will be returned to their rightful owners according to the ancient boundary markers and title deeds. Taxes will be paid by all, but taxes will no longer be raised and spent in the name of the common good, while robbing the hard worker in the name of sharing the wealth. The hardworking man will spend his own money and the state will not spend it for him. I am declaring a year of jubilee. All debts in the Vestland are hereby forgiven. Each citizen will receive a fresh start.

There are many who have committed crimes against the people of this city who will not meet the same fate as these who stand before you today. They were given a choice between the Pit and banishment. There are over two hundred of them, and they will be banished from Vestland for ten generations. They will be taken by ship to Naxosis with their families. They may take whatever possessions with them that they can carry. But their descendants must never return until the term of banishment has expired, under penalty of death."

As Prince Daylin instructed, there were no celebrations that day. The compliance of the crowd signaled the acknowledgment of their guilt and their complicity in the death of so many innocent victims. In sharp contrast to Abner's death, the condemned were neither stoned nor ridiculed. With hollow eyes and somber faces, the condemned marched to their fate to the sound of clanging chains. Only Karola and Raymaris, who were overcome by fear of old Komodus, cried and whimpered for pity. The sentence was carried out without further protocol. Prince Daylin's object lesson was thus forever etched on the stony hearts of the citizens of the Vestland.

****

The Consummation

There is an old saying among the Brotherhood: "New levels, new devils!" Urbanus was about to fully comprehend the meaning of this well-worn saying. A new day and a new order had dawned, but the populace was about to meet a new challenge, the likes of which made all others pale in comparison.

The tumultuous events of the day had ended. Prince Daylin was exhausted. He had rehearsed his lines so many times, in his mind that his head were numb. He needed sleep. The people had accepted the prospects of a new order, at least outwardly. Time would tell. It is one thing to take the people out of tyranny and quite another to take tyranny out of the people. A night's sleep brought the prospect of a welcome respite from the pressures of the day, but sleep would have to wait.

Just then the Jasper Stone began to glow intermittently with an intense light that illuminated his bedchamber. Prince Daylin leapt from his bed and shouted, "Guards, guards, come here now!"

He knew what it was. The utter blackness of the night and the absence of stars and moon created a smothering darkness that could be felt, reminiscent of the cave of bitter waters. There was a presence about it, a personality that animated the foreboding atmosphere. While the city slept safely and securely within its massive walls, Prince Daylin, the Rangers and the field marshals gathered in a central chamber of the palace.

As dawn awakened on the Ramsgate, the sun wrestled the darkness for a foothold on the landscape. The sun had risen, but to the watchman's eye, the twilight created an aura of dusk. Surveying the river, Daylin froze in a paralysis of fear. He rubbed his tired eyes in disbelief as he observed the ominous shapes of thousands of Black Ships that floated silently on the still waters of the Ramsgate. They had appeared like an evil apparition without sign or signal. For two days they had advanced like a plague of locusts from the western shore of Vestland toward their objective. The Ganza's infiltration of the westerns towns of Camesa, Santos and Pontus assured the invaders that there was little chance that Urbanus would receive advanced warning. The towns had been overrun and subdued without resistance. The massive force had moved toward Urbanus with an eerie silence and deadly determination. The Great Southern army was as mobile as it was silent. Sanballat and his terrible armada had arrived.

"Sound the alarm! Sound the alarm!" the watchman cried.

****

High above Urbanus the Artrax circled the countryside like vultures surveying the city's defenses and probing for weaknesses. On the western, northern and eastern walls, armies of untold numbers had surrounded the city, filling the horizon. Dressed in uniforms of black and red, their heads were crowned with silver helmets donning blood-red plumes. Black chainmail mesh covered their faces, making them indistinguishable from each other. Behind them marched the ashen faces and sinister, soulless eyes of untold numbers of Ghouls, their gaping, distorted mouths dripping with the fiendish stench of death and decay.

Without a word, the enemy hordes came to an abrupt halt just beyond the reach of bow shot, and stood motionless before the city walls. Hour after painful, fitful hour, they stood at attention like pillars of stone. The tension inside the city escalated and fear began to give way to panic. Imaginations ran roughshod over reason.

The silence was finally broken as sharpened stakes were abruptly driven into the ground and the captives taken from the western towns of Vestland were impaled alive upon them. The deathly silence was soon displaced by the tortured cries of impaled victims. Thousands of men, women and children screamed and writhed in pain to the perverted delight of their tormentors. The walls of Urbanus echoed with the sounds of the victims' agony, filling the city with horror and dread. Gradually, the screams of torment slowly diminished to pitiful whimpers as death became a welcomed release from their diabolical torment. The cold, carefully calculated effect upon the citizens of Urbanus had been achieved.

The unnatural twilight of the frigid winter's morning was now intensified by enormous black clouds of arrows and projectiles of shrapnel fired from whirlwind catapults. Drums and the beating of spears on shields created a deafening cadence that echoed off the city walls, creating a tangible terror. Dissonant trumpet blasts filled the city sending soldiers and civilians alike scurrying for their weapons as a lethal torrent of death rained down upon them. Fires erupted throughout the city from the whirlwind catapults' incendiary bombs. Desperate men and women rushed to save their homes, only to meet their fate from a volley of arrows that indiscriminately sought their fatal mark.

****

"The safety of the people comes first. I will leave the defensive measures to you. I will coordinate the evacuation of the citizens," Prince Daylin said.

"Evacuation? But where will they go?" asked Sandor.

"To the Pit," replied Daylin. "Souteneur can make all the arrangements. There's another city down there that few know of. Call for Souteneur and bring him here at once."

Urbanus resembled a helpless cork in the middle of an ocean tempest. She was surrounded, and the center of the city was a blaze. The Eagle Legions rushed to the walls, returning the enemy's fire with an initial volley of arrows and projectiles launched from strategically placed ballistae that shredded the enemy's center. The onslaught was momentarily repelled as the enemy retreated in order to regroup.

While the battle raged on, Souteneur revealed the numerous entrances to the Pit that were previously known only to him. Multiple tens of thousands could survive in the Pit for a few weeks, if supplies held. Water flowed through the subterranean honeycomb in abundance, but the Pit had not been designed to occupy the entire population of Urbanus. Disease was always a specter that loomed over the besieged city. The sick and the wounded would need medical attention. Illdikko was given the responsibility of coordinating it. With studied skill and calm resolve, she quickly organized a make-shift underground hospital. There would be no shortage of patients.

Using his old network, Souteneur quickly communicated the necessary instructions to the people. They were told to bring only what they could carry—food, bedding and medicine being the top priorities. Like ants retreating from the oncoming cold of winter, the frightened population scurried down the crude passageways into the large caverns. They needed little encouragement to move quickly. In matter of a few hours, the women and children were safely underground. All able-bodied men were expected to join the ranks of the Eagle Legions. The Pit was uncomfortable, but it was a safe refuge from the terror that loomed above them.

****

"They are regrouping and probing for a weakness on the walls and I believe that their next major assault will come from the water front. The walls are weakest there, and we have to plan to resist their assault. We have three to four hours at best. Bring Tribune Unitas here at once," Wain ordered.

"We will need to hold the waterfront at all costs. We must neutralize their ships before they land their forces," Wain said pensively.

"Yes, but how? We have no means of preventing it," Lothair said.

Just then, a legionnaire entered the room and said, "Sir, Tribune Unitas is here as ordered."

"Tribune, we are at a critical disadvantage. Do you have any means of neutralizing the Black Ships on the waterfront?" Wain asked.

"We have a very old and well kept secret," responded Unitas. "It is a weapon that was created by the founder of Urbanus centuries ago. Only select commanders of the Eagle Legion know of it. It is a weapon of last resort, fashioned for times like these. We call it the 'Dragon's Breath.' It is a mixture of oil, naphtha and pitch which are loaded into large barrels and then piped through a hose to a bellows. The mixture is then lit and sprayed onto the enemy ships," he said.

"Has it been battle tested? Does it work it? What is its range?" Quill asked.

"It has been tested, but never used in battle conditions," Tribune Unitas responded. "Even in the Great War, Urbanus never faced a threat like this. We will soon know whether it works or not. It is maintained routinely and is ready to be employed even as we speak."

The "Dragon's Breath" was well hidden within the parapets of the city's walls. On each of the city's walls, three nozzles were precisely angled over the span of the battlefield and waterfront. The nozzles could cover nearly a one hundred and sixty degree pattern.

The order was given to prepare the weapon.

****

Wain stood looming over the map of the city's defenses in a trance-like state pondering his options. His eyes widened and an expression of inspiration lit up his face. "What are you thinking?" Lon asked. "What do you see?"

Wain paused, drew a deep breath and asked, "What is the last thing such a powerful force would expect us to do?"

Quill responded and said, "Open our gates and leave the safety of the city and then go out to meet them head-on!"

"Precisely and that's why we may have an opportunity."

"What do you mean?" Lon asked.

"We came into the city by way of Beth Craven did we not? The enemy does not know of the underground passageways that lead into Urbanus from Beth Craven. We entered the city with Souteneur's help and by stealth and surprise we overcame Solon. We can use the same passageways to attack the enemy's rear positions and destroy those whirlwind catapults. We will attack them both from the front and the rear on the north and the east walls," Wain explained.

Lon looked into Quill's eyes and then said, "Maybe, just maybe, this will work!"

"Find Carty and have him, along with a dozen of his best men, proceed to Beth Craven at once and scout the enemy's position," Wain ordered.

"Who will lead this expedition?" Quill asked.

"This is a task for Samuel Alder, his Loyalists, and the archers of Zunderland. This is their native soil and they will relish the opportunity to defend it. Have them prepare to leave as soon Carty and the scouts return."

****

Carty and his scouts cautiously made their way through the Pit's labyrinth of tunnels to Beth Craven. Beth Craven was three and half dextors from the walls of Urbanus. The trek was slow and tedious given the twists and turns in the tunnels. And then there was Komodus. When anyone ventured too close to his lair his low pitched growls echoed through the caverns. Most of the passage ways leading to the dragon's lair had been blocked over time, but not all of them, and occasionally a man would go missing. It wasn't difficult to get lost in the subterranean maze. Sooner or later old Komodus would find him. The people of Urbanus had a saying: "The Wolf will hear it, the Eagle will see it, and Komodus will smell and eat it!" The fate of the man who lost his way in the maze was sealed.

At last their arduous trek came to an end as the portals that gave them access to Beth Craven came into view above them. The air was thick with tension and apprehension since they did not know if the enemy was occupying the ground above. Slowly they made their way upward and then with trepidation slid the cap stone covering the tunnel aside and peaked over the rocky ledge surveying the enemy's position.

To their amazement it was a far better situation than they could have hoped for. There was a half dextor distance between Beth Craven and the enemy's rear position. Sanballat's frontline troops had been amassed at the walls leaving only auxiliaries and their supply train at the rear. Carty nodded his head in approval and winked to his fellow scouts and then motioned with his right hand as he pointed downward to the maze. Without a word they hastily made their way back to Urbanus.

****

Samuel Alder and his bowmen impatiently waited for Carty's return. Each bowman carried twice his normal quiver of arrows along with a flask of pitch and strips of linen. Once fashioned together they produced incendiary arrows. This was the weapon that would prove to be the demise of the whirlwind catapults.

Carty finally arrived and reported to Samuel. Their spirits soared with eager anticipation at the prospect of attacking the enemy at his most vulnerable point. It was a bold and daring plan and they knew that although they could not deliver a mortal blow to such an overwhelming force, they might severely damage the enemy's morale and buy precious time for Urbanus.

"Men of Zunderland, this is our hour! Rise to meet it with courage and resolve knowing that we fight for what is good and just. We fight for freedom!" Samuel declared.

The battle plan was set. Samuel ordered half of his archers to attack the enemy troops from the rear. The other half would ignite their arrows and target the whirlwind catapults that were wreaking havoc on the city. Through the tunnels of the Pit they marched accompanied by Carty and his spies. Carty had stubbornly refused to be left behind, saying that this was his fight as well and he was not going to be denied an opportunity to strike a blow.

****

The southern walls of Urbanus were the weakest because the commerce of the city flowed through its docks located there. It had evolved over time due to necessity and was arbitrarily built and designed to meet the needs of commerce, not the military. The Eagle Legions had long known that the pride of Urbanus was also its bane.

In the meantime, several thousand Black Ships eagerly waited for the order to land their forces and storm the waterfront. Eagle Legionnaires, in turn, apprehensively occupied the parapets high above them, anxiously awaiting the order to release the Dragon's Breath and the ballistae.

At once a deafening trumpet blast signaled the order to release the Dragon's Breath. It shot upward and cascaded downward on the Black Ships that were preparing to offload their forces. Instantly the incendiary shower engulfed the ships transforming their decks into infernos. Men burst into flames becoming ghastly torches and everything and anything that was combustible ignited. The tortured screams of the enemy filled the air as chaos, confusion and choking fumes overcame them. With no route of retreat open to the majority of the ships, they were trapped as the flames spread from one ship to another. Those who managed to pull anchor and set sail became fire ships and floating torches, plunging like white-hot knives into the heart of the fleet. The spreading, scorching heat of the crucible was intolerable, sending even the legionaries in the parapets for cover. The attacking armies on the three walls needed no messengers to inform them of the fate of their comrades. The smoke and the odor of burning flesh was signal enough that one of their three fleets had been decimated.

****

The flames that engulfed Sanballat's forces were easily seen from Beth Craven. The black smoke filled the sky line, while flames of orange and red filled the night sky, creating a ghastly hue. This was the sign that signaled that all was ready. Samuel ordered the attack. The enemy was completely distracted and in disarray making the rear guards an easy target for the bowman of Zunderland. Volley after volley of arrows found their mark. The whirlwind catapults now became an easy target for their fire arrows. One by one they were set ablaze putting an end to the infernal misery and death that they had rained down on Urbanus.

The enemy soon realized the source of the attack and sent reinforcements from the front to deal with the threat. Several thousand Ghouls and a division of Sharokhan were sent to counterattack. Samuel knew that it was impossible to hold the line against such odds so he ordered a retreat. Carty led them down the portals and into the safety of the tunnels. The Sharokhan assessed the situation and hastily sent fifty of their number to reconnoiter the tunnels. But Carty had wisely anticipated that the enemy would discover the portals of Beth Craven and pursue them. He therefore chose the passageways that led straight to the lair of Komodus.

"Follow me!" Carty exhorted. "Tell every man to stay in line and not to stray off the path." And follow they did. A few brave men formed a rear guard action to protect the retreat by releasing volley after volley of arrows. It was difficult enough for their blind foe to pursue in them in the darkness of the tunnels amidst the lethal showers of arrows, but they had no idea what awaited them.

When the last man was safely through the passageway, Carty ordered the great iron door to be shut and barred. With a thunderous clank the door closed, signaling the doom of the enemy. The closing of the door resounded throughout the cave. None of this escaped the attention of Komodus, who sniffed the air with his tongue and detected what he relished the most, fresh blood. The Sharokhan were disoriented and hopelessly lost in the maze of twisting tunnels. Soon the air was filled with cries of agony and terror as Komodus chased them down and devoured those who dared to trespass in the lair of the "Watch Dog of Urbanus".

****

"No doubt they have ships, troops and siege equipment in reserve. They still possess significant strength, should they attempt to land their armies that now stand on our western walls. They must have two or three other fleets of the same or greater size," Wain said.

"I think you right in that," replied Tribune Unitas. It will only be a matter of time before they place their reserves in position at the southern wall for another assault. We only have enough Dragon's Breath to repel one more assault. The mixture cannot be transported safely from parapet to parapet and it must be mixed on site. However, it can be employed from the parapets on the remaining walls. These are armed and ready. If they try to breach the walls, we will roast them like pigs."

"If I were in their place, I would focus my attention on the north wall, Wain said. It's the weakest of the three. The Salisians must have given them intelligence on our defenses. Even if Samuel's attack on their rear positions is successful, I think we can expect a heavy bombardment from their reserve whirlwind catapults preceding their next attack."

"I agree," said Tribune Unitas.

"I believe that this is a task fit for Lothair. I know that he can be trusted to hold his ground and marshal our forces. This is no time for second guessing ourselves. The north wall must hold or the city is lost," Wain said apprehensively.

Wain's words were keenly prophetic in their accuracy. The night's sky was soon illuminated by tens of thousands of missiles all destined for the north wall of the city. Balls of burring pitch and caltrops—or the crow's foot—were hurled over the walls at the defenders. The flaming pitch ignited whatever it touched and the crow's foot crippled any unfortunate soul seeking to extinguish the flames or to flee from them. Fighting the flames became a losing battle since there was far more available fuel than water. And so Urbanus burned.

The barrage lasted for hours, giving no respite to the defenders. There was no time to eat, drink or rest. The defenders clung to whatever cover they could find, biding their time and waiting for an opportunity to counterattack. Suddenly the bombardment ceased as quickly as it had begun. An eerie quiet settled on the burning city only to be broken by the sounds of drums and lances beating against shields. The rhythmic cadence of marching infantry, replete with crude scaling ladders, approached the wounded city. The gruesome enemy hordes salivated in anticipation of administering the fatal *coup de grâce*.

But the attackers had no idea what awaited them. The fate of their comrades, vanquished by the Dragon's Breath remained a lingering mystery to them; however, it was one that would soon be solved. They would soon see to that. Boldly and with extreme confidence, they approached the north wall. After all, they reasoned, what could survive such a holocaust? On command, their ladders were readied and prepared to scale the walls. The Ghouls drooled with delight as they fanaticized the joys of their promised feast.

In the meantime, Lothair had taken command of the north wall and ordered the Dragon's Breath to be readied. The last stores of the elements comprising the Dragon's Breath had been loaded into the pressurized vessels and prepared for discharge. He then gave the order to fire, but to the defenders' shock, nothing happened. The deadly fluid leaked from the nozzle, but it lacked sufficient pressure to discharge the mixture.

Gripped by shock, the defenders watched helplessly as the flammable liquid flowed down the outer face of the north wall and to its base. Closer, ever closer the enemy marched.

Lothair immediately discerned their predicament. Instinctively and without the slightest hesitation, he snatched a small torch and ran headlong into the parapet, "For Kingdom, for Glory, for Dominion!" he shouted, thrusting the burning torch and his own body into the volatile black mixture, instantly igniting the Dragon's Breath in a savage fury of exploding flames.

As soon as the first enemy ladder touched the wall, a tidal wave of flames rushed out and over the attackers creating an avalanche of annihilation. The flames were so overwhelming that they consumed friend and foe alike. In seconds the heat's intensity slowly weakened and eroded the structural integrity of the wall, causing it to crumble, creating a massive breach.

Lothair's act of heroism bought precious time for the defenders, but the price was high as many brave and valiant legionaries sacrificed themselves that day to protect their beloved Urbanus.

The enemy's losses were catastrophic, but there was no thought of retreat. Replacements were already on their way from Kronia. The cost was more than acceptable to Sanballat, who had given orders that anyone who retreated including his generals were to be executed. The Ganza kept careful watch over the military and anything that they deemed as a sign of weakness or cowardice was made an example. This served as a stern warning to all his forces. It was not uncommon for generals to be impaled before their soldiers. Sanballat did not waver or compromise.

For the defenders the loss of so many of the legionnaires was a blow that they could hardly hope to recover from. Unlike the enemy, their resources were limited and time was not their ally. Lothair's sacrifice was a temporary victory that had simply postponed the inevitable.

****

Time was of the essence. Prince Daylin had the command center moved underground safe from the fire-storm that ravaged the heart of the city. Wain and the military leaders advised him that the best course of action was to escape to Beth Craven and then to Zunderland, but Prince Daylin refused. He knew that the enemy would soon follow after them and that many of the people would perish on the journey. They would make their stand here in Urbanus, despite the grim reality of the outcome.

"They are marshalling their forces, as we speak for another major assault, and this time it will come on all fronts. We do not have the resources to defend the walls. The facts are that there are far too many of them and far too few of us. We will fight to the last man. Expect no mercy from the enemy and give none. There will be no prisoners taken, not even the innocents hidden in the Pit. It is a war of annihilation not conquest," Wain said grimly.

"Gather every man who can fight and assemble them in the public square," Prince Daylin ordered. "I want to address them."

"It's far too dangerous; it's not wise," replied Tribune Unitas.

"This is no time to speak of danger. Wisdom will be judged by its outcome, not its assessment of the situation," Prince Daylin said firmly. Those in ear shot could not believe that this was a mere boy prince of twelve years old. "Assemble the Legions at once!" he commanded.

The Legions and any able-bodied man capable of fighting stood together at attention as Prince Daylin climbed the palace steps to address them. The air was filled with smoke. The once beautiful buildings of Urbanus flickered with flames like lamps bathing the square in a grotesque light. The air was tense and each man was deeply immersed in introspection. Like a drowning man, the sum of their lives passed before their eyes as they waited: sorrow, regret, marriage, home, the birth of their first child, the death of a parent, the loss of a friend or loved one—the good things that they should have done and the gratitude they felt for not having done all the wrong that they might have.

"I would have, I could have, and I should have, if only I had..." they mused. The collective cacophony of recollection and regret engulfed them like a riptide, sweeping them out to sea as it does to all men when death knocks upon their door. Animals expire never pondering what could have been. It is for men to inquire and ask, "Could my life have been lived differently?"

But Prince Daylin broke their trance-like state of introspection, and said:

> Soldiers of Urbanus, I need not tell you what your eyes can plainly see. The question before us today is not how nobly we have lived our lives. The question is how nobly we shall end them? The sorrow of regret will not serve us in this hour. It is our resolve to die for what is just, merciful and true that will sustain us. No man can determine his destiny

or his fate, but he can decide how he will face it. The line between courage and cowardice is very thin. Yet we must acknowledge that we stand here today because of our rebellion against King Sa'lem. What we see is the outcome of rebellion to King Sa'lem's law. Urbanus sowed the wind and reaped the whirlwind. Her glory is gone, but her future yet remains. I was told by King Sa'lem that this battle could not be won by the sword alone. It would require weapons of an invisible kind. King Sa'lem cannot intervene until we all acknowledge our rebellion and renew our covenant with Him. He will not take sides in this conflict, but He gladly invites us to join Him in conquest. We must be unified in spirit and intent on one thing, that whether we live or whether we die, we are committed to serving Him. If my words have meaning, and if you have an ear to hear them, bow your knees and acknowledge your rebellion, ask His pardon and swear allegiance to the Great King. Choose this day whom you will serve.

Laying their weapons aside, one by one they bowed their knees and raised their hands. Tears streamed down their faces as battle hardened soldiers and seasoned workmen individually confessed their wrongs and pledged their allegiance to King Sa'lem. It was a scene that had never before been recorded or recollected in the history of Urbania.

"Rise! In the name of the Great King Sa'lem, I declare that you, by this act of humility and submission, are hereby His covenant people and legal subjects. We stand as one. So be it!"

With these words, the sun broke through the horizon, announcing a new day. Despite the lingering canopy of smoke, they could see that the twilight had lifted and that the day was clear. But the interlude of calm quickly gave way to the impending storm. The sound of drums and the beating of lances upon shields thundered once again against the city walls. Each man ran to the walls, prepared to fight to the end. But this time they would not fight for Urbanus alone but for King Sa'lem and for each other.

Bravely, and with renewed determination, they mounted the walls and surveyed the looming tidal wave of enemy forces. They were greater in number and fire power than when the siege had first begun. The enemy commander had ordered that the banners of Mara bearing the insignia of El' Shay'tan—the Red Dragon—be waved signaling the all-out assault against the mortally wounded city. Archers stretched their bow strings to full tension as the whirlwind catapults ratcheted their torsion boxes to the full in preparation for releasing their instruments of death and destruction. The opening salvo of artillery would soon be followed by a chorus of infantry that was prepared to scale the walls.

****

But in that instant an interlude of calm penetrated the suffocating twilight. And just as suddenly, a silent hush settled over the Pit. Simultaneously the cries of the children, the moans of the suffering and the chatter of the multitude ceased. All eyes and ears perked to the roar of the tumultuous, inexplicable silence that engulfed them as they pondered its meaning. In the distance, a faint clicking sound could be heard and a powerful authoritative voice commanded:

"Come forth and live, the hour of reckoning and recompense has come!"

Illdikko did her best to keep the spirits of her nurses high while they comforted the wounded, but the fact remained that the situation was hopeless. Their care and kindness had prolonged the lives of the wounded and eased their agony, but death lurked like a specter over the dark Pit.

The clicking sound became louder and louder resembling thousands of hardwood sticks banging together. The clicking became almost deafening, and then the source of the sound appeared like an apparition. Slowly, the brittle mass of bones moved in unison animated by an unseen hand as if by the mysterious but commanding presence of an invisible maestro.

As the spell-bound audience watched, an army of dead bones emerged from the wretched lair of old Komodus. Komodus was fond of flesh and blood, but he had an innate disdained for the bones that had littered his subterranean haunt, and he preferred to heap them in enormous piles. But it was from these very piles of dead bones that a living host appeared, beckoned by the voice.

Paralyzed by fear and the prospect of imminent death, the people looked on in a trance-like state of shock and horror. Lifeless human bones were morphing into skeletons and as soon as they came together, muscles and tendons appeared on the bones. Finally skin covered the muscles and tendons, forming bodies. Silently they ascended from the depths of the Pit to the surface of the city, marching down the streets of Urbanus and mounting the walls. The ramparts were now defended by the bones of the innocent dead just as Abner prophesied.

The commanding enemy general raised his sword high and, with deliberation, brought it downward and ordered the assault. His sword had no sooner finished its downward arc than the sky over Urbanus erupted like an exploding star. Like an enormous boulder thrown into a placid pond, the ripples of energy swept out from its epicenter. The intensity of the light blinded the enemy troops while the wave of energy cut through their formations like a sickle through ripe wheat.

Dismembered bodies fell where they stood, never knowing what hit them. The Black Ships on the Ramsgate watched the spectacle in terror as the wave of energy instantly came towards them, cutting away their rigging and sweeping the decks clean of men and equipment, while the surging waters of the Ramsgate boiled beneath their hulls engulfing them.

The Black Ships went to the bottom as though the waters of the Ramsgate refused them buoyancy. The Black Ships on the Western Sea fared no better suffering the same fate. The speed and power of the blast left the defenders on the wall awestruck and wondering—'*What was this awesome force?*' The indomitable armada lay wasted. Not a single survivor was to be seen.

While the defenders on the walls looked to the heavens, an opening appeared that spread across the sky revealing horsemen on white stallions numbering in the hundreds of thousands. They were armed with flaming swords and golden shields. They circled Urbanus seven times and then abruptly came to a halt. Above them a regal figure dressed in white linen, donning a breast plate of gold, and wearing a three-tiered crown appeared before the host and said:

> "I have heard your contrite plea and the vows that you have made this day. I have pledged to help those in need, to aid those who call upon Me and who are, indeed, My covenant people. I am King Sa'lem and My word is law. You have sworn to keep my law and, therefore, I will keep my promise to you. Know this day that your enemies were conquered not by your might, nor by your power but by My strength. This battle has been won, but the war is not yet over."

King Sa'lem then reared His horse and signaled His army to follow him. They circled Urbanus one time and then set a course to the south.

****

Mara was now eerily quiet, like the unsettling quiet before a storm. The clamor and commotion of the previous days of preparations for the invasion of Urbania were past. The city now resembled a ghost town with only an occasional merchant upon the streets. While the skies shimmered on the red horizon and warm winds arose from the surrounding desert wastelands, Mara waited in a suspended state of anticipation for news.

Sanballat paced back and forth in his personal quarters free from the distractions of his daily routine, anxiously awaiting the news that Urbanus had been vanquished. "At long last" he mused. The coveted prize was now his and his alone!' He could now proceed with his unrequited desire—to rebuild the temple and cleanse Urbania of all inferior races.

Finally, he, and he alone, would be the honored one, worthy to declare the unchallenged dominion of the Great One, El' Shay'tan over all Urbania. Today I conquer Urbania, tomorrow the eastern lands. They would fall like autumn leaves before the fury of his forces. His predecessors had dreamt of this day, but it was he who would make those dreams a reality.

This was Sanballat's day and it was *his* victory, and only his. Yes, Sanballat the Great had succeeded where others had failed. He would share the credit with no one.

He could barely contain the euphoria that welled up in him. He beamed with the pride and the arrogant self-confidence of a strutting peacock. He reveled over the recent events of the invasion, all the while admiring his image in the large bronze mirror that hung upon the wall.

It was a beautiful day. It was only fitting that nature should celebrate his victory with a warm gentle breeze blowing off the Amar. The warmth of the sun and the gentle breeze conspired to create an intoxicating mood of tranquility. Peace was a rare commodity in Mara.

As he looked out over the city standing transfixed in a state of euphoria, he scanned the northern skyline and his eyes beheld a most peculiar sight. It appeared at first to be a small bright cloud, but the skies were clear and it seldom rained in Mara. Was it a divine sign? Were the powers that he had conjured converging on his chosen city to celebrate his victory?

But as the cloud came closer, it slowly took on the appearance of a man's hand, and the hand seemed to take the form of a fist. Bewildered by the sight, he focused his eyes by squinting for a more precise view. "How strange," he thought. "It was but a single cloud in an otherwise clear blue sky..."

While Sanballat stood mesmerized by the approaching image, the small cloud suddenly exploded growing exponentially in size and speed. It was transformed into a massive sandstorm sweeping across the desert sands. It was now an ominous force that sent a wave of energy slicing through Mara like a sharp blade through a ripe melon.

His face was instantly etched with fear. He gasped for breath as the very air was sucked from his lungs. His pride and arrogance were now exchanged for a countenance of sheer terror. His arrogant face dissolved into an oozing mass before his mirror. In an instant, Mara the magnificent was vanquished. Her gates, buildings and gardens were leveled by a force of incalculable power. Not one stone in the great walls that surrounded the city was left standing. Mara was now being judged by her own standard of judgment. The fate that she had long planned for Urbanus was now executed upon her. She was now drinking the very poison that she had prepared for her sworn enemies.

As her gates crumbled and fell with a whimper, a vast host in the heavens circled the city seven times. Trumpets blared to a resounding chant of: "Kingdom, Glory and Dominion." Just as quickly as they had appeared, the great host vanished. Virtue, after all, had been victorious and darkness was vanquished.

****

The war-weary survivors of Urbanus gathered in the great public square. They were dazed and numbed by the siege and its fantastic end. Victory was theirs, though vicariously won. "Victory," they thought; what a hollow word.

And then they recalled those immortal words, "The glory of war is for scribes to immortalize, for little boys to fantasize, and for the soldier to agonize. Victory in war is a myth embraced by those who have not paid the price for it."

The glory that once was Urbanus was gone. She had paid the ultimate price for building her house on sand. Her great buildings were now empty burned-out shells covered with ashes. The tyrant's dream was now a relic of the past, soon to be forgotten.

But that same cruel dream is never far from being revived by men who ignore the supreme reality that the key to maintaining liberty begins with a commitment to self-government rooted in the Law of the King. It is the foundation that supports the four pillars of the kingdom. Those who cannot rule themselves are destined to be slaves ruled by tyrants.

All choices have consequences. The ruin that was now Urbanus gave stark testimony to this eternal truth. As the Toon proverb says: "One does not plant a pumpkin seed and expect to grow a giant oak."

For now I bid you farewell, dear reader. May wisdom guide you on your journey. It is but the beginning—the dawning of a new day...

****

Postscript

The events described herein happened just as I witnessed them. All men view the world through the lens of their values and convictions, prejudging the outcomes. This lens makes objectivity as rare as the mythical unicorn. This humble scribe has taken great care to relay the events of those times as honestly and as accurately as possible. I trust that they will serve you well as a guide in your journey through Urbania and the times to come. Learn her lessons well and set your course on the path of wisdom.

Now lest I leave you wondering what became of Prince Daylin and the Vestland, I want you to know that Prince Daylin became the man and the prince that King Sa'lem had predicted. Historians of Urbania refer to his reign as the "Golden Age of the Vestland." It was a reign built on the foundation of King Sa'lem's Law. Mercy, justice and kindness were its hallmarks, and peace its legacy. Daylin was more than a prince. He was the servant-prince of his people. There is far more to this great story, but it shall come at another time.

For now I bid you farewell, dear reader. May wisdom guide you on your journey. It is but the beginning and the dawning of a new day.

So be it...

GLOSSARY

Abner the Seer	The Seer from the Northern Kingdom, King Sa'lem's messenger.
Agatha	Lady of the underworld who provided guidance and enlightenment for Daylin
Age of Acquisition	A time of and peace and prosperity in Urbania making it the target of the Dark Lords of the Southern Kingdom.
Age of Consummation	Last age of Urbania marked by tyranny and war.
Age of Knowledge	A period of 1000 years dominated by Argos when men sought knowledge at the expense of goodness.
Age of Laws	Time period of 1500 years dominated by Kronos when men sought order and created laws after their own understanding. In order to restore order, truth and preserve the race men King Sa'lem gave his laws to Kronos as recorded in The Book of Kronia.
Alderhaus	Samuel Alders house in Zunderland
Aletheia	Capital city of the Northern Kingdom and home of King Sa'lem
Amar	The life sustaining river that flowed through Mara the capital of the Southern Kingdom
Amenuus	Solon's personal scribe.
Aphrodinia	Lady of the underworld who sought to deceive Daylin.
Arche	Sanballat's counselors.
Argos	Capital city of the province of Terrarinia
Artrax	Winged Bat like creatures used by Sanballat for reconnaissance.
Ballistae	A large crossbow that fires long darts the size of spears and used as field artillery.
Beth Craven	Ancient ruins located northeast of Urbanus
Bjorn Svengarrd	Renowned woodsman and boat builder of Mattydale in the Great Forest.

Brantford	Capital city of the province of Lamburg
Brotherhood	Religious order who were known for their speculative prophetic interpretations of the ancient scrolls.
Brothers Fairn	Swain, Hull, Quill who were Northern Rangers.
Cannibas	The ferocious cannibals of Beth Craven.
Carty	Souteneur's right hand man and chief lieutenant.
Chancellor Doulos	Chancellor of Urbanus and loyal to King Sa'lem.
Charite	Prince Solon's daughter
Crosia	A city and a region of southern Hupsominia.
Crosian	Ethnic group of southern Hupsominia
Crow's foot, caltrop	Anti-personnel weapon consisting of triangular barbs, side is always pointing upward.
Cyrus Hanner	Father of Jurius Hanner keeper of the temple cornerstone and the Jasper Stone.
Daylin	Grandson of Jurius & Molly Hanner, the "Chosen One," destined to restore Urbania.
Dextar	A unit of measure the equivalent of 15 inches.
Dextor	A unit of measure the equivalent of 1.5 miles.
Doron Fay	School mate of Daylin.
Doulos	Chancellor of Urbanus and ally of Abner and King Sa'lem.
Dragon's Breath	Fire weapon used to defend Urbanus.
Drakontas	The name given to Neri for his legendary conquest of the dragons as the first ruler of Urbanus
Eagle Legion	Urbanus' professional soldiers of elite infantry and cavalry
Echidna	Elder of the Brotherhood
Einheit	City of Zunderland home to the Loyalists
Eirene	Compound of the Brotherhood located in Urbanus
El' Shay'tan	The red dragon, god of the Southern Kingdom
Esteria	Capital of Esterland and center of the Age of Acquisition 2500 years—
Esterland	The eastern most province of Urbania located on the southern bank of the Ramsgate

Eternal Age	First Age of Urbania comprised of one kingdom ruled by King Sa'lem
Forge of Lair	Renowned for its fine swords
Francesca	A throwing axe
Frid	Tributary of the Ramsgate lading to Mattydale
Ganza	Sanballat's secret police
Ghouls	Evil spirits inhabiting the bodies of the walking dead feeding on human flesh
Glennore	Name of Macoot's village used by outsiders.
Gordo	Captain of Ursus's Salisian Thema
Hans Jurgen	Loyalist compatriot of Samuel Alder
Hextor	Equivalent of 1.25 acres
Huiedien	Village of Hupsominia home to Sandor and Illdikko
Hull	One of the Northern Rangers.
Hupsoma	Capital city of the province Hupsominia
Hupsominia	Central province of Urbania
Illdikko	Ethnic Crosian from Huiedien of Hupsominia, wife of Sandor.
Inn de Fosse	Dwelling of Vixeena
Jasper Stone	The Jewel entrusted to Cyrus Hanner and given to Daylin
Jonas Eberhardt	Loyalist compatriot of Samuel Alder
Journey of Sorrows	The retreat of the survivors from Urbanus after its fall to Nergal Anshar
Jurius Hanner	Son of Cyrus Hanner and respected business man of Brantford of Lamburg.
Kampia	The first name of Urbanus.
Kantos	Fourteen foot lance
Karola	Mother of Raymaris the notorious con artist and thief.
Keil	Neri's slave master and captain of the fishing boat.
Kingdom, Glory, Dominion	The Ranger's motto.
Knarr	Gigantic Brown Bear of the Great Forest

Komodus	The great dragon that roamed the labyrinth of Urbanus
Kronia	Province of Urbania situated on the southern bank of the Ramsgate.
Kronos	Capital city of the province of Kronia and the name of the Law Giver
Lamburg	Central province of Urbania renowned for its husbandry.
Law & Covenant of Kronia	King Sa'lem's law given to Kronos.
Lon of Mark	Northern Ranger known for his wisdom.
Lon of Mark	One of the Northern Rangers.
Lothair	Northern Ranger, second in command and brother of Wain.
Loyalists	Disenfranchised citizens of Vestland living in exile in Zunderland.
Loyalists	Refugees and outcasts of Urbanus driven to Zunderland for sanctuary by Solon's tyranny.
Macoot	Toon chieftain, husband of Ursula
Mara	Capital city of the Southern Kingdom
Mattydale	Home of the men of the Great Forest
Meander	Ruthless leader of the Patrikos
Men of Invar	Thrace, Doran, Jergen, Egbert, Derek and Owen who were Northern Rangers
Menteur	Elder of the Brotherhood
Migdal	Pass through the Mystic Mountains of the Great Forest
Minex	An incremental measurement of a dextar equaling 1.5 inches.
Moldovinia	Northeastern province of Urbania
Molly Hanner	Wife of Jurius and grandmother of Daylin
of Fange	Desolate swamp and wastelands on the southern bank of the Ramsgate located in Kronia.
Mount Regius	The highest point in elevation in the city of Urbanus.

Mt. Medus	One of two mountains where Kronos cut the covenant with the people of Urbanus, literally Mount of Blessings.
Mt. Tage	One of two mountains where Kronos cut the covenant with the people of Urbanus, literally Mount of Curses.
Mystic Mountains	Forbidden mountain range of the Great Forest
Naxos	Capital city of Naxosis a province of Urbania.
Naxosis	Naxosis a central province of Urbania located on the Southern bank of the Ramsgate.
Nergal-Anshar	Emir of the Southern Kingdom during the Great War with Urbanus.
Neri	Fisherman who slew the dragons and became the founder of Urbanus.
Nestleton	The Toon name for Macoot's village.
Noraxe	The emblematic knife worn by Northern Rangers symbolic of their service to Sa'lem.
Old Quarter	A section of Urbanus known for its crime and sordid underworld.
P'Ones	Pinecone like creatures of the Toon forest that act as the Toon's eyes and ears.
Patrikos	The wealthy elite of Urbanus.
Pertrosia	Province of Urbania located on the southern bank of the Ramsgate
Petros	Capital city of Pertrosia Province of Urbania
Phalanx	A fighting formation consisting of interlocking shields and spears forming a mobile defense.
Pit	The underground city of Urbanus; hideout of Souteneur and home of Komodus.
Place de Mort	Place of public execution in Urbanus
Poison Arrow	A tactical maneuver employing a feigned retreat by cavalry consisting of a deceptive counterattack done by swiveling in their saddles and firing arrows at the pursuing enemy.

Prophecies of Arnos	Ancient prophecies given by Kingdom predicting the restoration of Urbania
Quill	One of the Northern Rangers.
Ramsgate	The largest river of Urbania
Rapids of Noor	Rapids on the Ramsgate descending from the Great Forest to Lamburg.
Rasputitsa	Common people of Vestland
Raymaris	Son of Karola the street urchin a con-artist and pick-pocket
Rill	A small brook; a rivulet; located on the north shore of the Ramsgate leading to Brantford.
Romona	House maid of the Hanner household.
Saga of Argos	Scrolls containing the history of Urbania
Salisia	A city and a region of Hupsominia
Salisian	An ethnic group of northern Hupsominia.
Samuel Alder	Leader of the Loyalists of Zunderland
Sanballat	The emir of the Southern Kingdom
Sandor	Ethnic Crosian from Huiedien of Hupsominia, husband of Illdikko
Shabakosh	Wastelands bordering the Southern Kingdom.
Sharokhan	Elite special forces of Sanballat
Silca	The living stones of Urbania.
Solon	Tyrant Prince of Urbanus
Souteneur	The godfather of organized crime in Urbanus
Strategos	A Thema's overall commander
Tagmata	Professional army regiments
Teleios	City of Hupsominia
Telos	A tributary of the Ramsgate in Hupsominia
Terra	City of the province of Terrarinia
Terrarinia	A northern province of Urbania
Thema	Small localized professional army groups
Theodus Cane	Friend and business associate of Jurius Hanner
Toon	Little people of the Great Forest renowned for their wisdom.

Trapezites	The corrupt bankers and financial brokers of Urbanus.
Unitas	A Tribune of the Eagle Legion of Urbanus
Unser-atem	The life force of Urbania
Urbania	The Kingdom comprised of ten provinces of which Urbanus of Vestland was the greatest.
Urbanian Calendar (Months of the Year)	Jervis Kanta Vida Vertrag Gerda Montag Solarum Mintra Vistra Ornos Zona Dura
Urbanus	Capital city of Vestland and the greatest of the ten cities of Vestland.
Ursula	Wife of Macoot, chieftain of the Toon.
Ursus	Ruler of Hupsoma who came to power by assonating the legitimate ruler
Varun	Son of Jurius Hanner and father of Daylin.
Verfall	Strategic valley in Zunderland providing the only direct land route between Zunderland and Vestland.
Vergil Bonner	Friend and colleague of Jurius Hammer of Brantford of Lamburg.
Verna	Capital city of the providence of Zunderland
Vertrag	The fourth month on the calendar of Urbania or the month of covenant.
Vertrauen	Tributary of the Ramsgate leading to Einheit
Vestland	Western province of Urbania whose capital city was Urbanus.
Victus	Filed Marshall of Urbanus' Eagle Legion vanquished at Verfall.
Vim Tuner	School mate of Daylin.

Vixeena	One of Souteneur's ladies of the night; the seducer of Wain
Wain	Captain and leader of the Northern Rangers, brother of Lothair.
Whirlwind Catapult	A light and mobile catapult employing no counter weights but using manpower instead to destroy fortified walls with heavy objects from long distances.
Zestor	Salisian soldier who attacked Ildikko.
Zunderland	Province of Urbania and refuge for the Loyalists

The Sacred Law and Covenant of Kronia

The sacred Law, solemn Covenants
And Statutes herein conceived,
Revealed and recorded, written and prescribed,
By the Sovereign King, Sa'lem,
Are hereby and forever declared to be,
In eternal and ineffable harmony with
The King's own perfect and peerless nature
And compassionate disposition...
Eternal, immutable, irrevocable
And universally binding.

The said Laws and Covenants,
Like the life-giving blood of the lovely sun-fed
Fruit of the vine, are conceived and sustained in
Flawless solidarity with the King's
Own inimitable and beneficent nature,
Even as the soft life-sustaining soil
From which the same sweet fruit is drawn.

****

Furthermore, let it be declared, understood,
And gratefully received, that the pure nature
And benevolent disposition of these
Laws and Covenants,
Like the same life-sustaining fruit,
Heretofore described, neither knows,
Prescribes or condones any other intent,
Or supreme purpose on earth,
Than to produce, perpetuate and preserve
Goodness, growth, life, freedom, health
And true happiness for the cherished souls
Of the sons and daughters of man.

Sovereign Transcendence, Loyalty and Submission

As a fundamental premise
And governing principle, absolute, unconditional
And free, submission to the rule and right
Of the Sovereign King, Sa'lem,
Is the unalterable bedrock of the Sacred Law.
The sacred Law is equitable, honorable and good.

Let it be herein declared that
The Sacred Law is Just and right and noble, and as such, Cannot,
should not, and shall not ever conspire
To engender doubt, denial or defeat
In the hearts and lives of its humble subjects.
Nor can it be, or should it be,
Ever reversed, remanded or rescinded.

The same irrevocable and irascible Law is,
As a testament to its own virtue and veracity,
Hereby declared to be, and evidently known to be,
Manifestly true and transcendent,
Operating and demonstrating its inherent integrity
And goodness in the very practice
Of its implementation in the daily lives
Of its subjects, or, by contrast, in the case of transgression,
In the disastrous, self-denigrating and self-destructive behavior of
Those who may be inclined or persuaded,
Of their own nefarious and self-serving volition,
To oppose and violate its righteous tenets.

Furthermore, let it be declared and known
That the sacred Law,
Flowing as it does from the benevolent nature
Of its preeminent Source, is eternally worthy,
Wholesome, desirable and commendable,
And can, therefore, only ever be inherently, entirely
And everlastingly good.
As such, and as it is written, the Sacred Law is

Inherently inviolate, perfect and incontrovertible,
Preeminently consistent with the inexorable
Principle heretofore affirmed,
That the said Law is the perfect expression
Of the very Person and nature of
King Sa'lem Himself,
And is no less believable and verifiable,
In its own mysterious, but observable
And visible nature, than is the inseparability
Of the sun from its own emanating
And life-sustaining rays.

Therefore, let it be herein affirmed that
The sacred Law
And its adjoining precepts are fundamentally good,
Right and wholesome, bestowing blessing,
And restoring goodness and freedom
To the human heart
Of every obedient and loyal subject.

On the basis of such an inherently
Beneficent disposition, revealed, reflected
And delineated in the present Law,
And flowing from such a pure and unfathomable Source as
King Sa'lem Himself,
The congenial expectation of
Fealty, loyalty and willing submission
Cannot, and must never be seen
As a particular and mitigating hardship,
But rather a just and equitable provision
For one's ultimate happiness.

Such loyalty and submission,
If its truest nature is to be discerned,
Is, and should be received, as the truest and fullest expression of freedom.
As a self-evident truth and governing principle,
That the gracious 'yoke' that a subject

(And not the Source) is compelled to bear,
Is designed not to impose hardship
Or to destroy, inhibit or enslave the one
Who is called and constrained to bear it;
But is, rather, a 'yoke' that its Sovereign Lord
Deigned and designed to protect,
Preserve and benefit for all generations,
The very life and happiness of the one who is called
To bear its blissful burden.

The structure and supervision of the supreme and
Sacred Law of Kronia is thus conceived
And duly administered by the
Sovereign King, Sa'lem,
In the form of a sacred, binding covenant.

The sacred covenant, thusly conceived,
Is the worthy sign and personal, penultimate
Promise to every loyal subject
(Irrespective of clan, gender, reputation, moral or social status)
That the content, declarations and terms
Contained in the Law are as true
And trustworthy as the One from whom they flow,
And for whose supreme and ultimate glory
They are freely and graciously bestowed.

Principles of Hierarchy—Image and Likeness

Let it be forever known in every kingdom and in every age,
That these Sacred Scrolls and inspired Prophesies
Reveal and declare, and established as true and irrevocable,
This one, self-evident, fundamental, absolute and undeniable decree,
That King Sa'lem, uniquely, eternally, and without equal or rival,
Is the only true and worthy Sovereign Creator and Supreme Ruler
Over the known universe, in all of its glorious expanse
And all-transcending, self-attesting harmony.

Let it also be known, recorded and declared that
The kingdom of earth, and the men who dwell therein,
Are, by King Sa'lem's flawless will and free intention,
And in the Exercise of His everlasting, just and gracious dominion,
Created in His perfect likeness, being thereby endowed
With every quality and perfection that is, without exception,
Reservation, variation, or trace of discord or disharmony,
The perfect and visible reflection of His own Nature.

And let it be understood and affirmed that the truths and declarations
Contained within these Ancient Scrolls and inspired Prophecies,
And hereby revealed to the children of men,
Are neither arbitrarily conceived nor frivolously offered by the
Sovereign Lord,
To human kind, but are freely and lovingly bestowed,
In concert with the King's own peerless and pure intention,
And in perfect accord with the King's own sovereign,
Self-sustaining nature and gracious disposition.

Let it also be affirmed and agreed that these same eternal truths
And tenets, hereby revealed, like their immutable and transcendent
Sovereign,
Are the true offspring and pure reflection of His own free and loving
nature,
To be sure, but shall be received, valued and exercised
By the sons and daughters of men with the same perfect love and care,

And the responsible and gracious exercise of obedience by which, and with which, they have been, forever, lovingly and freely bestowed.

For the created thing, while possessing and reflecting the very
Image and likeness of its Creator, cannot and must not presume to think
Or claim to possess the same eternal perfection and infinite, self-sustaining and self-creating independence, so as to seek to usurp or otherwise snatch, with finite hands, the infinite grasp and grandeur of its Creator... No more than as a child can never rightly Claim to have born his own father, or a simple clay pot to have formed the Potter's hands, to which it can but attribute its fragile existence.

Internal Precepts for Self-governance

Having created man thus, and so happily and freely endowed him
With every good gift to assure a peaceful and harmonious existence,
It is but proper and reasonable that the gracious, eternally wise and beneficent King Sa'lem
Should, in keeping with His own perfect and peerless nature,
And His equally benevolent disposition, seek to bestow upon His creatures
The freedom and ability, and, in accordance with His own nature,
The benefit and privilege of free and fruitful self-governance.

Indeed, it should not be surprising, nor should it seem unreasonable,
That the children of men, having been conceived and created
In the glorious image of their good and just Sovereign,
And thus endowed with every good quality pursuant to His own Nature,
In order to fulfill and to enjoy the eternal benefits and blessings
Of such privilege, should be expected to graciously comply
With their Sovereign's good and just intentions.

And so it should be, by submitting happily, freely,
And with a gratitude born of humility to his beneficent Sovereign's
Just and beneficent commands, and that,
Within the liberating refuge and restraint of willing obedience,
That every blessed child of man can and should enjoy
The perfect, enduring and self-perpetuating
Freedom and fulfillment of his Sovereign's presence.

Obedience—ethical moral relationships:

Indeed, a proper, respectful and grateful relationship with one's Sovereign
Is the only sure provision and prerequisite that can
And must, in turn, create the kind of responsible,
Industrious, respected and trustworthy citizen, co-laborer, courtesan
And model champion for the cause of all human endeavor,
Providing the only lasting assurance for the happy and peaceful
Survival, success and propagation of the human race.

The man or woman who is obedient, then, to His Sovereign,
And who acknowledges and respects the goodness and presence of his
Sovereign's signature work in the lives of others; and the man who,
being so freely and similarly endowed with the gifts of strength, skill,
intelligence
And a wholesome and grateful regard for his family, friends and neighbors...
Those two men, having both gratefully received and dispensed
Such purity and goodness toward others are one and the same.

The treacherous and perilous profile of darkness and lawlessness
Is visible to the heart and eye of man only when he turns
In ignorance and wanton foolishness from the free and
Glorious night-dispelling light of the eternal King.
The lawless acts that such treachery and turning breeds
Defies explanation, and is as mysterious as the forces
That conspire to create and perpetuate its hideous shadow.

The heart of man is susceptible to such darkness
Only when it retreats from the purity and protection of willing
Submission and obedience to the Truth, and yields to the
Terrible and self-refuting reality of lawlessness
Which is everything more, and nothing less than
The utter disregard and disdain of righteous authority
And willing abuse of true freedom.

Lawlessness is the unwitting, howbeit willing offspring
Of the marriage between self-worship and self-possession.
It is the unholy and perverse coronation of self-love and self-loathing.

In its unbridled disdain for sovereign authority, it bears and boasts a liar's
Mask of self-seeking mockery, naked independence and false integrity.
It blinds its own eyes and bites off its own blasphemous tongue,
Drowns goodness, and violates purity in the lifeless
Pursuit and perverted parody of its own pale deceit.

The stark and sterile nature of lawlessness and rebellion
Floods Eden's garden with the stench of rancid fruit and naked
Innocence clothed in lusty shamelessness; at last,
It stirs the fires and flames of a lover's wrath.

In truth, the price of freedom, freely spurned, can be none else
Then righteous retribution and the helpless, faceless cry
Of wordless choking grief in the face of unrequited love,
Or the senseless loss of a beloved child.

Statues Ordinances

Such is the nature and raw inevitability of lawlessness,
And so is born necessity of the Law,
At once the step-child and unwilling school-master of
The righteous King, Sa'lem, who, with pure intent
And gracious unprovoked desire to rescue and redeem the
Wandering child of man, conceived a just and
Unrelenting way to find, pursue, and lead him home again.

And so, in order to rectify and restore each wandering waif,
And casting radiant pearls about his dusty feet of clay,
The gracious King, Sa'lem, beckoned His eternal Spirit of unseen Light,
Beseeched every celestial cherub and every saintly soul,
And behooved every loyal scribe to convene and catalogue
A clear and binding list of changeless laws and principles
To govern, guide and gain the heart of man.

And so shall it be written and forever resolved,
Declared the righteous and merciful King,
That these clear and unchanging laws,
Proceeding from the very Soul and Heart of Heaven,

Shall henceforth, like the daily dawning of the glorious sun,
And brightness of midnight's Morning Star,
Enlighten, enliven, chasten and console,
Pursue, pardon, protect and preserve
Every precious soul of man.

Yet let it be at once and forever declared that
Should (ever) the weak and wandering soul of man,
When the darkness seeks to beguile and beckon
His fragile self, urging him to strive to rise above the sun,
Or raise his blinded eyes and spit into the vaulted sky...
Let him remember from whence he comes,
And who the Potter is who formed the lifeless clay!"
And so spoke King Sa'lem,
And thus the ancient Law was born, declared,
And brought to bear, but for his lasting good and happiness,
Upon the cherished souls of Man:

"Observe these laws, the blessed Voice declared
And echoed through the celestial spheres...
With the dawn of each new day, in every clime and every way,
Come rain or wind, or darkest night, or every gruesome glint,
Or devilish urge to stay and staunch the all-embracing Light.
Take to heart to follow every clear command,
And do, and be, what Light and Right decrees."

The Supreme Laws of King Sa'lem

Live every waking breath in willing submission and obedience
To your blessed King and sole benefactor, Sa'lem, the eternal Sovereign
And Source of all that is good and right. Be faithful and loyal
To Him, alone, and obedient to His every command.

Seek to learn to love and serve the Sovereign Lord of Life,
To heed His words and do His will, and to draw from His
Eternal well of kindness, living water to sooth your heart,
And cool and quench and satisfy your thirsty soul.

Meditate upon His right and gracious laws night and day,
To find wisdom and strength and comfort, Finding in them your daily
bread and soul's delight.
Follow when you cannot see the way; listen when you cannot hear;
Wait patiently in the night for the breaking of the day;
Seek to know and please your King, and to do His will,
For in doing so, you will receive the fullness of His presence,
And the wisdom that he freely offers every seeking heart.
Keep fear, worry, criticism, hatred and anger at bay;
Be thankful and grateful for every gift that He bestows;
And every blessing and benefit that He freely offers,
Seek to freely and generously share with others.

Be faithful and loyal to family friends and neighbors,
Respectful of who they are and all that they possess. Freely love
And freely forgive your fellow man, for you also have received
The purest of love, forgiveness, mercy and kindness
From the great King Himself.

Binding Precepts and Practices

And finally, practice these binding precepts and teach them
To your children, and your children's children:
Love the King above all others; love and respect your wives.
Respect the elders of your clan; honor and befriend your neighbor.

Work diligently; share your wealth and wine with the poor.
Comfort, console and care for widows in their distress.
Bind up the wounded and care for the sick; be generous to all.
Cancel all debts every seven years;
Befriend and receive the stranger and foreigner;
Eschew evil, and always practice what is good and right;
And above all, keep your hearts pure.

Sacred and Solemn Promise—The Binding Oath

"These precepts are the essence of the Sacred Law.
In keeping them there is great reward.
Obey and practice them, and you will know
The fullness of the King's divine blessing,
And the benefits of life and peace
And eternal happiness."

The Subject's Solemn Oath

"I hereby swear faith, allegiance, love and loyalty
To the Sovereign Lord, Sa'lem.
I further promise, on penalty of death,
Faithfulness to Him, and obedience to his every command.
And will, by the force of his strength and guiding Presence,
And as long as I am granted life and strength,
Live according to these supreme precepts,
And teach them to my children. So be it.

Consequences of Disobedience, Defiance and Disloyalty

"I, King Sa'lem, the only true and Sovereign Lord
Of all the earth, and every earthly kingdom
Of every child of man and nation of men,
Hereby declare, by sacred, solemn oath that:

The person who disdains and denies his sovereign King,
And who refuses to submit to His loving rule,
Rejecting and repulsing His laws and precepts,

Rebelling against his Sovereign's eternal and benevolent truth,
By which and for which he is created, conceived and destined...

And who, refusing forthwith and forever more to either
Receive mercy for himself, or to extend mercy, pardon and grace
To others, or to humbly seek to be forgiven,
Or to offer the same to his fellow man...

Shall, without hope of mercy, be judged and condemned,
And shall, in this life, suffer a whirlwind of affliction from
The storm of rebellion that he has sown...

The same rebellious soul shall, furthermore, and forever more,
Suffer eternal remorse and separation
From his Sovereign Lord, and from any and all others,
Whose love and forgiveness, grace and goodness,
He has so blatantly and cruelly denied...
And shall, himself, forever forfeit such love and happiness,
In this life and the next...

Let the one who has ears to hear, hear.
And let him who has nothing to offer, come
And freely receive...

And the one who, though seeing and well-clothed,
Is blind and naked in the presence of the King,
Humble himself and come,
For the day is near.
The Sovereign King, Sa'lem's Law and Oath,
Conceived in love and goodness, and bound with the
Unbreakable cords of mercy and everlasting justice,
Eternal, unchanging and irrevocable,
Is hereby forever solemnly sealed So be it.

Saga of Argos

Tana'khil I.—Prolegomena—Pre-Dawn

Mik'raim 1.
It is written in the sacred parchments and shiftless sands of time
That the sublime Law-giver and Righteous Ruler of the eternal Realms
Decreed to forge an everlasting, sacred bond
And freely bestow upon a beloved, unborn race
The blessed, pure-born gifts of friendship, brotherhood,
Virtue, peace, humility and blissful harmony...

Mik'raim 2.
And so it was, that the Eternal Spirit of the Northern spheres
Pierced the fragile fringe of time, graced the emptiness,
Grasped the black and lifeless void, and, like a life-giving Potter
With lifeless, joyless clay, fathered man, perfectly conceived,
Bestowing strong and loving hands, and purity of heart,
And thus To create, quicken and awaken breathless blessedness...

Mik'raim 3.
And so it was that the new-born earth first birthed and blossomed;
Peace filled the verdant plain, and rain and river and rock, were locked
In blessed harmony; and then, from shapeless forms, life and voice,
And sacred sounds and scintillating sights were forged,
Bursting, blushing forth, from nothingness, baptizing light and laughter
For the beauteous daughters and blessed sons of men...

Tana'khil II.—Creation and Conception

Mik'raim 1.
Silence, sweet pilgrim of a long-forgotten realm! Rest your tired,
Night-encumbered, tear-filled eyes, and *Listen* to the sacred
Raging silence of earth's first dawn, when the searing, soothing, life-giving

Light of day first burst upon the cold surface of the primal earth,
aroused the sleeping form of prepubescent man, awaking his finely

hewn and Blood-bequeathed mortal frame to the stranger soil and
solace-filled Expanse of time...

Mik'raim 2.
Be still, I say, and listen closely, softly as the wind-named Man
Progenitor of the blessed sons of men, first freely woke
To the friendly warmth, and splendid light-inducing celestial symphony
Of the spheres, each whispering sweet infant songs and finely tun'ed
Harmonizing strains, filling new-born earth with perfect, undulating,
Heart-fulfilling hues of peacefulness...

Mik'raim 3.
Watch once more as the curious planets' peerless brother, frail mortal
Witness to earth's happy birth, peered with perfect eyes upon the bright,
Blessed beauty of time's beginning ... And watch as young sons of men,
Offspring of the prototype and priestly caretaker
Of the Righteous Realm, drank deeply, yeah freely, from the pure,
Blessed streams of paradise, and who, scaling it dome'd heights and
reveling lamb-like,

Mik'raim 4.
Sit silently, again, and watch the first primal glint of dawn, before deep
Darkness held the ancient world in its death-like grip, as, unashamed,
Searing bursts and bright white threads of laser light pierced
The cold surface and hidden lifeless lesions of mother earth, as, in a rush,
Like the child-like cry of purity and innocence, bursting from
Its mother's tender sacred womb, as a fresh glimmer of hope was birthed...

Mik'raim 5.
And so was ordained, and so it was thereafter when
The glorious kingdom of men first drew breath,
All bathed in blessedness, built with bright, rightly hewed stones,
Keenly cut from the clear rock face of the mountainous
Northern realms of light where virtue reigned and the strong clans of
Mother earth each drank from a common, crystal clear and peaceful
stream...

Tana'khil III.—Corruption and Conflagration

Mik'raim 1.

But then it came, late one black day, at the setting of the Western sun,
A cold, sinister ancient form crept out of deep darkness, and,
Seizing the light within its vile grip, like *Komodus's* deadly, diseased claws,
A ravenous form, prowling the dark underworld in the dead of night...
So the dark creature aimed his hungry, yellow predatory eyes and fetid fangs
At the helpless child of man, and pounced upon its fickle prey...

Mik'raim 2

At once, every gruesome guardian of the grateful dead gave up its
Cherished post
Unleashing death and darkness upon the new-born world, and slowly,
The predatory, pestilential wave of darkness swallowed light, spewing
pride and
Hate, cruelty and blood-lust, crushing hope and happiness;
Hideous, fiendish hordes gorged themselves in venomous glee upon the
shallow souls of men;
The very pillars of Light shifted and shook, but stood firm...

Mik'raim 3.

It is recorded that with the relentless death-bearing storm of darkness,
The eternal soul of man, though shaken, survived the unholy
onslaught of evil,
But not without a long death-struggle, nor bitter sacrifice and loss of grace;
For when the darkness came, strange and savage thorns of greed and envy,
And self-exalting pomp, ravaged and pillaged the tender heart of man,
Weakening his fragile, fearful flesh and will, and stealing innocence...

Mik'raim 4.

Yes, it is true; the spreading darkness obscured the sun's bright light,
And spread a cold, death-like, bloodless pale upon the fragile face of earth,
But the pain and pallor of the all-seducing plague went deeper still...
Fetid currents of sickened self-will flooded the pure and placid,
Freely-flowing streams of the kingdom, silencing the strong voice of

Spirit and Reason until, at last, the Silent, sacred, silver cord was severed, And vile hellish fiends loosed their rabid brood.

Mik'raim 5.
There have been self-serving 'prophets,' and there will be again, who,
Seeing the death-dealing veil of seducing darkness,
Turned and tuned their deadly, deep-deceiving craft to the
Sickly voice of doom, offering their seditious soul-seducing aptitude
And spirit-trade to earthen spirits, babbling hollow Prayers and slobbering oaths to the Dark Lord,
Cruel Keeper and Vile Custodian of the wanton
Southern wastelands of earth...

Mik'raim 6.
For while the prophets prayed and preyed, themselves whitewashed tombs,
Dark, billowing clouds without rain, Luxor's living dead and unrighteous
Guardians of Hades's horrid, hidden gates...
With black hearts and lying tongues,
Growled and groveled in wretched glee, releasing death from its putrid den,
To feast and forage, blood-crazed, upon the sons of men...
And all the while, the same writhing, wretched hellish horde,
Beckoned and beguiled by the ancient Dragon, seething and serpent-like, hatched a vile and wicked scheme to wrest Truth and Righteousness from The Sovereign Source and timeless Throne of Light.

Prophecies of Arnos

Tana'khil I—The Coming Light

Mik'raim 1.

The darkness, though pernicious and pervasive, penetrating and
Permeating every layer and hidden corner of the Kingdom,
Could yet not cancel out the sun or blight the Eternal Light of Day;
The hearts of men would not soon recover from the spreading doom,
but the rock-hard helm of truth and justice stood fast as the rock-hard
fortress of truth and justice would once again prevail,
Certain coming and the promised appearing of the Child of Righteousness...

Mik'raim 2.

What is written in these sacred Ancient Scrolls is certain, irrevocable;
And the formidable pillars of Righteous Rule are firmly anchored in the
The ever-knowing, time-transcending, all-embracing, truth-dispensing
power of The Unseen One, The Great King Sa'lem,
The supreme Source and Fountain of Self-sustaining Love.
The One known throughout the kingdom of men
And to the descendants of the Southern clans.

Mik'raim 3.

But the blind, brutal forces of deep darkness will ne'r renege in their
Relentless scheme to seize the power and usurp Sa'lem's Righteous throne,
Nor will they bow to the wishes and warnings of His truth-sayers, but will,
By unholy decree and blasphemous lies, seek to pacify and purge the
Light-filled land of honor and truth, spawning and spreading seditious
Falsehoods, exchanging truth for lies, and wolves for sacrificial lambs...

Mik'raim 4.

So it is written, and so it shall be,
As pomp and pride, and power impose their collective, seductive gaze
And mesmerizing slow sleep of death upon the unsuspecting
Hardened hordes, before the dreadful, awful, final day,
When endless black gales assail great Urbanus's fragile shores,
And assault, with evil's full and gathering force, her weakened citadel...

Mik'raim 5.

But eye has not yet seen, nor heart known, nor ear heard...

Nor can the darkness perceive, blinded by its own ignoble, dead intent,

The ancient secret of the lion and the lamb,

Or the spell-binding choice of children over sages,

Or the pitiful plight of strong tyranny in the face of child-likeness,

Or the sweet song of the weak, when the strong lay whimpering insure defeat...

Tana'khil II—Admonitions

Mik'raim 1.

So beware; strong evil will not retreat quickly from the Light...

Darkness is a subtle foe ... It was not with an accursed scream or

Awful shout that pernicious evil first burst upon the unsuspecting world,

But a quiet, lurid, lifeless, ruthless, bloodless thing with black

Penetrating eyes and hideous death-fangs, coiled and bent in foul intent to bend, bind and break others in its venomous embrace...

Mik'raim 2.

And so, dear child of earth, listen well to the Author of these Scrolls,

Ask for wisdom, and it shall be soon given;

Guard your heart from the tyranny of the tongue, and the

Sweet seductive lure of power and passion, and unrestrain'ed greed,

And resist the unseen Foe, the Enemy of all that is true and pure,

Reject the false step-father and fomenter of lies and dark deception...

Mik'raim 3.

Beware the wide, well-traveled road oft' taken

By the sons of men in every earthly clime...

For even now the fetid fire-worm wends its wretched way northward

From the pallid, festering, lifeless Southern wastes

To engage and disengage forever more the shallow, hollow hearts of men,

And bend their twisted, helpless hearts to its control...

Mik'raim 4.

Beware of vile Komodus and his vicious grisly kin,

Beware the sinister Southern shore and her ancient sisterhood,
Where, long ago, before the celestial sun's healing rays
Burst upon the distant shore, and Vucub-Cadix, Lord of Darkness and
denizen of the night sky, seduced and stalked the twin sons of Huracán
And sought to seize the rightful throne of *Yam Hu naab ku*!

Mik'raim 5.

These are no easy foes that lay siege to holy heights, or conspire
To lay waste the glorious Kingdom realm,
And sever the taproot and sacred pillars of blessed Urbanus!
But take heart, pilgrim; the final victorious day is near, when truth will
conquer Reigning falsehood and faith replace the fear that
Holds her in its death embrace,
And King Sa'lem rescue, with intervening love, his wandering sons!

Tana'khil III—Birth-pangs

Mik'raim 1.

Listen, my children, to the full and finale chapter of the Sacred Scroll,
And the glorious day of Consummation, long ago foretold...
It shall not come with wise words, keenly felt and hewn from the
depths of Man's brightest dreams or visions, however well conceived,
But by the sovereign strength of Love itself, unsolicited and free,
Pure and condescending Love, dispensing truth and liberty.

Mik'raim 2.

Think not, when the deepening darkness comes and seizes mortal kind
And terror chokes and drains the keenest soul of hope, that victory,
By clever ruse or blind submission must bow in dumb retreat to a Dark
Lord, but resist his lying schemes and bend in strong humility before your
Sovereign King, and stand with conquering weapons of truth and purity...
The Sacred Citadel shall n'er succumb to our Enemy's dark design.

Mik'raim 3.

Put no trust in the skillful arm of man, or a warrior's trusted steed,
For no weapon, deadly honed, shall pierce the tender, contrite soul,
Nor foulest flood bear its blessed victims beyond the blackest pale...

Nor fetid force still the cries of helpless poor and wandering waif,
But humble hearts and bended knee shall lead a host to victory...

Mik'raim 3.
Surely, the day is coming when the ancient ruins will be rebuilt,
And peace and justice restored, and hope revived,
Throughout the grieving land, and the sword of justice
Ring anew like a smith's strong hammer in the forge of Lair, and
endless mercy flow like warm spring rains from sun-filled clouds...

Mik'raim 4.
But before that great and blessed day,
The converging powers of darkness will be bound and blinded
At breaking dawn by the sovereign strength of the rising Sun
And bright Morning Star, the enemies' bowstrings will be severed
And their sharp swords broken like twigs in a mighty wind,
And they shall be utterly consumed...

Mik'raim 5.
The Voice and Glory of ages past will bring healing to the land
Where the seeds of hatred had been sown and grown unchecked
In the raging storm; cruelty will be uprooted and mercy planted,
From the frozen north to the barren Southern waste.
No more will death and darkness reign, and shadows stalk
The Kingdom's majestic forests and mountain vales...

Mik'raim 6.
No more will fear and violence stalk the land,
Or gluttonous greed devour the hearts of man;
Once again doe and buck, and morning-dove
Will grace and graze among the tender valley grasses,
And plump grapes and sweet figs, and fresh fat grains
Flower, flourish and fill the fertile fields.

Mik'raim 7.
Let he who has ears to hear, and eyes to see,
Understand the hidden secrets of this prophecy.

Yes, the day is coming, and is near, at the very Ramsgate.
Listen to the rushing, soothing, whispering waters of the ancient Rill.
Death and darkness, disease and decay shall never more see the Day,
Never again inhabit the warm and welcoming land...

Mik'raim 8.
On that Blessed Day, old men and nursing mothers
Shall sit in the quiet shade of stately oaks and myrtle
And watch their children play in the morning Sun...
No more shall evil stalk the sons and daughters of men;
Peace and freedom, love and gaiety shall be the lot
And legacy of every child of man...

Mik'raim 9.
In that final day, a day that will test men's hearts,
A Righteous Branch shall appear in the barren land,
One chosen from the simple ranks of the sons of men;
To him revelation shall be given and honor restored,
And authority granted to lead a righteous remnant to the city gates
And repulse the rush and rise of wickedness in the land.

Mik'raim 10.
This is the Eternal Stone, coveted and cast out...
When the Kingdom felt the first onslaught of dark forces...
This is the same Living Stone that lay buried, undiscovered,
In the secret place, among the sacred
Scattered debris at the foot of Sa'lem's holy throne.

In that terrible, but glorious day, the ancient Cornerstone
Shall reappear and return to its former resting place...
This is the Eternal Stone which the builders rejected
When the Kingdom felt the first onslaught of dark forces...
This is the same Living Stone that lay buried, undiscovered, in the
secret place
Among the sacred, scattered debris at the foot of Sa'lem's holy throne.

Mik'raim 11.

But take heart! Watch and wait. The end is near.
Man's ancient foe and his vile minions are at the very gate,
Like hungry rabid wolves at the wintry door, poised to pounce
And unleash an unholy war against the children of men
Let the reader understand, and listen, and beware;
Night is darkest just before the birth of day...

Tanakh III—Kingdom Consummation

Mik'raim 1.

Yes, let the one who has hears to hear and eyes to see...
Listen and learn children of men, the song of mercy and victory...
On that final glorious day, *the Northern Star* will arise at mid-day;
Regulus will rise from distant Leonis's celestial womb...
In the fierce heat of battle, *a lion's whelp* will appear on the wasteland,
To quench and quell the burning, devastating heat of day.

Mik'raim 2.

On that dark day, the frozen, faceless sun, time-worn and worthy,
Now shunned by the encroaching darkness,
And stunned by the force of descending night, will be darker still;
The once-white moon, worthy brother of the light of day,
Will slowly shield its weary wounds; shed its warmth and splendor,
Turn blood-red, and fall to earth like a wounded warrior in his final hour...

Mik'raim 3.

Again, on that final day's dark night, the blackened, beleaguered,
Agonizing earth, like a poor woman, great with child, in the final painful
Moment of travail, will writhe and moan like an ox at the slaughter-house,
Or a helpless dog, eyes glazed with fear, clawing and whimpering
At the 'wintry door...,' or a brave warrior, wishing for a painless demise
Among the blood-stained battle-field of 'the happier dead ...'

Mik'raim 4.

But alas, from the ashes of that final hour,
A timid but worthy root and tender shoot will surge forth,

Nurtured by unseen rains and unseen hands,
Growing strong, and green, and tall, will rise
Unhindered and unknown, from the charred and thirsty forest floor,
A strong shelter and ready refuge for the surging storm...

Mik'raim 5.
He will arise on that dark day, daylight dauphin,
The beauty-bruised, embattled, emboldened morning-dove,
Will arise, ascend, and re-ascend, with healing in its wings,
The chosen child of man, driven and buffeted by relentless winds,
And dark pelting rains will rise on eagles' wind-filled wings...

Mik'raim 6.
On that new-born, hope-filled day, a first-born son, an infant child,
Fresh from his beloved mother's lifeless womb,
Will thrust his tiny trembling hand in the coiling Viper's nest,
Seize the deadly serpent's tail, and hoist his sharpened fangs,
Now forever stilled, upon a victor's blood-stained lance,
Silencing, in one fell swoop, the sound and scent and fatal scourge of death!

Mik'raim 7.
Herein, pilgrim is open wide the Fount of Truth and Mercy;
Herein lay the hope of Kingdom: On that great day, when at last
The deep darkness is dispelled; peace shall flow in abundant streams
From the mountain heights, and ceaseless joy from King Sa'lem's
Eternal throne of endless light. Forever more.
So it is written, and so it shall be!

Tana'khil IV—Summa Prophetica

Mik'raim 1.
Thus ends, cherished reader and scribe,
The prophecy and predictions of the Sacred Scrolls...
Let the reader understand and take heart.
Let no honest soul disdain, deride or distort, or forget
The sacred truths and signs of this prophecy,
But at the price and peril of his life.

Mik'raim 2.
Be warned and take humble, heart-felt heed...
Be not slow to hear or blind to see, or quick to ignore these words,
For they are truth and wisdom, opening the sacred door;
Be child-like wise and accepting, careful not to forget,
Or glibly discard, deny or disgrace the blessed message and
Binding meaning of these Ancient Scrolls, for they are life!

Mik'raim 3.
Blessed be the one, then, who hears and heeds and believes...
The words of this prophecy; for herein is a great and merciful promise:
Dispelling darkness, defeating death, dispensing mercy and compassion,
Defeating every foe, disrupting and diverting every evil scheme,
Delighting in truth and goodness, declaring healing and victory
And peace to the pure of heart and delivering hope.

Mik'raim 4.
Thus ends the prophecy and promise
Of these Sacred Scrolls. So it is written, and so it shall be.
Blessed be every man or woman,
And every cherished child of the noble race of man
Who hears and heeds... and the eyes that see,
And the humble heart that receives the truth herein recorded.

So ends the sacred words, signed and sealed, forever,
By the eternal King, Sa'lem's, good and righteous hand.

Made in the USA
Lexington, KY
14 September 2018